Coffee Beans
of
Northern Minnesota

Book I in the "Hearty Boys" Series

Bill Pearson

"The older you get, the more you realize you have no desire
for drama or conflict. All you want is a warm place to live,
a strong faith in Jesus, and someone who can remember how you
like your coffee." - Arvid Ellison

This story is dedicated to Baby Boomers of all ages.

*"Therefore, we do not lose heart. Though outwardly we are wasting
away, yet inwardly we are being renewed day by day.
For our light and momentary troubles are achieving for us an
eternal glory that far outweighs them all.
So, we fix our eyes not on what is seen, but on what is unseen, since
what is seen is temporary, but what is unseen is eternal."*
2 Corinthians 4:16-18

Much of the 'wisdom' included in the story is
from the Mount Holy Waters University boiler room
and was inspired by the teachings of *Ole*: boss, mentor
and friend to young minds.
Read on.

Dedication

This story is dedicated to my senior friends-
many older than Baby Boomers. Most endure daily pain, frequent
medical appointments, large pill boxes and face the end of life on
this earth which draws nearer with every breath.

These are the bravest of souls, especially those who labor on with a
smile in their heart and on their face. It's called faith. Lord, bless
them all. They deserve respect, praise, and love.

Acknowledgements

My daughter, Beth, made this book happen when all I wanted to do
was write the story.

My wife, Carol, assured me it would be worthwhile and satisfying.

The unforgettable residents of independent senior living
communities, with whom Carol and I worked for many years,
provided the passion; especially those I named
Mrs. Koepke, Mr. Elston, and Louise.

Through the process, Gizmo (our Maine Coon), sat on my lap.

Hope brings a spark into the soul for a moment but can soon be
forgotten. Still, for that moment, a life is happy.

Chapter 1

"Boys, stay as young as you can for as long as you are able.
Growing old is a different ball game altogether. Heh heh."
- Ole

"The wise people will shine like the brightness
of the sky. Those who teach others to live right will shine like stars
for ever and ever." Daniel 12:3

"So, there will be only four of us again this year," Arvie said to his friend Carl, as they traveled north on 169 toward the lake-cabin in the woods.

"Yup, a far cry from what it used to be," responded Carl. "I remember, not too many years ago, we packed the cabin with 13. That year, we had 'em sleeping on the floor and couch and in sleeping bags on the deck. Man, that was fun. Amazing how many we've lost since then."

Arvie sighed, took a deep breath and responded, "I'm sick of funerals and putting old friends in the ground, a crypt or a brass jar on the mantle and I'm tired of trying to say something meaningful in a room full of grieving people."

"I know what ya mean, but we're always going to try to help a family celebrate the life of a person we loved, right? Though sometimes, I wish others were helping us. We're grieving over losing our friends, too."

Arvie nodded and thought for a moment before responding, "Well, we do have a unique perspective, having spent so many years as friends – particularly the college years. It does make for a lot of memories and who better to tell some of the more colorful stories?"

Carl was rubbing his chin, experiencing the feel of his "day one scruffiness". "Do you think *Ole* is watching all this from up there, waiting for another former employee to join him at the heavenly coffee bar?"

"I want to believe he is," whispered Arvie, hopefully, "and I don't think he'll be totally satisfied until all his boys are reunited up there. He truly cared for all of us. I wonder how many are on his list after all the years?"

"Arvie, he did all the maintenance at old Mt. Holy Waters College for what – 40 years? Let's take a guess. I'll say he hired, on average, ten guys every year so that's 400 guys."

Arvie thought for a minute, "Hmmm. I'll bet it was even more than that. Remember all the guys who only worked part-time, an hour or two a day, maybe only on weekends or one day a week? And then there were those who worked the summers. I'm guessing the number might be double that. I wonder if any of those who came after us have their own version of *The Ole.* Ya think?"

"Probably. Why not?" asked Carl.

"Well, *we* loved the guy," Arvie said softly. "Gotta believe the others did too. Wouldn't be surprised if there are *Oles* all around the country. Anyway, we're going to continue to remember him. For these few days, every summer we get to talk of all the memories; the good ol' days: cleaning boilers, shoveling snow, chopping ice, mowing grass, painting dorm rooms, hauling furniture and whatever else needed to be done across the campus. Aahhh, those were the days," he said with a wave of his hand.

"He was such a good leader, wasn't he?" asked Carl. "I mean, who else could've gotten us to do all that work and walk away loving it and wanting more?"

"And the smile," Arvie mused. "I don't think I ever saw him without that infectious smile. Even when he was ticked off, he would let us have it with a grin. There really was something magical about the guy. Or perhaps it was just the coffee?" Arvie nudged Carl. "Think about it: so many dirty jobs, like you said, and his men, well, his boys, fell over backwards volunteering for the dirtiest. I seem to recall that he who took on the dirtiest and completed it honorably and in respectable time, would be asked by Ole to sit on the stool next to him at Reds for a, "cuppa". There was no greater honor to receive in the entirety of the maintenance department at Mount Holy Waters. Agreed?"

"Yeah" answered Carl. "This is what makes *The Ole* so great: telling and re-telling the stories. It's my favorite part. Each year, the tales get a bit bigger and more unbelievable and the excessive exaggeration is part of the draw. This, 'getting old' stuff can get kind of painful at times, but, even that, makes for great stories when we're catching up each year. I just love everything about it."

* * * * * * * *

"How long have we been on the road now?" asked Arvie.

"Well over an hour. Probably still an hour to go. Why?"

"Well, Bart's sending me constant reminders that relief is long overdue. Be at ease, Bart" he mumbled.

"Who is Bart?" asked Carl.

"Bart's my bladder and he's getting a bit anxious." Arvie had been on a first name basis with his bladder for some time now. "I'll be on the lookout for a suitable roadside establishment," he added.

"Got it," responded Carl with a smile. "Ya know, you sound like my wife, God rest her soul. I used to give her grief all the time about frequent stops when we would make road trips over the years. Glad I don't have to admit this now, but these days, I'd be grateful for the relief. My bladder seems to be in touch with its feminine side these days. Why is that? Old men need to pee as much as women. I don't get it," Carl chuckled while taking another swig of cold coffee from his travel mug.

"I'm afraid I know exactly why we are becoming our wives. It's the prostate. That little sucker has made my life a battle over the last year. I had a bad blood test. *'Elevated PSA*,' they said. *'Take a couple biopsies*,' they said. SEVENTEEN biopsies, two more blood draws and a couple doctor visits later, they tell me I'm fine and even if I had cancer, I'm too old for anyone to care. Apparently at our age, something else is bound to take you out before the prostate cancer grows big enough. *'It's a slow grower*,' they said. Bottom line, *'you'll experience frequency and urgency*,' they said. Well, I already knew that. That's what brought me in the front door to begin with! Come on now. Perhaps the prostate is the one and only mistake God made, ya think?"

"Well I don't know about that, but this aging thing is pretty tough. Seems like there should be an easier way to creep to the finish line. I'm going to have to speak to the Big Guy about that when I arrive," Carl said with a grin.

"Well, physical stuff is one thing, but I even read an article about the baby boomers the other day. It was talking about the huge number of boomers and how they will retire. We are kind of leading that group through the Golden Years, aren't we? With social security, medical problems and coverage issues, I just wonder what will happen to everyone. A lot of people have to be worrying about their future, don't ya think?" Arvie let out a sigh. "Right, Golden Years."

"Well, I can tell you that it's all a bit above my pay grade, that's for sure," Carl stated. "I end up turning off the TV these days and can't read a lot of the news, because it makes me crazy; yes, even my conservative channel. Don't roll your eyes. It's all just overwhelming. I can't do much about the big picture, so I'm just going to do what I think is right in my little speck of the universe. How's that?".

"But you're the one with the answers, right?" Arvie goaded. "It's those Democrats: tax tax, tax, spend, spend, spend, spend, grow the government and big brother will take care of you. Isn't that what you tell us? I'm only saying it because it's true, right?"

"Yes, exactly," began Carl. "It's always the…. wait a minute. Seriously, Arvie, knock it off." Arvie burst out laughing. "Don't get me started. I'm a senior and my heart can't take it anymore. Besides, this is vacation. I'm here to relax."

"Alright. Alright. I just couldn't resist, man. You make it too easy. You're right though. About all of it, but mostly about doing what we can with our little piece of it. I need to keep my eye open for more opportunities, I guess." Arvie's voice trailed a bit as he watched the big pines roll by.

Carl nearly shouted, "Relief is in sight."

"Ah yes, Bart is feeling pleased," Arvie announced.

Carl navigated into the gravel parking lot and pulled up next to a wooden porch. Arvie unbuckled quickly and was halfway to the door when he realized that Carl was having trouble extricating himself from the front seat. He went back to lend assistance.

"Knee not working, huh?"

"Ahhh, damn scar tissue. Next week they're gonna scrape it out. Almost got it." One more grunt and an additional yank and he was out. "We never should've done those deep knee bends with the weights on our shoulders our sophomore year."

Arvie nodded. "Yeah, but it sure helped our jumping that year. Would you want to trade all those dunks just to have two good knees today?"

"Good question. Dunking was exciting, but, maybe I would." They entered the store.

* * * * * * * *

Once the bathroom needs were taken care of, they went exploring. Arvie followed his nose and found a little hand-written sign on a stand that proclaimed, "Now Brewing," and a Mr. Coffee right next to it, proudly boasted a full, steaming pot. *They knew I was coming* he whispered to himself. He lifted the pot to show Carl as the big guy came shuffling up beside him. "You bring in your mug?" Arvie asked.

"Naw, I've had enough."

"Ok then." Arvie filled his travel mug and screwed on the lid as Carl wandered off for further exploration.

Sitting next to Mr. Coffee were two shiny black cans. On the front of each was the single, bright red word, Forever. *Neat can and good marketing,* Arvie thought to himself. *I've never seen a coffee can like this before. Never heard of, Forever coffee, either.* He picked up a can for further study and found on the back, in very small letters, the phrase, "A fine coffee product of Northern Minnesota."

"Look at this, Carl." He caught up with his friend and held out the can. "I didn't know they grew beans up here."

Carl moved close for a good look. "Isn't that interesting. I didn't know they grew beans up here either. Lived in Minnesota my whole life and never seen that can on a shelf before."

"Yeah. Me neither," Arvie responded. He took another sip from his travel mug. He thought about four Swedish coffee drinkers in a cabin for four days and took the can with him to check out.

It was a ramshackle counter. The glass top had duct tape running in all directions, an obvious attempt to help it survive an imminent collapse. In keeping with the ancient counter top, there was a very old man hunched-over on a stool behind the old counter. He had coke bottle glasses resting at the end of his nose and looked up slowly to speak, in a painfully hesitant cadence, "I see you'd like the coffee." (Wheeze.) "That coffee means a lot to me." (Pause.) "I've been drinking it now for over 100 years." (Slight smile.) "I hope you enjoy it as much as I do." (Gasp.) "Since you bought a can, I've only got that one can left." (Burp.) "I don't know when I'll have any more." (Wheeze.) "Are you sure you wouldn't want to buy the second can too?" (Shudder.) "You will be glad you did. I can promise you. (Gulp.)"

Arvie thought for a moment about the upcoming morning breakfasts and how many hours would pass with the boys just sitting on the deck pouring down the coffee. He quickly decided that, yes, he would take the second one as well and walked back to get it. Returning, he placed it gently on the glass/tape counter top alongside the other can. The very old man said, "I know you will be glad you bought both cans." (Gasp.) "Since I started drinking at least four cups a day (Sucks air.) back in 1912, I've never had a doctor's appointment." (Swallow.) "I hope you have a wonderful day (Passed Gas.) and thank you. (Gag.) Enjoy your get-together."

Anxious to be on the road, Arvie handed his money to the old man, said a thank you, scooped up the sack and travel mug and headed out the door with Carl. As he paused to shut the door behind them, Arvie felt certain he saw the old man looking at him, a knowing smile stretched across his thin, pale lips.

* * * * * * * *

Back on the road again, Arvie had a hot cup of brew in hand and both men were thankful for their empty bladders.

"Life is especially good at a moment like this," Arvie exclaimed with a toothy grin. "Wow, this is terrific coffee," he said as he took another sip. *I can almost hear Ole asking, 'How's the coffee?'* "You sure you don't want a sip?" he asked Carl.

Again, Carl waved it off. Arvie, glancing down at the paper sack containing his recent purchase said, "I am anxious to brew a pot of this for you and the boys in the morning."

"I'm looking forward to it," grunted Carl. "Now then, beside your prostate issues, how are you doing, really?"

"All things considered, not too bad. All my other organs continue to work, it seems. I've told you about the weekly senior Bible study at church, right? Where we have 150 - 175 show up every week? I listen to a lot of conversations there and I feel truly blessed. Last week, one of the men at our table shared that he's got a brain tumor and his surgery is next week. That's got to be a difficult surgery to face. And then I overheard two women comparing the upcoming stomach and throat surgeries: cancer, they said. It goes on and on, from one table to the next. There are 20 tables with these conversations going on. You and I have discussed "organ" concerts before and every Wednesday I get to be a part of this rather large and unique event. The worst surgery I'm facing is for another hernia; no big deal and quite simple. But some of these folks, given the surgeries they have, can't bet on waking up afterwards. Did you ever talk to your folks about old age and what it's really like?"

"Never did. I don't think I ever thought about it back then."

"Yeah. Back in the day, when we were playing basketball we wanted to know every piece of information possible about our next opponent, so that we could be well prepared, right? So how is it that we wouldn't do the same with aging? Why didn't we think to prepare?"

Carl grunted and then stated the obvious "Maybe we didn't want to know. We saw the elderly all around us and didn't want to think about being like them: stooped over, unsteady, bumping into things because they couldn't see and talking too loud because they couldn't hear. And those were just the obvious things. We had no clue about what was happening on the inside. Aww, I don't know. Did you ever ask old people what it was like?"

"Only once. I think I was maybe ten years old and I asked my grandpa what it was like. I remember he compared it to a popcorn popper. One day his popper quit and he threw it out. He said we're just like that popper: only as good as our worst part. I thought I knew what he was saying."

"That's a pretty good analogy," Carl responded. "But, things have changed some with the advances in medicine. They can now suck our blood, run some tests, and tell us what's needing to be fixed. Then we schedule more appointments, drive some more miles and get some more prescriptions filled. I should have gone into the drug business."

"Yeah. Ain't that the truth. There was one other thing Grandpa told me. He said that when I got old I should keep a smile on my face, no matter what. I remember thinking *sure, that's easy*. But back then I didn't understand the part about the body wasting away."

"In other words, it's easier to keep a smile on your face when you're young and everything is working like it's supposed to and nothing hurts."

"Yeah. Back then there weren't senior moments like the one I had this morning."

"Huh? What happened this morning, Arvie?"

"Well," Arvie began. "At about 2:30, I woke up on the floor. Apparently, I had fallen out of my bed and ripped off my ear lobe."

"What?" Carl looked at him, shocked and yet giggling uncontrollably.

"Thank you. Your concern has been noted." Arvie continued, "When I woke up, I was lying on my back trying to understand what had just happened. I felt a trickle of something dripping onto my left cheek and *that* woke me up. Blood maybe? I tried to get off the floor but my head was stuck between the nightstand and something that was stored under the bed. I felt some panic right then – you know, I felt like I couldn't move – claustrophobia or something. Finally, I rolled over onto my stomach, got to my feet with some effort and made it to the bathroom. Blood was running from somewhere around my left ear, down my cheek, and was dripping on my pajama's. I couldn't see where the problem was, so I soaked a wash cloth with cold water and held that against my left ear, hoping to stem the flow.

"As I looked at myself in the mirror, I remembered fighting something during my sleep. I had a vague recollection of a dream. It must have been a good fight though but how could I have ended up on the floor on my back with my head wedged where it was – if I had won? I couldn't figure it out and how had I managed to cut something around my left ear? I pulled the wash cloth away and took another look. Something was very wrong with my ear lobe.

"To make it worse, Hannah woke up whining about the bright lights in the bathroom. When I told her I had cut my ear or something, she was up in a flash and yanking my ear toward the light. She was saying something like, 'Oh, Good Lord. What *have* you done?'

"After a thorough 15 second examination, she said I had ripped off my ear lobe and she was going to call Bren. I was accused of being a dumb man, Carl. Can you imagine that? I think her exact words were 'You men can be so exasperating.' How many times have we heard that? Then she went for her phone and Bren told us to head up Highway 61 to the emergency room. What else was she going to say when Hannah's telling her I'm bleeding to death at 2:30 in the morning?"

At that point, Carl was nearly hyperventilating.

Arvie continued and would never admit how much he was enjoying the reaction, "We spent four hours in the waiting room because, apparently, ripping off an ear lobe isn't life threatening. When we finally got home after, Hannah chewed me out for leaving a trail of blood from my side of the bed all the way to the bathroom. Like, somehow, I'm supposed to clean up, as I go, while I'm bleeding to death. She just kept mumbling about men, particularly the old ones."

Carl regained his composure after a couple slaps of the steering wheel. "Oh, my gosh. You can't make this stuff up. Truly – great stuff, man. Can't wait to hear you tell the boys. So that happened *this* morning?"

"Yup. See all this fishing line hanging out?" asked Arvie pointing up at his left ear lobe.

"Good grief," grunted Carl.

"Here's the good part. Hannah told me to call you guys and tell you that I couldn't make The Ole. I reassured her that I have the pills and creams, it doesn't hurt, I can take care of myself, and I won't go jumpin' in the lake getting it all infected."

"How'd she take that?"

"She told me to go jump in the lake," Arvie quipped. "But it's starting to hurt a little now," he added. "They froze the left side of my face for the sewing but I think the feeling is starting to come back. The doc put five stitches inside and five outside. I don't understand what it means to have stitches on the inside and the outside." Arvie switched subjects midstream.

"I've got to think about that dream. What was it I was fighting when I ended up on the floor?" He giggled thinking about falling out of bed. "When's the last time you fell out of bed, Carl?"

Carl just shook his head, still giggling.

The Minnesota landscape continued to fly by. In the trunk were the suitcases and the coolers. In the back seat lay all the fishing equipment and a box containing the popcorn popper and all the required accoutrements. Carl had always appreciated anything that could be used as a conveyance of butter. When they were roommates at Mount Holy Waters, the popper sat on top of the Hi Fi speaker. A little hot plate sat on the floor adjacent to the speaker; a small pan and spoon at the ready, just waiting for the butter. They washed the pan and the spoon every two months whether it was needed or not. Arvie had always been the master of popcorn and butter and he was totally prepared to convey a lot of butter over the next several days.

Carl had finally stopped his giggling and was serious again. "You know that business about not asking our parents and grandparents about getting older? I think a lot of that had to do with us wanting to get back outside with our friends to play. That's all I wanted to do: basketball, football, kick the can after dark and all the rest of it. I wasn't thinking about growing up, 'cause I had the important stuff of being *young,* front and center."

"That's right. Yeah" agreed Arvie. The car went quiet for several moments as two old minds remembered the days of youth.

Arvie broke the silence. "Will we get to the cabin ahead of Freddie and Bert?" he asked.

"Yeah, but not by much. Freddie stayed at his sister-in-law's place last night so he didn't have far to go this morning. Bert might not make it until mid-afternoon."

"So, Freddie is bringing all the good food as usual because he knows a butcher in Lincoln, Bert's bringing a huge bottle of Jack, I presume. I've got beer and wine. What did you bring?"

"Well, let's see. I've got TP and sheets and blankets. I have to wash that stuff once a year. That's probably overkill but I do it anyway. There's a box or two of kitchen stuff and then some other stuff for the fridge."

It was then that they caught the first view of Mille Lacs Lake. What a picture. "Look at that, Carl," said Arvie. "All these years later and I still can't see the shoreline on the other side."

As Carl prepared to turn west off of 169, Arvie watched a McDonalds roll by. *"Last year I had to stop there to use the facilities,"* he muttered to himself. *"Huh, and I'm still drinking coffee?"* He drained the last of it from his mug.

* * * * * * * *

"Carl, did you hear what that old guy behind the counter said when I was checking out? He said, 'Been drinking it for 100 years.' Did he really say that? And then he said he hadn't been to a doctor since 1912. The guy must have dementia. But did you hear that? And then he said as we were leaving 'Enjoy the get-together.' Just for a moment there, I thought he knew all about, The Ole."

Carl shook his head negatively while saying, "I don't think I heard any of that."

"So now I'm hearing things. That's part of being a senior too, isn't it?"

"Sure is," Carl said as he reached across and punched his friend in the shoulder. "At this stage in life, we're old guys getting older by the minute – well the *second* really. Time is running out on us and we are filled with doubts, regrets, some fear, a little hope, lots of thanksgiving, and a faith in a God who loves us dearly and will greet us one day with a, 'Well done.' At least we hope so."

"That's a nice sermon right there and ain't it the truth."

The Ford was quiet for several minutes as Carl negotiated the back roads leading to the cabin. Finally, he took a right turn and came to a stop behind a vehicle with Nebraska plates and said the obvious, "Freddie's here".

The cabin sat at the east end of Eagle Lake so when the prevailing west winds blew, the deck on the backside of the cabin was the place to be – always cool. And the sunsets from there were always spectacular. Best of all, if they ever happened to run out of gas while out on the lake, they could just relax, open up another cold one and let the westerlies blow them gently to the dock. How nice was that?

Arvie reached for the sack of coffee as he got out of the car. After he shut the door he went around to the other side to give Carl a hand. The big guy was grunting while trying to bend the bad knee, twisting in the seat to get a better angle. "Pull my foot out, Arvie," he said. A moment later, Carl was once again, extricated and together they marched – well, technically, Carl limped a bit, to the deck and the backdoor of the cabin. They'd bring in the rest of their supplies later.

At 75, Arvie remained in reasonably good shape; still 6 feet tall when he purposefully stood erect. He couldn't change the usual sagging that is common in a man of his age, but overall, he could navigate quite well and was proud of the fact that he could get off the couch or out of an easy chair without grunting or having to re-adjust his position several times in order to get his legs under him, well, most of the time. He'd had both knees replaced and two neck surgeries, the biggest of which fused seven vertebrae and forced him to give up golf a few years prior.

Carl was the biggest of the boys at 6' 2". Of course, after a couple of snorts of Jack, he could be measured up to 6'4". Back in the day, he was a muscular 195; the quarterback of the football team and the leading scorer on the basketball team. He had drifted a bit to a "healthy" 260 pounds and had had both knees and hips replaced (one hip, more than once). One of the knee surgeries hadn't gone quite right and that was what caused some challenges when standing up and/or exiting a vehicle.

Freddie, back in the day, was so skinny he couldn't create a shadow when he stood sideways. He had become a bit overweight and could no longer move around without making a multitude of unusual sounds. He had survived a cancer surgery but had never gained any metal implants over the years. He also let his hair go crazy, having lost affection for scissors and razors. Joyce must not have minded a man who looked like he hadn't been down from the mountain in years.

Bert had always looked older and more mature than the rest. That's why all the girls thought he was especially cute and interesting. When brave enough to ask, he never had any trouble getting a date. Trouble was, he never could find the courage to ask. He was terribly afraid. Said he had no experience with girls, "They just don't have 'em where I come from." Then, Gayle had come to Mt. Holy Waters and everything changed.

The greetings were usually one of the best parts of the reunion. Arvie always got a little choked up and that year was no exception. However, the emotion quickly dissipated as the event got underway. All worries had left the premises; there were no mountains to climb, no problems to solve, no rivers to cross, no bills to pay. The plumbing in the bathroom worked and there was a fresh roll of paper. Freddie brought the beef, the pork, the bacon and sausage. Arvie was proud that he was known for bringing the humor: he hoped he still had some. All they needed to focus on for the next four days was how to enjoy each moment.

Bert arrived mid-afternoon as expected and the hearty welcomes continued. By late afternoon, Arvie and Freddie were on the deck watching the setting sun slowly making its way into the pine trees at the far end of the lake. A Loon was calling to a friend out there, somewhere. Mosquitoes stopped by for their evening introductions and extractions, and the talk was of all that had happened over the previous year: family, friends, health. *Here's a picture of so and so*, and *here we are downtown at the play*. The night was spent catching up.

Freddie said, "Dweeb's wife isn't doing so well. Seems like a lot of things have caught up with her all at once and the doctors' appointments are almost daily. Even with all the medical expertise, there is still no clear diagnosis." Down on the dock, Bert and Carl were conversing, perhaps about the same subject.

Dweebs was on the track team at Mt. Holy Waters and continued to run. Everyone knew his wife Carolyn. She had been the homecoming queen their senior year. This was the second year in a row he hadn't been able to attend.

More and more old friends were suffering the effects of, "wasting away," as it is called in the Bible and each reunion featured time spent discussing those who have moved on to the better place. Both Arvie and Freddie remembered that, not long before the previous reunion, Carl had lost his wife to Alzheimer's following a very brave and lengthy battle. They knew, full well, that someone would be next. Freddie said, "Arvie, we'll be having this conversation every time we get together, or we won't."

With that, the conversation turned to thoughtful silence and, as they watched their friends below, the darkness took over.

Arvie suddenly realized he had, in all the catching up, forgotten to call Hannah to let her know that they had arrived safely. She didn't need anything additional to worry about. Life had been a challenge since her anxiety diagnosis 15 months earlier. There had been so many appointments: psychologists, psychiatrists and counselors. Then there was the orthopedic surgeon and internist. Hannah had learned, just prior to finding out about the anxiety, that she would need back surgery. It was a routine operation, not extremely invasive, but it was a back surgery nonetheless, and she had heard her share of stories about back surgeries. An anxiety diagnosis explained all the emotional outbursts, the times of tears, and the inability to get out of bed in the morning. It helped to understand why she didn't want to leave the house, why her mind would run away from her, how she dealt with all things negatively, thus promoting more emotional, gut wrenching moments, *especially for me,* he thought. *Men think it is their responsibility to fix things, and I have only the feeling of absolute helplessness. I have learned from the doctors that I am only her support; a source of love, and I am the stable one for her to lean on. Beyond that it's a waiting game. I can't fix anything. But I can call.* And so, he did.

Arvie and Hannah talked for a few minutes and he was pleased to hear her sounding ok. She had not been happy about it for several months: his leaving her for four days with the boys. But the kids lived close by and arrangements had been made for them to drop in and spend time. They had made it very clear to her that he needed the time away. Daughter Brenda would be spending the following evening with her mom. Arvie said, "Good-bye. I love you. I'll call again tomorrow evening and yes, my dear, the ear is still attached and doing fine. It's all good."

Once the line went dead, he considered what she was doing right then. He knew: shedding a tear or two and feeling very alone. For the 1,000th time he asked himself *where did this anxiety mess come from and why did it choose her?*

* * * * * * *

Arvie took his share of the barbs on day one, especially about the ear incident: "Why have you got fishing line hanging out of your ear?" "You got a couple ugly ears. Can't blame ya for wanting to take 'em off," "Hey! Over here on your left...can you hear me?" "Don't let 'em mess with you; it looks good on you;" that sort of thing.

Dinner would feature Nebraska Rib Eyes that were so large, a second plate would be needed to hold everything else: baked potato, corn on the cob, salad, dinner roll and the huge slab of butter. The corn was the night's primary butter conveyor, although the potato and roll were excellent options, as well. Supper would be served on the deck overlooking the moonlit waters of the beautiful lake. Carl had the grill going at the far end of the deck. The others prepared the slabs of beef, set the table, boiled the corn and mixed the greens. Dinner would be a late one, as it usually was the first night. Conversations would be all over the place. Everyone knew that time was precious and that particular night would not come again.

Arvie, done with his salad duty, popped open a beer. Bert headed for the bathroom. On the way, he rose off the ground and slammed a beer can into the trash while exclaiming with pride, "That's how I dunked against St. Procopius back in '57." Everyone had a good laugh remembering that Bert had, at best, a two-inch vertical leap back then. No one reminded him that he did not make the basketball team, let alone fly above the rim to dunk in '57. Once back on the floor and stabilized, he limped down the hall to take care of more pressing business. *"Growing old does have its advantages: wonderful memories appear out of nowhere. Some might even be true,"* thought Arvie.

At the dinner table on the deck, Freddy asked Arvie to again tell the story of Freddy and his pitching prowess for the Mt. Holy Waters baseball team. "But Freddy, this is only the first night. Are you ready for it this soon?" asked Arvie.

Freddy, smiling broadly said, "Absolutely. I've been waiting a whole year for this moment."

Carl and Bert mumbled back and forth with each other saying something about, "Not this again. Please!" Bert said, "Can I take my food down to the dock?"

Arvie gnawed on an ear of corn for a moment. Butter dripped from his chin, splashing into a pool on his baked potato which was in need of more butter anyway. "Ok." He shoved back from the table and said, "I've got to be standing to do this."

Bert leaned towards Carl and pleaded in a whisper, "When he can't stand up any more, can we be done with this story?"

Carl let out a guffaw, reached quickly for his napkin and placed it over his mouth to keep the food in where it was meant to be as he laughed through his nose.

Arvie assumed the position of a pitcher standing on the mound peering toward the catcher for the sign. Holding that position, he leaned towards Freddy and said, "Ignore those two. They don't love the game like we do." He resumed his stare towards the imaginary catcher crouched at the end of the deck.

"Now remember, Freddy's wind-up was reminiscent of the great Warren Spahn. The only problem was that by the time he completed his wind-up, everyone in the ballpark had lost interest, including his catcher." Once those words were out of his mouth, Arvie began the demonstration of the wind-up, very slowly, by raising his hands high above his head. The narration continued, "The ball, in Freddy's left hand, was tucked deep in the pocket of his glove". Again, Arvie paused the description for effect. As he raised his right leg, his foot was extended to a position high above his head. His back dropped into a position parallel to the floor of the deck and he, inevitably, like so many times before, lost his balance, and staggered off in one direction or another. The audience was mesmerized with Arvie's pliability at such a ripe old age. Even better, he was able to right himself once again. That had not always been the case.

Once, with all the wives in attendance at the corn boil down in Illinois at Old Wills farm, Arvie fell backwards for effect during the telling of the story. He struck his head on the edge of a picnic table on the way down. The orator was silenced as a new story line developed; one with the makings of life and death: a bleeding head wound, a farmer/vet with questionable analgesia and a needle most recently used on pigs and a surgical procedure performed in the middle of a field. That, however was a story for re-telling on another day.

"Back to Warren Spahn," Arvie announced as he regained his footing. "Despite the beautiful wind up, Freddy's first inning of work continued on and on, because he could get no one out. In the middle of the inning, I think four runs had scored, the bags were filled and there was still no one out. The opposing coach called a time out, marched across the field and asked our coach, Coach Bibbs, if he had somebody else that could actually *throw* a ball? That was it: Freddy's pitching career." Every time Freddy and Warren Spahn were mentioned in the same breath, laughter reigned. Arvie looked forward to re-telling the story every summer.

Nobody wanted night one to end but old men tire easily and early, and one by one they departed for sleep. The next day was coming: a day on the lake, most likely. They would troll for those lunker bass and jump in the water to cool off; except for Arvie, of course. He wouldn't be enjoying the water because of his newly decorated ear.

Arvie sat on the side of the bed replaying in his mind the day's events. He felt deeply for Dweebs and Carolyn. He knew what Dweebs was feeling, wanting to come but also wanting, and needing, to stay at home. Hannah needed *him* back home as well but he had so looked forward to these precious few days with the boys. He walked down the dark hall to the bathroom and realized he hadn't been there since he arrived at the cabin some six hours ago. *Well, that's interesting*, he thought. *Must've been all the excitement, the fun, the food, the laughing, the old stories, and wine? And a beer or two? And I also made contact with Jack once or twice. Humph.*

On the counter beside him was an old issue of 'Pietisten' and on the cover page he recognized the article written by Boldy. It was the article entitled "Let there be Light," from a few years back. That was a good story. Boldy must have paid some attention in the creative writing class. After all, he had been a jock so what could he know about words and grammar? The story was about his heart transplant and was a real gut-grabber.

It felt good to lie down. It had been a long day. He couldn't believe he'd been up since 2:30 that morning. He had been waking up earlier recently and had begun to enjoy the solitude and peace of that quiet time. However, on this particular morning, those hours had been extra early and were spent waiting to have an ear re-attached. He couldn't help but smile at the thought.

Chapter 2

"No matter your job, do it like a man. Heh heh."
- *Ole*

"Lord, heal me, and I will truly be healed. Save me, and I will truly be saved. You are the one I praise."
Jeremiah 17:14

Arvie's feet hit the floor. The cabin was still dark and quiet. No one was stirring as he sat clearing the cobwebs and reaching for shorts and a T-shirt in his suitcase. He felt refreshed. *Man. That was a good night's sleep*, he thought. *I didn't move all night, and I don't remember getting up in the middle of the night for a bathroom run. When was the last time that happened? Oh, and I didn't fall out of bed either.* He couldn't suppress a giggle.

He made his way to the kitchen to start the coffee and flicked on the light over the sink. *Get it going without making any noise. Let the old boys sleep,* he thought. The clock on the wall said 5:10 and he judged that to be about right as he looked into the darkness down the length of the lake. He opened the black can of Forever. "Can't wait for the boys to taste this," he muttered. He loved the smell of it as it perked: a unique aroma.

In general, Arvie loved early mornings and the cabin was extra special: the quiet of the north woods, full cup in hand and a mystical view out the cabin window. Nothing better. Even at this hour in the dark, Arvie considered the detail of what was out there and how the imagination takes the pieces of what's seen and adds whatever details are needed to form what is not. *Six months from now while the snows of winter have me homebound, I'll remember this moment,* he thought. He was about to wander out on the deck when Carl shuffled up. He put a hand on Arvie's shoulder and with all the creativity he could muster at such an early hour said, "Its dark out there." Arvie motioned toward the kitchen and said, "I've got the good stuff brewed and waiting." Carl headed that way with a grunt.

As he moved out the sliding door onto the deck, Arvie wondered, *how do they roast the beans? Where do they roast the beans?* Then he thought, *what beans? They can't have coffee beans in Northern Minnesota. What is that taste? Black berries or maybe Black grapes mixed with a touch of rum and brown sugar? Wow - it's really good.* Carl came alongside and said astutely, "This is really good coffee."

Bert arrived a little later, not saying a word until he'd filled his cup and taken a sip. There emerged a low growly sound, and then, "That's good." So the quorum had begun to form, three of four agreeing on the quality of the coffee with only Freddy yet to cast a vote. Arvie felt good about yesterday's purchase.

Freddy, the group's breakfast maker, hadn't stirred yet. Arvie, Carl and Bert sat at the table on the deck sucking up the coffee and discussing anything, everything and nothing at all. Carl told a joke but no one got it except him. He laughed uproariously while the other two looked at each other with upraised eye brows. Bert mouthed the words, "Was that supposed to be funny?" The first pot of coffee complete; Arvie got up to start the next. Just then Freddy arrived and complained about no coffee. Arvie assured him that he would have his cup in a matter of minutes. Freddy mumbled something about the, "crummy service at this joint," while scratching his navel.

After consuming his first cup, Freddie got energized and headed to the kitchen to begin work on breakfast. While he crash-banged in the kitchen, Arvie set the table with all the necessary accoutrements. It wouldn't long before the plates would be piled high with scrambled eggs, bacon, sausage and fried potatoes. Texas toast was served on the side with the ever-present, huge slab of butter. It was another feast to behold. Arvie kept the cups filled with Forever.

With bellies full and kitchen clean-up accomplished, it was time to don the swimwear, grab the fishing gear, load the pontoon and get out on the lake.

Arvie fumbled for his swimsuit which wouldn't get wet today but while searching for it, he discovered his pill box. *Holy crap,* he thought. *I didn't take my acid reflux pill last night before supper. It's still here.* He couldn't believe what he was seeing: that big purple pill was still sitting there. *That huge steak I devoured... and the beer? That would always bring on the reflux. But, I had no problem last night. I should've been up gagging and coughing and searching the fridge for a diet Pepsi, which seemed to help on occasion.*

Confused, he pulled on his swim shorts and a t-shirt and sat down on the edge of the bed, deep in thought. "What's going on?" he muttered while he continued to stare at the pill with unbelieving eyes. He had also forgotten to take two of the four antibiotic pills. Oops. He was beginning to grapple with the thought that he had had no pain from his ear since arrival at the cabin. And finally, as he remembered the previous day's long hours into the evening without a bathroom break.

"Arvie, move it, let's go. We'll be on the pontoon," came the call. Totally confused, he took several more moments to get put together, but finally he lethargically, almost reluctantly, retrieved his fishing gear and headed down the path to the dock. He went through the motions that morning but his mind was untangling, with little success, what had happened with his stomach the night before.

Carl was the first in with a cannonball that doused everyone still on board. Next in were Freddy and Bert, splashing and laughing in the cool water. Arvie asked if it had been an hour since breakfast because, "When growing up, mom had made it very clear that you'll get a cramp and drown if you don't wait one hour." They all decided they were going to drown at any moment. Though nothing more was said, Arvie noticed that within seconds the three had quietly paddled within arm's reach of the pontoon. Ahhh, the power of suggestion.

It didn't take long for them to re-board the boat. Once settled, they trolled awhile. No one really cared if any fish wanted to play or not, but Freddy was able to bring in the first: a very nice bass. Bert asked if it was the same fish that Jonah got acquainted with many years ago. Everyone agreed it was not, or Jonah was smaller than most, but actually the determining factor was the question of how that fish from the Mediterranean Sea could swim into this lake so far away. "Well, it could have been a simple miracle," Carl suggested.

Two of the four were biblical scholars. Both Carl and Freddy had spent their lives ministering at several churches through the Covenant denomination, preaching, teaching, loving and caring. Arvie had bailed on the seminary shortly after beginning and had worked in a variety of sales and marketing tasks over the years. He often wondered about that seminary decision, sorting through his memory in an effort to determine why he had not continued. At the time, he was tired of studying and struggling to learn and the upcoming classes intimidated him: subjects like Greek, philosophy and theology. The latter, he feared, was well beyond his intellectual capacity. But, there was something else going on at the time. He and Hannah had met that year and they were ready to do life together. They were married in the spring of the following year. Yes, it was Hannah's fault.

Bert had spent his life in libraries throughout the upper Midwest and had the diploma that proved him qualified. His wife Gayle was educated in that discipline also. At one library in northern Illinois, they had a memorable experience that made 60 minutes, the network TV news show. Every one of the old boys and their families were glued to the TV during that time. As it happened, a man had spent his entire life in a hidden room in their library and no one was aware. But that's another story for another time.

* * * * * * * *

Through lunch, Arvie hadn't noticed anyone going to the little boy's room. He made a mental note of that. He'd been thinking all morning about his own bathroom habits since arriving at the cabin. *I don't get it*, he thought. But the three of them had all been in the lake. Maybe that's it - they had used the lake. Once the quick lunch on the deck was concluded, it was back to the pontoon for the afternoon frolic.

The afternoon was much the same as the morning. By mid-afternoon the decision was made to head to the cabin, get out of the sun and give thought to the preparations for supper. It was on the way in that Carl asked, "Arvie, are you with us? You've been quiet all afternoon."

"Guys, something is bothering me," Arvie replied. "Something is not right here."

Carl cut the motor. "What's up?" he asked, concern in his voice.

"I don't know where to begin, so I'll just begin. Number one: I was digging out my swimsuit this morning and I happened to grab my pill box. I realized some pills were still in the box from yesterday including my acid reflux pills. I generally take one before supper and another after. I didn't take either one. And what did I have for dinner last night? Only a great big hunk of Nebraska beef with half a dozen ears of corn on the cob dripping with butter and salt and pepper, a huge baked potato; again, with butter, salt and pepper. I have never eaten a meal like that and survived without having taken, at least, one pill. I don't understand why I wasn't up in the middle of last night with all the usual gagging and coughing. That's the first thing. Let's move on to number two.

"Yesterday on the way up, we stopped to tinkle about 50 miles down the road from here. On the way out of the convenience store I bought a cup of coffee for the road. Carl, you said you'd had enough coffee and refused more in your travel mug. We got to the McDonalds in Garrison where I've had to make a bathroom stop every other time I've been up here, but not this time. Then once we got here, I popped open more liquid refreshments and didn't hit the bathroom til bedtime around 11:30. So the question is, what's going on with my bladder since I normally go so frequently?

"And now for number three, and a question for each of you. I noticed that absolutely none of us went to the bathroom when we were back in the cabin for lunch. Does that mean all of you drained the tanks when you were in the lake before we came in for lunch, or are we not feeling the need for urination suddenly? I didn't get in the lake because of my ear problem but I had no bathroom urge for how many hours? Perhaps our bladders have increased their capacity. And I don't believe that's possible.

"But wait, there's more. Number four: I haven't taken an ibuprofen since I left home, 24 hours ago. I don't have any aches and pains from any arthritis or anything else, including the ear. This is the best I've felt in for ever. And I don't believe it's all because I'm with you guys; your aura, your wonderfulness, or anything like that.

"Finally, one final question: have any of you noticed anything different, or is it just me?"

Blank stares from all. Dead silence, save for a fish jumping somewhere nearby. Wheels were turning. Arvie waited.

It was Freddy who asked, "Arvie, where are you going with this?"

"Freddy, I don't know. Maybe I've had a stroke or something. That's a possibility at my age. If that's what it is, so be it. If however, any of you have noticed anything, any change at all in your physical well-being – or not, well, maybe it can lead somewhere. But I'm pretty much in tune with my bathroom habits and I know that something quite dramatic has changed there. How about it Freddy? Did you go in the lake or did you hit the john at lunch? We all had multiple cups of coffee this morning. Where did it go?"

"I didn't pee in the lake and I didn't hit the john at lunch," said Freddy with a quizzical look. "Come to think of it, I haven't even thought about taking a leak."

"You know, I didn't go either," said Bert, looking at Carl.

"Me neither," said Carl. "I would agree that's most unusual."

Freddy jumped back in. "Arvie, I don't know if maybe this will help or make things worse, but I've got acid reflux, big time, as well. I took my pill last night before supper and didn't have any problems. You should've had a problem but you didn't. So what have you done differently?"

Arvie stared blankly at a tree on the shoreline. Freddy's comment seemed to be on target. *I should have been sick last night but I wasn't.* "So maybe it's just me," he mumbled. But he still was waiting for someone to comment on where this morning's coffee went.

"Guys," said Bert. "Let's head in. It's about time we think about dinner. Let's let this question settle a bit and we can all give it some thought. I don't have an explanation for the bathroom question, but it does give us something to think about. Maybe Arvie, there is something very logical that transpired here that we are not coming up with. Let's head in. Frankly boys, I always think better after a couple rounds of Jack."

With that, Carl cranked up the motor and the drive to the Lake's eastern shore commenced. There was no conversation. Even the loons were questioning their bathroom habits now and were therefore quizzical and silent. This wasn't the way an evening at the reunion was supposed to begin.

Once on shore, Carl got the grill going and then leaned on the deck railing and stared west. Freddy, preparing the gigantic pork chops, paused to stare east out the kitchen window, and as Arvie mixed the greens, he stared blankly at lettuce leaves moving about in the mixing bowl. Bert stood on the deck with knives, spoons and forks in hand gazing at the sun sliding lower in the western sky.

Arvie thought about his upcoming appointment on Friday with the Urologist. They will draw his blood and the PSA number would drop back to wherever it's supposed to be. He just knew it. He felt it. There had been some kind of major miracle and no one in his doctor's office would have any kind of explanation. He could hear the urologist saying, "I don't understand it."

Freddy asked quietly, "Arvie, are you going to take your pill before supper?"

"No. I need to know what will happen."

Freddy replied, "Then I'll join you. Better that you have a friend who's up sick with you all night, than to go it alone."

"What a guy," Arvie answered with a grin.

The sun was dropping closer to the far end of the lake as they sat down to eat at the table on the deck. Bert arrived at the table with four shot glasses of JD and said, "Boys, we could use some of this." The pour, the clink of glasses, and the Jack was consumed with great relish. The meal began.

Carl munched on his first thick slice of pork chop when he pushed back from the table, stood, and slid over to the railing, thrusting his hands deep into his pockets. "I know where Arvie's coming from, since he gave us some examples earlier. How 'bout the rest of us? Any examples going on that have you guys wondering? I'll tell you what's been rolling around with me.

"Three things: my bump, my back and my knee. First off, I've had a funny bump on my left thigh: a round circle thing about the size of a quarter. I've been watching that since I first noticed it, maybe two months ago. It's been getting bigger. When I was sitting on the pontoon today, rubbing my thigh I realized that I didn't feel it. I looked down and it was gone. Totally gone. I was actually wondering if it was ever really there. I know it was, because I almost called a skin doctor last week to have 'em take a look.

"The second thing is my back; my lower back. When I leaned down to pick up the bag of charcoal to start the grill, I felt nothing in my low back. Maybe it's because we're all focused on this that I noticed, but I actually put the bag back down, stood up and then leaned over and picked it up again. Nothing. I felt nothing and let me tell you, that is significant.

"The third is also significant. You all know that since I had the right knee replaced I haven't been able to bend it far enough to do much. I can't seem to get out of a chair, wash my foot or trim the nails or to climb the ladder to get back on the pontoon, without a real struggle. The first time I climbed the ladder today it was like old-times: simple. And now, look what I can do." He pulled his right lower leg back, and the bend at the knee was near 90 degrees. "See that?" he said, looking with astonishment at the others. "I have an appointment with my orthopedic guy in two weeks. He said he could fix this thing. Said there's a little scar tissue in there that can be removed with arthroscopy and once that is done the knee will be flexible again. I think it just fixed itself. Or something appeared out of nowhere and, unbeknownst to me, just climbed in there and got it done. How do we explain that? And, why all of sudden, today?"

"I climbed the ladder today and I distinctly remember not getting in the lake at all last year," said Freddy with a bit of emotion in his voice. He took a deep breath and said, "I decided to give it a try since I lost some weight and am in a little bit better shape. Now you're making me question my big muscles and toned physique.

"But seriously," Freddy continued, I've had a back thing going too. Been thinking I should go in and have it checked out. It kind of reminds me of the pain I had before that cancer lump had to come out, several years ago. I know I've been procrastinating because I don't want to have to deal with it, all over again. Today? No issue. I also noticed that stupid skin rash that I get on my feet. It was there two days ago. Today? Gone. It could be a coincidence. Maybe it's still too early to draw any conclusions," and his voice trailed off as he lapsed back into thoughtfulness.

Bert picked it up by saying, "I know I'm the cynic and it's hard for me to become invested in something like this. But, there is this one thing that I can't quite figure: my head; sinuses and allergies. I've been doing a lot more honking over the course of this past winter and spring. Can't go anywhere without my handkerchiefs. And I mean it's a constant thing, the drainage. When we got in from the boat just a little bit ago, I discovered my handkerchief on the chair. I didn't take it with me. I haven't needed it. Maybe it's a little thing but, it does make me wonder."

"All right, guys. Sounds like there's enough reason to consider Arvie's question," said Carl. "So, again, what has changed? Something had to change for Arvie yesterday because of the reflux thing last night, and, obviously, something changed for the rest of us today. If we are in agreement that indeed, something is going on here, what is it that we do about it? Shall we sleep on it tonight and meet at the breakfast table with thoughts and ideas? I'm just asking here – is that a reasonable plan?" The other three were nodding heads, indicating an unspoken agreement. With that, Carl passed gas, acknowledged the applause, resumed his seat, and all got back to the business that had been left un-eaten.

Shortly after kitchen clean-up, Freddy disappeared down the road, out front with his phone stuck to his ear. Obviously, he was in need of a conversation with Joyce. Bert walked down to the dock and took a seat on the pontoon with phone available for the upcoming conversation with Gayle. Arvie found a spot on the deck and dialed Hannah. Carl opened up his laptop and sat down at the dining room table.

Later, Bert poured and delivered another round of JD. As the dark settled in, one by one those outside gave up the battle with the Minnesota state bird and made their way inside. Carl, unbothered by the flying interruptions while inside, continued to type away. The first full day of the reunion was being put to bed as one-by-one the sleepwear was donned, the lights were turned out and with grateful sighs, the snores began.

Chapter 3

"When you can't remember what you are supposed to do, mop the floor, paint a wall or clean a boiler – whichever you prefer. Just do something. Heh heh."
- *Ole*

Blessed are the poor in spirit, for theirs is the kingdom of heaven.
Matthew 5:3

Arvie reached for the cell phone, pushed the button and saw that it was 2:45. All was dark and quiet. No acid reflux. It would have occurred by now. He couldn't sleep but it was too early to get up. He crawled on top of the covers and just laid there looking out the window into the dark. *Lord*, he thought, *what is happening here? You know all things, what's in our minds, whether spoken or not. There are questions, Lord. Stir in me what I know but don't remember, can't recall. There is something there. You know what it is. What am I missing? Help this humble servant. In Jesus name, Amen.*

Several minutes later he gave it up, sat on the side of the bed for a moment before reaching for clothes. He dressed in the dark and then padded into the kitchen and did what was necessary to bring the Mr. Coffee to life. He stood at the sink looking out the kitchen window to the east. Wasn't much to see. Even though there was some moonlight flickering in and about the dense patch of woods across the road, it was just too dark to see anything out there. So, looking *inside* was the alternative, and that's what he needed to do. Something had happened on Monday that he was overlooking. He had to re-do Monday, that was reunion arrival day. *OK, Arvid, let's take Monday one step at a time and begin at the beginning.*

Falling out of bed and the ear thing started the day at 2:30. He wondered about the antibiotics he received at the hospital and decided that couldn't be it because they hadn't helped with the acid reflux. He poured himself the first cup of the morning and headed to the deck.

He put the cup down on the table and realized something was nagging at him, a-back-of-the-mind sort of thing. He had just missed something. *What - just now?* He stood and retraced his steps back into the kitchen and stood again at the kitchen sink. *I got out of bed and came here to the kitchen to make coffee. I had poured water into the Mr. Coffee and added the coffee and turned it ....* his eyes fell on the black can. He picked it up and held it close for a moment, again looking out the kitchen window into the dark as he said to himself, *Forever: a fine coffee product of Northern Minnesota. Could it be the coffee?*

Back on the deck he placed the pad of paper and a pencil on the table and took a seat. There was just enough light creeping out the window for him to write his notes. So, with a degree of excitement pulsing through him, he began.

> "Heading north on 169. Potty stop. Convenience store. Pull in. Hit the john. Leaving. See coffee brewing and coffee in a can. Filled my mug. Picked up a can. Headed out. Wait. Picked up two cans. Paid at counter. Really old guy. Looked like Native American. Said he'd been drinking the coffee since 1912-never been to a doctor. How old was the guy?"

It's 2013 now, so if he started drinking at birth he would be 101 years old. He definitely looked that old. Maybe he started drinking it at 15 so he would be 86 or so but had lasted 101 years without a Dr. appointment? Was he full of crap? Did he want to sell his two cans that bad? Arvie continued his notes.

> "Kind of talked into the 2nd can. Said something like, "I won't have any more of this for a while so maybe you'd like to get the last can" – or something like that. Started drinking the coffee at around 4-4:30. Scheduled bathroom break and McDonalds in Garrison – skipped it. Kept going. No bathroom break 'til bedtime? Next morning, boys drink their

first cups, three or four pots full, from wake-up through breakfast.

I had filled my travel mug the day before, so that's why the need for potty breaks was gone and why no acid reflux Monday night, really? Is it possible? Could it work that fast?

"Good Lord," Arvie exclaimed aloud. "It's a magic coffee that heals stuff in the human body!"

He was excitedly pacing the deck, about to head in to refill his cup, when the door was pushed open and Carl shuffled out. "Hey," said Arvie nearly skipping with glee to Carl's side. "I'm really glad you finally hauled your butt out here. Let's get a cup. I think I got it. I wanna run it by you. Come on. I'm pumped." Carl didn't offer any resistance as Arvie grabbed him by the elbow, pushed him inside to the pot, grabbed a cup, filled it to the brim and led the way back to the deck.

Arvie told him what he had been thinking, read his notes about the coffee purchase and revealed the conclusion he had drawn. When he finished, he looked up into the eyes of his friend. "What do you think?" he asked, as his excitement continued to mount. If there was any chance it was for real, well, he didn't dare to think about what it could mean. The big guy, obviously not fully awake or in any state of understanding, reached for a "weed" (also known as a cigarette).

As roommates, back in college, they had had many conversations and many more in recent years. Arvie could remember none that had ramifications as significant as this one could. He knew that Carl would not respond to the question until he had mentally studied it from every angle. It might take a while. Arvie knew it wasn't his turn to speak. He gave his friend time to cogitate on the matter.

Finally, several minutes later, Carl drew himself up, took a breath and said, "I don't believe it." Then again but slower, "I …. can't …. believe …. it. Do you realize what you are proposing?"

"Yes, I do," Arvie said hesitantly. "Well, I think I do."

"Given what the old guy told you when you bought the coffee, and if he wasn't lying through his eye balls, you purchased *miracles in a can*. We have all spoken of things that have suddenly been cured. Can I really say that? In each of those cases, the cure happened in less than 24 hours, and those were only a few aches and pains that quickly came to mind. Won't we have to be paying attention to our physical and mental health for months and months to be sure of any of this? Can you imagine: healing for sale for only six dollars a can?

"So, we should base our reaction only on what we know. As of right now, that consists of the few things that we talked about at supper last night. And if everything we described is truly fixed…. I don't know if I can say this, but I think we have found …. the *Fountain of Youth*?

"Wait. Wait a minute. Let's be practical here. Did you buy two, two pound cans? How much is left? How much more of it can we buy back at that store? Can we buy it in truckloads? Trainloads? What a great name, Forever. If what we suspect is true, why hasn't your old friend built himself a huge business? I'd be happy to help him set up the distribution side of his coffee business; take it international. No. Wrong. We need to buy him out."

Carl had taken to pacing while sipping and talking. His weed had been forgotten in the ash tray. There was a spring in his step that no one had seen since sometime back in the mid 60's.

Arvie joined him in the pace. Back and forth they went and occasionally there would be some giggling as they passed one another.

Carl then paused in his pacing, saying, "Ok. Let's get real. Think of the applications for this coffee. If it is a fountain of youth for humans, what can it do for animals? Should they lap some up? How about werewolves? Or mummies… or the walking dead? Ooh, now there is one for you. Could this stuff un-dead the walking dead? This does get interesting because we must also ask, 'Can the dead drink coffee?'"

"Enough," Arvie laughed. "But I wanna be the one to write the movie script."

"Arvie, can we find that place again? Well, of course we can. It's just down the road. He began to pace again mumbling, "Miracles happen to those who believe in them - Bernard Berenson – the Renaissance Art Critic."

Arvie looked at him blankly and said, "Huh?"

"Oh nothing," mumbled Carl. "Just a Berenson blurb on miracles that came to mind."

"What's an art critic know about miracles?" Arvie asked.

"I've wondered the same thing," Carl said with a shake of the head.

"Yes, we can find the place again," answered Arvie. "My only concern is if the guy has any more to sell. He clearly said he didn't know when he would have more. No matter what, I think that we gotta talk to the guys about going back. We'll have to start at the beginning with them and see if they arrive at the same conclusion we have."

The slamming of a cupboard door in the kitchen signaled the imminent arrival of at least one of the boys. "Shall we wait for both to arrive or shall we proceed as they arrive one by one?" asked Carl.

"I'm too anxious to wait. I'd like to let 'em in on this as they arrive," Arvie suggested. Carl nodded in agreement.

It was Bert, the cynic, who shuffled out the door onto the deck moments later, sipping on Forever. "You guys got to stop making all this noise so early in the morning. Some of us older guys need to get our sleep."

Carl replied, "Bert, tell us when your brain is activated because we've got something to discuss."

"We might as well wait for Freddie. He's standing in front of the mirror in the bathroom picking his nose hairs or some such nonsense."

"I heard that," Freddie hollered through the screen door as another cupboard slammed shut.

It seemed like an eternity, but eventually Freddie appeared in the doorway, "How long have you guys been up? Good coffee, by the way."

The newcomers wiped the sleep from their eyes as Carl began, "Arvie was out here long before I was, writing down the details of Monday. He discovered what made his Monday different from ours and may be responsible for our little health miracles. Why don't you begin there Arvie; with those same notes that you read to me."

So, Arvie read through the notes, looked up at Bert and Freddie and said, "That's it guys. Does that make any sense? What do you think?"

Arvie held his breath through another long pause. Freddie was the first to speak, "This is crazy." Arvie turned to Bert and asked, "How about you?"

"Well, this is pretty far-fetched if you ask me. No, I don't believe it. For us to discover this – this – whatever it is, makes no sense to me. There are questions, boys, like who made this coffee? How did they make it and with what? No, a healing coffee makes no sense at all."

"Well," Arvie continued, would you be interested in going to buy some more; I mean, go back to that convenience store and find out if there is more? Don't you think we should at least do some investigation?"

"I think we should see if we can get some more and if the old man is willing to have a little talk," said Carl. "I want to ask him where he gets it, what's in it and if there is a chance to continue getting it when we get back home."

Freddie nodded in agreement while Bert frowned. "This is going to be a huge waste of time," he growled under his breath.

Carl continued, "Bert, what if this coffee *is* the Fountain of Youth. Have you seriously considered that possibility? Is there any way your cynicism could deal with that? Think of it – what if it is? Shouldn't we at least check it out a little bit more?"

Bert replied hesitantly, "Ok. I guess it would be unwise not to check it out. I'm in. If nothing else, I get the right to talk about all of your stupidity at next year's Ole."

"Let's not get ahead of ourselves," said Freddie with a big grin, "the real priority is to do a good breakfast." He rose from the table telling the boys to sit and relax for a few minutes while he got things going. "We can go buy more miracle coffee after we eat the most important meal of the day."

* * * * * * * *

The mood was pensive as the white Ford headed south on 169. Carl drove because he was saving so much money with every mile. It was a hybrid and Carl loved it. "I'm going to be wealthy any day now," he had stated several times.

"You know," said Arvie, "I'm going to guess the store is 45 minutes, or so, south of the Garrison McDonalds. The one thing I know for sure is that it will be on the left as we head south and it's a bit south of the casino. It is not much to look at: old, not very big and I don't remember any sign. I think there was another store just next to it but in the same building and then gas pumps out front, I think. Anyway, let's be alert." Even with many miles to go, three sets of eyes were set on the scenery to the left. Only Carl didn't look around. He had this odd habit of keeping his eyes on the road when he drove.

"There *are* gas pumps, right Carl?" Arvie blurted out, "and the store next door is a liquor store but I think it's out of business – closed up. Is that what you remember?"

"Yeah, I think so," said Carl. "But I really wasn't taking notes or anything."

"Wow, Arvie," said Freddie. "It must be the Forever, because you never could remember anything *for ever*." He giggled and gave Bert an elbow in the back seat next to him, "Did you hear how I used Forever and *for ever* in the same sentence? That was pretty good, huh?"

Bert had known Freddie *for ever*. He sighed and said, "Yes, Freddie, you have *for ever* had a way with words. Even from the pulpit." Freddie gave a loud, "Amen."

The miles rolled by as did a number of little bridges over Brandy Creek. It seemed that every three or four miles there was another bridge with another sign reminding them that they were passing over it, yet again.

"Is that it?" asked Freddie, pointing ahead. Arvie and Carl both nodded and the white Ford slowed and turned left into the dusty lot. They passed two rusting pumps and pulled into position just in front of the weathered wooden front porch. They got out of the vehicle and paused outside the door. Arvie and Carl exchanged a look that silently said, *Ok, this is it*. And in they went.

The inside was darker and even more decrepit than Arvie remembered. Of course, when they entered the last time, they were on a mission. This time, they were taking it all in. Arvie walked to the front counter. The counter top was a beat-up piece of oak. *What happened to the cracking glass and duct tape?* Arvie remembered that clearly. The slab of oak appeared to have been there forever. *Where is the old man? Where is the coffee pot full of freshly brewed Forever?* Instead, there was a young girl behind the counter staring down at a cell phone, as all young girls do. She was wildly chewing a large wad of gum while spinning strands of red and green tinted hair in one hand and manipulating her phone with the other.

The boys had fanned out around the little store. Arvie walked to where he thought he had found the Mr. Coffee but there was none in sight. Instead he looked at a stack of old t-shirts promoting Old Style beer, sized small, a couple of straw hats, sized 4X and a display of stomach remedies, Gas-X, Tums and Rol-Aids.

He turned to the counter and interrupted the girl's study of her phone. "Aaahh, excuse me. Do you have any coffee?" he asked.

"No coffee," she answered; eyes never leaving the phone.

Arvie tried again, "There was a man behind the counter Monday afternoon when I came in, a very old man, wearing a funny hat. Can you tell me where I can find him?"

She replied, "I don't know of any old man who works here or any old man who has ever been behind this counter." With that said, she raised her head and eyes abruptly and moved her hand to sweep away the multi colored hair so she could see something. Yes, she was young, perhaps 16 or so.

He tried again. "I bought two cans of Forever Coffee that day. Do you have any more I can buy?"

She said, "We don't sell any coffee." Her eyes dropped to her phone once again, obviously wishing this conversation would end. Arvie realized that he'd lost her and turned away.

Bert had been observing from a distance and decided to lend a hand. He asked the girl if the owner of the store was available, hinting that perhaps, that would be her father. She shook her head no, and mumbled without looking up, "Ain't got no father. The owner ain't here. He's hardly ever here. Ain't been here for weeks."

The boys continued to circulate through the decrepit store. Arvie wondered what had drawn him into this joint in the first place. *Why this place?* He headed back to the bathroom, pushed open the squeaky door and went in. It was a tiny, cramped space. He didn't remember it being that small, but again, he was on a mission when he was there the first time. The porcelain throne was there and filthy, as well as a crust-covered little sink sitting on a pedestal at an awkward angle. There was no soap or paper toweling. He didn't remember it being that bad. He used the facilities as he had done before and reached down to flush. It didn't flush. He was sure that it had worked before. The way it looked, it may not have been flushed for quite some time. *Is this the Twilight Zone?* he wondered. *Is this a Rod Serling creation? Did I hallucinate my visit here before? Maybe I was never really here. Where is the old man? How could he have never been here? Good grief.* He opened the squeaky door and hurriedly moved toward the exit.

The boys had already left. Arvie could see the three of them through the grime covered front window. He navigated his way through a narrow path to the front door, knowing there was nothing worth buying in there.

He reached for the door handle when something to his left, caught his eye. On the wall, hung a small, felt-covered cork board where push pins were used to hold business cards, announcements and community information. With the collection of dust, yellowed newspaper clippings and felt that no longer appeared felt-like, he could tell that it hadn't been disturbed in a very long time.

"There he is!" he exclaimed with elation. *That's him. That's him. That's him,* he thought. The gal behind the counter rolled her eyes and was irked with such a disruption. Arvie didn't notice and burst through the front door and hollered, "Guys, you've got to see this." They filed back in and he pointed to the clipping pinned to the lower right hand corner. All four bent their heads sideways together to read:

> *"Jacob Whitefeather walked the Road of Spirits in peace on Friday, July 18. Outdoor services will be held at Woods & Waters Cemetery at 4:00 P.M, Tuesday. All*

who knew him are invited to attend the celebration of life. He is survived by his many friends."

The picture was a simple head and shoulders shot of Jacob Whitefeather wearing his pork pie hat. He was wearing an open collared shirt with a loosely knotted necktie and a vest. *That's what he was wearing on Monday,* thought Arvie. The newspaper clipping was dated July 20, 1963.

Without a word, as each finished reading the clipping, they silently slipped out the front door. Nobody was talking as they piled back into Whitey, the Ford. Silence can be very special when enjoyed for all the right reasons but not when it is experienced following such disappointment. Arvie was dumbfounded as he replayed the recent shopping experience. *How does someone die 50 years ago this month and yet sell me coffee just two days ago?*

"Anyone want to tell me what just happened?" Arvie asked. "How is someone dead for 50 years, but show up two days ago to sell me some coffee? Huh? Huh?"

Arvie knew that it would take Carl some time to ponder, so he gave a push to those in the back seat, "Will someone say something back there?"

Freddie said, "I remember a Steven King novel I read some years ago where someone died but not really. I didn't get into it because I believe that there is only one person who ever died and then rose again. I never thought I would be a part of a story like that. Seriously, do you think what you saw on Monday was a real person? Could you have had some type of vision? Or maybe you imagined something?"

After thinking for a moment Arvie said, "I handed the person, the vision, or the figment money when I paid for the two cans of coffee. I'm not real sure a vision or a figment would be able to make change. That leaves a real person so that's what I'm going with. It was the way he talked that made him a real person. His breathing was forced and irregular, and frankly, difficult. I don't know for sure but I doubt very much if a vision or a figment would have difficulty breathing. Now that I've said that, though, I'm wondering how it makes any more sense to claim that he was an alive dead guy as opposed to a vision or my imagination. I don't know, I'm just sayin'. I want to go to the cabin and get to some Jack."

Bert threw in a mumble about not knowing how to speak to this situation either, but would agree with the Jack part.

Carl kept the car between the ditches and was quiet for several miles before asking, "Is there anything he might have said to you that you may have forgotten, any other scrap that could give us additional information?"

"I'll think about it," Arvie said, but he felt sure that in the darkness of that morning, while sitting on the deck, he had captured the entirety of the encounter. And yet, he would replay it over and over in his mind whether Carl had asked him to or not. How could he ever get this out of his head?

When Whitey the Ford pulled up behind the cabin Arvie broke the silence, "Why was it me that happened to make that purchase on Monday? You guys all came by that place on the way up but it was me that had to use the bathroom right then, not any of you. My bladder caused this to happen and I'm sick and tired of my bladder. If I had anybody else's bladder I would have been able to keep right on going and then Jacob Whitefeather would have had to sell Forever to someone else. Then *that* person would have had to deal with a dead person who isn't dead. *That* person would have to deal with all this in *his* little puny p-brain and I could just go on with my life or I could tell that person, 'you're just going to have to deal with this dead/living/coffee whatever it is situation so suck it up, figure it out and stop your whining you little ninny!'" By then Arvie had opened, exited and slammed the car door and was marching his way back to the cabin talking very loudly to no one in particular.

Carl chuckled and said, "That's just what I was about to say Arvie, but I couldn't have said it any better." They exited the vehicle, including Carl without giving it a thought, a smile playing across their faces as they headed inside for some quality time with Jack.

Everyone and everything received a toast that afternoon, especially *Ole*, mainly because he was the pre-eminent coffee lover. He had taught the boys how to love a good cup. They had all climbed aboard a stool at Red's, sat next to The Man and sipped the brew. At those times, there wasn't any conversation. *Ole* stirred the coffee for several minutes while staring into it deeply and waiting to know, *it is ready now.* He approached a cup of coffee with reverence. It would not be hurried. There was no sound. It was always peaceful there; at the counter in Red's. They would all sit in a row, quietly looking into their respective cups, stirring and stirring until the coffee spoke to The Man. When the time was right, he laid down the silver spoon, hoisted the cup gently to his lips and all followed suit. The coffee was sipped, enjoyed, respected and honored with thoughtful silence. The Man would say, "Amen," climb down from the stool and bark "let's get to work." Ole's chapel service was concluded. All climbed down from their stools in unison and waited patiently for The Man to open the door and lead them back to campus.

Bert mumbled with raised glass, "No one in the history of our planet loved coffee as much as *Ole*. And now we have Forever coffee. Is it truly a healing blend? To *Ole*, every coffee was a healing blend. His words echo down through the ages, 'Honor each cup. Respect it. Pay tribute to it and it will heal what ails you.' How many times did I hear him say those words? Especially the last part, '*it will heal*?' Yes. He actually said that. It makes me wonder if healing is associated with hope. Maybe every time *Ole* sat down with a cup of coffee he believed he was being healed. Did he harbor that hope deep inside? The way he drank coffee makes me believe he found hope in every cup - hope for healing of some kind. Perhaps it was for the healing for stuff like we talked about. Maybe it was for developing a closer relationship with his crew or with God. Maybe God, to *Ole*, was really in that coffee cup. Perhaps he worshipped God in that way? I never thought to ask him those kinds of questions and now he's gone. Gone forever. But I will believe it that way. I can if I want to so I will. Thank you *Ole*. You have taught me. And I believe."

Except for the mumbling of Bert, the room had been in total silence. No one had moved. No one had breathed through the oration. The room remained quiet until Freddie exclaimed, "Damn. Bert, that was really good. You are still the best preacher I never heard. Be honest with us, you must have used that theme in a sermon before, right? Maybe a sermon that you gave to the people in the library? Huh? Come on, you didn't just make that up, did you?"

"Freddie, you forget that I never preached a sermon, but if I had, they would all have been ad lib, off the cuff, created with no forethought whatsoever." And then with a wry smile, "Most likely, much like yours."

"Yeah, right."

Arvie picked up on the theme and said dreamily, "Forever coffee. Will any more be found? And Jacob Whitefeather: where was he and how does he make the stuff? Maybe he comes back to life every 50 years to sell some coffee to deluded old men. I mean, who else would so easily believe in the fountain of youth? It's easy for this group to believe. It only took one day of Forever to start to work. And then I say to you guys, 'Here, let me lead you down the garden path by telling you that I have been healed by a coffee named Forever.' And away we go; skipping down that garden path. Do do do do, do do do do. Serling. Are we now, to be forever young? Will ripped off ears heal perfectly before the dawn of another day? Will Forever fix our failing minds as well? Is our belief in Forever actually proof that our minds are failing? It says in the Bible that the bodies of old waste away. Are the four of us the only bodies that will not waste away? Stay tuned to this and other informed news and weather radio stations."

"If I would've had my phone on during that, it would've been a big hit on you-tube. That was brilliant," said Carl. "By the way, how much Forever is left?"

"The can in the kitchen is half empty." answered Arvie. "But, I've got the second can, too. I'll split it up so we'll all have some to take home to heal our loved ones, and whoever else happens to share our pot."

A quick lunch was put together and the rest of the glorious sun-filled afternoon was spent either aboard the pontoon or in the cool waters of the lake. Arvie fished off the back of the pontoon while the others were cavorting in the water. There was laughing and splashing and jumping and diving and no-one needed assistance in climbing the ladder. Freddie said, "Before Forever, I couldn't negotiate that ladder and now I climb it easily. I don't know what to think." Arvie couldn't help wondering if he shouldn't just jump in and swim. *No chance of infection when you're drinking Forever…* but… Hannah would kill him.

Back in the boat, Freddy began the discussion of his true passion, "Tonight we will be blessed with a big steak and buttery, salty, peppered corn on the cob, a big Caesar salad and some red wine to compliment the beef. Did I say we were having Porterhouse? Not just any Porterhouse, but Nebraska Porterhouse from the sand hills where Crazy Horse roamed free. He led his people in search of the perfect piece of beef for the grill, right? Everyone knows that. We'll also do some other stuff to make The Last Supper memorable. As they did at that first Last Supper, Arvie has agreed to bathe all our feet with an oil of some kind. Thank you Arvie."

The food was wonderful but the foot-wash and oiling did not happen. No one wanted Arvie fondling their feet, never mind the fact that, the only oil in the house was some cheap brand of Neetsfoot oil that was used on Carl's ball glove about 100 years before.

Arvie had also taken note of Bert's bunion and said, "Ummmm…. no."

Freddie thought that tending to feet would've been good for everyone. "But come on boys. After all, if it was good enough for the disciples, it should be good enough for us. Next year it will be done. I'll bring expensive oil: 40 weight Pennzoil."

"Oh, that's a super idea, Freddy," chided Bert.

Following the clean-up, it was toasting time again while all leaned on the railing and watched the sun go down. They toasted the setting sun. They toasted Freddie's weight loss: nearly 30 pounds since the last reunion.

Everyone proposed a toast or two for someone who needed to be remembered: a young man who had just been shipped out to Afghanistan, a young single-mom of four battling severe depression, senior friends battling one illness or another. Special memories were honored as well. Someone even toasted English muffins. The most fitting conclusion, however, was the toast to aging bodies. There was a lengthy silence after that one.

Arvie excused himself, "Boys, I'm sorry to break this up but I must attend to some business in the little boy's room. If you'll pardon me a moment, I'll return shortly."

* * * * * * * *

He was in the habit of sorting through the reading material Carl made available in the bathroom. "The New Yorker Literary Journal." "Pietisten." "Saturday Evening Post." "Moby Dick: the short version." "This week in Baseball." "Golf World." "Politics for the Intellectual." Arvie picked up the latter and threw it in the trash can under the sink.

Business completed, Arvie returned to the old boys who were now toasting Siamese cats in a northern province of China.

"Hey guys, can I read you something? I just found this among Carl's reading material in the head."

"I didn't realize that there was something worthwhile to read in there," voiced Bert. "Was it in the New Yorker or that old April Fool's edition of our old Mount Holy Waters Weekly Newspaper?"

"I don't know," replied Arvie. "I think it is the Pietisten. This page was lying open at the bottom of the pile. Listen to this. Does any of this remind you of something?

> *The Ojibwe believe the fundamental essence of life to be unity, the oneness of all things. Harmony with all living things is the mission. People cannot be separated from the land with its cycle of seasons and the cycle of all living things; birth, growth, death.*
>
> *The Ojibwe are also said to be the faith keepers; keepers of the sacred scrolls of the Midewiwin Shamanic Society of Healers. Generations of Ojibwe Midewiwin, knowledgeable in the ways of all things, have provided healing to those in need. It is known that Midewiwin were sent by Gitchi Manitou, God and Creator of All, to*

resolve many mysteries of mother earth and master the harmonies that flow through life.

The Midewiwin were taught how to live in oneness with mother earth; how to use the elements of mother earth to benefit those who dwelt as one with her. Every blade of grass is useful. Mother earth provides healing through nature. The Midewiwin have been shown the secrets, taught to use earth's many miracles. Mysterious powers were given them by Gitchi Manitou. They see within a person, even within the soul. Healing may come even before illness. Those who are healed before the illness are unaware that healing has occurred. The gift received passes with a thankless spirit. It is the way.

In their Medicine Lodges, the Midewiwin call out to the Great Spirit and by so doing can divine the hidden, both in body and soul, cure misery and bring hope. In the earliest sun of a new day, hope rises to joy with praise given to Gitchi Manitou for the matchless gift. Living in oneness gathers all creatures in great joy.

Arvie concluded the reading and looked up at his friends. Bert was hiking up his shorts and re-cinching his belt. Freddie was yawning while he scratched his navel. Bert apologized and said he couldn't follow the entire reading; said he needed sleep and headed inside. Freddy also excused himself stating a lack of mental clarity after a bit too much time with Jack.

It was obvious, however, that Carl would not be jumping ship at that point. When Arvie looked in his direction, Carl was focused and staring intensely back at him. "Are you thinking that article has something to do with Forever: the Ojibwe blend a magic, healing coffee with all-natural ingredients or something? Is that it? All of that happens even though there are no beans grown up here?"

"I guess so. It's possible, isn't it? These magicians go rake up some leaves and roots, chicken droppings, squirrel fir, and possum remains, throw in a shovel of magic dirt, and sell it off as coffee? Can it be any more than that?"

"I don't think so. But … there has to be more to it than that."

"How would you *know* that?"

"I don't know anything about any of this stuff," exclaimed Carl. "I'm going to bed. I'm beat and my mind is fried." He poured himself another Jack, "Well, maybe one more." He leaned on the railing, gazing west into the dark. "Been a little different this year, hasn't it? All because of our Forever mystery."

"Yeah," replied Arvie. "This morning was a shocker. We got some answers but not any that we wanted. I wonder if arteries can be scrubbed out, cholesterol levels can test out at nothing and arthritis could be a thing of the past. Imagine: arthritis disappears like polio and so many other horrendous diseases of the past. Beat up knees won't be bone on bone anymore. Where does it end? What would this life be like if all pain was eradicated? I'm afraid there is something wrong with this entire synopsis, Carl."

"And, of course, there is the ultimate question, if it heals the human body and if we had an ongoing supply, would we die – or would we live *forever*?" Carl posed the question softly, even reverently; almost like a prayer. They looked at each other for a long, quiet moment. Carl continued, "Are we talking about heaven on this earth? This earth so filled with evil and so much pain."

"Do we want to be responsible for something like that?" whispered Arvie. "I mean, God went to a lot of trouble sending Jesus down here to die for us and our sins so that, through his Grace, we could spend eternity in Heaven. We don't have to fear death because on the other side, it's all good. And here we are, Carl and Arvid, discovering a healing coffee that takes away all pain so we can have heaven on this earth. Really? I'm not sure I want a role in that play." There was a long quietness that descended over the two old friends.

Several moments later, Arvie continued, "Carl, do you remember the movie The Green Mile? Tom Hanks played the jailor, and the big guy who was convicted, wrongly of course, of killing those two little girls had to be put to death. At the end of the movie the jailor guy said he was something like 125 years old and God would not let him die because he had helped put the innocent man to death. All he wanted to do was die and he couldn't. Is that the same fate for the four of us? We are messing with God's plan, aren't we?"

"Yeah, I'm afraid you're right. But now that you've brought it up, I don't want to be at odds with God so I'm going to bed. I don't want to think of all the ramifications of that," Carl said through a massive yawn. "That's way too big a concept for me to handle. If you figure it out tonight, tell me in the morning at breakfast." The big guy shuffled off.

Arvie was left on the deck in quiet confusion. "Wow," he muttered and began to pace. *What is going to come from all of this? I'll split up the remaining coffee in the morning. Everyone will take some home. But now, what do I do with this responsibility? I'm in possession of a magic coffee – well, at least it seems so. I've got to use this for as long as Jacob will get it to me to bring as much healing to older folks as possible. I can't think of it in any other way.*

He headed inside and down the hall to the bathroom pondering the dream that kicked him out of bed and broke his ear. *Maybe this is what it was all about – messing around with God's plan. Maybe the dream was a warning to stay away from Forever. But how can I not help people if I'm able? This is a real quagmire and I'm afraid I'm not smart enough to figure it out.*

Chapter 4

"When it's hard to say good-bye, don't say good-bye.
Heh heh." - *Ole*

"Be strong and brave. Don't be afraid and don't be frightened, because the Lord your God will go with you. He will not leave you or forget you."
Deuteronomy 31:6

Morning arrived and everyone did their very best to cover up the ugly truth that another *Ole* was coming to an end. The emails would begin as soon as the following morning, about how quickly the next 12 months would go and, Lord willing, how all would return the next July.

Arvie made note of how good the breakfast was and vowed to savor every bite because there wouldn't be one like it for another 51 weeks. Why? Because for all the intervening weeks they would be eating *healthy* to increase their chance of enjoying each other's company once again. *Maybe*, Arvie thought, *with this new magical healing coffee, we don't have to be concerned with all that healthy eating stuff. Wouldn't that be nice? We'd be able to eat food that tastes good all the time. But how and where will we continue to find the coffee?*

Throughout breakfast, every time someone at the table reached for their coffee cup, Arvie was paying attention. He noticed that there were no quick sips rushing to get back to the bacon. Everyone seemed to stare at the dark contents of their cup before taking a slow sip and, only after a moment of enjoying the flavor, was it swallowed. They all appeared to contemplate that each sip could be providing health benefits. Two days prior, when Arvie had brought up the subject on the pontoon, they had all contributed something to the conversation about their seemingly improved physical health.

Arvie brought these thoughts to the attention of the group and said, "Guys, I'm bothered because our get-together has been consumed by this coffee thing. Regardless of whether we do or do not believe in magic or miracles, that may be exactly what's happening here. Perhaps we will know more in a week or two. I hope, should any of you discover something that might be related to all this, that you'll let the rest of us know."

It remained quiet around the table, but there was nodding and grunting assent that passed for agreement from all. "By the way," Arvie continued, "a little something for you all to take home with you. These containers hold about 30 pots of Forever each. Take 'em home and use them as you wish. If I get lucky and stumble into more, I'll send what I can to each of you. Let's all pledge to do the same." More affirmatives followed from the group and that was the last of the coffee related conversations.

Freddie left almost immediately after breakfast. Bert left an hour later.

Carl and Arvie lived about 40 minutes apart in the Twin Cities and would get together, perhaps, once a month. They would sit with cups of coffee and discuss their writing, talk about authors and good books and, in general, just spend time together. Carl was working on a book that he hoped to get published one day. He hadn't yet decided on the title. It was going to be a fun discussion about many of the stories found in the Bible. Carl would read his latest chapter aloud and they would discuss and enjoy it together.

Since retiring, Arvie had had time to write as well. He had been the editor of the College News, back in the day, and during a time in broadcasting had written many articles for the local papers. He enjoyed writing; the act of telling stories. He had discussed several ideas with Carl and the big guy had been very supportive.

After watching Bert depart, they went to the table on the deck for one last "cuppa". Carl said with a giggle, "Arvie, this thing with the coffee. Just think of the possibilities for memories at *The Ole* next year. How much fun is it going to be to look back on this one?" They grinned at each other, knowing what the following year's recap was going to sound like. It would begin… *and what the hell were we thinking with that coffee thing last year?* Everyone would laugh and then recount what part of their body they thought was being healed. *We drove 100 miles, roundtrip, trying to find this Indian guy - who died 50 years before - that Arvie had bought coffee from...* and on and on it would go.

"Carl, I want you to pray about this whole coffee situation. We talked about it last night briefly and I'd like to get God's approval on us healing old bodies. I prayed last night about it and I plan to continue with it. You've got a better line to Him than I do, so I want you to pray as well."

"I will, but your connection to Him is every bit as good as mine," Carl responded. "How do you feel about getting answers to your prayers?"

Arvie considered for a moment and answered, "Pretty good, I think. There have been times when I've been writing and hit a wall. I couldn't determine where to go next and in the middle of the night I'd wake up and there was my answer. Now maybe that's just my advanced brain functioning as I've trained it to do over the years, but maybe God put the answer there. Maybe he was talking with me right then, very softly, of course. You know, sometimes I've wished that I would've prayed a lot more over all the years. I wish Hannah and I had prayed about everything."

"Ok. I get a little nervous when we get on this subject. You say I have the better line to Him, but I've got a way to go to get to where you are, I think. Anyway, I promise to help out with it and let's keep each other in the loop as those answers come to us – if they do."

"Thanks Carl." The two old friends enjoyed a youthful fist bump.

It was mid-afternoon when they pulled away from the cabin. They had swept it out, washed the sheets and pillowcases and cleaned and put away everything in the kitchen. Through it all, they had talked about Carl's upcoming trip to California to see Boldy and his family. Carl planned to leave first thing the next morning and promised to stay in touch via email, text, and occasional phone calls.

Arvie had suggested that he be on the look-out for black can opportunities during his trip, "If I could stop at a convenience store and find it," he had said, "it could happen to you too."

Arvie further suggested that perhaps every Native American tribe from coast to coast had a Midewiwin that comes back from the dead every 50 years to roast some beans. "Stay alert," he prompted, "the next can that comes may come to you".

Heading towards home they discussed the Twilight Zone. Carl said that the coffee situation made him feel like the guy on the plane. "You know, that episode, or was it the movie? Anyway, he sees the creature or thing on the wing of the plane while flying at night. How do you deal with that? If he tells people …. if WE tell people, we may look as crazy as that guy." They laughed and agreed that their coffee dilemma had put them in a unique position.

* * * * * * * *

It stands to reason that, as time goes by and the human body deteriorates with age, one can expect to feel as good today as he ever will. That makes sense. Of course, there will be some good days and then some bad days, but on a large line graph of how a body feels, the line is dipping south, perhaps not plunging, but heading in the general direction of downhill. Forever coffee, however, seemed to be battling with that southerly direction. Arvie had not taken any of his pills for arthritis, acid reflux or anything else since departing for *The Ole* and had said to himself more than once throughout the trip that he was feeling really good.

As they drove for home, the discussion continued to return to coffee and the hope it had inspired in the group. "Perhaps coffee beans are imported to Minnesota from some place where they grow beans and then they get roasted up here by someone who is dead?" suggested Arvie. He continued, "I'm thinking that the magical healing ingredient comes through because of the dead guy. Or, wait! Maybe it's the rabbit droppings or something from the soil of Northern Minnesota. Huh? Huh? Waddaya think? No, never mind. I still think it has something to do with the dead guy who's doing the roasting."

"Nope," retorted Carl. "I feel confident that whatever it is, it's something totally native to northern Minnesota. Could be the soil or the trees, wildlife or water. Maybe something unique up here that has never before been identified. Could be that we are on the leading edge of something that's never before been identified. What would you think of that?"

"I don't know but I can tell you that my mother would be laughing at us right now and she would say, '*You boys are smarter than that. What's the matter with you?*'"

Carl chuckled, "Sounds like my mom too. Hey, and how about Bert? He was a spoiled sport over all this. Did you notice that?"

"Yup," answered Arvie with a shake of his head. "Course he's always been slow on the uptake. Look here - we've got a gas station coming up on the right. Do we need gas?"

"Yup, we do." Carl left the highway and pulled up to one of the four pumps. He began to pump gas as Arvie went inside to use the facilities.

This store is as old as the one the other day, Arvie thought. Once inside a quick look around didn't reveal anything familiar as he headed to another old counter. An attendant had been leaning on the counter watching as he came through the door. As Arvie approached, the man said, "You paid for the gas outside. What else can I help you with?"

"Information please. I was in a store around here on ……."

The attendant interrupted by asking, "You heading south?"

Arvie was puzzled by the question but answered hesitantly, "Yes, in fact, I am." The man leaned down behind the counter, his head bobbing around as if looking for something. Up he came with a well-used paper sack. He opened the sack and pulled out a black can and ceremoniously presented it across the counter. Arvie didn't move. He was frozen in place. He looked at the shiny black can with one red word printed across the front, Reunion.

Slowly, he reached toward the can as the man said, "I was told to give this to you."

Arvie's mind kicked into gear as his hands encircled and caressed the shiny black can and he haltingly asked, "How did you know it was me you were looking for?"

"They told me I would know," he answered.

"If I need … more … one day," Arvie asked, "how can I … get some?"

The Native American thought for a moment before answering, "He will know when you are in need and that's all you need to know." With that, he turned and walked to the back of the small store, opened a door that said, "Private," exited and closed the door behind him. Arvie had more questions but his mind could not form them. Even if it could, his jaw had become disjointed from the rest of his skull. Nothing would work.

Jay Silverheels came into his mind. Arvie could still see the picture of Tonto, the Lone Ranger's faithful sidekick, from that early TV series: Jay Silverheels. That's who this man behind the counter looked like. *So, this Silverheels must know Jacob, the Midewiwin. He had to know him. Oh Lord, have mercy. Are you really at work here through the Ojibwe healers? But how did "they" know we would stop here? We didn't even know we would stop. Jacob had given the black can to Silverheels and told him to give it to me. And now I have, Reunion.*

Arvie walked to the door Silverheels had closed behind him thinking, *Oh, what the heck.* He reached for the door knob expecting it to be locked. The knob turned easily and the door opened into an entry way of sorts, a small narrow room with no windows. The room was totally empty. The only light in the room came through a small pane of plastic, which served as a window in the door to the outside. He walked to that door, pausing to look through the scratched-up piece of plastic. He saw nothing but trees. That door hadn't been opened in a while and squeaked painfully as Arvie pushed. There, before him, was a small grassy area completely enclosed by a pine forest. Barely visible was a hint of a path leading into the woods. Silverheels was nowhere to be seen. *He must have gone in there,* Arvie thought, and with that in mind he stepped down into the grass and walked to that hint of a path. *No way. This is no path. No one has walked back into this anytime lately.* He stood there considering the tangle of closely packed tree trunks, which looked even less inviting with vines and foliage intertwined. Pine needles covered everything. "Silverheels," he muttered, "where on earth did you go?" Maybe that was, indeed, the right question. Maybe he didn't go anywhere *on earth. Oh, man.*

Arvie turned and looked back at the door. The little patch of grass he was standing on was totally enclosed by this thick stand of trees on three sides. As he walked back to the door he looked for a way Silverheels could have walked around a corner of the building and made his way back to the parking lot out front. But it was the same dense thicket all around, and he guessed it had to be at least 30 feet of this stuff to get through – on both sides, before reaching a front corner of the building. He saw no evidence of an escape route or a trail. No one had ever messed around in these trees. So, where did Silverheels go? He simply vanished.

As Arvie stood there, it occurred to him that the building, including backyard, was put there just 30 minutes earlier. It was just plopped there in an otherwise empty space, along with the gas pumps, giant underground tank and the parking lot. *They put all this here just because they knew I was coming? I guess maybe they didn't need any big tank in the ground. They could've put some gas inside one of the pumps or maybe all four pumps are linked together and then if I had needed gas, I would've gotten it no matter which pump I chose to use. And, because they are in total control of this space, they don't have to worry about anyone else driving in because they have it all rigged so that I'm the only one that can see it. Arvie, Arvie, Arvie. Listen to yourself. You sound like a perfect idiot. Perhaps this is what senility feels like, hmmmm.*

He realized that he had been holding the shiny black can in his two hands this entire time. He raised the can to eye level and stared it down. The mid-afternoon July sun was beating down on him and the perspiration was beginning to run down the middle of his back. The can was identical to the two cans of, Forever already in his possession. Well, not two any longer. Only his allotment of Forever remained. *And now, I have a can of Reunion. The printing on the can is identical.*

He went back the way he came, through the empty narrow back room, into the back door of the store, through the store where no one stood behind the counter, and met up with Carl who was on his way in the front door. Arvie held up the black can and let Carl read the front. He told his friend what had happened.

Carl wanted to see where Silverheels had disappeared so Arvie walked with him out the back door. They stood just outside the door trying to understand where he might have gone. Carl, holding, Reunion in *his* hands, whispered, "This mystery is getting deeper and deeper. What happened here, just now?"

They walked back through the store and out the front door. They stood on the front porch analyzing the situation. Arvie said, "Your car is the only one in the parking lot. There was no other car in the parking lot when we drove up, right?"

"No other car," answered Carl with disbelief on his face.

"So," continued Arvie, "Silverheels came and left by another means. There are no other buildings sharing this parking lot."

"That's right," agreed Carl. They left the porch and got in the white Ford.

"Carl," said Arvie, "once you pull back onto the highway and head south, this building will no longer be here. All this was put here so that I, we, could get another shiny black can. I asked Silverheels how I can get more and he said, 'He will know when you have a need and that's all you need to know?' But I didn't know that I had a need right now. Why did he have to get me another can this day? How could *he* know that I had a need when *I* didn't know that I had a need? And if I do have a need, what is it and who is it for?" Arvie sang the Twilight melody, "Do do do do, do do do do. Yeah, there's the guy out there on the wing of the plane again. It *is* me."

They sat in the car quietly for several minutes just looking at the front of the building. No one else pulled into the parking lot. The building sat there totally devoid of any living being, with a small circle of grass out back which was totally surrounded by impenetrable forest. Why was that small circle of grass out the back door? What purpose did that serve for our visit today? Wait. Silverheels hadn't asked him to pay for it. What might *that* mean? Probably nothing. "There goes another car heading south, Carl," said Arvie quietly. "Do you think that driver saw this building? Maybe the building is only visible to us, just us who, apparently, have a need."

"I've never been involved in anything remotely close to this before," said Carl with a hint of excitement in his voice. "Wait a minute." He jumped out of the car with a nimbleness that took Arvie by surprise. *We'll need to talk about that move* Arvie thought. Carl walked several paces towards the highway, then turned around and snapped several pictures with his phone. He took several steps to the left and then to the right, clicking off at least ten shots. Quickly he was back in the driver's seat saying, "Now we've got some pictures of this place to prove it was here. What if we came back next week and it wasn't?"

"Good grief," was all Arvie could think of to say. "Oh, by the way, do you realize how quickly you jumped out of the car to snap those pictures. On the way up, before we knew anything about Forever coffee, you could barely get out. Remember?"

"I guess … I can't ignore it, huh? I'm amazed. I … I really don't want to say it, but … I think it fixed my knee. I wondered about that day when I first brought it up, but now I gotta say it feels fixed. You know how exciting that is? I've been walking around for two years like I got a wooden leg," he said with a big smile.

"So," Arvie continued, getting back to the business at hand, "if this store isn't here next time we come by, it proves one of three things – no four things. They took it away and put it in their storage yard until their next need for it, it was torn down by someone for some reason, it was never here, or I'm totally nutso."

"But look here," Carl said pushing his phone in front of Arvie, "Yes, there are indeed several pictures of the building, the pumps, the drive. Phew. We've got proof that it was here for at least as long as it took us to get gas, walk inside and get the can of coffee from a man who walked out the back door and vanished."

Carl looked for traffic coming from the left, looked in his rear-view mirror at the building that would be gone in a moment and turned right and headed south.

"So where did Silverheels go, Carl?" asked Arvie.

Carl could only shake his head back and forth with raised eye brows. "It's beyond me," he mumbled softly.

How would Arvie explain all of this to Hannah? He knew he would have to because it was important that he pour her a cup soon after he walked through the door. It would be approaching supper time when he arrived home and the first question she would ask, after she asked, "Why are we having coffee?" would be, "Is it decaf?" He would begin by replying that he didn't know, but that he was sure it didn't matter. He would tell her just what had happened and that's all he could do. It wouldn't make any sense and that would be ok. *She can be as puzzled by all this as the rest of us.*

"Which one should I brew for Hannah when I get home, Carl? Now, there are two to choose from: Forever or Reunion. Does it really matter? What do you think?"

"Well, I think I'd want to keep Reunion unopened for as long as possible, so I'd go with the Forever."

"Yeah," answered Arvie putting his head back and closing his eyes. "I think that's right. Here's another thing I don't understand – and that's the word *need*. Silverheels had said, 'He will know when you are in need and that's all you need to know.' I guess that means that 'he', whoever he is, will get it to me, or us, somehow. So, should I be thinking about where the need might be? I was given this coffee because 'he' knew of someone who had a need for healing. Hannah will get her first cup soon, for her anxiety of course, but now with another full can, who else is in need? I think my family is well, so who else might it be? Dweebs? It must be Dweebs. Carolyn is having troubles and they can't figure out the problem." Arvie grabbed his phone and dialed him up, something he should have done days ago. The phone rang and rang and he got Dweebs' message. He told Dweebs to call just as soon as he possibly could and, "It's important". Dweebs returned the call about a mile down the road.

Arvie put the phone on speaker and asked Dweebs about Carolyn's health. Dweebs stumbled around for a moment or two and said nothing to indicate that she was getting any better and that she was home, but would be back in the hospital the next day for another test. Arvie explained briefly about what had happened at the cabin. There was silence at the other end of the line.

After what seemed like forever, Dweebs replied, "Guys, I just got home from Walmart and let me tell you what happened. I was in a hurry and racing through the store getting what I needed because I never want to be away from her for long. You aren't going to believe this, but an absolute stranger walked up and handed me a paper sack with something. He said, 'This is for you. I was told to give this to you.' I looked down, and…"

Arvie couldn't contain himself and interrupted, "Did the guy look like he could be a Native American? Could you tell?"

Dweebs thought for a minute and responded, "Yes he did, come to think of it. As soon as I took the paper bag he said, 'It's paid for,' and then he walked away. Holy cow. This is the coffee you're talking about. Now I've got some?" Dweebs asked.

"What does it look like?" Arvie asked.

"It is a black can and that's about all I can say," said Dweebs. "I took a quick look in the bag and it sure looked like a can of coffee. A big can."

Arvie asked, "What was written on it?"

Dweebs said he didn't know. He hadn't noticed. He thought it was strange but was in such a hurry that he just dropped it into his cart and figured he'd check it out when he got home.

"Where is the can right now?" asked Arvie.

"Still in the trunk"

"Can you go and get it, please?" Arvie pleaded. "We'll wait."

They heard a door open, sounds of walking and the muffled sound of a trunk being opened and closed. Finally, "Ok, I've got it. It says Reunion in big red letters. The can is black and really shiny." Carl took a right turn at the next opportunity, pulled over as far to the right as he could on the gravel road. He shut off the car and Carl and Arvie both got out. They had to stand and walk for this talk.

"Dweebs," Arvie said slowly, calmly emphasizing each word by waving his free arm all over the place, "make a pot of that coffee right now and get Carolyn to drink a cup as soon as she possibly can. Don't ask us any questions, just do it - please. And after she's had a cup or two, call me back when you have a chance to talk because I've got a lot more explaining to do."

"What are we really talking about here, Arv?" Dweebs asked.

"I'll explain later, but right now, just go make a pot of coffee and get her a cup. Call me back after, when you've got a little time."

"Will do," came the response and the phone clicked off. Carl and Arvie marched side by side down the road a bit. They eventually stopped and stared straight ahead at a point where the road disappeared over the top of a little rise, turned around slowly and began walking back to the car. Their minds were running in circles again. Still.

"Ok," began Arvie, "let's think about this. They – whoever "They" are, already knew about and took care of Dweebs and Carolyn. So, who needs our latest can? I bet I picked up this can of Reunion from Silverheels at about the same time Dweebs was getting his can at the Walmart in Indiana. So, maybe Hannah is the only reason I have a new can. Or maybe there IS someone else. Maybe more than just one someone else. Maybe, even, it is me. I just hope I know who it is when I see 'em."

A few minutes later, with scenery whizzing by the windows again, Carl said, "Now I'm thinking that on my trip out west, there's a real possibility I could stumble into a black can of something. Huh?"

"I'm sure of it," answered Arvie. "You'll get a can and I'm thinking it'll be for Boldy for all the reasons we know of, or it'll be for something we don't know of, even Marlene or someone else in their family. How did we get put in this situation anyway?"

"Wait a minute Arvie" Carl blurted out with laugh. "What do you mean, 'WE?' Seems to me you stumbled into this all on your own."

"I guess you're right," answered Arvie. "When do you take off for California?"

"First thing in the morning. I've got tonight to get organized."

"Here's a thought. Maybe we're supposed to make coffee for anyone and everyone. Maybe it's not necessary to know who actually needs it. Maybe we just assume everyone has a need for it. After all, Paul told us that every human body is in the process of wasting away; dying is an appropriate word. Make coffee for all and quit the incessant questions. Now I feel better. I think that's the mission."

* * * * * * * *

The 45 miles or so rolled on by and after he and Carl had said their goodbyes and unloaded Arvie's stuff in the townhouse driveway, Arvie grabbed his coffee supply and headed inside.

Hannah was waiting for him and she looked good. It was a long hug to make up for those she hadn't gotten over the past few days. Finally, she asked if he had a good time. He told her he had and that he had a mystery to tell her about. She took a long look at his ear and nodded, "ok."

"But before we do anything else, I have to make a pot of coffee." She took a seat at the table and asked, "A pot of coffee at this hour? Is it decaf?" He smiled and assured her that soon she would understand. He grabbed his allotment of Forever and loaded up the coffee maker. After he pushed the "on" button, he wondered again if Forever and Reunion were the same or if there was a difference. He didn't have any earthly idea about what was in one or the other, or if one was designed to work on problems A & B, while the other would do a job on problems C & D. Of course, it didn't help that he didn't know what problems were represented by A, B, C, and D to start with. Come to think of it, he decided that he didn't know anything about anything and had been drawn into the whole magic coffee thing because his acid reflux had disappeared and he had come to believe that he was supposed to help people with their physical and mental issues. Surely that wasn't too much to hope for, or was it? He reminded himself to just brew coffee and stop with the questions.

Hannah said that she had heated some soup a while ago, since she didn't know what time he would be home, and asked if he was hungry. He told her that he wasn't the least bit hungry. They sat and they talked and when the brewing came to a halt he poured two cups. Then they sat and talked and he poured two more cups. By that time, he had told her the whole story. He didn't get into all the questions, just the basics. He watched her very carefully, every time she took a sip. He was waiting; waiting for her to take a sip, smack her lips a few times and then leap to her feet, raising her head and her hands to the ceiling light fixture while yelling, "I'm healed. Praise God and Jacob Whitefeather, who has been dead these many years yet came back with a black can just for me."

She didn't even make her usual "this is really good coffee," comment. They just talked and hugged until her eyes became heavy and it was time for her to head to bed. As they hugged one last time that night, Arvie looked over her shoulder and was proud to see the nearly empty coffee pot. After she left for the upstairs, he turned it off, silently giving thanks for the several cups she had consumed. *Now I'll just wait, watch and listen.*

His thoughts were interrupted by the ringing of his phone. *Dweebs*, he thought, and then saw the name on the screen, punched the talk button and said aloud, "Dweebs."

"She had two cups of the coffee," reported Dweebs and then asked if that was a good thing. Arvie said that, indeed, it was and he proceeded to tell Dweebs all that had transpired over the previous days with 'a fine coffee product of Northern Minnesota.' Arvie told him that Hannah had just consumed her first two cups, too. The two friends agreed that they would wait, watch, and listen together and keep the other informed. Arvie also told Dweebs that he had made the decision to stop asking himself all of the questions and just brew coffee for people. Just do it. Dweebs said, "I understand, and yet I really don't understand. I do get what you mean though: don't ask, just do, for now anyway." They said, "Goodnight," and, "Sleep well," and the evening drew to a close.

It was way past his usual bedtime when he brushed his teeth and headed for bed. He was ready for sleep but he feared it would not come quickly. He pulled the covers back a little but just flopped down on top of everything as his mind rolled on. The next day, at 10:45, he would meet with his Urologist and get the results of the latest PSA test. The Doc had taken all those biopsies the last two times, searching for the reason for the high PSA levels and found nothing. One blood test showed high PSA levels and the next revealed a normal result. No one could explain it. *Maybe this is one thing that I can put out of my mind*, he thought. *Regardless of the results tomorrow, maybe this coffee will bring the number ridiculously low in the future. That will be a relief.*

He wondered if more cans would come and if so, when. He recommitted to himself that he was just going to brew the coffee and stop with questions. He'd use the cans that he received and "just brew it," he said aloud. And sleep crept in.

...He is in a packed auditorium, standing in front of perhaps 4,000 cheering people - all thanking him for healing them and Ole walks up to the microphone and asks the crowd "Wannacup?" Someone screams out, "I have a need." Black cans descend from the ceiling. Hundreds of them. No, thousands. They are piling up. And

then a blurry image is coming closer and, though he can't see who it is, the image asks for a cup of Joy. Ole explains that we aren't pouring Joy, only Forever and Reunion. Ole gives the image a pour from the pot in his right hand. He hands a black can to a smiling little girl and says, "Get this can to whoever needs it because they need it." Jacob and Silverheels are in the front row of the auditorium clapping as Ole pours coffee from both black pots. Charlton Heston arrives in a gold chariot followed now by Ole in a black chariot. Ole is wearing black armor with red trim. There is a Mr. Coffee plugged into his chariot's dashboard and he's standing, with coffee cup in hand, telling Charlton that he's brewed a pot of the Redeemed blend. He asks Charlton if he would like a, "cuppa." Charlton says he would and Ole hands him a black cup with the red word, Redeemed printed on two sides. Suddenly, Charlton is in the wilderness with a mob of people. They have long, scraggly hair and are dressed in dirty robes and rotted sandals. They scream wildly for healing. Charlton bangs his staff into a big rock and out gushes steaming, freshly brewed, Forgiveness and the mob rushes forward to fill their shiny black cans, black pots, black mugs, and black buckets. Flash to Ole in the Walmart Deli. He is packaging sandwiches with sliced meats and calling them, "Trust," "Mercy." and "Grace." Customers ask why they don't owe anything and Ole shouts, "It's all been paid in full." Meryl Streep leads a parade of the walking dead and they chant, "In life there are no mistakes," as the whole crowd walks into a swimming pool of French-pressed, "Freedom." When they climb out on the other side they are no longer dead. Jacob Whitefeather waves from across the pool and yells, "Arvie, Arvie, Arvie. It's me (Wheez), Jacob." A man in a white coat walks into a room laughing, pointing toward his groin. He says, "Your prostate. It's huge and still growing. Still growing! STILL GROWING! Think of the pressure. The pressure on your bladder. Surely you need to pee. Need to PEE. Don't you need to pee?" He leaves the room just as Ole walks in with a pot in each hand and asks, "Wannacup?"

Arvie bolted upright gasping for breath. He was soaked with sweat, needing dry PJ's and a visit to the bathroom. *Doc was in my dream*, he thought. *Ole was in my dream, and Charlton too. Mercy, please mercy. I hope that was a dream. But isn't "Mercy" the name of a coffee?*

Chapter 5

"When I was your age, I mowed Cook County Highway grass on the Eden's Expressway from Highway 96 to 180th street. I was the only one to do that - ever. I take a lot of pride in that.
Heh heh." - *Ole*

"But the people who trust the Lord will become strong again. They will rise up as an Eagle in the sky; they will run and will not need rest; they will walk and not become tired." Isaiah 40:31

As was his custom, he awoke early the next morning. Hannah was sleeping soundly as he put on the coffee. Once his cup was filled he headed upstairs to the computer. He needed to do some writing, get creative, but he couldn't do it. He just sat there. He stared at the wall over his desk. He stared at the keyboard. He stared at the coffee cup holding his pencils. He stared at his coffee cup holding his coffee. How would he respond that morning if the PSA level hadn't dropped back to normal? What that would mean, simply put, would be that the miracle coffee wasn't meant to cure any prostate thing – that's what it could mean. And really, if the Midewiwin were who he thought they were, they wouldn't be trying to solve his prostate issue anyway because at his age it just doesn't matter. They would focus their divining and their healing on those health issues that they could cure in those much younger; those who still had a chance at the full life he had already enjoyed.

He went for another cup of coffee. It was more Forever that he had brewed that morning. He wanted to keep the can of Reunion sealed as long as possible. He smelled the now-familiar aroma and the thought *I believe in you* flew through his mind. He roamed the townhouse while he sipped, looking blankly out the windows. He especially loved the view to the west because it was so easy to be back on the deck of the cabin overlooking the lake. He showered and shaved, got dressed and had breakfast. He read <u>Jesus Calling</u> for the day and felt inspired because of it, as he felt about it every day. The reading concluded, he offered a short prayer for all his ailing friends at the Bible study. After he said "Amen," he began another prayer that asked God for guidance regarding the healing coffee. It was time to hit the road.

He had left Hannah with at least four cups of coffee in the pot and a note urging her to remember their conversation the night before and enjoy several cups this morning. He added that she should pray for good news on his PSA test and he would get bananas on the way home.

The prostate Doc officed some 40 minutes away, down 35E and then east and south on 694 to Woodbury. He had just entered 35 and was heading for the split when his phone rang. He knew it was Dweebs even before he looked. He punched talk and said, "Hey Dweebs. What's up?"

Dweebs reiterated that Carolyn had two cups the night before and then another cup that morning. He asked what he was supposed to be looking for, but quickly shared that he thought there had already been something to note. Given Carolyn's lower abdomen pain and the meds she was on to combat that pain, she rarely slept through a night and would be awake two or three times a night, simply walking around the house. However, the night before, she had slept all night long. He knew that because, since this all began several months ago, he had become a very light sleeper. He was always on the alert for those restless times and trying to think of ways to help her. He, like Arvie, had realized that his role was to be there for her, and beyond that, there was nothing more he could do.

Arvie said, "That is very positive. Keep on the watch because we need to learn what this coffee thing is all about and why these people go to so much trouble to deliver it to us."

Then Dweebs told him about a very good friend of his who just found out his cancer is back after being in remission for several years. "Maybe the Reunion came to me," he said, "because of him. Ben is a terrific husband and father, a leader in his church and volunteers on a regular basis with under privileged kids."

Arvie advised Dweebs to have Ben over for coffee as soon as possible and see what, if anything, happens. Might be best not to tell him anything about it, but it sure is worth a try. "You are right,

Dweebs, maybe you are supposed to get this to your friend. You and I have received this coffee because someone we know is in need of healing."

Arvie told Dweebs of the prostate appointment he was headed for and gave him a brief history of his PSA tests. He was sure the Forever had fixed his prostate. He asked Dweebs if he should bother telling the doctor about the coffee. There was a pause, and then Dweebs answered, "If you tell him that, he'll begin proceedings to have you committed, heh heh. But, seriously, good luck with that and give me a call after."

Arvie didn't have to remind himself that this was an important moment in this journey he and the others were experiencing. *All of this mystery is about hope*, he thought. Everything that transpires these days reveals more and more about what this hope is; a dream of the elderly to be without pain, to experience happiness and joy. He smiled to himself remembering a commercial for some medicinal product where a woman looks into the camera and says with heartfelt sincerity, "If I didn't have this pain, I would feel better." *Duh!*

* * * * * * *

He wandered into the office, announced himself to one of the ladies behind the counter, received a form that amounted to four pages of questions and answers regarding his urinary history. He'd filled out one of these on every visit. Apparently, his urinary health was constantly changing and the doctor needed to be updated each visit. "What if my visits were daily?" he thought. "Would I be answering these questions every day? Would my urinary health change overnight?" So, he wandered to a chair in the corner, ball point in hand, prepared to circle an answer of either Always, Frequently, Sometimes, Seldom or Never to the four pages of questions.

Question #1: How often do you experience the need for elimination? He studied his choices. He couldn't circle *always* because that would mean he would never leave the bathroom. He couldn't circle *never* because that would mean he never entered a bathroom. He decided that the right answer must be *frequently*, *sometimes* or *seldom*. He circled *frequently*. He continued down the list of questions and became totally upset by the frequency of his circling of *frequently*. He gave thought to scratching out all the *frequentlys* and circling all the *nevers*. That could make for an interesting visit with the doctor. Instead, he left it as it was.

He picked up a magazine from six or eight months ago from a small table loaded with outdated magazines. All these magazines in waiting rooms didn't have a clue about what being current meant. But then, who sat in offices like this, concerned about the health news they were about to receive, and looked in these magazines for articles of critical importance that would draw them into an in depth study of some something. *It doesn't matter if these magazines are five or 10 years old,* he thought. *Anyone sitting in this chair just waiting and waiting doesn't really read anything anyway. All we do to pass the time is flip through pages. Look at that old man over there, flip, flip, and flip again. He doesn't care what he's looking at. Wonder what information he's waiting to get today?*

Could the following five or 10 minutes validate the coffee? No, it would not. He asked his knee to stop bouncing. A good report: a number back down in the three's, would only indicate that his prostate health had improved over the course of the last six months. He had been drinking, Forever just since the prior Monday, so no real validation there. And yet, somewhere inside, he knew that the introduction of Forever into his system had been the cure. He didn't know what the current report would show, but was certain that PSA results would not be an issue in the future. Specialists wouldn't be able to explain, but Arvie could. His knee began to bounce again.

Ok, stop that he thought, and he stretched out his legs and crossed them at the ankle. He heard a feminine voice call, "Arvid?" It always took a moment for that name to register. He just knew all the other people in the waiting room were suddenly looking at him saying to themselves, "Oh, that poor old man is named Arvid. What a shame. Such a nice looking man, too." Arvid had been perfect for his dad and his uncle but he was not Arvid. "My name is Mickey," he mumbled under his breath as he stood and smiled at the nurse at the door on his left, "Mickey Mantle." *Now there's a cool name.*

Nurse Sharon and he were now on a first name basis. He felt he knew her rather intimately because she had dealt with his prostate biopsies. They greeted each other with smiles and she said that he was getting to be a regular. She asked how he was doing and he responded with his usual inane response to that inane question, "Really good." She led him down a door-filled hallway and parked him behind the 4th door on the left, announcing, "He is running right on schedule and should be in shortly." Arvie picked out a sports magazine from the rack on the back of the door with basketball players posing on the cover. *Oh good. A review of this year's March Madness,* which meant the magazine was only a few months old. Of course, as he inspected the publication, he realized it was a review of the tournament which concluded 15 months prior, not three. He replaced the typical doctor's office magazine from whence it had come and sat down empty handed.

Now it was time. All the formalities had been concluded. There was nothing more to do but wait for the light tap-tap-tap on the door followed by its opening which allowed the Doctor to enter. *Wonder where Carl is right now.*

He heard the taps on the door and "He" entered. They completed the customary hand shake and sat down and the latest test results were quickly revealed. The PSA number had returned into the three's, just where it was prior to the last two tests, and the doctor could not explain how. The prostate is indeed a mysterious organ. Arvid was told he would not have to have another PSA test for a year. There would never again be a need to dig out additional specimens, there was no need for surgery and, "Please call if you have any changes or further questions." They shook hands again and Arvid thanked the Doctor. He exited the room, headed for the lobby, scheduled the appointment for the following year and left the building. On the short walk to his car he mumbled, "Ok, I guess that was good news."

Back in the car he dialed up Dweebs. He got his message again so he left one confirming that his PSA had dropped back to where it was over a year ago and that no one, including all the prostate specialists in the building had an explanation to offer, or even any kind of an imaginary daydream. He told Dweebs to ring him up whenever he had news of Carolyn.

Yes, it was good news, he thought as he entered the northbound ramp to 494. Maybe it would have remained in the threes from that day forward, no matter what, but Arvie knew it would now, thanks to Forever.

It's hope. And it's faith. And it brings joy. Because "they" picked him - Gitchi Manitou picked him, he will pour the coffee until his time is done – or at least until it runs out.

Chapter 6

"Stop asking, 'How?' and 'Why?' Just do it. Heh heh."
- Ole

Jesus said, "Don't let your hearts be troubled.
Trust in God, and trust in me."
John 14:1

Arvie realized he was wide awake, staring at nothing in the dark. No use rolling over and making a futile attempt to get back to sleep. He had tried it before. Waste of time. *Just get up* and so he did.

Hannah was sleeping soundly. He could tell by her steady breathing. Quietly, he grabbed his clothing out of drawers and a closet and tip-toed down the stairs to the kitchen. Yes, the coffee was ready. *Get dressed, fill a cup, open the blinds, sit down at the dining room table and see what the weather looks like. It looks like "dark" weather out there.* He decided to take a walk and watch the sun-rise; fresh air and quiet contemplation to begin the day. He took the first sip, re-filled the cup to the top and headed out the door.

His usual trek took 25 minutes or so. He thought he would do it twice that morning.

It was Saturday and also the Saturday of the month that Hannah and he would volunteer in the bookstore at Church for the 4:00 and the 6:00 services. It was a great time and they both looked forward to it each month. Since beginning to attend Dove Creek Church, nearly 12 years prior, they had sought the right place to volunteer. He had always loved books and, after their first time volunteering in the bookstore, it was a no-brainer. They had met so many people, developed many friendships and found a great sense of belonging. Even though Hannah sometimes got anxious about going, once there, she was always good behind the cash register and with the customers. By the time they got home, she was always so thankful she had served in that way.

Nearly two years prior, Hannah and one of her friends had decided to start a small group of 50+ year old, Dove Creek women, living nearby. Almost immediately, 12 ladies signed up and the 14 of them began. The association with that small group for Hannah had been a godsend. They met every other Monday evening and she so looked forward to it. She worked very hard on the home work and dedicated many hours preparing for those evenings. She had said that the small group allowed her to get close to the women and share life experiences, as well as, give and get help with life's trials. Most of all, she believed it was the best way to hold herself and each other accountable in their day-to-day walk with God.

Arvie hadn't found a group yet and as he walked along in his solitude he thought about that. If he found a small group he would have another opportunity to brew a pot of coffee and pass along some healing. *Let's call that possibility #2. Perhaps Jacob Whitefeather and Silverheels knew of that possibility and that was another reason I was chosen. Obviously, possibility #1 are those occasions when the kids come over and maybe the Fantasy Golf Group and when people just stop by to say hi.*

What might possibility #3 be? Just next to the bookstore at the church was the coffee shop. Long lines would form before every service for the specialty brews; lattes, frappes, cappuccinos. Near the seating area was a serve-yourself station with the full-strength and decaf brews of the day. *How many people might there be in a church this size that need some healing - some hope? After all, 5000-6000 people attend services at this location each weekend.* Perhaps Arvie's Native American friends knew of this possibility. *Am I supposed to volunteer in the coffee shop?* With four services each weekend, two on Saturday evening and another two on Sunday morning, it was obviously a huge opportunity to reach more people. *Let's call this possibility #3.*

Maybe there were other options. He considered that there may be shut-ins, retired people or others who had no way to get to church. *Maybe I could bring a cup of coffee to them once a week and have a conversation. I'm retired. I've got virtually every day free. I get Hannah to her medical appointments but other than that, I have no commitments. I could become known as the 'traveling coffee guy.'*

And maybe I should do this for men only? Senior men only? Everyone seems to think of the older women. How about the older men? Is anyone paying attention to them? Is anyone insuring that they get a good cup of coffee every day, or at least once a week and have someone to talk to? Old guy brings hope; will travel. I like that. Possibility #4.

And then there is possibility #5. He kept thinking about the man who was always standing on the corner of Charitan and the 35W exit ramp near downtown Minneapolis. Every time he took Hannah down to the University of Minnesota for her therapy, they would see him there and the image made Arvie uncomfortable. The large man had an old white lard bucket that he would sit on while holding his sign. The sign let passers-by know that he needed money to get home for Christmas, Easter, Thanksgiving, or his mom's funeral. Arvie had never given him a penny. That thought brought with it a feeling of guilt. *If you don't help even the least of these, you don't help Me*, he paraphrased. *That guy sure looks like he could use a good cup of hope.* He guessed the old man was, at least, his age, if not older. He thought that same sign had been used for the two years he and Hannah had driven by. Since his mom's funeral has been indicated on that sign for that length of time, Arvie thought it reasonable that the mom's health was not good, *and that surely is too bad. Hah.* He thought he had been clever with that thought.

So, there are five, count 'em five, possibilities and he thought if he continued walking, he could have 10 or 15 more.

So, if he were to take coffee on the road, how would he carry it? He thought of the old milk man from the days of his youth. Les was his name and he had a hand-carrier that would hold six or eight quart bottles of milk that he carried with him on his journeys from his vehicle to the front door of every house on his route. His horse was named Daisy and she would pull the little cart up and down all the brick paved streets, six days a week. *Thank goodness I won't need to find a horse to pull my cart. And how old am I to remember Les and Daisy?*

He walked in the door and found Hannah sitting at the dining room table staring out through the sliding glass doors, a coffee cup held just under her nose.

"Good morning," he said while leaning over to give her a kiss on the top of her head. "I've been thinking about what to do with the coffee thing and I've got ideas for six or seven ways to pour the Forever. First, I'm going down to 35W and Chariton. If our friend with the sign is still there, I'll pour him a cup and talk a bit. He looks like an old guy who could use some healing. What do you think of that?"

"That's nice dear, but before you go, can we have our cereal and devotions?"

"Of course. By the way, do we have a really good thermos for hot stuff?"

"Yes dear. I think it is out in the garage on the top shelf on the left."

"Let me go get that and then I'll fix the cereal." He headed to the garage and found the thermos right where she said it would be. Back in the kitchen he put it on the counter near the sink. He'd need to clean it up a bit on the outside, but first he unscrewed the top and peered down inside. Yes, it was glass and it appeared to be intact. He opened the cupboard to grab a couple of coffee cups. It was when he was fishing around the backside of his coffee cup stash, searching for his least favorite cups that it hit him. *I will take my favorite two cups down to the old man.* He placed them next to the thermos, took down two bowls and the cinnamon cheerios, grabbed the milk and served the breakfast.

They ate and talked, read <u>Jesus Calling</u> and prayed. She told him all that she was planning to do here at the table this morning and that he should go and do what he feels he must. "Wait. What day is this? It's Saturday, Arv. We've got the bookstore tonight. We leave here at 3:00. Right?"

"You are so right dear" he said while washing off the thermos. "I'll be back in plenty of time." He filled the thermos with Reunion and then searched the pantry for a carry bag of some kind. He found a cloth bag that Hannah used when she went to her knitting group. He returned to her side, patted her on the shoulder and gave her a peck on the cheek. "I'll be back in a little while. Enjoy the beautiful morning. By the way, I noticed your birds are back again. I wonder where they go sometimes. Ok, see you later."

"Have fun and good luck. I'll be anxious to hear all about it," she said. "Oh, and if you can remember, I am totally out of gum. Just gum of any kind."

As he headed for the freeway he noticed a big line of black clouds stretched across the western horizon. *Storms this afternoon* he thought. *Those are some really black clouds.*

He took the entry ramp south toward Minneapolis. The line of clouds appeared to be approaching very rapidly and could arrive much sooner than he had earlier thought.

Jacob Whitefeather and Silverheels returned to his mind. They were never very far away. *It's because of you guys that I'm off to find some guy I don't know with the intention to give him a cup of coffee. What's his name? I don't know. Does he like coffee? I don't know. Will he be in his usual spot? I don't know.*

What do I know? Well, he's an old guy with a lot of facial hair. Where will I park the car? I don't know. What will I say to him when I approach him? I think I'll use the Ole approach – Wannacup? What if he says, "No, that stuff makes me vomit?" Well, I'll tell him that this is magical coffee and it will fix whatever is ailing him. What if he laughs in my face? Well, I suppose I'll tell him that I'm serious; that this coffee is going to fix him right up. What if he asks how much it will take before he's all fixed up? I'll say I don't know exactly, but that he really needs to trust me on this. And he'll ask why he should trust me and I'll have to say again that I just don't know.

Doubt jumped in with its own set of questions. *What are you doing, Arvie? When is the last time you went out for coffee with someone you never met before? Huh? Don't you usually go for coffee with someone you know? Well, don't you?*

"God, I'm trusting in you this morning. I believe that I am motivated by faith that I am doing the right thing. I have my doubts of course, but don't I have them every day? It is so easy to doubt and then shy away from doing something I feel called to do. I feel that I am called to do this and so I am going to do this. It's Romans 15:13; *Now may the God of hope fill you with all joy and peace in believing, that you may abound in hope by the power of the Holy Spirit.* I believe that, God. I believe and I am filled with peace and joy and hope. It's the Holy Spirit in me. You have brought me to this place and to this moment. It is hope that I am going to give to this stranger and with your guidance, perhaps there will be others."

The sign said, "Chariton - ½ mile," and his stomach completed a sudden lurch. *What if the man is not there?* But as he took the off ramp, he could see him up at the stop sign. *Good. He's standing in his usual spot. I'll need to turn right to find a place to park.* Arvie stopped at the light which gave him the opportunity to study the old man. *He's got to be older than me – he's at least 80. Good Grief. How does he do this?* Businesses along the road had parallel parking but nothing was open. He turned right up a side street with parking on both sides. *It's only a two block walk back to him. No hill for a climber.* Arvie grabbed the sack and exited the vehicle. As he began to walk, he smelled the rain and felt the wind. *It's almost here.*

Arvie waited for the stop light. *I'm going to keep this simple: walk up and introduce myself.*

"Hi. I'm Arvie. Thought you might like a cup of coffee."

The old man turned to look at him, sized him up for a moment and then . . . "Ahhhhh, yeah, sure. And what's the catch?"

"No catch. Thought you might like a cup of some really good coffee." *This guy is way over 80. Whew. I need to stand upwind.*

"Sure. You just walk up, you don't know me and pour me a cup of coffee? What dja do, pee in the thermos?"

"Certainly not. Here, just smell it. If I took a leak in the thermos, you'd probably be able to smell it, wouldn't you? At least it would smell kinda weird, wouldn't it?"

"Why should I drink a cup of your coffee?"

Giving away a cup of coffee isn't easy. "Well, I really like coffee. I think there are a lot of people like me who like a cup of good coffee. I've seen you out here many times, and some of those times the weather wasn't so nice. I don't have money to give you because I'm on a fixed income, and it's turned out to be a real tight situation. I do buy coffee and it is something I like to share. Well, I told you my name. What's yours?"

"Call me Zeke. Here, let me smell that stuff."

"Sure."

"I don't smell no pee. You're right. It smells good."

"Good. How long you been on this corner Zeke?"

"Long time."

"Can I ask how long is a long time? I'm just askin' because I know I've seen you out here every day I've driven by for maybe two years."

"Twice that."

"How come so long, Zeke? How's the coffee taste?"

"Does it matter?"

"Just that I happen to like coffee that has good flavor."

"Not that. Why does it matter how long I been here?"

"I was just wondering, that's all. Storm's coming. Is there anywhere you go when the weather gets bad?"

"No. This is just going to be some rain. It'll clean my clothes."

"You just stay here, in the rain?"

"Why not? More people feel sorry for an old guy standing in the rain."

"I see. How much do you make on an average day?"

"Not much."

"Here. Let me refill that cup. I'll drink one with you."

"Why you doin' this, man?" Zeke asked between swallows.

"Because I've thought of it for a long time. Just want to, I guess. You don't look like you believe that, though."

"Nope."

"Well, it's the truth." Arvie looked up at the incoming storm clouds. "I've been bringing my wife around this corner two mornings a week for the last two years – on our way to the University of Minnesota Medical Center, right down there, for some therapy. Five hours a day, two days a week. She sits in a group and they share information and learn about anxiety from Psychologists. She was diagnosed with anxiety a while back. I don't understand. It's all very strange to me. Anyway, I've seen you here many times. Would it be ok if I come back sometime and bring you some more coffee?"

"That's up to you, man."

"Zeke, are you ok? I mean your eyes and nose have been running since I got here. Sinuses? Allergies? What 'ya got goin' on there? Have you been to a doctor about that?"

"Don't know. Just the way it is. Been like this for years. Got no money for a doctor."

"Can I give you a handkerchief?"

"Don't need no handkerchief. I got my sleeve. You better go now. Here's the rain and your cup."

"I'll see you again one day. Take care of yourself."

"Yeah. Ok."

The light changed and Arvie walked away from Zeke. Once on the other side of the road, he turned and looked back. Zeke was, once again, sitting on his white lard bucket facing the incoming traffic. His sign was in position. Cars stopped at the light. Those that didn't stop, barely slowed at all. Arvie stood in the light sprinkle as the storm announced its approach. No one stopped to hand Zeke anything. Maybe this day was not going to be a good day.

Arvie picked up the pace as the sprinkle moved quickly into a shower. The sky darkened, and in only a moment the area was consumed by a downpour. He jumped in the car in time to miss the worst of it. There was pounding thunder, lightning and buckets of rain. He made no attempt to move the car. The gutters on both sides of the street filled with rushing water but it couldn't move fast enough to escape what seemed to be a waterfall coming down from the giant faucet turned-on from above. He couldn't see the building across the street. The rushing water crept steadily up the grass of the terraces, approaching the sidewalks. And still it came. Traffic had to be at a standstill out on the freeway. Visibility couldn't have been more than 10 feet. Lightning flashed across the gloom and then another huge clap of thunder. And then the storm rolled quickly east towards Wisconsin. It was over. The gutters were again able to contain the water racing down the street. *Now that was a real Thunderstorm.* He was thankful for his car. Zeke didn't have a car. He probably sat on his lard bucket through that downpour. *Why is that, Lord? The poorest of us have no place to go to get out of the weather. So they just sit on a bucket through the storms.*

He pulled away from the curb and moved slowly down the street and took the first left. Then he took the first left again. Now he was approaching Chariton where he would take another left in order to get back to Zeke's corner. When he got to the corner he was thankful to have a red light. He looked over to his left. Zeke was sitting, still holding his sign and facing the traffic approaching the stop light. *Did he even move during that downpour? He's probably happy because his clothes got washed.*

All the way home he thought of Zeke. The man's face was heavily lined with many years of squinting into the sun. Maybe his eyes are bad and he squints all the time. Arvie had also noticed several scars on what little of the face he could see. They could have been caused by almost anything, he supposed. Most of his face was covered by the long gray beard and mustache. For an older guy, he still had a good head of hair. Arvie wondered when he had his last hair cut? When he stood down wind, it was very apparent that Zeke needed a shower and his clothes needed soap and water too. *What is his story* Arvie wondered? Perhaps it will take several visits to build up some trust? It was obvious all he accomplished this time was to give the old man two cups of coffee and learn his name. He wondered if Zeke really was his name?

Arvie had plenty of time to get home so instead of the freeway, he opted to take the back roads to the northeast. He turned north on a street he'd never been on. Glancing down at the dashboard he suddenly realized he was running on fumes. In his haste to get to the old man he had paid no attention to the gas gauge. But he needed gas right now, and it couldn't come soon enough. He did not know this road so he wasn't sure that he would find a gas station in time. Now he was consumed with the small red outline of a gas pump on the dashboard that had been there for – well, he didn't know how long. He thought he had read in the Honda CRV Owner's Manual that when this light appeared, there was approximately one gallon left. That meant 20 miles or so of grace. This road was traveled enough that he was comfortable there would be a gas station soon. The only problem was he didn't know when that red light had appeared so he had no clue how much of that gallon remained.

He was looking for a Holiday sign or a Super America sign. Those were the usual ones in this neck of the woods. There is a Mobil and a Shell and BP here and there, but they were not as prevalent as they used to be. The leading edge of panic had arrived as he topped a rise and then down the hill he saw the sign: Gas.

That's all it said – Gas. Good. That's all he needed. As he pulled in, he realized there was no pay at the pump. Needless to say, the pumps were old like the building itself. At one time, there had been a service bay but that had been some time ago. That area now was a mini convenience store. Gum. Hannah had requested gum.

He went in to ask about paying by credit card. The elderly lady behind the counter tamped out her cigarette before responding with "go ahead and pump and then come in to pay. You see that little crank on the side of the pump? You just turn it clockwise and that will reset it." Arvie said thanks, and returned out front to do as he was told. He was not a first-timer at this cranking thing.

He remembered a station in Colorado Springs when stationed at Fort Carson with the 5th Infantry Division Mechanized. It was a coin-op. Turn the crank to reset, put the nozzle in the tank, drop in the quarters, squeeze the handle and voila. Gas poured into the tank. What was the cost back then – 15 cents a gallon? He couldn't remember. Right now gas is running into his tank at the rate of $3.29 a gallon. That's some real inflation. But at least he didn't have to feed it quarters.

The tank full, he walked inside to pay. He handed the lady his credit card and she asked, "How much?"

"I don't know," he reported and then asked, "Don't you have it in here?"

"No. If you'll tell me how much I can run your card."

"Ok, I'll be right back."

He walked to the pump thinking *I am not out in the north woods somewhere. I am either in Minneapolis or one of the northern suburbs and I have to tell the cashier how much I bought? How would she check? If I walk in and say $36.68, is she going to walk out to see if I'm an honest man? If so why isn't she walking out here now? So I'm going to say $36.68 and then out the door she'll go to take a look for herself. Seems like a lot of time wasted in this system. Maybe some of the new technology makes some sense after all especially when it allowed her* to see the pump price at her register. But he looks at her through the window and thinks *it has been a good long while since she has done anything resembling a physical effort, so I could probably say $10.25 and that would be the end of it.*

So, he walks back in and say's "$36.68," and she says, "ok" and that's the end of it. He was proud that he did not succumb to temptation, yet he still wondered if he could've gotten away with it. *Why do I think like that?*

"Do you have any gum?" Arvie asked. She pointed to what used to be the service bay and said, "Over there." He said a thank-you and headed through the door. He found the gum and as he stood there pondering which flavor, he knew by the smell that there had been a lot of oil changed in here. How many years ago was that because it smells like it could have been yesterday. *Yes, he'll purchase the Wrigley's Spearmint with the burst of motor oil flavor. And thank you.* He picked up two packs and was about to walk out to pay the lady when he almost broke his neck because of the double take.

It was a shiny black can with the word Redeemed in red letters. *He felt instant sweat rolling down his back.* They couldn't have known he would be in here today. He has never been in this neighborhood or on this street before in his life. But he is here and so is this can of Redeemed. He reached for the can, turned it around and read "a fine coffee product of Northern Minnesota." Still looking at the can he moved through the doorway and made his way to the lady, laid two packs of gum on the counter and asked, "How long have you had this can of coffee?"

"Maybe an hour or so. Why?"

"Just curious. Do you know who left it? Was it one of your usual suppliers?"

"Yes, it was the candy guy. New guy. We changed companies not long ago. Oh, and he did tell me something about that can. He said, "I'm leaving this in there. He'll be in today to pick it up. Tell him it's been paid for."

"Oh. Interesting. Just curious, did the new guy look like a Native American by any chance?"

"Well, yes he did, come to think of it."

"Do you have a phone number or an address for this company?"

"I do. Right here. Here, I'll give you a sticky."

"Thank you so much. How much for the gum?"

"$2.87."

"Thanks again."

"Sure."

Back in the car, he sensed she was watching from inside; from her perch on top of her stool. His mind returned to the Thursday before. He and Carl had been sitting in the car. They stared at the building where Silverheels had been, before he vanished into thin air. *How soon before this one is vaporized? Why has no one else pulled in here since I've been here? It is another of these convenience stores that appears for a moment, just long enough for me to walk in and stumble into a shiny black can that someone left there knowing that I was going to stop by. How do they do that?*

The ringing of his cell phone jarred him out of his stupor. "This is Arvie."

"Arvie, its Carl and you're not going to believe this."

"Oh no. Not you too?"

"Why? What?"

"Ooooh no. You called me. You first."

"Ok. I left this morning and I'm on the road at 7:00 am, heading down 169 to Mankato. I stop at this little place to get some breakfast. Afterwards, I go up to the counter to pay and I notice a little closet area just behind the counter stocked with candy bars and gum and stuff. I ask if there are any stomach remedies in there like Rolaids you know? The gal says, 'Yes,' so I go back there. I barely get in there and ...."

"You found a shiny black can."

"How'd you know?"

"I didn't, but I just found one too in a little gas station grocery area on a street that I have never been on in my life. Was it a can of Redeemed?"

"Yeah. You got one too?"

"Sure did. How do they do this?"

"I asked the lady if they have this kind of coffee all the time and she said, 'No.' She'd never seen it before but the lady who delivered it had said that she left a can of coffee back there for a man who would be in later to pick it up. She also said that it had already been paid for. I asked her what would happen if someone else had come in before me and how she would know she had the right person. Do you know what she said? Get this – she said the delivery gal said, 'There wouldn't be anyone back there before he arrives.' So, Arvie, they can control traffic in and out of some of these places to make sure the coffee is there when one of us walks in. What do you think of that?"

"Or, perhaps they have access into the minds of every person on earth. They know what we are thinking, and if we change our minds, a light flashes on a screen somewhere and alarms go off to alert them. Perhaps they know what we are going to be doing and when. And because they know the mind of everyone, they look at everyone's timetable, pick a slot of time that's open, drop off the can a few minutes before we walk in the door. Wow. I'm just sitting in my car outside this place looking at my black can and I'm thinking that when I get home I'm going to perk some Redeemed and sit down with Orwell's 1984. It's the big brother is watching thing as you know. Is that what this is?"

"Well, now I know what you've been feeling since this all began. How did they know I was on the road this morning? Nobody knew the route I'd be driving. Shoot, I didn't know myself."

"Apparently they know what we are going to be doing before we do. How does that work?"

"Yeah. What did they say when you found *your* Redeemed?

"There was a new delivery guy on the route today, so I asked the lady if she had a phone number to call. So, I got that. I'm going to wait to call until Monday and I'll let you know what I learn – if anything. In the meantime, make sure you keep your eyes open for the next one because I'll just bet you'll find at least one more before you get back here."

"You said you were on a road you've never been on before. Where are you?"

"I'm heading back home from the intersection of the freeway and Chariton and didn't feel like I wanted the freeway type of drive."

"Do I want to ask what you were doing at that exit?"

"That'll take a little explaining. I'll send you an email, but it all has to do with this same subject."

"I'll be looking for the email. Peace and Love my friend."

"And to you as well. And don't forget to be careful out there."

"It's hard to focus on driving when I've got coffee on my mind."

"I understand." Carl clicked off.

So now Carl is getting coffee. That makes three of us including Dweebs. How soon will the phone calls come in from Freddie and Bert? Arvie thought he'd better get away from this gas pump before they take this place away. He wondered if it would be all bad to go with it? If he did, maybe he could learn how this all works? He started the car, took a left and headed north on whatever street he was on.

Looking at the dashboard clock he was suddenly pulled back to reality. He had to get home and get ready for church. *Enough of this for today.* He'd probably see Pastor Anne at church and he'd ask her how he can get names of senior men who don't get out much anymore. Maybe there is a group that meets at the church and he is suddenly reminded of the senior Bible study that takes place on Wednesday mornings at the Deerwood campus. There are usually 150 or more seniors who attend. Why didn't he think of that this morning on his walk when he was thinking of all the ways to pour coffee for people? He and Hannah would go this coming Wednesday and Arvie decided he would find out if he can provide the coffee. Yup. Good idea. That's opportunity #6 and a good one. Or was that #7?

Hannah was in a bit of a panic when he came in from the garage. "I just got started getting ready too late. I'm going to wear the same thing again. Do you think anyone will notice?"

"I don't think so dear. Everybody dresses so casual these days you know. You will look gorgeous as usual. I've got to hurry up too. You won't believe my day today, and yes, that guy was at his usual corner. His name is Zeke. Well, that's what he told me anyway. Kind of stand-offish a little bit but he did drink two cups of coffee so I was pleased with that. I'll go down again next week at least once. Oh and by the way, I'd like to go to the senior Bible study on Wednesday morning. Will you go with me? I'm thinking that's another coffee opportunity."

"Yes, it is. I think that's a good one. You'll have to make sure to get me up on time. We'll have to do some shopping that day too. Oh, I just don't know if there will be enough time. What time does the Bible study start again?"

"It starts at 10 and it's down at Deerwood. Remember?"

"Yes, dear. Oh, I just don't know if we'll have enough time? Do you think we will?"

Today is a real anxiety day. "Yes, dear. Time is what we have plenty of. Isn't that right?"

"I guess so. I'll be down in a minute. Why is everything such a rush these days? Do you feel like everything is a big rush?"

"Yes, I suppose so. We need to hurry if possible. I guess it's ok if we miss the prayer time. Oh, and one more thing. When I stopped for your gum, I got another can of coffee. This time the name on the can is, Redeemed. I was sitting in the car having just found the can and I got a call from Carl. He's on the road to California and he got a can of, Redeemed when he stopped for breakfast. Isn't this crazy?"

"It seems crazy to me. I don't understand any of it. I'll hurry."

By the time they pulled into the volunteer parking lot, every spot was filled and he had to double park alongside a minivan at the end of a row. "Do you think the church issues parking tickets for parking illegally?" he asked.

"Oh, dear me. Do you really think they would do something like that? How much do you think that would cost? We don't have any money in our budget for that. Maybe we'd best go over into that other lot."

"We'll be fine right here. Anyway, if they do hand out tickets, it'll come right out of our tithe."

"Is that ok to do? Do we need to ask someone if that's ok to do?"

"No. I'm sure that's ok. I think I read something about that in last week's bulletin. Well, maybe it was the week before. Anyway, we're parking it right here."

"Well, that's good then."

Saturday night in the bookstore was wonderful. The volunteers took turns going to one service or the other so the store was never left untended. Arvie got a chance to talk to Pastor Anne about the retired 'old guys' and she said she would get him some kind of a list by midweek. She even suggested that if he really wanted to get into this, it could probably fill up his entire week, especially with the addition of the 7th campus which opens soon. Arvie said it would be best if he focused on just this campus to begin with and she thought it was wonderful that he'd do this. Arvie did not mention anything about "magic" coffee thinking it would be best if he kept that bit of information to himself. So that opportunity is now up and running.

He also had a conversation with Roberta, the manager of the coffee shop next door to the bookstore. He asked if she had any openings for additional people, since he was considering volunteering a second Saturday a month, maybe a third. "As a matter of fact" he added, "I'd consider taking a Sunday morning too." But she's all staffed up right now but should things change, she'd let him know. She asked if he wanted to be behind the counter making the specialty coffees or at the self-serve area where the tables are? He said he would prefer the latter, and she added that if he worked there, he would come a little earlier to brew the coffee and fill the pots. Well, now he knew how that worked. He said, "Yes. I would like to do that, so please keep me in mind, and since we are in the bookstore on the 3rd Saturday, any other Saturday would be great." She assured him that she would contact him as soon as she had an opening. And with that, another opportunity is off the ground. Arvie had this brief moment when he felt Jacob Whitefeather standing beside him through that entire conversation nodding his head and murmuring his approval; "oh that's really (gasp) good. Yes, (wheeze) very good. Really excellent (burp)." Well, he *is* 116 years old.

As they pulled in their townhouse driveway, a large cardboard box was quite obvious sitting on their front porch, right under the porch light. As soon as the car was parked, he was on the porch inspecting the box. His first thought was that there was absolutely no identification on it whatsoever. Well, it's dark out here. He'd get it into the kitchen. As he hoisted it into position, Hannah asked, "What is that?" He responded, "I don't know. We need to get it into the kitchen and find out." Hannah opened the door and pushed the button to put the garage door down. He entered the kitchen and placed the box on the counter.

It took only a moment for him to realize that indeed there was nothing on the box, no words, no little plastic pouch stuffed with documentation, no identification numbers from UPS or FedEx. Nothing.

"I don't know where this came from or how it got here" he mumbled. Hannah asked, "Why don't you open it and see what's inside?" "Good idea. Let's do that." As he reached for a knife to cut the tape, he realized that he knew what he was about to see.

As the box opened exposing the contents, Hannah peered inside and said matter-of-factly, "Well, some more coffee. How nice," and walked away. He reached inside and carefully extracted a shiny black can. On the front of the can was printed the word, Forever. He knew what was printed on the back of the can, but turned it around, just to make sure. Yes, those words were the same. In all, 12 cans of Forever filled the box. *What do they think I'm going to do with all of this? Maybe they know about Wednesday's Bible study? How do they get the information so quickly? Was it Jacob Whitefeather who delivered this box? He thought not.* At 116, or however old he is, Arvie doubted he could manage the weight of that much coffee. Must've been Silverheels. *Wake up Arvid. Must be more people involved in this than just the two of them. Maybe hundreds, thousands even?*

He cleared another shelf in the pantry and reverently placed the 12 cans of Forever in perfect order. Standing back in order to see the big picture, his thought process envisioned knocking down walls to expand the pantry. Or, perhaps the garage is the answer. Leave the car out front. Fill the garage with shelf units to house the inventory. *God, I guess it is not necessary for me to understand what's going on here. I feel that you are urging me to continue moving forward with this. Is this your answer to my prayer of the other night?*

As he drifted off to sleep later that night, Jesus' words "Feed my sheep" kept rolling through his drowsy mind. He wasn't going to feed them. He was going to make sure at least some of them got a good cup of coffee and, hopefully, more than one. *Those 12 cans of Forever are the sign to pour as much coffee as possible. He wants me to heal as many as possible and create a heaven on earth. Heal them!*

Chapter 7

"I know the Good Lord said that Sunday was a day of rest. Well, it ain't – unless you put in a good eight hours first. Heh heh." - *Ole*

*"But the Lord looks after those who fear Him,
those who put their hope in His love."*
Psalm 33:18

He'd set the coffee on auto for a 5:45 brew. It was pitch black inside and outside the townhouse as he shuffled down the steps and into the kitchen. He hit the light switch. 'Numnum,' their precious, patch tabby Maine Coon for the past 11 years, squinted up at him as if to say, "Man, that light is so bright first thing in the morning. Could you just light a candle instead?"

He fixed Numnum her breakfast and then with great relish, poured himself his first cup of Reunion. He opened the pantry door for a quick reminder of his inventory: Forever - 13 cans, Reunion - one can nearly full, Redeemed - one can unopened. The inventory had grown substantially with 12 cans received the previous night. Then Silverheels was beside him, whispering quietly, *He will know when you have a need. Keep the Faith. Gitchi Manitou is involved here.* Arvie wandered the downstairs as he sipped the coffee

Sundays had become very interesting since Hannah had been diagnosed with anxiety. Wonder of wonders, she had become a fan of golf and football. How could that have happened? Arvie had no answer, but it sure made for wonderful Sundays. PGA tour coverage would begin at 1:00 and conclude at 5:00, unless there was a playoff in which case the coverage would last until whenever. The remainder of the evening would be filled with coverage of either the European or LPGA Tour. What a great day.

There had been so many years when he had to watch golf and football all by himself got the evil eye if he so much as flicked the TV channel to a second game. He didn't like her anxiety at all, but it sure made for some super Sundays and with fall on the way, there would also be Monday Night Football to watch together. Go figure.

Chapter 8

"If you're always begging someone for a favor,
chances are you are in the wrong line of work. Heh heh."
- *Ole*

*"A good person can look forward to happiness,
but an evil person can expect nothing."*
Proverbs 10:28

What would he do with the day? What a great feeling it was. He had wondered if the feeling of retirement would be one of instant euphoria as opposed to muddled confusion. It was really some of both. But, how nice; to be in total control of his time.

He decided he would begin writing or journaling, or whatever people called it, when they sat down and fumbled with words. He sat down at his computer and opened an empty page in MS Word and began. The entry that day would be about coffee, the north woods, disappearing buildings and people. He would write about the dead Native American Midi who sold him coffee and the steps he had taken to build his plan to bring hope and healing to the masses. He would write about his acid reflux disappearing. Maybe the entry would lead to his first book. He wondered if miracles would help sell a book?

He knew as he began to write that he needed to call Pastor Sayles and ask about making coffee the following Wednesday morning: what time would he need to be there and would he make the coffee there or bring it? Maybe, with a little Forever, the usual organ concerts that begin each Bible study would diminish considerably. Yes, the "organ concert." He couldn't suppress the quiet giggle.

When the old folks come together, the conversation is dominated by discussion of the organs. This, "organ concert" then, has absolutely nothing to do with music: "It gives me so much trouble; the occasional pain is just awful." "Well, with me it's my heart. It runs in the family. Mom suffered with it all her life." "I don't have any organs left to worry about." "Oh, it's my kidneys. Doctor says, one day they'll just quit". "Mel, how's that pancreas?" And the ever present, "George. How's your prostate?" Then there are the various other issues that are also discussed during the concert, but may not be exactly about an organ: "Gladys, I can see that your arthritis has got a good grip on you today." "How many of us at this table are getting new hips in the next 60 days? Two, three, is that all?" All the issues come together in a full-bodied orchestra that is known lovingly as, the "organ concert."

Put 100 seniors in a large room. Wander around and listen. Yup, it's truly an organ concert without the music. Why should it be any different than it is? The people don't work anymore. There are no longer issues regarding a job, promotions, co-workers or rush hour traffic. Kids are long out of the house and busy with their lives. Health becomes a major focus of life.

When so much time is spent with doctors or in transit to and from appointments, it only makes sense that this would monopolize the discussion. Potential sub-topics never end: body fluids, worts or bad skin with pending biopsy results arriving by mail or with a phone call. Patients hope for results by mail because it is well-known that when a doctor calls with results, something isn't right and when something isn't right, it means more donations of blood, fluids or tissues for more pending results. Therefore, seniors become somewhat obsessed with the daily mail: test results could arrive at any time. In addition, seniors become best friends with medical people who work in the labs of clinics and hospitals and with Pharmacists in drug stores as there are always prescriptions to be refilled.

There is no other way to spend time as a senior citizen – unless someone comes up with a magic coffee. Arvie became quite sure that a couple of Wednesday mornings with the senior Bible study group would answer at least some of the questions regarding Forever.

He decided to make those phone calls and postpone his journal writing. He dialed the number for Pastor Noah Sayles.

Noah answered on the second ring. "Good morning. This is Noah."

"Good morning Noah. Glad I caught you. This is Arvie Ellison. How are you?"

"Arvie. Good to hear from you. It's been awhile."

"Yes, and we're sorry about that. But part-time work is now a thing of the past so we will be re-joining you on Wednesday mornings."

"Well I'm happy to hear that."

"Noah, I'm calling to find out if there is a chance I can buy you a cup of coffee somewhere, wherever is convenient for you. I've got something that I need to talk to you about in person. Do you have any time today?"

"I could do something this afternoon, say around 2:00, or so. Yes, that would work. Where would you like to meet?"

"Tell me what's convenient for you."

"Well, there is the Grandpa Brothers' Coffee at the freeway and county road 14. How about there?"

"That's great. I'll see you there around 2:00, and thanks."

"I'll look forward to that. Bye."

That's good, Arvie thought. *Now let's see if I can find out anything about the delivery of that can of, Redeemed to the gas station on Saturday.* He had no idea where he was calling as he dialed the number. Could be Iowa.

"Good morning. Northern Food Supply. Can I help you?"

"Yes ma'am. I purchased a can of coffee this past Saturday and I was told that it had been delivered by you. I want to know how I can get more of that brand?"

"Certainly. First of all, what was the location where you purchased the coffee?"

"It was just north of Minneapolis. The lady told me that it was your, 'North 27' route and the gas station was on – I think it was Central."

"All right. You said the route was the North 27?"

"Yes, that's what she told me."

"Well, this is a little confusing. I'm sorry to tell you that the North 27 route was discontinued nearly one year ago, back in August of 2013, so it couldn't have been us that delivered that coffee. We went through a re-organization last year and there were many changes."

"Interesting. The lady at the store must not have received the memo. So, it has been almost one year since your company worked that route?"

"That's correct sir. I'm very sorry."

"I appreciate your help ma'am. Thank you."

Hannah suddenly appeared. "Hi. Good morning."

"Well, you sure came down the steps quietly. You're up early today. Good for you."

"Yeah, up and at 'em. Who were you talking to?"

"When I stopped at that gas station on Saturday and found that coffee, I asked the attendant for the name of the company who delivered it. She gave me the phone number and that was them. I learned that it couldn't have been them because they no longer deliver in that area. They haven't been to that store for over a year. So, another dead end."

"Is the coffee ready?"

"Yup, sure is. I can't ever seem to get any information on where this coffee comes from. It says on the can, 'a fine coffee product of Northern Minnesota,' so why does it even say that? Even knowing that much, I can't find out anything else. Who was it that put that can in that convenience store for me to find on Saturday? Who was it that put the box on our front porch Saturday night? How did that someone find out where we live? Did you sleep well?"

"I'm sleeping really well, it seems. I want to get out of bed earlier in the morning. Morning is my hardest time. Why is it so important that you know where it is coming from? Why do you have to keep asking so many questions about this? Can't you just accept the way it is and go do what you feel you must do?"

"Well now. I think you just delivered an important message to me. Accept the way things are and move along with your life. Do what is needed and stop all the analyzing, huh?"

"Isn't it the same thing you've been telling me about my anxiety? If all I do is continue to ask myself so many questions, questions that I have no answers for, I'm really not moving forward with anything am I? I think that makes sense for me and I think it makes sense for you too. Doctor Blower said, 'Paralysis through analysis,' the other day. I'm beginning to see how that fits. You were talking to someone else, earlier, weren't you?"

"Oh, yes. I called Noah about the Bible study on Wednesday morning. I want to see if I can provide the coffee. If ever there was a perfect setting to test our theory that this coffee improves our health, this is it. Anyway, we are meeting this afternoon at Grandpa Brothers' at 2:00. I'm going to tell him the whole story so he'll know why I want to provide the coffee. Of course, he may smile at me and be very nice and once I leave he'll make a call to someone about having me committed."

"Well, you couldn't be put away by a nicer person. He is such a fine man and yes, he really is committed. But that's what you should do. Figure out what you can do and then go do it. Good for you. I've never been into Grandpa's. Have You?"

"Nope. Never have. I've seen it there but never stopped in. Let me get you your first cup of the day. I think I'll take a can with me. Just to show him what I'm talking about."

"That's a good idea. Oh, thank you. It smells so good."

"And it warms your hands at the same time."

"Maybe you should open up a coffee shop. Wouldn't that be kind of fun? And then you could really pour a lot of your coffee for a lot of people."

"I hadn't thought of that. So, you are suggesting I go out right now and open a coffee shop? But I'd have to think about so many things before I could ever do that, don't you think?"

"Sure. But just don't overdo the thinking, the analysis. Get some information, think about it, pray about it, make a decision and trust your faith."

"Huh. That sounds simple. Where is the right place to open up a coffee shop around here?"

"Oh, maybe right down the street. There is that little strip center where the liquor store is. You know, some others have opened up in there but haven't been able to stay open very long. Must not be enough traffic."

"Interesting. I think a good coffee shop generates its own traffic. You might be right. Just across the way is that Fast Stop and that place generates a lot of traffic. And think of the morning traffic coming through from Wisconsin headed toward I35. We'd have to have a drive-through window. I'll bet rush hour every morning would generate good business. Wouldn't you think?"

"How about finding some kind of traffic analysis? Who does that kind of thing? The city?"

"I don't know, but that's a good thought. We can ask around and make a call to find out what the rent is in that building, how big the available space is and all that stuff. That's not too much analysis, is it?"

Hannah shook her head and took another sip of coffee with her eyes closed.

Arvie continued, "So then, this retirement thing is over before it really begins and I've been enjoying myself these few days doing only what I want to be doing."

"Now dear, don't get carried away. It doesn't hurt to look into things. And just the looking and the thinking can be enjoyable, don't you think?"

"I suppose so. That case of coffee that showed up Saturday night has me wondering. I had thought that I would be receiving it one can at a time and then here comes a whole case and that got me to thinking. Carl and I had a talk before we left the cabin last week about this healing coffee. What if it really heals, and what if we're so healthy we don't die? Now I know that's far-fetched but, what if? We wondered if God wouldn't approve because, wouldn't the absence of pain mean a kind of heaven on earth situation? Aren't we supposed to die and go to heaven before we live forever? Isn't that part of His plan of redemption? So, after Carl and I talked about that, we agreed that we needed to pray. I did. I asked for some sign of approval, and then we find 12 cans on the front porch. I think that's a sign, don't you?"

"Oh, mercy. What a question. But, yes, I think that could be an answer to prayer. And now that you are thinking about opening a coffee shop, maybe it's also the answer to buying coffee in bulk – you know, a whole truck load. Or am I getting a little carried away here?"

"That could be possible Hannah. If we opened a coffee shop we would want to buy in bulk to keep the cost down but we still don't know how to find these people to even start the process. I guess we know, at least, that they'll deliver more than one can at a time. It's a start. Do you think they'd continue *giving* it away? That would be nice. Aahhh, I don't know. Lots of unanswerable questions. The one question that really matters is about our faith. How good is our fath, really?"

"We have to always ask ourselves that question, don't we dear?"

"Yes, I suppose so. And now, where is that grocery list? I think I'd like to go get the shopping done before I head down to meet Noah. Here it is. Not much on here. Can you think of anything else we should get?"

"Are those mini ice cream sandwiches on there?"

"No, they aren't. I'll write that down. Anything else? I've got salad, rolls, bananas, soup, crackers, 60-watt light bulbs, AA batteries, ibuprofen and I think I'll get two more good thermos bottles."

"I think that's all. I'm sure you'll look around a bit in case you think of something."

"Soup and crackers for lunch?"

"Sure."

"Ok, I'll see you in a few minutes."

Arvie headed to Walmart. It wouldn't take long. He knew his way around the store. As a rule, he disliked shopping, but had learned that the secret to a good shopping experience is to know the store and to have a list. *Get in and get out and then get back to your life.* That's how he rolls on a shopping trip.

* * * * * * * *

He was almost to Cassie's register when he thought of yogurt. Of course, yogurt was in the dairy section which was all the way at the back of the store. And then he thought of coffee. He would be going past the coffee on his way back to dairy so he would take notice. It was the store that he usually shopped so he wanted to get in the habit of checking the coffee inventory. Just in case. But, *no shiny black cans today,* he thought. He even went to his knees to check the bottom shelf. At that precise moment Assistant Store Manager Aaron happened on the scene.

"Oh Arvie. I'm so sorry. You've fallen and you can't reach your beer. Or is it that you are looking for a brand of coffee that we usually stock far back on the bottom shelf so no one can get to it?"

"Well, since you asked, the latter is correct. Aaron, if you ever see coffee in a shiny black can, please set it aside for me. I will go down on my knees in search of coffee, but I wouldn't do that for a can of beer. You know, we all have our priorities."

"What's the brand of the coffee?"

"Interestingly enough, the name on the front of the can changes, but the shiny black can with red lettering is always the same. And I am serious. If you see the shiny black can, or cans, grab it or them and keep for me. Ok?"

"Must be some good coffee. Where does it come from?"

"Northern Minnesota."

"They don't do coffee in Northern Minnesota."

"And what's really interesting, is that it's roasted by a Midewiwin of the Mille Lacs Ojibwe who has been dead for 50 years, or so I've been led to believe."

"Did you take a hockey puck in the forehead this morning? What are you talking about?"

"Aaron, it is such a long story. If you think I'm losing it, you just might be right. I'll tell you the story one day."

"Should I bring a 12 pack?"

"To tell this story, a case would be better. Good to see you."

"Take care, Arvie."

He left the coffee section and headed for yogurt. With that secured in his cart, he was off to find Cassie.

As usual, she had a line. After many years, she had created quite a following. Everyone wanted to talk with her. Arvie wondered if he shouldn't seek out the rudest cashier in the store. Chances are, her line would always be one of the shortest. But, then he wouldn't get to have his few minutes with Cassie.

Several minutes later, "Hi Cassie."

"Have you got any coupons today, or price matches?"

"Not a one."

"Well, good. I'll get you outta here ASAP."

"You are so thoughtful that way."

"How's Hannah doing?"

"Pretty much the same. This anxiety never ends."

"I know that very well. You tell her, 'hi' from me. Oh, and by the way, I've got a little brown bag for you to give her."

"Isn't that something. These little brown bags continue to appear. Thanks Cassie. You are very thoughtful. See you next time."

As he turned out of the Walmart parking lot, he noticed in the rearview mirror a black Ford sedan pulling into traffic two cars behind him. He took a right on 8th Street and watched in his rear-view mirror as the black Ford took the same turn. He paid no further attention as his mind drifted back to the subject at hand. *They obviously know where I live. Why would Jacob not just deliver the cans to my front porch as he did the other night? Why should I have to keep checking the coffee displays at every store I pass by? Why would they go through the extra effort of leaving a can at a store, and then, have to make sure that no one else gets in that store, or at least that aisle, before I get there? Or do they know every schedule of every human being? If that was the case, then they could just regulate my schedule to somehow get me to that can at a time when no one else will be there.*

"Guess what I've got for you?"

"Another shiny black can?"

"No. Another kind of crumpled up little brown bag with something inside."

"Cassie?"

"Yup again."

"I wonder why she does that?"

"I think she enjoys doing it. I think she is a good, caring person."

"Well, thank her again, next time you see her. Oh, look. She sent her usual can of Chicken Noodle soup, and look at this cute card."

"I sure thanked her," Arvie said. "Did you heat up some soup?"

"Yes. On the stove."

"Smells good. Thank you dear."

"There's crackers in the cupboard."

"Yup. Got 'em. What will you be doing while I'm drinking coffee with Noah?"

"I'm starting the work for Monday's small group session. We are beginning Colossians. Francis is going to lead this one."

"Oh, good. That should be a good study."

"I think so. Paul did so much back then to encourage so many. I wish that I could have done more of that over all the years."

"I have always thought of you as an encourager. I've seen it in the way you've interacted with people over the years. Remember that no matter how much we've done, we'll always wish we would've done more. Don't you think?"

"Yes. I'm sure you're right."

"I'll see you in a little while. Good luck getting into Colossians."

"You have a good time and be sure to say, 'hi' to Noah from me."

"I'll do that. See you in a little while. And thanks for the soup."

* * * * * * * * * *

Arvie headed for the freeway thinking about the can of Forever sitting next to him. Noah would ask about it; probably say something like, "Whoa. Now that's a good looking can."

Wait. Here is that little strip center Hannah mentioned. I'll drive through and take a quick look, especially for the realtor and a phone number.

The liquor store occupied one of the middle spaces. There were four middle spaces and one at each end. The end spaces appeared larger. He wouldn't want to be in the middle spaces anyway because he would need a drive-through. *But why couldn't the middle spaces have a drive through at the back of the store? Duh.*

Which end looks the best? As he looked at it from the front, the west end looked better than the east because it seemed slightly larger and sat closer to the main road heading to the freeway. The west end with a drive-thru would be faster to access than the east. *Everyone is in such a hurry - should keep that in mind. The west may be better because of size; more seating and comfortable seating - critical in a coffee shop these days, as is a variety of table sizes and placement.*

An intimate interior is important. Color scheme is important too. Fireplace. We're in Minnesota. Warmth is important and it contributes to, 'cozy.' One negative to all these storefronts is that they face north. There will be no warmth from the sun entering any of these choices. Facing south would be nice. We would have to provide Wi-Fi too. Yes, we could get creative with window blinds to keep the cold look of the north to a minimum, so the northern exposure is not a killer. Ok, enough of that. On to Noah.

Wait. There's the sign. He pulled over and wrote down the name and the number.

Back on the road again, he was headed to a coffee shop he'd not been in before. He would study it carefully and make notes: likes and dislikes. The coffee shop opportunity could be a better idea than he originally thought. However, of all of his ideas, it was the one that would require the most attention, time and work, to say nothing about cost. But then he could really be thought of as 'the coffee guy,' or quite possibly "The Coffee Guy." That would lend credibility to his efforts to get in with the coffee shop at church, or doing the coffee for Noah at the Bible study and anything else coffee-related. He came to County14, exited, and there was Grandpa's.

Grandpa Brothers' was on the east end and faced south. The drive-through seemed quite busy on a Monday afternoon. There was plenty of parking; much more than at the other strip mall. He parked and walked to the front door. He opened the door to enter, pausing to allow two young ladies with computer bags thrown over their shoulders to enter ahead of him; neither took the moment necessary to thank him for his chivalrous deed. *Did I lock the car?* He let the door close itself and headed back into the parking lot to make sure. He pushed his remote lock button from about 20 feet away, heard the familiar beep, turned immediately back towards Grandpa Brothers' and had to wait for a car to pass in front of him. *It's another black Ford sedan.* He noticed the two men in the front seat looking straight forward and then went inside to find Noah. *There he is. He's already got us a table.*

"Noah. Good to see you."

"Afternoon, Arvie. Get yourself a cup and come join me."

"I'll be right back."

"Yes sir. What can I get for you?"

"What have you got brewing? You sell it by light, medium, and dark roasts?"

"Yes sir."

"Which do you recommend?"

"I like the medium. To me, it has the most flavor and it smells the best. I brew it at home. I just like getting up in the morning and smelling it ready and waiting for me. And, it's our most popular. Most everyone who comes in has the medium."

"Well said, young man. Let me have a medium medium."

"Coming right up.

* * * * * * * *

"Noah. Thanks for meeting with me today."

"Happy to. I always appreciate another opportunity to drink some coffee. Did you say you've been here before?"

"No. First time."

"Did you get the medium?"

"I did. The young man at the counter said it's the most popular."

"Glad to hear you'll be coming back to the Bible study. You said, on the phone, that there was something you wanted to talk to me about."

"Yes. Who makes the coffee on Wednesday morning and what brand of coffee is used?"

"Well, Moggy and I usually make the coffee since we are the first ones to arrive. And it is most always a Folger's or a Maxwell House, I think. The church buys it and I'm sure they are very price conscious, so it is whatever we find in the cupboard that day. Why?"

"Let me show you … this."

"Ok. It would look to be a can of coffee. I don't think I've ever bought coffee in a black can before. Forever? Is that the name of the coffee? I've never heard of that."

"That's what I wanted to talk to you about. The first can of this I bought was called Forever and I got it at a convenience store on 169 on the way to a cabin for a reunion with some old college friends last week. Matter of fact, I bought two. The third can I received was labeled Reunion and it was given to me at another convenience store on 169 as I was heading home from the cabin. The fourth can was labeled Redeemed and it also was just handed to me at another convenience store on Central Avenue in Minneapolis. This is more Forever. I found a case of it on our front porch Saturday night when we got home from church. No matter what the name on the front, all cans have looked the same, the shiny black color with the red letters."

"Ok again. Interesting how you are receiving the coffee. I'm curious. What's the story?"

Arvie told Noah the story of last week.

* * * * * * * *

"Unbelievable. So, you're telling me that this coffee actually fixed up you and your friends?"

"Well, we certainly thought so and I can still say that my acid reflux is gone. We all identified something within us that the coffee fixed or at least improved. But there are so many questions: I bought coffee from a guy that had been dead for 50 years. Maybe that's why I couldn't find him again – he is still dead. And then Silverheels told me that 'he will get me more when I have a need for it'. How would he – whoever 'he' might be, know that? But now, since we are all back to our normal ways of life, the coffee continues to miraculously appear.

"I feel like I have to get this coffee poured for everyone I encounter, Noah. I know that those who are sick want to be healed, but I have also come to believe that those who are not sick but are about to be sick can be healed of what's coming that is about to make them sick. How about that? I see no logical explanation for what is happening, but I want to believe in a magical coffee that can heal. That's why I want to do the coffee on Wednesday mornings. Where else can I see, in a matter of perhaps two or three weeks, a positive difference in the health of people?"

"I see that, Arvie. Now you understand why my involvement for so long with Seniors. It's helping others, serving them during their later years. I take it then that you are familiar with Organ Concert's?"

"I'll say. And now that I've gotten older, I find that I can more readily participate in the concert myself. When seniors get together it seems we have nothing else to talk about but our organs, our aches and pains, pills, doctors. I think I need to do it. Pour my coffee, I mean."

"And that's fine with me. Moggy and I'll be glad to have you. And since you are being provided with free coffee, we'll save the church some money. Seems like it's a winning idea on many fronts. You know, over all the years of service in the church, I have had one or two similar opportunities like the one in front of you now."

"Really Noah? Like what?"

"I felt that the Lord wanted me to do something and so I did. I kept doing it until I felt the urging subside and then it seemed that the reason to continue to do it didn't exist any longer so I stopped. I wondered what exactly I had accomplished by doing it. I couldn't come up with any answer to that, but I also realized that nothing had been hurt by my doing it. It sounds like that same thing is now going on with you. God has convicted you to pour this coffee for everyone you meet. We *can't* know the mind of God but we *can* sense Him leading us to do something. So we do it because we trust Him. We don't need to question Him about it because the urging is so strong. God works in mysterious ways, Arvid."

"This one seems especially mysterious to me. Jacob Whitefeather was here even though he couldn't have been, and so he wasn't and therefore isn't. I don't think I said that right. Anyway, I paid him for those first two cans, but I haven't paid for what I've received since."

"I admit that is most interesting and unusual, especially since everything about this world we live in revolves around money. I have a thought - what if pouring this coffee is a stepping stone leading you to something else, something you are really meant to be involved with? Perhaps you are being led to something infinitely more important?"

There was only the din of the coffee shop heard while Arvie deliberated Noah's question. "I hadn't thought of it that way. I feel like pouring this coffee is very important. I've been told that there are those who have a need. Perhaps they have a need to be healthy a little longer so that they can finish their cure for cancer, or the common cold, the complete understanding of the human brain or maybe just to provide love to someone. If pouring someone a cup of coffee enables the completion of such a project, how could I do anything more important? I could be the instrument used to get the healing from Jacob to whomever. The very fact that I am playing one of many roles in this process is vital in and of itself. – isn't it?"

"*I* think so. Back when the Jewish people were slaves in Egypt, God spoke to Aaron and said, 'Go find your brother.' You know the story - Moses had escaped from Egypt years earlier because he had killed an Egyptian guard. He ran away to the wilderness where he began a new life. He found himself a wife and they started to build their life together. Aaron had no idea where Moses was. He assumed he would have gone to the wilderness because that seemed like a good place to hide from the Egyptians. He could have started analyzing the whole thing. He could very easily have thought that he misinterpreted a dream. He could have said to himself that it would be a waste of time to go on such a search."

"He could have talked himself out of doing anything."

"Yes, he could easily have done that. What he didn't know at the time was that release from captivity in Egypt, freedom at last, was just around the corner. It was to be Moses who would lead the Israelites out of Egypt. So it was really important, obviously, that Moses return. All Aaron knew was that he was to find Moses and bring him back. Do you know this part of the story? Do you know what he did?"

"I know that it was Moses who led them out because I watched Charlton Heston part the Red Sea. No. I know nothing about how Aaron found him. What happened?"

"Well, Aaron left immediately. Other than knowing that he was going to the wilderness, he had no idea how he was going to find his brother. He didn't question doing this. He just did it. His faith was such that he knew that God would lead him to Moses. That's real faith, Arvid. Most of us don't have a faith that strong."

"So, off he went. I wonder if God believes that I have Aaron's faith? I will go pour coffee for people never understanding why? But

I don't need to know why. I should be content knowing that I'm doing what God has called me to do. Aaron did what he was told to do. I should do the same. Can it be that simple?"

"Yes, Arvid. It is that simple."

"Ok. Do we then have your permission to brew Forever for everyone on Wednesday morning?"

"Absolutely. I would not want to stand in the way of a God-directed mission. You'll want to be there by 9:00. Moggy and I'll be there to help you get the lay of the land. You realize the work you are going to cause me, don't you?"

"Ummm. No. I guess I don't."

"I have to put a circle around Wednesday's date on my calendar. I have to keep track from now on about every phone call I receive and every phone call I make. No matter who I am talking with, I have to keep copious notes on each and every comment made about health. I will need to monitor it all because what if your coffee is really magic? What if it does heal? What does it heal, and what doesn't it heal? Wouldn't we want to know all of this information?"

"But with God telling us to do this, isn't that enough? We do what we are told to do. We are his instrument for getting healing to the people. Isn't all this record keeping stuff something we do because in this world that's what we do? Do you think God means for us to keep track of everything?"

"I think you make a very good point, Arvid. Perhaps, as you said it, you are to be his instrument to get the healing to the people. We, however, being of this world, could be a little curious about what happens, don't you think?"

"I totally agree. So, I do what God tells me to do. Then, if I want to keep some records on the side, I can do that after hours."

"I think that's about right. I have to tell you, the story about the healing coffee has aroused my curiosity. I will be paying very close attention to all the conversations from Wednesday forward. In your story about last week didn't you say that you noticed a change in just a few hours?"

"It seemed so, yes. So should folks who arrive early at 9:30 and grab a cup first thing experience something before they go home at noon? I think it is possible that by then the process of healing something has begun. Realistically a change won't be noticed until later, but we should begin hearing something within a few days for sure.

"I have another question Noah. This came to me as I was driving here today. Do you think there might be some benefit to telling the folks what we are doing and why?"

"Mmmmm. Let's think about that. Tell them of your experience last week? You experienced healing of some kind. Your friends did also. We would be speaking honestly. There could be the 'Placebo' effect, people thinking they are getting something they are not, but they feel better anyway."

"Or, would we be setting them up for disappointment? Maybe those things we thought got fixed last week are the only things that get healed, and if a person has other issues, nothing gets healed in them at all. Now that I think about it, my acid reflux appears to be gone and when Freddie went without his pill that night, he didn't have a problem either. He was excited about that the next morning. But maybe we don't know enough yet? Maybe it would be better to say nothing and just pour the coffee? If something positive happens to someone, anyone, well, that would be a good thing. What do you think?"

"I agree with that Arvid. Let's wait and see. Maybe we tell them if something good happens? Perhaps we do nothing other than share a knowing smile with each other. Yes. Let's leave it at that for now. Have you other pouring plans?"

"Well, I've some additional ideas. There is no doubt in my mind that if I volunteered in the coffee shop at church two or three weekends a month, many could be exposed to my coffee; that is, if they allowed me to use my own. I've thought of making house calls on seniors who are shut in's. There is a guy who is always standing on the corner of 35W and Charitan. I've poured for him once already and I'm going back tomorrow. I'm trying to get Hannah to drink more and more Forever. I want to see if it can have a positive effect on her anxiety. Anytime anyone comes to our place for a visit I'll have a pot brewing. I've also thought about opening a coffee shop – like this one. Wouldn't you like to select from choices named

Forever, Redeemed, and Mercy? Maybe Forgiven will be next? Who knows what names are still to be used?"

"You've got some really good ideas there. Don't get too many things going. You are not getting any younger, Arvid. Perhaps you should focus on doing a few of those things well."

"Yeah. I suppose so. Yet, I continue to hold out hope that this coffee is the fountain of youth. The more that is consumed the faster the ageing process is reversed. I'd like to dunk a basketball again Noah. I'd like to experience that feeling one more time. What do you think? Possible?"

"As you know Arvid, with God, all things are possible."

"One final question Noah. I've been wrestling with this one since all this began. If everyone who drinks our coffee is healed, perhaps even of everything, is it conceivable that people will not die? And should that happen, are we creating a problem as we consider eternity? Aren't we to live forever in Heaven? Will God be displeased with us?"

"Arvid, I can help you with that one. God will be pleased if you help eliminate pain. After all, He wants us to be happy while we are here. He knows very well what happens to us as our bodies fail. I doubt very much that this will do more than perhaps postpone death a bit, because something inside of us will stop working and the end is inevitable. Science is causing us to live longer and I think God is ok with that, and I think He'll be happy if your coffee eases things for us along the way. If anything, I see you bringing hope.

"And remember Arvid, we can't take our imperfect body with us to heaven. We will leave it behind and journey on with our soul. There is a wonderful thing that comes with age and that is wisdom. Because of all the experience we accumulate over the years, we are better equipped to understand and make more intelligent and practical decisions. So, we are in a stronger position to lead those who come along after us."

"Isn't it backwards, Noah? Wouldn't it be better for us to be born with wisdom so that we don't make as many mistakes in our early years? Why is it good to only acquire wisdom late in life when all we can do is sit in our chair because we are not physically able to do anything other than that?"

"Now, Arvid. There will always be those questions, but I believe even the greatest of minds agree that since we cannot know the mind of God it is fruitless to ask them. You are driven to pour this coffee. You don't know why this has fallen on your plate. You have realized there are many questions and there are no answers. So you are going to do it anyway. Isn't it the same with life? We don't know the answers but we live it anyway. We are, after all is said and done, just people doing what people do. And it's in the doing that we learn. The young *do* and the older have learned because they have *done*."

"Well. I like the way you summed *that* up. Not to change the subject but Hannah asked me to ask about Moggy. She has missed their Wednesday conversations. She is anxious to know about that back problem she was living with."

"It's one of those things that will always be there. It is not going to go away unless your coffee is truly blessed with magic. But, I must say, she does well in spite of it and in my opinion, she continues to age gracefully. Thank you for asking. And how about Hannah's anxiety?"

"It's still there. She is coping with it the best she can. This thing comes with lots of ups and downs. She has a wonderful psychologist."

"How are *you* coping with it?"

"I am up and down as well. Some days my patience is good and I feel like I am helpful to her. Other days I am overtaken by a real impatience with the whole thing and I'll catch myself trying to fix her. It's a bit taxing."

"Yes. I've heard others say the very same thing. We will continue to pray for her. I must be getting back but before we go, let me pray. 'Father, how much we appreciate these moments of fellowship. We pray for this adventure that Arvid has embarked upon. Thank you for planting the seed within him, to bring hope to many who suffer from that which we all must go through, the failing of our humanness. Thank you for hope. You sent Jesus to us so that we would have hope and ultimately - joy. You love us so. Thank you for caring for us. We love you. Amen."

"Amen. Thank you, Noah."

"Wednesday at 9:00. I am really looking forward to this. Hi to Hannah."

"And a warm hello to Moggy. See you both Wednesday."

* * * * * * * *

"I am home. Is anyone here? Anyone - anywhere? Hello."

"Well of course I'm home. Where did you think I would be?"

"Oh, there you are. Noah and Moggy send greetings to you. They are looking forward to seeing you on Wednesday."

"Is she doing ok?"

"Noah says her back is much the same but she is doing a better job of dealing with it. And he has given us permission to pour our coffee. We need to be there at 9:00 to get it ready because people show up as early as 9:30."

"Well good. What did he think about your story?"

"He enjoyed it and he thinks God wants me to do what I'm doing, you know, figuring out ways to pour more coffee."

"Are you going to stand up and tell your story to everyone?"

"Noah doesn't think that would be a good idea. He wants us to get it ready and then let them do what they always do – consume it. We'll see what happens. But no, we will not share the story with everyone because that could set up some false expectations and he doesn't want to do that. Now you'll have to help us with the listening. We probably won't hear anything about healing until next week. So, Noah and Moggy, and you and I are going to be paying close attention to hear if anyone experiences some healing. Think you can help us with that?"

"Well, yes. That won't be too difficult."

"Good. Remember, we don't say anything about the coffee story. Got that?"

"Sure."

"Ok. How's it going today?"

"Pretty good. I'm better than I was yesterday."

"I'm sure glad to hear that. How much coffee did you have?"

"I had my usual two cups."

"Good for you. What's for supper?"

"I thought the bratwurst and sauerkraut would taste good. It's thawing now."

"Sounds good. I'm going to go down to see Zeke again tomorrow morning."

"Who?"

"Zeke. He's the guy at the Chariton exit off the freeway that we used to see all the time on our way down to the U. Remember?"

"Oh, of course. He sat on that bucket with that look of despair on his face. Every time it was the same look. Didn't you think so too?"

"Yeah, I sure did. I told him I'd be back down to see him this week. I think I want to do that tomorrow."

"Will you leave me some coffee?"

"You bet. If you're feeling that good today you need to put a smiley face on the calendar. I haven't seen one there in a long time."

"I did that just before you got home."

"Good. Have you read any more of that new book we just got?"

"Yes. She writes very easily. I mean, what she writes is very easy to understand. I am getting something from it. And you are right, she says if you've been diagnosed with anxiety, accept it and don't fight it. The sooner you accept it, the sooner you can take the steps necessary to overcome it. Maybe I have been fighting it. I'm not going to do that anymore. You are so smart."

"Well, that's why I am in such demand. Whenever there is a question about the brain, the mind, I am the first one they think of to call. I am getting tired of all these incessant consultations but someone's got to do it. I guess it's all for a good cause."

"Oh, good grief. You make yourself out to be such a goody-two-shoes."

"Hannah my dear, as you so very well know, I am very unselfish in giving my time to help mankind."

"Yes, and that is why I love you so much. Oh. Brenda called. She's coming over tonight for pizza and a movie. She's bringing the pizza and the movie which she thinks we'll like. Well, she said she thinks *you'll* like it."

"Did she tell you the name?"

"I think she called it, "The Book Crook", or something like that."

"The Book Crook? Well, I'm not familiar with that one. But it sounds like fun. Glad she's coming over. Didn't you say a few minutes ago that you were thawing Brats for tonight?"

Hannah clapped her hands together "Yes, I did. I'll get them back in the freezer."

"Any idea when she plans to get here?"

"Should be anytime now. She wanted to do it early because she has an early morning tomorrow."

"Sounds good to me."

"I'm going to go freshen up a bit."

"Ok. I'll be right here."

Arvie reached for the morning paper, fumbling through it looking for the sports section. Finding it, he glanced at the headlines and realized he wasn't at all interested. Putting the paper down, he got up and walked over to the sliding glass patio doors. It was a very warm Mid-July day. There were no clouds up there to block the sun even a little bit. Usually he would go outside and sit on the patio, but even sitting under the umbrella it would be hot. How interesting that he didn't pay any attention to the heat when he was out earlier. But then, he was on a mission.

He thought of Zeke sitting on his lard bucket hunched over his sign. It's too hot to be out there today, Zeke. And he'll get some more coffee tomorrow. He'll think I've got a screw loose or maybe more than one if tomorrow is like today and I show up with hot coffee. Wonder what the forecast is for tomorrow? He was turning away from the patio doors when he noticed again a black Ford sedan parked half way down the block. Those cars are everywhere. They must be the least expensive car there is. Paying no further attention, he returned to the table, picked up the sports section again but turned it around to the back page. Ahhh. That's more like it. Increasing clouds through the day with a chance for rain tomorrow evening, and the temps will be down 10-12 degrees. "Sounds like a good coffee day to me" he mumbled mostly to himself.

"Sounds like a what?"

"Hey. I didn't hear you come in."

"You know me, Daddy. I'm known as the quiet walker. (Hug) Sounded like you said it was a good coffee day, or something like that."

"I didn't know I said that out loud."

"Let me put the pizza in the fridge and this cat food in the pantry. Mom tell you about the movie?"

"Well, yeah. She said something about "The Book Crook" or something like that."

"Yeah, something like ……… Hey, Dad. What's all this?"

"Huh?"

"What is this? Looks like I'm in a coffee store. Did you find a special on coffee at Walmart today?"

"Oh. Yeah. Well, not exactly."

"Now Dad, I'm not one to be nosy, but this is a lot of coffee? This has got to be over $100 worth of coffee here. Probably $150. You win the lottery or something? And what's this stuff called? Forever. I count 13 cans of Forever, one can of Reunion and one can of Redeemed. I assume that you like Forever the best? And what kind of names are these for coffee anyway? And here on the back it says, 'A fine coffee product of Northern Minnesota.' They don't do coffee in Northern Minnesota. Ever since I went to Texas Tech you have loved black and red. I get the colors. But you are worrying me a little bit with all this. You are definitely not the stockpiling kind so, you want to tell me what's happening here? The pantry is now so stuffed with coffee there is no room for cat food."

"Ok. Ok. Why don't you sit down at the table? I'm going to put on a pot of coffee and then I'll tell you a story. Might be kind of a long one."

"It's too late in the day for coffee, so just tell me the story."

"My dear, after you've heard the story you'll know why it is never too late in the day for coffee. I'll be right there. How are things at work? Oh, damn."

"Scuze me?"

"You work in a hospital. You are surrounded by people in need of healing. This is … what? Opportunity #8? You may very well be the reason. They knew all along and it has taken me this long to put two and two together. Oh, for Pete's sake. I know I'm losing it now. You are the reason."

"No, I'm surely not. Dad, you are probably the most logical person in my world. At this moment, you make no sense to me and you have always made sense to me, always. Oh, hi Mom." Hannah had reached the bottom of the stairs. "Well don't you look nice."

"Thank you dear. (Hug) I knew you were coming so I just cleaned up a little."

"Is that a new sweater?"

"Oh, this old thing? No. I have had it for ages."

"Well it looks very special on you today."

"Well, thank you dear. Isn't that nice - Dad's pouring us some of his special coffee."

"What's so special about it? I was just asking him about it after seeing all those cans in the pantry."

"Yes. He's going to build shelves in the garage to store it all, so we can keep track of the inventory. He just never knows when more of it is going to show up and it doesn't cost us any money. And it helps people. Isn't it wonderful?"

"What?"

"And an Indian gentleman who's been dead for 50 years sold him the first can."

"I'm going to sit down now. Dad. Will you please get in here?"

"I'm coming right now. Here we are. Everybody enjoy. Doesn't that smell good? Go ahead. Taste it."

"Ok. Smells good and tastes good. Please tell me what's going on."

And so, he did.

* * * * * * * *

"I don't believe it."

"Honey, do you think I can believe it?"

"So, the only coffee you've paid for was the first two cans you got from Jacob who has been dead for 50 years?"

"Isn't that amazing?"

"Unbelievable. That's what it is."

"Here is the question for you my dear - what health concerns do you have right now?"

"Me?"

"Yes, you."

"Well, one thing, in particular, that I'd like not to talk to my father about."

"That's ok. You don't have to talk to me about anything. What's important is that you write down anything that's going on right now. You're taking home a can of Forever and that is what you begin every day with. And, for that matter, you could end each day with some more. Pay attention to those concerns over the next several days and see if anything changes. After I realized that things had changed with my reflux and told the boys, they thought about it and it got interesting."

"This is crazy."

"Yes, it is. Do you believe in miracles?"

"Yeah. I do. At least, I want to think I do. I don't think I have seen one but I think I believe they are possible and probably happen all around us every day. So, it was the guy you called, 'Silverheels' that told you they would get it to you, right? It's silly to ask that question because it has already happened, hasn't it?"

"Yes. It was that case of 12 cans that was delivered to our front porch that got me wondering why I need so much. Prior to that, I had been getting a can here and there. Somehow, they must have heard that I'll be providing the coffee at the Bible study. That must be it."

Bren finished a lengthy sip, put her cup down and said, "I'm guessing that since I am surrounded by people in need that you are going to supply me with coffee so that I can push a cart around the halls of the hospital loaded with coffee to give to every patient and then hang around long enough to make sure that each one of them drinks at least one cup, if not more, each and every day. Is that a reasonable synopsis?"

"Perfect. And then you update a chart you'll keep on every patient so that we can measure the results. How about that?"

"Here's an idea. Why don't you come down to the hospital and get a volunteer job pushing a coffee cart?"

"Is there such a job?"

"Sure. Haven't you been in a doctor's office or a hospital waiting room and a volunteer has pushed a cart up to you and asked if you'd like coffee or water, or something?"

"You're absolutely right. Do you have a contact for me?"

"Yes. I can get you to someone in all four of the hospitals I work in and I know a person at the hospital you go to. So that's five hospitals. Is that enough? Will that keep you busy?"

"Thank you dear. You are wonderful."

"I know that. Now … you remember Emma, don't you?"

"Well of course. She has called us Mom and Dad since we met her way back when. She's the contact at which hospital?"

"Your hospital: Cottage Hospital. She's not the contact there but she knows everybody so she'll know who is. I'll call her right now and we'll set it up. What day and what time?"

"Let's go with anytime Thursday or Friday. Should I say anything about instant cure coffee at the interview?''

"Aaahhh, no. I don't think that would be a good idea. Let's get you in the door first and then you can introduce that thought over time and *then* let people wonder if you are totally off your nut."

"Ok. That would be terrific. And thanks. So, you are going to call Emma right now?"

"Right now. And by the way, the movie is called, 'The Book Thief', not 'The Book Crook'."

"Hannah, she is calling Emma down at the hospital to get me set up as the volunteer coffee guy."

"Well, that's a good idea. How do you know they'll let you serve up *your* coffee? Won't they expect that you'll use what the cafeteria makes?"

"Yes, I should think so. Maybe over time I'll find a way to introduce the Forever idea, but we'll not be worrying over that question right now. The first thing is to get Emma to set me up with an appointment with whoever is in charge of volunteers."

"You look like you've been crying again," Arvie continued. "Another emotional day?"

"Yes. That's what today has been."

"I'm going to say this again. If you are a Christian and you have Jesus in your life, how can you have these emotional times? Is your faith not strong enough?"

"I … just don't … know. I guess … ahhoo … I don't. What will … happen when … you're not here … to help me?"

"Where am I going? If I'm going somewhere, I wish someone would let me know."

"Oh, you know … what I mean."

"No, I don't. I'm not going anywhere my dear. I will be here for you. You must stop playing these 'what-if' games. Remember now – we don't worry about tomorrow, we don't even think about tomorrow because we can't do anything about tomorrow until it gets here. You know that. We have enough to think about just focusing on today. And God gives us enough strength to get through today, isn't that right?"

"Yes. I just can't wait for my appointment with Marion. She gives me so many good things to think about. I'm wondering if maybe I should be going to her more often than once a week? Or do you think once a week is enough?"

"I really do think once each week is just fine. I like the way she gives you things to remember and her advice to you is to start each day by re-reading those things."

"And what's the subject here?" Bren asked as she re-entered the room.

"We were talking about your mother's weekly appointment with Marion," Arvie began. "She was wondering if maybe she should be seeing her more often than once a week."

"I sometimes get so worried because I don't know what I would do if your dad wasn't here," Hannah added with some emotion.

"Now Mom – he is here. It's all good. Keep your mind on today. Do you take notes every time you meet with Marion?"

"Yes, I do. I re-read those notes most every day till the next appointment. Well, a couple times anyway. Her advice is so good."

"That sounds good," Bren replied. "I think you should keep on doing what you are doing. You'll learn more and more about how to deal with it.

118

"Now, let's have a fun night tonight. I'm going to start on the pizza. We can eat and then watch the movie. I just know you are going to love it.

"Dad, you're set for 10 a.m. on Thursday. The ladies name is Wilda Maring. Go to the front desk and ask for her. Simple, huh?" It was obvious that Bren was attempting to brighten the mood a bit.

"Thank you so much. It will be fun to see where this might lead," Arvie replied.

He thought for a minute and then said, "By the way ladies, I have an announcement to make. I've decided that I want to be baptized at the 4:00 service on Saturday. Now dear, I'm not putting any pressure on you but I sure would like for you to join me. I would like to do it. I feel that I need to do it. We aren't getting any younger. Will you join me? What do you think?

"Oh, this is such short notice. I just don't know. Oh, I suppose so. Bren, what do I wear? Is it difficult? Is the water cold? Are you sure the baptism that we had as babies doesn't cover us? Why do we have to do it again?"

"We got sprinkled when we were babies, and that decision was made by our parents, not by us. I want to be responsible for getting baptized, and it is very important to our church. I love our church and I feel like I've put it off too long, and there will always be a reason to wait until next time. I just don't want to wait any longer. I've had it on my bucket list for a long time and I would like to cross it off. Matter of fact, it is the only thing on my bucket list. I really don't want for much. I would like to register both of us. Will you do it with me?"

"Mom, it is really simple. Put on a swimming suit under the clothes you wear to church, bring a towel and a t-shirt in a bag. You'll go into the church as you usually do, sit towards the back somewhere and they will tell you when to go out. You'll go to the bathroom and get ready, come back out and get in the line. Take your towel with you and there will be someone there to hold your towel and your glasses. I suppose there will be between 50 and 75 people so you won't be the only ones. Then, after, you'll return to the bathroom and take off the wet stuff, put on some dry undies and your clothes and head for home. Believe me, it is really simple and when you're in the car heading for home, you'll feel so good. I'll be there because I volunteer to help with the Baptism's. Maybe I can work the line so I'll be there to hold your towel. Oh, and by the way – I'll get you two t-shirts. They've got those in the bookstore, so I'll get those for you. What do you say Mom? I'd be really excited for you.

"Well, right now it feels like I can do it, so let's do it."

"Super. Thank you dear. It wouldn't have felt right for me to have gone it alone. Now it will all be right. But, Bren, you don't have to buy the shirts. We can get them."

"No, no. I want to do that."

"Well, thanks for that. It will be much appreciated. Oh, and by the way Bren, tomorrow morning I'm going down to Charitan and the freeway. There is a guy who sits there holding a sign wanting money to get home for his mother's funeral. And he's an old guy. No matter the weather, he's always there. It's been at least two years if not longer. You'd think she would have been buried by now. Makes you wonder how they have her preserved?"

"Ice, Dad. Ice."

"How much would that cost? Two or three years of pouring ice on the old lady; just think of that?"

"I doubt that she knows that she's so cold. Don't you think after a couple of years she'd be used to it?"

"I suppose so. Just so you know, I'm really enjoying our conversation. And by the way, when you have friends over, make a pot of coffee for them too."

"I get it. Ok, folks, grab your plates, napkins and silverware and let's head into our theater. It's time for 'The Book Thief', our movie of the week."

Chapter 9

"If you're going off to see someone you don't know to do something you've never done before, maybe you should just stay home. Heh heh." - *Ole*

"I give you a new command: Love each other. You must love each other as I have loved you. All people will know that you are my followers
if you love each other."
Mark 13:34-35.

With the coffee made, Arvie filled three thermos bottles, tucked them in a canvas bag he had found and headed to the garage. He opened the passenger side door, turned around to the shelves that lined the side wall of the garage, selected what looked like a medium sized, black trash can, turned around and placed it on the front seat. The canvas bag slipped easily into the black container. The remaining space was filled with a towel to eliminate any movement. Stretching the shoulder harness seat belt from the upper right to the lower left held the container securely in place. He had spent some time on this yesterday. He wanted to transport the hot coffee in the front seat of the car. He wanted it to be easily accessible but safe. He thought it would be unpleasant to have an accident in the first place, but to have an accident and then have hot coffee sloshing around could be really unpleasant. Or, perhaps catching a flying thermos in the back of the head could be unpleasant as well. Everything in place, he tugged on the black container and found it to be nicely secure.

Five minutes later, he was heading south on the freeway. It was a beautiful mid-summer morning. If he were Zeke, this would be a morning when it would be a pleasure to sit on a lard bucket and beg for dollars so that mom could finally get out from under all of the ice. Arvie couldn't suppress a slight giggle. He wondered if Zeke ever thought about how long he had used that same sign. He thought it unlikely that he and Hannah were the only ones that had noticed. It was likely that someone had pulled up to the stop sign, rolled down the window and asked, "Where's the funeral?" A reasonable question to ask. Most likely Zeke would have said, "Duluth," to which the inquirer would have responded, "Pretty cold up there, huh?" Zeke would have said, "Especially during the winter." And then the final question, "So you only have to keep her on ice during the summer?"

Arvie's mind moved to Thursday morning and his appointment with the Volunteer lady at Cottage Hospital. Wilda. Wilda Maring. He decided to take a thermos of Forever and offer Wilda a cup. He wanted her to think his coffee was really good. If she did, it stood to reason that he would then have a better chance to, one day, be able to use it in the halls of the hospital. What an opportunity and an endless supply of so many people in need. One hospital is enough. He didn't need to run to different hospitals five days a week. Maybe he could work in a few other days during the week now and then.

He exited at Chariton and headed up the ramp. It's somebody else today. Zeke isn't here. *Well, maybe this guy would like a good cup of coffee and I'll find out about Zeke.* First, got to find a place to park. Take a right. Take the first right after that and see if there is a space. Maybe get the same place as the last time. Whoa. There's one. Not the same as last time but close enough. *Doggone it. There's that same black Ford sedan. Couldn't be the same one. Or could it? It looked like one of those cars the police used when they want to go unnoticed. If I notice it, I believe it is not going unnoticed* he thought. *I've watched too much tv.*

It was a totally different guy. Much younger and not nearly as tall. Clean shaven too. Nice looking man and that's not to say anything negative about Zeke's looks. When he drove up the exit ramp he drove slow enough to get a glimpse of what his message was: "Vet. Just back from Afghanistan. Will work for food."

The car parked, Arvie walked around to the passenger side to retrieve the coffee bag. With the door opened, he carefully extracted the bag from the black trash can. He slipped the bag over his shoulder and was about to close the door when, on the periphery of his vision, he noticed a black car moving slowly down the street towards him. *Here's another black sedan. I didn't know there were so many. Why am I all of a sudden noticing black Ford sedans?*

He stood up while adjusting the bag on his shoulder, closed the passenger side door and turned towards the sidewalk. He glanced at the black sedan as it moved slowly past. Two men in the front seat, both intently focused on looking straight ahead. Black sedans. There are red sedans, blue sedans, white sedans and sedans of every other color. Why are there so many black ones? Might be seeing the same one again and again? Well, no. Can't be. There's another one parked right over there.

At the stop light, he stood on the corner studying the man with the sign while waiting for the light to change. Finally, the traffic slowed and then stopped as his light went to green. He purposefully strode across the busy street, the coffee bag swinging gently to and fro. "Hi. My name is Arvie. What's yours?"

"What's it to ya?"

"I'm the coffee guy. Can I interest you in a cup?"

"Kinda hot for coffee, isn't it?"

"It's never too hot for a good cup of coffee. Here, let me pour you one. I'll have one too. Here you go. Best coffee anywhere."

"Smells good. So, you go around the city looking for people who beg for money, or at least show people a sign that begs for money, and then you pour them a cup of coffee?"

"Well, that's kind of what I do. I used to see Zeke here in all kinds of weather. We came by here on our way to the University two days a week and would see him out here every day, rain, snow, whatever. Where is Zeke, by the way?"

"Who is Zeke?"

"He's the old guy, big guy, lots of facial hair. A few scars on his face. He's here all the time."

"Oh him. He's not out here today. From what I heard, he's got a bad cold or some kinda infection. I heard he wasn't going to be here today so I decided I'd take his place. This is a good corner, ya know. The coffee's good."

"You are welcome. Can I warm it up a little for ya?"

"Sure."

"I was hoping to see Zeke again today. Just met him last week. I told him I'd be by this week to bring him another cup. Think he'll be back tomorrow?"

"Have no idea. Wouldn't be a bit surprised. He's a tough old guy."

"You live here or are you just passin' through?"

"I live here. Kind of in between everything right now – place to live, job. Henrik – that's his real name, Henrik and the boys let me stay with them. Have you known him long?"

"No. I just stopped here last week to give him a cuppa coffee and we talked for a bit."

"So, let me ask again. You brew whatever coffee you brew, fill up them thermos bottles, get in the car and drive around looking for someone to drink a cuppa coffee with you. Are you a really lonely guy or just plain weird?"

"Ha. Well, when you put it that way, I guess it does sound a little weird. No, I'm married. Got a wife and a couple of kids. Well, they are grown up now. I just retired and I'm enjoying not having to go to work every day."

"So, one more time. Why are you out pouring coffee for people you don't know or for someone you just met last week?"

"You wouldn't believe me even if I told you the real reason."

"I'd be interested in hearing the reason."

"Well, ok then. This coffee is magical. It heals things in people."

"You got magic coffee that heals things in people?" he said with wrinkled forehead. "Like what?"

"Well, don't have a lot of answers for that question just yet. But I know it heals acid reflux. I had my first cup of this stuff just a week ago yesterday and my acid reflux is now a thing of the past. And it sure fixes things in the prostate. My PSA had gone up to record levels and after a couple cups it had returned to below normal levels. I don't yet know what all it can heal. And you know the most interesting thing? I found out late last week that the guy who sold me my first can had been dead for 50 years. How do you think that could happen? I sure don't understand. You know about all the Native American people living up 169 in the Mille Lacs area?"

"I've heard there's a tribe or two up there and what d'ya mean you bought coffee from a dead guy?"

"Yeah, true. He was a Native American and he sold me the coffee on Monday of last week. Then later in the week I go back and he's not there and then I see this little bulletin board on the wall and there's a newspaper clipping about his death and his funeral and all that, and it was dated in 1963. We just couldn't figure it out."

"Are you and your friends followed around by large men in white coats carrying butterfly nets? It all sounds pretty strange to me. I know the guys I live with are into drugs of all kinds. And let me tell you something – they dream up some of the wildest stories imaginable. You sure you weren't on some really good stuff?"

"No. We don't do anything like that."

"Then why are you here looking for Henrik - Zeke? Everybody knows he can fix you up. Anything. Whatever you want. Isn't that why you had a need to find him?"

"Huh? No, no. I just wanted to pour him some of my coffee."

"Sure. Some of your magic coffee. I think you've got an issue, *pal*. Do you know how that sounds? Have you any idea how ridiculous you sound? And you're the right age to have been smokin' all that stuff back in the 60's. So you got hooked back then and can't kick the habit. Is that it?"

"No. Not at all. So, do I understand you correctly? You cannot believe in any way, shape, or form that one small, simple miracle can happen? You couldn't or wouldn't be able to believe in a coffee that could bring healing? Have I got that right?"

"You got that right. And don't start in on me about believing stuff that I can't see either. I've had enough of that in my life to last me ten lifetimes."

"Now who is sounding ridiculous here? There is no possibility in your mind, not even the smallest of possibilities, that something you haven't seen could be possible? You can't see air but don't you believe it's there, especially when you need to take a breath? How 'bout fear, sadness, joy? You can't see those either but you know they're there. Don't you? I do hope you'll think on that but right now, the driver of that car is waving money at you. I won't bother you any further, but I will see you again. I didn't get your name?"

The man did not say a word but handed Arvie the coffee cup, a rude smirk playing across his lips as he turned and walked towards a dollar bill. Arvie watched him walk away as he screwed the cup onto the top of the thermos. He put the thermos into his bag, hung it over his shoulder and turned away. On his first step he again noticed a black Ford sedan in the Mobil station across the street. He also noticed two men in the front seat, one of whom was apparently looking at him through binoculars. He mumbled to himself *I think I'll go home now* as the light changed to green.

His head was whirling as he walked down the block. *Am I just making this up; are men really following me in black Ford sedans? How is that possible? Why?* He turned the corner and looking down the street he saw them. Two men in black suits and white shirts and black ties were standing in the street next to his car. They weren't trying to hide at all because they were looking at him, waiting for him. The day was warm but it wasn't because of the heat index that he felt perspiration coursing down his back. *What have I done and who are these people?*

They were now teamed up and walking towards him on the sidewalk. *What movie is this from? I know I've seen this one – 12 o'clock High? No. A Schwarzenegger movie. Arnold beats the crap out of these two guys.*

"Mr. Ellison. May we speak with you a moment."

Arnold would want to talk with them first. He would want to find out what they knew. Once he found out what they knew he would beat the crap out of them. And why do they know my name?

"Yes. Of course. Do I know you? How do you know me?"

"I'm Agent Owens and this is Agent Settles. We're with the FBI." They both flashed their badges in his direction. "Sorry to bother you but we would like to know what business brings you here?"

Arnold would want to know why they wanted to know why he was here before he beat the crap out 'em. "May I ask why you have an interest in why I am here? What have I done that would be of interest to you?"

"How long have you known Henryk von Barstow?"

"Who?"

"Henryk Von Barstow."

"I don't know Henryk von Barstow."

Agent Owens reached into his inside coat pocket, *He's going to shoot me with his Baretta. Wonder if he'll use a silencer,* and retrieved a small spiral notebook.

"At approximately 11 am on Saturday last, you were observed having conversation with Henryk von Barstow at the Chariton exit off 35W. We just now observed you having conversation with Agent Slicer of the FBI at that same location."

"Agent Slicer?

"That was Agent Slicer you were talking to."

"So, who is this Henryk guy?"

"Why were you talking with Henryk von Barstow last Saturday morning?"

"Is that who I was talking to last Saturday? He told me his name was Zeke. You're talking about the old guy who always sits there with a sign begging for money?"

"That's him."

"All right then." Arvie shifted his weight to the left side while he fumbled for some words. "Here is the story. My wife has anxiety and for nearly two years had group sessions over at the University – two blocks further down over there." He pointed in the general direction. "We live up north and we drove down the freeway and exited here at Chariton. We noticed this old man sitting on his lard bucket every time we made the left turn here. Last week I was at a cabin up north on a small lake near Mille Lacs for a reunion with some old classmates from college. While there, we discovered a magic coffee – well, that's what we thought. Anyway, it performed some healing on each of us. I bought the first two cans from a Native American who we found out later had been dead for 50 years." Arvie immediately noticed the two wrinkled foreheads. "Yeah, we wondered about that too. Anyway, we all decided that we were given this magic coffee to give to others. I thought of Zeke, well, he told me that was his name, sitting over there on his bucket in all kinds of weather and thought he might need something healed, so I came down Saturday morning and brought coffee for him. I was planning to give him some more this morning because I had noticed that he had a bad cold or a sinus or maybe an allergy problem. That's the story and if you hook me up to a lie detector I'll tell the same story again."

"Did you get that all written down, Settles?"

"Well, most of it, maybe."

"Make any sense to you?"

"Not a bit of it. There is more to this story."

"I'm thinking that as well. Do you mind, sir, if I take a look in your front seat?"

"Of course not."

"You've got this small black waste paper basket strapped into the front seat with the seat belt. Inside of the waste basket is a canvas bag. In the canvas bag are three thermos bottles. One is empty. One is maybe half full of what I presume to be coffee, and the third is full, again, it smells like coffee. Mr. Ellison, will you open the rear door please?"

"Certainly."

"Settles, we've got a plastic ice scraper here. There is also a second ice scraper that has a glove attached. Nice. The hand stays warm while scraping ice. A big golf sized umbrella, black and white in color. Or maybe its white on black – can't really be sure. Two small umbrellas: one black, the other red and white with a VFW logo on it. There is also a black hoodie with the Nike swoosh. Got that Settles?"

"Yeah."

"Good Grief, where are my manners?" Arvie interrupted. "May I offer you gentlemen a cup of coffee? Here we go - this will only take a moment." He fumbled with two thermos lids which became cups and filled them up. He gave each of the two agents a cup and then filled the third for himself. He noticed the furtive glance exchanged between the agents as they sniffed at the coffee but were hesitant to drink. *Of course – arsenic.* Arvie remembered several movies dealing with arsenic. He raised the cup to his lips, a quick sip and then another. The agents waited for the arsenic to take effect. It was when he went for the third sip and he was still standing that they decided to drink the coffee.

It was quiet for several moments as the three of them stood in their small huddle, eyeing each other. Salient questions were not asked. Perfect answers to unasked questions were pondered. Noisy sips were the only sound.

Agent Owens broke into the silence of the sipping contest: "So, Mr. Ellison, you want us to believe that you came down here to give Henryk von Barstow a cup of coffee. You did not know him as Henryk von Barstow – his name to you was Zeke. You are in possession of magic coffee. You did not come down here to purchase illegal drugs. You did not know that Henryk von Barstow deals in drugs of all kinds and is believed to be the biggest single source of illegals in the upper Midwest. You were hoping to heal him of some disorder by giving him a cup of your magic coffee. You just gave us some of your coffee hoping to heal some disorder in each of us. Just last week you got this magic coffee from an Indian that had been dead for 50 years. How did you know he had been dead for 50 years?"

"I saw a newspaper clipping to that effect. It was old and yellowed. There was a picture of him. It was him."

"And what year was the clipping dated?"

"July 1963."

"Agent Settles, would you think that someone dead for 50 years might smell bad?"

"I would think so, yes."

"Mr. Ellison, when you bought your coffee from this guy, did you smell anything at all? Did you smell something dead?"

"No. I didn't."

"That could be," said agent Settles, "because after 50 years there wouldn't be anything left to smell bad."

"Mmm. Hadn't thought of that. I suppose you're right. Mr. Ellison, I'm going to have to ask you to come along with us. You can tell your story to Special Agent Woodhull. If I were to tell him this story, he wouldn't believe me. Our car is right here."

"Can I bring the coffee? Perhaps the Special Agent would understand better, you know, while sipping on some good stuff. I still don't know why Zeke isn't at his usual place. Certainly, you must know. Anything you can tell me?"

"Climb in the backseat here and watch your head. All we know is that Henryk, or Zeke as you know him, was rushed to the hospital sometime very early this morning. He's in the ICU in critical condition."

"Oh no. Do you know what happened?"

"An apparent overdose of something. At 82, and after the hard life he has led, it wouldn't take much of something to put him down."

"Do you know what hospital?"

"Cottage."

"That's my hospital. And how do you know he deals in drugs?"

"Believe me, we know."

"Well if you know, why haven't you put him away?"

* * * * * * * *

FBI Special Agent Titus Woodhull stood behind his desk, facing the large glass pane that separated his office from the main work area. He held the folder he studied with its top edge just below eye level, allowing him to read the folder while at the same time observing the activity in the room outside his office.

Special Agent Woodhull was not a big man. He was, in fact, precisely five-ten, his weight scarcely varied from a trim 155 pounds and yet, he noticed the way people tended to take a second glance upon seeing him for the first time. He studied the folder, reaching absently to touch his abundant black, curly hair, touched up by Ms. Gustafson at 7:20 a.m. that day, just as she did six days each week. A pencil-thin mustache, also black, extended from corner to corner of his thin upper lip. During studious moments, he tended to stroke his mustache between the thumb and first finger of his left hand. This was one such moment.

He folded the dossier and gazed thoughtfully out over the work area. He buttoned the top button of the jacket. Woodhull took great pride in his perfectly fitting, three-piece, black pin-striped, Hickey Freeman suite - one of a closet-full he kept perfectly cleaned and pressed. He then unbuttoned it again. He caught the eye of Agent Owens and beckoned him to enter the office.

"Owens," said Woodhull when the agent entered, "Is that the man? Ellison?" He pointed with his chin toward the slightly overweight, balding, older man standing quietly in the entrance hallway beside Agent Settles.

"Yes sir. That's him."

"Do you believe his story?"

"No. Why would he want to give someone he didn't know a cup of coffee?"

"He drove 30 miles to do that, correct?"

"Yes sir."

Woodhull gently massaged his mustache and mumbled, "I've been looking for you, Mr. Ellison."

"He says he didn't know it was von Barstow," Owens continued. "He didn't know von Barstow's name; called him Zeke. And here's the kicker: he says it's magic coffee and it heals what's wrong with the human body."

"Very interesting. Do you have his DL, Owens?"

"Yes sir. Right here."

"May I see it, please?"

* * * * * * *

Arvie looked at Special Agent Woodhull through the office window. Arvie was reminded of a British detective from some old movie. *That suit fits perfectly. I never looked like that when I used to wear a suit. No - I never looked like this guy.*

Agent Owens opened the door of the inner office and said, "Mr. Ellison, Special Agent Woodhull will see you now."

"Thank you, Agent Owens," Woodhull said with a slight wave as Arvie walked in. Agent Owens exited and closed the door gently behind him.

Special Agent Woodhull began "Good morning, Mr. Ellison. Won't you please sit." It didn't sound like an invitation. It sounded like an order so Arvie sat, taking the canvas bag off his shoulder and gently setting it on the floor beside his chair.

"Well, my wife will wonder … where I am," Arvie said hesitantly, "and I don't understand why you want to talk to me."

Woodhull nodded, looking at the folder in his hand—like he was thinking really carefully about something.

"I'm wondering how you know Mr. von Barstow? As you are aware, we observed you having a lengthy conversation with him last Friday."

"Okay, but I did not know him until I met him that day," Arvie said with a bit more confidence. "I had seen him on that corner many times. You see, I had to bring my wife to anxiety counseling group sessions just down the street at the University." Arvie explained to the Special Agent why he had brought the man a cup of coffee.

Woodhull stared at Arvie with his steely eyes, not moving a muscle except to massage his mustache. When Arvie finished talking, they sat silent for several uncomfortable moments.

"That is an interesting story," Woodhull finally responded in a voice barely heard. There was another pause as he fingered his upper lip, still looking at Arvie.

"What day of the week did you drive north?"

"It was Monday morning, last week."

"If I heard you correctly, you said that you bought coffee from an elderly Native American who had been dead for 50 years. Is that correct?"

"Well, that's what happened."

"And the name of this Native American?"

"Yes sir. His name was Jacob Whitefeather."

"Jacob Whitefeather. Is he in fact, native American?"

"Yes sir, I believe he is. Oh, may I pour you a cup of coffee?"

For just a second, he looked surprised. Then his face smoothed over again. "If you'd like."

"Here you are - a hot cup of Forever." Steam curled up from the cup Arvie placed on Special Agent Woodhull's desk.

"And this is the coffee that healed you of acid reflux?"

"Yes sir, it is."

Special Agent Woodhull raised the cup to a point just under his nose and took a quick double sniff, then asked, "How did you know that it was doing something for your health?"

Arvie explained what happened at the Ole and about talking it over with the boys. "So, the way I figure it, the only thing I did different was drink the coffee. So, it had to be the coffee, see?"

While Arvie was talking, Woodhull paced slowly back and forth, behind his desk.

It was quiet for a long moment. "Mr. Ellison, I understand you received a large cardboard box on Saturday night, left on your porch?"

"Yes, we did."

"Would you mind telling me what was inside that box?"

"Sure. Coffee."

"Just coffee?"

"Yes sir. Twelve cans. Matter of fact, Forever Coffee: the same as I bought from Jacob Whitefeather last week."

"So, when did you place the order?"

"I didn't place an order."

He gave Arvie a questioning look. "How would the company know where to deliver if you didn't place an order?"

"I've wondered the same thing. But they know when I'm going to need more, and they just get it to me, somehow."

Arvie could tell he didn't believe him. "Where do you send payment?" asked Woodhull.

"This may sound funny, but I don't pay for it. Well, I did pay for the first two cans, but I've not paid for anything since."

Woodhull stopped his pacing and stood behind his desk, raising a finger towards his mustache. Instead, the finger pointed at Arvie, waggling back and forth as he began to speak.

"Mr. Ellison, in our society we pay for what we take. If we don't, it is called stealing, and we can go to jail for a long time."

"Yes sir. I know that. I always pay for what I get. Say, aren't you going to try the coffee?"

"But you told me you did not pay for the coffee. Why didn't you pay for the coffee, Mr. Ellison?"

Arvie told him about the coffee he bought on the way to the cabin and again when he stopped for gas and Hannah's gum on the way back from his first visit with Zeke - or von Barstow, or whatever his real name was/is - and how the attendant said the coffee had already been paid for. Arvie talked of the message from Dweebs, where he was told the same thing. "And when I got the box delivered to my house that I also didn't place an order for, there wasn't an invoice, or a payment address, or anything. So, I guess they're just giving it to me? So, I can pour it for more people? I mean, the guy told me they would know when I had a need and he would get it to me. So, maybe they want it to … do more good, I guess?"

Woodhull looked at Arvie, his lips curled up a little bit. It would have been a smile, but nothing else on his face moved. "Mr. Ellison, I don't think you understand what's going on here. You were brought in under suspicion of involvement in selling illegal drugs here in the Twin Cities. The man you were seen talking to on that street corner is involved also. Now then, let's start over. Why don't you tell me about your involvement with the Cienega cartel in Peru. When and how did you become involved with them?"

It was then Arvie became confused, and worried. "I'm sorry … what was your question?"

"We've been doing some background work on you, Mr. Ellison, and we know about the years you spent in South America working with cartels on a drug distribution method to North America. You've got a history in Columbia, Peru, and Venezuela. We have you ID'd in Lima from years ago. Why don't you make it easy on yourself and tell me about it? I was specifically asking you about the Cienega cartel in Peru."

Before Arvie knew what he was doing, he had jumped to his feet. And then it hit him. He laughed loudly and smacked his forehead. "I got it now. Carl and Bert put you up to this. Didn't they? Those guys! Where did you run into them?" Arvie's giggles continued as he sat back down, shaking his head.

But when he stopped laughing and looked up again, Special Agent Woodhull was not chuckling. He wasn't even smiling - or pretending to.

"Mr. Ellison, I've been in this business for a very long time. I have learned that people like you are all the same" he added with disdain. He carefully seated himself behind his desk, humming a tune under his breath. It was a Sinatra tune: "Watertown," one of few that Arvie knew. Woodhull looked at Arvie while he continued to massage his mustache, now with the fingers of his left hand. A light seemed to go off in front of his eyes. He got up from his chair and sat on a corner of his desk, a hint of a smile playing across his face. He was smoothing the crease in his trousers as the office door opened.

It was Agent Owens. "Everything okay, sir?"

"Yes, Agent Owens. Everything is fine. Just fine." He thought for a moment again, now looking at the ceiling to his right.

"Owens?"

"Yes sir."

"I want you and Settles to go out to Mr. Ellison's place. Rosenius says that a box was delivered to Mr. Ellison's front porch on Saturday night by a man on foot, perhaps a neighbor. Continue to maintain surveillance on Mr. Ellison, of course, but pay attention to that whole subdivision, 24/7. I'll have Rosenius and Craver play 2nd shift. Get on that till further notice. I'm not exactly sure what you are looking for, but if that box was delivered by a neighbor, then who delivered to the neighbor? Drive around. Keep your eyes open."

"Got it." Owens turned to leave.

Woodhull's eyes moved back to Arvie while still speaking to Owens. "I asked Mr. Ellison how he gets more of the, ah, coffee, and he was told not to worry because he would - how did you put it, Mr. Ellison - know when you had a need and would get it to you." He looked at Agent Owens. "What does that suggest to you?"

"It sounds like he is a regular and they knew he was almost out and they got it to him anyway they could - and a lot of it."

"Exactly" Woodhull agreed, snapping his fingers with flair. "They only work that way with deep pocket guys. It sounds as if our Mr. Ellison here has a very good line of credit."

"Huh" Owens whispered, a surprised frown upon his face. "After tailing him for a few days, I wouldn't have expected that." As Agent Owens was closing the door, a young woman stepped in.

"Yes Ms. Wong. What is it?" questioned Woodhull.

"I've got the information you were requesting" she answered.

"Good. Let me see it."

She handed him a folder, as Special Agent Woodhull resumed his pacing, perusing the information. As he read, his eyebrows arched several times.

"Mr. Ellison, part of my job is to vet people. Do you know what that means?"

"Well, I always thought a vet had either served during a time of war, or provided services to sick or injured animals. So, no sir, I don't know anything about vetting people."

"It means that I will find out who you really are, where you have been, and what you have done. In your case, you were not difficult to vet. Let me tell you about yourself, Mr. Ellison. You were born in Lubbock, Texas. Your dad was Navy, 110%. Yours was a military family that moved frequently - every two or three years. You graduated High School in Newport, Rhode Island. You attended West Texas State University in San Marcos, Texas - I believe it's now called Texas State.

"You obtained a degree in engineering with a major in oil exploration and refining. As I understand it, you learned how and where to find oil. You were drafted into the army and spent two years on active duty with the 9th Tiger Infantry Division, at Fort Benning, Georgia. You were honorably discharged. You then worked for an oil consulting firm in Houston and were involved in oil exploration projects in Venezuela, Colombia, Panama, and Peru, from the late 60s into the early 80s."

"Excuse me, I ..." blurted Arvie, turning a bit pale.

"You directed the creation of the drug distribution plan to North America and assisted in the organization of the Cienega Cartel to implement that plan. It seems your college roommate was a family member. Several of those years, you seemed to disappear and, unfortunately, the information we have is rather incomplete. This is typical of that time however, because the drug cartels ran everything throughout South America. They controlled the courts, society, education, politics, governments—basically everything."

It seemed as if the Special Agent was talking to himself rather than to Arvie, testing a theory, perhaps.

"Ah, Mr. Woodhull—" Arvie tried again.

Woodhull did not respond to Arvie, so engrossed was he in his lecture …. "It appears that your center of activity was Caracas or perhaps Lima. And, as you so well know, that's the territory that von Barstow controlled for many years." He looked at Arvie. "I can go on, if you would like?"

"I … I don't know what you are talking about. If you believe I know anything about all of what you just said, you are badly mistaken."

Special Agent Woodhull handed the folder back to Agent Wong. "Stay with it a while longer. Mr. Ellison doesn't seem to remember much of his background, especially the paragraphs pertaining to South America. See if you can find a definitive connection for me that will fill in the blanks for him. Thank you, Agent Wong. Please continue your work."

"Sir, I may have that definitive information coming to me as we speak—a picture being sent by the authorities in Lima."

"Ahh, excellent. Good work. Bring it to me as soon as you have it."

"I will, sir."

Agent Wong left the office. Special Agent Woodhull stepped to his doorway and motioned for Agent Settles.

"Agent Settles, please stay with Mr. Ellison while I attend a five-minute meeting."

"Yes sir."

Agent Settles and Arvie moved to a bench across the hall from Woodhull's office. Woodhull walked over to a filing cabinet and retrieved two folders. As he walked past Arvie, he paused and looked down at him. "An honest man, one with nothing to hide, does not approach strangers to give away a cup of coffee." He moved quickly down the row of offices, disappearing into the last one.

Arvie leaned forward to stare at the floor, trying to wrap his mind around all he had just heard. *According to their records, I've sure had an interesting life, so far* he thought.

"Are you all right, Mr. Ellison?" Agent Settles asked.

"To tell you the truth, I don't think so. I … don't know what to think. It seems like he thinks I'm someone I'm definitely not."

"It'll all be okay soon. I promise you."

Arvie looked at Agent Settles and Agent Settles was looking back at him. "I hope you are right, Agent Settles. Why is it so hard to believe that I just wanted to share a cup of coffee with an old homeless man? And then, why is he telling me that I've spent all those years in South America?" Arvie's coffee was almost gone. He reached into the bag and extracted a thermos. He needed another cup.

Just then, a hand was extended to him. Arvie looked up to see whose hand it was.

A friendly young face was looking down at him. "Hi. My name is Sandy Marsh. You've been in here a long time. I saw you when I first came in. Hi John," he said to Agent Settles.

"Hi, Sandy."

Arvie shook his hand. "Hi, Mr. Marsh. I'm Arvid Ellison, and yes, I have been here for a long time."

"Call me Sandy. So, what bad business are you involved in?"

"Oh, they think I'm a good friend of someone that I don't know. I'm waiting for them to tell me it's okay to go home."

"Where did they pick you up?"

"Freeway exit ramp at Chariton."

"Whoa. Were you buying or selling drugs?"

"Neither. Why?" Arvie was continued to be confused.

"Well, that particular location has been known as a place to go if you're in need of drugs, or, you know, anything illegal."

"Really? Is that what this is all about?"

"Sounds like it. You don't want to be hanging around that corner. But you are sitting here. You're not locked up in a cell and you're not in handcuffs. I'm not an expert on these things, but I should think you could leave any time you want." Mr. Marsh looked at Agent Settles.

Arvie continued before Agent Settles could comment. "Well, I would like to hear that from Agent Woodhull. And I need my phone."

"Oh, so you are talking to the man in the suit."

"Yeah. He is with the FBI."

"Yup. He's the FBI guy that gets called in on a lot of DEA cases—drug stuff. You were picked up in the wrong place at the right time, or the wrong time, or something like that."

"I had no idea. I was just trying to give a guy a cup of coffee. Huh. Why are you here, Sandy? Do you have business here?"

"Well, yes. I'm a reporter with the *Minneapolis Daily* and I spend my time around places like this - firehouses, city halls, county courthouses, police precincts—all those places that our tax dollars support. I just hang out, looking for stories."

"That sounds interesting. Can I give you a cup of coffee? Actually, my love of coffee is what got me here."

"I'd love a cup, and what do you mean?"

Arvie poured a cup for Sandy Marsh and one for Agent Settles and then, once again, he told the story about stopping to give a beggar a cup of coffee. He had barely finished the story when Woodhull came back from his meeting.

"I didn't intend to be away for so long" stated Special Agent Woodhull. "And a good day to you, Mr. Marsh." The reporter nodded a response.

Arvie stood and addressed the Special Agent "Will it be much longer? I really need to get to my car so I can get home to my wife. She is going to be very anxious. And you took my phone, so I can't call her. Can I get my phone back?"

"Your phone will be here in a moment. Can I see you for a moment, Mr. Marsh?"

"Certainly." Marsh followed Agent Woodhull into his office, where they talked briefly. The reporter took out a small notebook and a pencil and began writing. Woodhull ushered him out of his office and invited Arvie back in. Arvie was sipping on the last of his Forever as he went back inside.

"Mr. Ellison, why don't you tell me what you were doing down in South America for all those years after you got out of the military?"

"Sir, I have never been to South America."

"We know that you spent a long time down there working for Hutton & May Consulting out of Houston."

"Who? I've never worked for them, I have never heard of them nor have I ever worked in Houston for anyone at any time."

Woodhull tapped his mustache with a forefinger. "You are going to stick to your story that you've never been to South America - is that it?"

"Of course," exploded Arvie. "I've never been to South America and I've never even had a passport."

"So where did you live all your working years Mr. Ellison?"

"We lived in the Quad Cities from '64 until 2002, when we came up here."

A brief knock on the door, it opened admitting Agent Wong. She handed Agent Woodhull Arvie's phone and a piece of paper. He studied it intently.

"Mr. Ellison, your passport is stamped many times and from everywhere, including Caracas, Bogota, and Lima—even Morocco, Japan, and China." He looked at Arvie with an expression of satisfaction on his face.

Arvie tried again. "I've never been outside the US. Couldn't have been my passport you were looking at anyway, because I've never had one – I think I said that a moment ago."

"So, did you fly in and out of South America using those air strips up in the mountains?"

"I know nothing about air strips in the mountains. No sir. I have never …. flown outside …. of the United States …. Ever. Is that clear?"

Agent Woodhull ignored the response. "Here is your phone. Just a couple more questions. You and your old friends that got together last week; what school did you go to and when?"

"We attended and graduated from Mount Holy Waters College, Theological Seminary, Music School, and Academy in Chicago, Illinois. We were in the class of 1960. Two of the four of us have been preachers."

"Preachers? Do you mean ordained ministers of the gospel?" It seemed the Special Agent was making an attempt at humor.

"Yes sir."

"Why would they do that? Wouldn't their income have increased exponentially if they had involved themselves in any other line of work?"

"They weren't in it for money."

"I've never understood that motivation. Are you saying you did not attend school in San Marcos, Texas?"

"I *am* saying that. I've never been there, either."

"What years did you work for Hutton & May Consulting?"

"Again, I've never worked for them. I've never even heard of them." By this point, Arvie's was speaking loudly, obviously irritated.

Woodhull dropped the piece of paper on his desk, though he continued to look down at it.

"All right, that's enough for now. You're free to go. But Mr. Ellison, I wouldn't leave the Twin Cities if I were you. The authorities in Lima are sending us a picture of you. When we get that, maybe that'll help you remember."

"A picture of me? Down there? That's not possible. I don't understand any of this. Why are you doing this to me?"

Woodhull held the door open. "I'll see if Agent Settles can give you a ride back to your car."

"I can help with that, Titus," Sandy Marsh said. He was sitting on the bench outside the office door, his open notebook still in hand. "I'd be glad to drop him off."

"Very good then."

* * * * * * *

They had just driven out of the parking lot when Marsh asked, "So why is it Woodhull is asking you about South America? I couldn't help but overhear a part of your conversation."

"He thinks I worked down there in the drug business back in the 70s and 80s."

"And you didn't, I guess?"

"No. I've never been there. Never been outside of the country."

"Where did you live during those years?"

"Down in the Quad Cities."

"Well, that shouldn't be hard to prove. Okay, back to your coffee; what did it heal for you?" Sandy turned onto Washington Avenue heading towards 35W.

"I no longer have acid reflux. I don't feel such frequent need to get to the bathroom any more. My PSA numbers have dropped back to normal. We've just found this coffee so recently. It is still so new and it's exciting every time I think about it; there's a lot I don't know."

"Interesting. So how did all this begin?"

"It all began a week ago yesterday when I was on my way north to a cabin, up near Mille Lacs."

* * * * * * * *

"Now that's a good story," Sandy Marsh said when Arvie finished. "You've got all the ingredients there: drama, intrigue, mystery, magic ... And now the FBI has you pegged for a drug lord. All you need is a beautiful woman in a black, very short dress holding a smoking gun beside her slender, shapely thigh. What do you think?"

"I think I gotta get home. Hannah will be wondering."

"We'll be at your car in a few minutes. So, tell me again; when did you meet up with von Barstow—or Zeke?"

"Last Friday."

"And you took him the coffee because?"

Arvie looked out the window, silently wishing they were already at the Charitan exit. "I don't know ... I mean, maybe I've got it all wrong about the coffee. But thinking that it really does heal, it gives me hope, you know? Hope is a wonderful thing. So, I decided I wanted to pour Forever for everyone, and I decided that I'd begin with that beggar we'd seen so often at that corner."

"Interesting. So, you took coffee to him on and that's when they got interested in you, because they were watching him. They've been sticking with you ever since?"

"Yeah, like glue ... Hey, do you see a black sedan in your rear-view mirror?" Arvie interjected.

"As a matter of fact, yes. Let's see ..." Marsh changed lanes. "Yeah. They changed lanes too. Wow. I've never been tailed before. This is kind of fun."

"I'm glad you think so."

"So, back to your panhandler. Von Barstow is as bad as they get - well, that's what I hear at the precinct, anyway. You talked to him. What'd he seem like to you?"

"He seemed very normal to me—I mean, for somebody who lives on the street. He was a little rough around the edges and very suspicious of everything. I am bothered that he is in intensive care right now, because if there is some magic in the coffee, why didn't it fix whatever caused his problem? I've been wondering if there are some things it can cure and other stuff it can't. Anyway, I'm going down to the hospital to see him tomorrow, if they'll let me see him. Maybe they would let me give him another cup? I mean, what could that hurt?" *When are we getting to the Charitan exit?*

"What time are you planning to go see him? Is it Cottage? I think I heard that's where he is."

"Yeah. Sometime early in the afternoon, I guess. I'm pouring Forever for a senior Bible study in the morning. Have you ever sat in on an organ concert, Sandy?"

"An organ concert? No. I've attended some piano recitals but never an organ concert."

"Hah." Arvie explained his humorous turn of phrase. Sandy liked it almost as much as Arvie and asked where the gathering took place.

"It's at the Dove Creek Church campus in Deerwood."

"I know that church. Do you think it would be okay if I stopped in? I try to be a good Lutheran."

"Can you get along with a bunch of old Baptists?"

"Are you kidding? I've been getting along with Lutherans my whole life."

"Hah. Yeah, that sounds tough. Actually, it was originally Baptist, but now I guess they say they're nondenominational or interdenominational, or something like that. I guess that means that even Lutherans can come."

"I'd like to listen to the concert. Mind if I ask your age, Arvid?"

"I'm 75."

"It seems that you are doing really well for 75."

"I guess I've been lucky. There are several in the group tomorrow morning with cancer. At least one is terminal. There is another man awaiting surgery for a brain tumor, several are awaiting new hips, and boy, are there lots of funerals. Oh, I'm parked on the north side of Charitan, a block west of 35W. Down the first side street."

"Okay. We'll be driving past your favorite corner."

"Yeah. There's agent Slicer, the FBI agent, or maybe he's a DEA guy. He's still there. They really want to find out who might come by asking for Zeke - I mean, Henryk." Arvie directed Sandy to the side street where he'd left his car. He breathed a little easier when he saw it there and it wasn't sitting up on cinder blocks.

"I sure want to thank you for the lift."

"You're welcome. Hope to see you tomorrow."

"I'll be looking for you. Thanks again."

* * * * * * * *

"Hello?"

"Bren. Is that you?"

"Dad. Where are you? Mom's been having a fit."

"I'm on my way home. I'll be there in 20 minutes or so. I'll explain everything when I get there. I've been in a police station for hours and hours. Hah."

"How nice. Won't this be fun to hear about."

"Yeah. They took my phone. I guess they wanted to find out who all the bad people are that I talk to all the time. Hah. You ever heard of a Henryk Von Barstow? Bad guy I guess. Drugs, kills people, things like that."

"Good Lord, Dad. I won't tell mom about that. I'll tell her you are on the way. She's been trying to call you for hours."

"Why don't you tell her that I misplaced my phone. Wouldn't that make it easier?"

"Perhaps. We'll see you in a little bit."

* * * * * * * *

The drive home was uneventful. He wondered if it was Agents Owens and Settles in the black Ford sedan motoring north just behind him. As opposed to the last couple of days, they made no effort to be inconspicuous now. There was something comforting about having the law traveling with him.

He pulled into the driveway, skirted the left side of Brenda's Rogue and pulled into the garage. As he entered the kitchen, Hannah literally ran to him, throwing herself into his arms."

"I have been so worried. You didn't answer your phone. Are you all right?"

"Yes. Yes, I am just fine. Sorry I couldn't call."

"Brenda said something about a police station. What was that?"

"It was all a misunderstanding. It's all straightened out now, though the police are still following me. See the black car down the block?"

"Where? Oh. I see it. Why are they watching you?"

"They think I might know something about something and they are not sure that I am really who I say that I am. It is all because I stopped to give that guy a cuppa coffee on the corner of Charitan and 35W. He's the one we have seen out there so many times. The FBI and the DEA guys saw us talking the other day and thought I was a bad guy too. It seems that they have been trying to get the goods on that guy in order to put him away. I'm guessing that he's a bad guy who is really smart or he is a good guy like me, totally innocent. Anyway, they had me confused with somebody who had spent some 30 years or so in South America doing what drug guys do – selling stuff over the borders, killing people, whatever it is those kinds of people do. I told them that I was going to pour coffee tomorrow morning at ten o'clock to 150 seniors at the Dove Creek Campus Bible study. And then tomorrow afternoon I'll be at Cottage Hospital pouring coffee for that bad guy who is in the ICU. That way, they would know my schedule and they wouldn't have to be following me around but you can see how much trust they have. They followed me anyway. I want them to know that I'll not stop pouring coffee just because they can't find out who I am."

"Good for you, dad. I've thrown together a sandwich and soup for your supper and then I've got to run. I've got another paper due tomorrow so I can't do our usual Tuesday night movie."

"We understand and thanks for being here for your mom."

"Sure. Have fun with all your friends in law enforcement and good luck at the Bible study in the morning. Heal somebody of something."

"Thank you, dear. Good luck with your paper."

* * * * * * * *

They ate supper quietly and both agreed that neither one had any interest in tv. Hannah had made plans to go see Marci. Marci suffered with depression and Hannah had been very faithful in keeping up with her over the years. Usually they got to talking and Hannah wouldn't get home until late. When Hannah left, Arvie relaxed in his easy chair and dozed off in a matter of minutes.

* * * * * * * *

When he awoke, he pulled himself out of the easy chair, and headed upstairs, anxious to get into bed where he could really sleep. He fumbled with the toothbrush and toothpaste. The tube was empty but he had been finding just a little bit more for several nights, and knew he could do it again. The Bible verse "in this life there will always be troubles" resonated in his mind. *Today was an interesting example of that* he mumbled.

Once in bed he couldn't find sleep. His mind wouldn't quit. He decided he needed some water. He went down the stairs to the kitchen. He drank a glass and then filled another. With glass in hand, he moved to the patio doors, looking down the street for the 'coppers' that had dogged him all day. Still there. *What do they do all night?* He stood in the dark for several minutes just watching. It didn't matter that he couldn't see anything except for the shadow of 'copper-car.' He watched anyway.

He crawled back into bed wondering if he might as well stay up. But he found a comfortable position and felt himself relax…

BOOM. A flash of searing bright light penetrated the room and was gone. Pain. He felt pain. He raised his hand to the side of his face and immediately knew he had been injured. He looked at his face in the mirror and saw an ugly red wound running from just above the right eye straight up his forehead, disappearing somewhere up in the scalp area. The right side of his face dripped with blood. From his forehead, it ran into the right eye, down the cheek to the chin, coming all together for one brief moment before it began a steady drip onto his shirt. "Oh, God. I need stitches" he cried to no one. She touched him and he looked at her and he understood. But as he looked into the star filled night sky in the mirror above the sink, he saw reflected the numbers '10-10-10' encircled in flames. There was a full, very bright moon. A winding road. A barbed-wire fence. A thick forest of pine and birch, walnut and oak. A heartbeat. A faint, distant heartbeat. The wind moaned through the trees. No. Someone was groaning. Singing? There were many.

He awoke with a start, threw the covers away and sat on the edge of the bed. This wasn't the first time. He had seen this dream or nightmare before. He stood shakily and moved out of the bedroom seeking light, paper and pencil. This dream was very clear. As he jotted down what he could remember, he wondered why he could remember so much? *I don't have dreams like this* he mumbled to himself. He'd try to figure out when it meant in the morning.

Chapter 10

"When you are stirring your cup of coffee, put your head down, close your eyes and ponder the mysteries of the universe. You'd be surprised how many of the world's problems you can solve before that first sip. Heh heh." - *Ole*

"The wicked are ruined by their own evil, but those who do right are protected even in death."
Proverbs 14:32

It was a glorious Wednesday morning. The bright sun was apparent even through the closed blinds. He moved to the window, pulled the cord and immediately filled the bedroom with glory.

"It's too bright. It's too early." Hannah wanted to roll over.

"No, my dear. It is time for us to be up and about. Remember? We are going to the Bible study this morning. We get to make our own Forever coffee and watch all the seniors consume it and then be alert for any comments of immediate healing. Remember? This is going to be a great day. So, let's get up and get going. The coffee is ready. C'mon, let's get a cup. Isn't that something to look forward to? You are up. Here's your robe and slippers. Let's go."

"I wish you'd get me going like this every morning."

"I can do that if you want me to. How's Marci doing?"

"Not so good. I'm glad I went over. Would you pour me a cup too?"

"Sure. I've got it for you right here."

"Thank you."

"You are welcome. Let's sit down and do our devotions right now."

"What's this?"

"What's what?"

"This piece of paper with some writing on it."

"What does it say?"

"Something about an explosion, a bright light, blood dripping onto a shirt … …"

"Oh, let me see that. I had a dream last night. It woke me up. I felt that I should write it down, at least what I could remember. I got up, came down here and tried as best I could to get most of it. It was strange, though. The more I wrote down the more I knew that I'd had this dream before. Isn't it interesting how the mind works? I sat here trying to make some sense out of it, trying to remember when I might first have dreamt this dream. I couldn't come up with anything. I don't know if I have dreamed this 100 times over the last two nights or two times over the last 100 nights. There are four or five things here and I'm not sure if they relate to different events or if they are all tied together. First, there is this explosion, the bright light and then blood dripping from a gash in the head. Touched by a woman and a feeling of understanding, whatever that means. Then, reflected in the mirror, there was a star-filled night with the numbers 10-10-10 surrounded by a circle of fire. And a full moon. Finally, a winding road, a fence, a forest, a heartbeat, the sound of groaning, of singing maybe, and then the words 'there were many'. What do you make of that?"

"Sounds like a bunch of gibberish. Do you think it gets more confusing the more you think of it?"

"Yes, I do. I don't think I'll think about it. But I'll leave this piece of paper here for the next time – if there is a next time. Maybe that's the way to approach it. Start a piece of paper and add to it or change it should I have that dream again. Ok. Enough of that. We need to leave here at 20 minutes to 9:00. So, we have an hour to have devotions and get ourselves ready."

* * * * * * * *

"Coffee ready yet?"

"No. But now that you've finally showed up, maybe we'll get some action on that front."

"You bet. Hi Moggy. It is so good to see you again."

"Arvie and Hannah. How many years has it been?"

"Almost five. Can you believe it?"

149

"Hannah, you don't look like you've aged a day."

"Now I remember why you are my favorite friend, Moggy."

"And I hear you're bringing magic coffee. How exciting is that?"

"Here you go" began Noah. "Measure out 12 of these per pot. Filters are here. Water loads automatically. What button do you suppose you'll push when you are ready to begin?"

"Gosh, let me think. How about this one? It says, 'start.'"

"Arvie, you are smarter than you look. Go get 'em. We usually fill up four of these vats to begin with. We put two out on the table and keep the other two back here. Doesn't take long for the first two to drain down and then the other two go out. Sometimes folks will hang around after, sit down at a table and drink some more coffee. So, we want to stay on our toes so we don't run out."

"Thanks Noah. We'll watch this stuff. You go lead the parade."

"We are so glad you and Hannah have come back to us."

"And don't forget now, if you see someone you know that has some issues, let me know. I'll want to give them a little special attention."

"Arvie, have you forgotten already? These people are all seniors. Everyone has a body that is deteriorating. Prepare yourself to give everyone your special attention."

"Ok. I think I've got it."

"Here's Mel and Gladys. They always show up early. They'll be your first customers when the coffee is ready. Enjoy yourself."

* * * * * * * *

"So – what do you think Arvie?"

"Noah, that was fun. And to top it off, I heard a lot of folks say they liked the coffee."

"That's good. I should think we might hear some comments about improving health this weekend or for sure by next Wednesday. You know, when I was listening to Gracie and her list of those needing prayer back at the beginning of the study, I was reminded of precisely how much work there is to be done. I counted 16 names on her list; longer than usual. And there were many serious concerns today – at least half of them had cancer involved."

"Yes, I noticed that too. Noah, you and Moggy attend services at this campus?"

"Yes we do."

"Ok. That's good. We go to the central Campus. Now would you say that most of the people that were here today go to services at this campus?"

"Yes. The great majority."

"Noah, you've got my phone number. Please call if you hear something interesting. Will you please?"

"I sure will. By the way, I couldn't help but notice the younger man you were talking with a couple of times. He wasn't a senior, that's for sure."

"No. His name is Sandy Marsh. He's a reporter with the Minneapolis Daily. I met him yesterday when the police hauled me in."

"What?"

"Yes. They thought I was involved with a drug dealer. They picked me up on a very busy drug corner. I had no idea I was at a known drug corner. I had seen this old guy on that corner many times over the past two years or so and I just wanted to get a cup of coffee to him. Anyway, I spent most of the afternoon in a police station. Oh, and Sandy told me that police found a body early this morning and it was a guy that was a good friend of Henryk von Barstow, the man I was seen drinking coffee with on the street corner. His throat had been cut and Sandy said that's how the gangs in South America take people out. He said I'd probably get taken in again and asked about *that* guy."

"Why would they think you might know something?"

"They think I spent 20-30 years down there in the 70's, 80's and 90's. They got me confused with somebody else. Actually, we spent our whole lives in the Quad Cities area of Illinois and Iowa. But for some reason, they can't find us there. That's what all the confusion is about."

"Lord have mercy."

* * * * * * * *

On the way home, they talked about their morning. Hannah reviewed several of the usual conversations that take place at every organ concert. "I told several people who were talking of stomach disorders to go get another cup of coffee." She said, "I told them I had heard of a lady who was having that very same problem and she started drinking the same coffee as we are serving here and it's totally gone away. Should I not have said that?"

"I think that's just fine. I think that was pushing it a little bit, but no harm done. Did they go get some more coffee?"

"Yes, they did."

"Good." They turned up the drive and into their garage. "Hannah, I'm going to get some coffee ready to go. I'm going down to Cottage to take some to Zeke. Well, if he is still alive. Do you want to ride along? You can wait for me in the cafeteria."

"No thanks. I think I'll stay right here and take a little nap. It was a late night last night."

"Marci doing all right?"

"Not really. I think she's trying to do too much."

"Did you tell her to slow down?"

"I sure did."

Ok then. I'm gonna make a sandwich and the coffee and take off. I shouldn't be gone very long."

* * * * * * * *

He pulled into the ramp adjacent to Cottage Hospital and rolled the window down in order to push the button to get the parking ramp ticket. *Hot and steamy today. The humidity must really be high.* Ticket in hand, he rolled up the window and wondered how anyone survived before air conditioning. He found a parking place on the level of the skyway.

He had a full load of coffee; three thermos bottles packed neatly away in his canvas bag and stowed neatly in the black trash can sitting next to him. He undid the seatbelt and lifted the bag with its precious contents. He was thinking of Henryk von Barstow as he swung the strap of the bag over his shoulder. *Will I find him alive this morning? Will he be alive but in a coma? Perhaps he'll be back to himself and be as gruff as he was the other day.*

Arvie stopped at the information desk and asked directions for the ICU. The lady pointed down the hall on her left. "Go down that hallway to the elevator bank on your right. Go up to the 4th floor and it will be in front of you as you get off the elevator." He thanked her and headed down the hall.

The elevator door opened and he stepped out into a sterile white expanse of walls, halls, floors, chairs, tables and counter-tops. He made his way to a white desk where a young lady dressed in white, while twiddling a white pencil with the word 'Cottage' on it, asked if she could be of help.

"Henryk von Barstow. How is he doing?"

"Are you a relative?"

"No. I am a friend. Can I see him?"

"No, I'm very sorry but he is not allowed visitors and I'm not allowed to give out any information on his condition."

"Is he expected to regain consciousness?"

"I can't give you any information. I'm sorry."

"Ma'am, he likes my coffee and I brought him some."

"Coffee? I don't have any idea when he might be drinking a cup of coffee again. He's hooked up to an IV and every other kind of apparatus we have. I doubt he'll be having coffee any time soon."

"I didn't think to bring a styro-foam cup and a lid, but I would like to leave him some."

"Right behind you, is our little break room. Through that door you will find some cups and lids and you can leave him a cup. I can't promise he'll drink it. I can't promise that his doctors will allow him to have it even if he does wake up."

"I understand. But just in case, I'd feel better if I could leave a cup for him. How about you? May I leave a cup for you too? Here is my coffee. Have a smell and tell me if it smells good to you."

"That smells very good. Well sure. I'll have a cup."

"Good. I'll be right back."

He entered the little break room and easily found the cups and the lids. He poured three cups, put lids on two of them, re-slung the bag over his shoulder, and very carefully carried the coffee out the door and across the hallway.

"Here you are. This is the best coffee you've ever tasted. I'll drink a cup with you."

"How much do you carry around with you? Is that what you've got in the bag?"

"Yes. Usually three thermos bottles."

"And you just give coffee to anyone you happen to bump into?"

"Well, yes I do."

"May I ask why?"

"Would you laugh at me if I told you it is a magical coffee? It heals things in people."

"O come now. Like what?"

"Since last week it has cured my acid reflux. A friend of mine no longer has a psoriasis problem. We only found this coffee a week ago Monday and we are still learning about it. It was Saturday that Henryk had two cups."

"This is very good. Can I buy this at any food store?"

"I don't think so. Please don't laugh but it just comes to me. It is as if someone knows when I need more and it just appears, sometimes one can at a time, but three nights ago we found a whole case on our front porch. It's a rather long story."

"How interesting, and a little weird, isn't it?"

"Perhaps, and very exciting at the same time. What if it heals everything? How many cups would you like *then*? Well, I should be going. Thank you for being so kind. I do hope Henryk will get the cup. It could help him. By the way, I'll be back tomorrow so think about your own self. Perhaps one cup can help you in some way. Pay attention to what aches and pains you've been having and see if they improve at all. May I refill your cup?"

"Sure. So, you come all the way down here from I don't know where to give someone like this Von Barstow a cup of coffee?"

"Why do you say it like that?"

"See the policeman sitting in the hallway down there?"

He turned and looked down the hall. "Yes. I see him."

"He is sitting outside Mr. von Barstow's door. He is there to guard Mr. von Barstow. Usually when we have police guarding a patient, 24 hours a day, there are some questions regarding the character of that patient. Know what I mean?"

"Yes. I think I do. I only met him once and he was kind to me."

"My name is Missy. I'll be looking for you tomorrow."

"My name is Arvie. I'll see you then."

Missy, still twiddling her white pencil, watched him walk away. She shook her head from side to side as the words *poor old man* crossed her mind. She put the lid back on the cup and placed it gently in the waste basket under the counter.

* * * * * * * *

"Arvie." It was Sandy Marsh hailing him. "On the way out? How's Von Barstow?"

"They wouldn't let me in to see him. A policeman is guarding his door. He is apparently still alive or they wouldn't be guarding the door. That's about all I know."

"So, he didn't get a cup of coffee."

"No. But I left a cup with the nurse at the desk. She said if there was an opportunity - well, you know."

"Being with the newspaper I can sometimes get some information. I'll ask around."

"Thanks, Sandy. Any information could be helpful."

"Any more stops to make?"

"No. I think I'm going to spend what's left of this afternoon and tonight with my wife. Tomorrow morning, I have an appointment right back here to talk with the lady responsible for volunteer services. I'm going to volunteer and push around the coffee cart. I'll let you know how that goes."

"Good for you. Hear anything yet from the seniors this morning, or is it too early for any results?"

"Heard nothing so far but I've got a lot of people listening for me. I'll let you know about that, too."

* * * * * * * *

"What shall we have for dinner tonight my dear?"

"I was thinking about that piece of steak. I took it out of the freezer and its thawing in the cupboard. It looks pretty good. Does that sound ok?"

"Sure. Sounds great. Since I've got some time, I'm going to do some work on the grill."

"Why don't you just throw it away and get a new one? You've been trying to fix it for two summers now. It's a piece of junk."

"Oh, now, it's not that bad. Just because the handle fell off the lid and the hinges rusted off doesn't mean it should go in the trash."

"How many times have I heard that? You'll never get it fixed."

"I can get it fixed. Besides, it still works perfectly. And why do we need a lid that is still attached to the bottom part anyway? It doesn't need to be attached to cook a good steak."

"That thing is junk."

* * * * * * * *

He didn't want to admit that she was right. He had made the mistake of telling her that he could fix it and that he didn't want to spend money on a new one. It was a guy thing. Now he had to prove to her that he could fix it.

But as he stood there looking down at it he had to admit that he knew not where to begin. He thought he could rig something to work as a handle, but the hinges were another matter. He had been to the hardware store and purchased two small metal hinges, small bolts and nuts. All he needed to do was drill the holes through the back of the grill. He had the drill and the bit in the garage. Maybe he could do it after all. He hated trying to fix something. His tendency had always been to not make the effort. Throw it out and go buy new. But he had made the mistake of telling her he was going to fix it. *You are a stubborn jerk, Arvie Ellison* he mumbled to himself. He knew full well that he should just wheel it down to the street and put a 'Free' sign on it, get in the car and go buy a new one. But, he had assured Hannah he could fix it. And so he must. He went for the drill and the hinges.

He marked one hole and drilled it. He inserted a small bolt through one of the four holes in the hinge just to make sure he had properly measured the size of the bolt. Good so far. He spun on one of the nuts and stood back for a moment to analyze. *It's going to work. Doggone it. I am good. Of course,* he muttered to himself, *there is that slight rust problem. I've got to put the hinges where the rust is the worst. There could be a question of them holding at all.* He removed the nut from the bolt and placed the hinges, the bolts and the nuts on the patio table. He'd finish that part later.

It was the repair of the handle that he was most concerned about. He had purchased a 16-inch length of one inch dowel rod. The plan was to drill two holes through the dowel rod and then use two sheet metal screws to attach the rod to the lid via the 'fingers'. There were two ½ inch 'fingers' extending out from the lid where the original handle had been attached. The handle had been wood but what he couldn't tell for sure was *how* it had been attached? He still had the handle and had spent considerable time studying it as well as the two 'fingers', but to no avail. He didn't understand, unless the handle had been attached with a super glue of some kind that just disintegrated over time. Of course, he was never the first person called to fix something. Everyone in the family knew he didn't want to fix anything. He had more important things to do than fix something.

So, the plan was to drill out the fingers, screw in the sheet metal screws and hope they grabbed hold of something inside the fingers. He thought it would work. The guy at the hardware store named 'Nester' thought it would work. Additionally, the two of them had spent ample time measuring both the drill bit and the screws. 'Nester' knew this subject well since he had spent his career working in sheet metal. Well, that's what he said.

He was ready to drill out the 'fingers' when his phone rang. Brenda. He hit the answer button and said, "Hey, what's up?"

"Dad. What 'ya doing? Have you got a minute?"

"For you, sure. What do you need?"

"Well, I'm ripping out carpet upstairs and I got to thinking that if you had an hour or so to run over here and give me some help, I could get it all downstairs and into the garage. It would speed things up a lot. If you can't I'll understand."

"Sure I can. Your mom is in the middle of a bath and then she is planning to take a nap and read a little. I'll be there in 20 minutes."

* * * * * * * *

"Thanks, dad. That didn't take us very long. Sure was easy with two people."

"I can't believe you pulled it all up yourself. That was a lot of work. Have you already bought the hardwood?"

"Yup. Can't wait."

"That's going to be nice. What are you doing for supper?"

"I hadn't even thought about it. What are you guys doing?"

"Why don't you come over? We've got a piece of steak we are going to put on the grill and I don't care how big it is, cause by the time your mom is finished trimming the fat off of it, there won't be much left. But whatever is left we'll split three ways instead of two. She says we eat too much meat anyway so when we sit down to eat a piece of steak about the size of thumb-nail she's as happy as a kitten in a room full of empty paper sacks."

"That sounds really good and very filling. So, after eating not much for supper, what do you do to get some nourishment?"

"What do you think?"

"A really big bag of your popcorn with butter and salt, maybe?"

"However, could you have known?"

"I'm in. What time shall I be there?"

"The sooner the better. Anytime."

"I'll see you in a little bit. And thanks again for the help."

* * * * * * * *

"Where did you go?" Hannah asked from the couch.

"Over to Bren's. She called to see if I could come over to help her get all the carpet she had ripped up out to the garage. She is coming over for supper. I told her you had pulled out this great big steak for tonight so there would be plenty for her."

"That's nice. Do you really think there will be enough?"

"Sure. I told her that you do some fat-trimming and that our portions seem to be getting smaller and smaller. Plus, I told her that there might be an opportunity for my popcorn for dessert. And that did it."

"Now don't use so much butter."

"You know me. I've cut way back on the butter lately. I'm only interested in healthy eating these days."

"Sure you are. When is she going to get here?"

"Any time now."

"You going to use that old grill?"

"You have to admit that it still does the job on a piece of steak."

"Well, you had better be careful. It's still a piece of junk."

"Maybe the kids would get us a new one for Christmas. We'll see about that. I've just about got this one fixed."

"Uh-huh. She just drove in. She's here. Light the grill."

"Ok. Great."

There is nothing wrong with this grill, he thought as he reached down and opened the propane tank. In that position, with his head down and even with the closed lid, he could hear the gas rushing into the grill. At the same time, he heard the patio door slide open and Bren's voice asking, "Dad, can you help me unload some boxes?"

"Sure. What have you got?"

"Several boxes of old family pictures. Remember all those you and mom framed several years ago?"

"How could I forget those beauties."

"Hey, now. There are some great memories there."

"If they're so great, how come you're bringing them back?"

"I'm re-doing everything and I haven't got room for anything. Where shall we put 'em?"

"Let's put 'em against the wall right here."

"Ok."

"There. When will you be wanting all these back?"

"I'll let you know."

"Glad you're here. Gotta get the grill going. Why don't you come out on the patio and we can talk?"

"You bet. Hi, Mom. How you doing?"

"Let me get you two some lemonade for the patio. Oh, Brooks, Katie and the kids just pulled in the driveway."

"It's our five-year family reunion. Who knew?"

He was reaching down to open the propane tank thinking that the steak wasn't nearly big enough. Unfortunately, he just happened to flick his Bic long nosed lighter at the wrong time. BOOM...

* * * * * * * *

The family exiting the car in the driveway ducked at the sound of the explosion. There were four sets of wide eyes looking around apprehensively, wondering what just blew up? CIA? Special Ops? Covert Ops? WWIII? Or just maybe – Dad in the backyard.

In the kitchen, Hannah dropped the glass pitcher filled with lemonade on the floor. The pitcher shattered and the beverage, once released from the pitcher's bondage, leapt with joy at its new-found freedom and raced around on the floor, frantically seeking the lowest point to come together again and huddle up. Hannah shrank back to the edge of the counter for some needed support as her knees began to give way, her other hand moving to cover her heart as she loosed a rather muffled scream of terror.

There was much activity on the patio. At the same time as all were flinching against the sound of the explosion, the grill destroyed itself. The lid, void of anything to hold it to the base, flew skyward, but was detoured in its upward flight by Arvie's head. The sound of sheet metal striking a skull was a sound never heard before by Brenda. Arvie was not fortunate enough to hear the unique sound due to unconsciousness which immediately followed impact. He was knocked dramatically backwards and would have landed in the bed of lilies were it not for Brenda who, while inadvertently trying to escape the disaster by curling up into a little ball in her patio chair, raised her legs and tripped her father who was gliding backwards towards the lilies. He landed on his shoulder on the concrete of the patio which was a fortunate landing indeed: it kept his head from bashing itself into the aforementioned concrete.

Brenda, an RN for over 20 years, had opened her eyes almost immediately after the explosion and watched in awe as her father rapidly passed by, traveling backwards, before ending up in a heap on the patio's far side. All her years of helping the injured and infirmed had prepared her for this moment. She sprang to her father's side and began her inspection of the damage.

The top of the grill may have cleared the approximate 22-foot tall evergreens which surrounded the patio if it had not come into contact with Arvie's skull. After impact, it took an immediate right turn, denting the aluminum siding on the townhouse. The collision with the house slowed its high rate of speed and upward direction. As Brooks came around the corner of the townhouse, he watched in awe as this black object soared lazily through the hot haze of the early evening sky before seeming to pick up a late burst of speed as it dove for the lilies. It was a beautiful splash of color that erupted as the grill lid slid through the lily bed spewing red, white, yellow and bronze skyward. Brooks had never seen anything like this before. He reached for his phone to capture this memorable moment and then realized he was too late. It was over.

Peace and quiet returned, except for the grandkids racing about frantically asking no one in particular a barrage of questions like 'No, but what really happened? Will grandpa be ok? Is he bleeding from his head? Why is he laying on the patio? Why is grandma holding her heart? What was that noise? There's water, glass and ice cubes on the kitchen floor. Was that a black Frisbee we saw?"

As Brenda reached her father's side, she heard him groan, and helped him as he rolled onto his back. He looked up at her and said, "What happened?"

"Dad, you just blew up your grill. Now you really do need a new one. But it's too bad you missed the show. It was a heck of an aerial display after the lid bounced off your head. Hey Bro," she said to her brother who was standing there with mouth agape, "would you get me a bowl of warm water and a wash cloth?"

"Huh? Oh. Ok."

* * * * * * * *

The steak remained in the fridge. Two large pizzas were ordered and delivered. The seven of them enjoyed supper around the dining room table. The patio, littered by interesting fragments of undistinguishable debris, was left unattended for the remainder of the night.

After a careful inspection of the damaged cranial area, Brenda announced that dad had survived and would likely recover all his faculties, once the headache subsided. However, she would be taking her father to the Emergency Room to check for a concussion. They would be back as soon as possible.

* * * * * * * *

"No stitches were required," Bren reported, and the meandering wound, which extended from just above his right eye northward into the scalp, was bandaged masterfully. The healing process had already begun. As talk around the table continued into the evening, Arvie was heard giggling several times, apparently proud that he had succeeded in providing the family with a memorable evening. Also, he would no longer be faced with repairing the grill and could now, in good conscience, go buy a new one – which he had wanted to do all along.

At one point in the evening Brooks had asked, "Dad, how did that happen? I know that was an old grill and we should have had it replaced a couple of years ago, but to totally blow it to pieces wasn't really necessary, was it?"

"I could've kept that thing going for a long time. It really wasn't my fault since I was interrupted several times by my daughter. Bottom line, the gas was on but I had forgotten that I had turned it on earlier just before she asked me to help her unload boxes of unwanted framed photographs. There wasn't any wind at all so inside, it was about as full of gas as it could get. I had opened up a rusted place in the bottom and I was in the habit of lighting it through that hole. This time, I happened to flick on the lighter as I was reaching down to open the valve on the propane tank – which unfortunately I had opened several minutes earlier, and BOOM, thar she blows. I think I wet myself."

Chapter 11

"Sometimes a man's just gotta play hurt. Heh heh." - *Ole*

"But I have hope when I think of this: The Lord's love never ends; his mercies never stop. They are new every morning; Lord, your loyalty is great. I say to myself, "The Lord is mine, so I hope in him."
Lamentations 3:21-24

What a headache. Arvie didn't want to get out of bed. He reached to massage his aching skull and felt a forehead of gauze and tape. The memory of last night's debacle flooded back. Despite the ache, he could not suppress a smile. The boys in the black sedan must have been surprised. He wondered if they had slapped iron when the explosion occurred, slid down in the front seat to stay out of the line of fire, searching for a target and finding nothing except an old bald guy on his patio and a flying grill lid.

He has an appointment at 10 with Wilma Herring at Cottage Hospital downtown. He wanted to call her and re-schedule but he thought if he got up and got ready, perhaps he would feel better. As he stepped into the bathroom, he caught the first glimpse of himself and had to suppress an intense gag. He wasn't into watching the walking dead programs on tv and now that he had seen himself in the mirror he would not have to watch to know what they looked like. He was now a little concerned that Wilma wouldn't want him as a volunteer because he had just stepped off the walking dead set. So, he went to work.

10 minutes later he studied himself once again. Better, he thought. He had washed up, applied the anti-biotic crème and went with a smaller piece of gauze and much less tape. He thought he looked better this morning than he did last night, though any inference that he looked 'better' than anything else was a real stretch. Lately he had been trying to stay away from looking at himself in the mirror because he did not like what he saw. He looked old. Most of

the time he didn't feel as old as he looked. But no matter what he felt like, he looked old. He looked a lot better when he smiled. So he tried to wear a smile all the time. Maybe that's what Grandpa was telling him with that story about the old popcorn popper – you don't look so old when you smile.

He thought again about calling to cancel the appointment. He thought it to be the most prudent course of action, given the continuous throbbing that was totally unaffected by the two aspirins ingested when he first walked into the bathroom. He laid two ibuprofens on the counter as a reminder to chuck them in a pocket after he got dressed. He decided at that moment that he was going. *I'll feel better in a little while* he told himself, and then he made a concerted effort to believe. He realized that the Forever was waiting downstairs. *That'll fix me. Why am I so worried?* He trekked down the steps in his underwear, making his way quickly to the Mr. Coffee and filling his favorite cup to the brim. He took his first sip of the steaming brew, eyes bugging wide at the realization that the coffee was hotter than expected and it was searing the roof of his mouth and his tongue. He immediately took another sip while reminding himself that this is Forever and repair of any damage is already underway.

Breakfast held no interest for him. He threw down a bowl of cereal while standing at the counter, then grabbed a juice glass from the cupboard and headed to the fridge for vitamins. He grabbed a handful thinking how silly this is. *They sell us all these pills because they are good for us – so they say. This pill is good for this, especially if you eat foods such as these and those. And, should you take this pill over here, then you should take that pill over there to counter-act the negative effect of the first pill. It's all crazy. The government and the pharmaceutical companies have sold us a bill of goods.*

After returning upstairs to finish dressing, he filled up the three thermos bottles and stowed them neatly in the canvas bag.

His head was throbbing as he placed the bag in the wastebasket and secured it all with the seat belt and then got in the car. It continued to throb during the 35-minute trip downtown to Cottage Hospital. It was throbbing as he walked up to the information desk and asked for Wilma Herring. The lady peered into her monitor, then asked, "Is that spelled like the fish, h-e-r-r-i-n-g?" Yes ma'am, I think so," he replied. The nice lady tapped away some more. "I'm sorry, but I find no one by that name either as a patient or an employee."

"I have a 10 a.m. appointment with her because I want to volunteer here."

"Oh. I'll bet you mean Wilda Maring. She's the head of the volunteers. Right down that hallway. You'll go past Radiology, the Cafeteria and a bank of elevators. Then you'll see Oncology. Once past that, turn down the hallway to the right and keep going. You'll see human resources on your left. Just go in and ask for Wilda. They'll get you to her."

"Thank you."

He turned towards the hallway as directed and began the journey, pulling his little Day Timer out of his hip pocket. He flipped to today's date and looked for the name at 10 a.m. "Wilda Maring. Right there in black and white. *And what name did I come up with? Wilma Herring? Good grief. That's what blowing up a grill will do to ya.*

The rest of the morning went no better. Wilda reminded him of the Wicked Witch of the West in the Wizard of Oz. She was maybe, 4'10", middle-aged and skinny. She had the long and pointy nose. She was dressed totally in black, wore a black scarf and carried a black handkerchief. But it was her black pointy hat and the black broom that really caught his attention. (Arvie was sure those two items were somewhere close by.) She spoke in a kind of a halting screech. Her long, pointy fingernails were painted black and she wore black lipstick, black eye liner, and had a black beauty mark where a dimple in her right cheek should have been. She had deep, very black eyes as well. Who would have expected anything else? Her notebook was black and she wrote with black ink. She handed him a form on a black clipboard, handed him the black pen that wrote in a black ink, and asked him to fill it out completely, her eyes flashing a black fire of sorts. Arvie wondered about her parents? Did she have any? Ever? If so, did they ever wonder?

He filled out her form. There was no one to give it to, Wilda having flown off on her broom, so he proceeded to pour himself a cup of coffee. It was a beautiful sip and for the first time today, he was feeling some better.

Wilda climbed off her broom upon re-entering her office, and screeched "That smells like coffee."

"Well, it is. It is my favorite coffee. May I pour you a cup?"

"Sure." Arvie cringed at the sound of her. It was as if a three-pound tarantula was walking north inside his backbone. He unscrewed a lid which also served as a cup from another thermos, filled it, and handed it across the counter, down to where she sat. Her desk top was black. He noticed a series of black cubes lined up down the left side of her black desk. Each cube had a greenish-orange letter on it. Wilda had them arranged to spell 'WHELP.' Who would have "WHELP" spelled out in greenish-orange on their black desk? The tarantula moved north another step.

"I see you would like to volunteer to pour coffee. Why would you want to do that" she screeched?

Arvie said to himself, 'O what the bloody heck,' and then to her asked, "Do you have a few minutes? May I tell you a story?"

"Sure." There was that sound again. It wasn't quite like fingernails on the chalk board but it really was. In any event the tarantula twitched in jubilation or irritation or whatever.

They drank coffee for several minutes while he told the story. Fortunately, she remained silent.

* * * * * * * *

It wasn't Owens and Settles in the black sedan that followed him home. He supposed they had remained down the street from their house. These were two men new to him. *Who cares? I suppose they still think I'm connected to Henryk somehow. How is this going to end?*

He wondered what was going on with the boys? He'd heard nothing from Bert or Freddie and he couldn't help but wonder if they had been on the receiving end of some black cans. He'd give them a call when he felt better. However, at that moment, he was headed home for a nap.

He thought of Carl out in California. It must be about now he's at Boldy's place. The thought crossed his mind that he doubted he'd ever see Boldy again.

Every time he thinks of Wilda he shivers. Maybe it's just his head. Maybe after a good nap he'll be himself again. He hadn't felt right all morning.

They had had a reasonable conversation after he told her about buying coffee from Jacob, the Native American who had been dead for so long. She didn't bat an eyelash. It was as if she had bought items from dead store clerks many times. Arvie was gratified that she had said, as far as she was concerned, he could work at Cottage as a volunteer, but there must be a background check first. That can take up to a week, but she would call him about a week from today and let him know officially. They shook hands. He was amazed that she even smiled at him as they said goodbye and the tarantula didn't move. *That's because she didn't speak. Perhaps if more people smiled instead of talking, the world would be a better place. He wondered.*

As Arvie closed her office door, he happened to glance through the glass that sided the door frame. She was standing at her desk and he could just see her head above the black counter top. Her head was surrounded by what appeared to be a halo. It was a reddish halo. Like a 'circle of fire.' Did she have that during the entire time he had been talking with her? No, she did not. It just appeared now. He moved away but decided he needed a second take. Yes. A halo of fire. He had never seen that before, flames licking at her hairline.

* * * * * * * *

It was 3:30 in the afternoon when he rolled over and looked at the alarm clock. He'd slept for over three hours and wonder of wonders; the headache was gone. What a relief that was. He got up, made his way to the bathroom and splashed some cold water on his face. As he was patting his face with a towel, he noticed that the jumbo-sized band-aid was falling off. He pulled it the rest of the way off and then took stock of his forehead. Not too bad. Frankly, if there would be a little bit of a scar remaining, he could deal with that. He turned his head up and down and from side to side, looking at his forehead all the while. Yes, that could be a good look. All the ladies would notice that scar and realize that he was the one that had won the battle with the grill because he is still upright. The grill is gone.

He was wondering what he might look like if he had a halo of fire? And what about Wilda? What was she doing with one? He'd never seen anything like that before.

He thought of the dream that had awakened him the other night. It was so vivid in his mind that he had found pen and paper and had written down everything he could remember, and there was something about a ring of fire. That piece of paper is around here somewhere because Hannah had found it and asked him about it. Hannah. Where is she? What's today? Thursday? Yes. Brenda was going to pick her up for lunch and they were going shopping. Good. All is well. Now, where is the piece of paper?

Yes. It's here. He read the notes once more to jog his memory. Then, he remembered one more thing. It was the faint image of a state highway sign. It read 'CR JW.' No. it was not a state sign, it was a county road sign. He added that to the notes. 'County Road J, West.' *Where is that? What county? The '10-10-10'? No clue. Too many questions.*

He moved on to focus on the 'She' in the dream. He had thought of 'her' several times but the image was so vague, so hazy. *How did I know it was a 'she'? I didn't know. Perhaps it was the finger that touched him? A very thin, very feminine index finger. I didn't recall nail polish or any facial expression. So why did I write down 'she'? It must have been a feminine face.* He admitted that he didn't know for sure.

But he was touched by that finger and 'he knew.' What did he know? Maybe there was more to be dreamed. The circle of flames. She touched him. He knew. Wilda Maring. She had a circle of flames. There was still the 10–10–10 business and people groaning, and the trees and the fences to figure out.

After pondering all that again, he sat down at the computer to write the boys an email and bring them up to date with what had transpired over the past week.

* * * * * * * *

He moved the mouse to the maroon send button and sent it on its way. It was, without doubt, the longest email he'd ever written. He had fun talking about getting picked up by the DEA and hauled away for a scintillating afternoon at the jail house. He explained Henryk von Barstow and why he delivered coffee to him and that the DEA and FBI found his history in South America over a period of 30 years doing the drug thing. He wrote about pouring Forever at the organ concert the day before and the case that was left on the front porch. He wrote about how he obliterated his gas grill and how it fought back. He included several paragraphs on the Wicked Witch of the West and her halo of fire. Since Carl and Freddie had all spent their working years leading churches, he asked if they knew of any Biblical references to halos of fire. He hadn't been able to find any but had seen the paintings of Jesus wearing one – it wasn't fire, just a regular halo made of paint. He made no reference to the dream.

* * * * * * * *

The ring of his phone startled him. He had to find a different ring, something less severe.

"Hello".

"Good afternoon, Arvid. This is Noah. I hope I'm catching you at a good time."

"This is a very good time. What's on your mind?"

"Did you see this morning's Daily?"

"No. Why?"

"You didn't make the banner headline on page one but you came close. You got a nice spread just below the fold and it continues on the back page of the front section."

"What are you talking about?"

"You better go get a copy of the paper and find out for yourself. You're not mentioned by name but I've already taken a couple of phone calls from friends asking if I know the coffee guy that was mentioned. By the way, he refers to you as the, Good Samaritan and the question he is asking is why aren't there more folks that try to bring a little hope to people. He is making you an example of what we all should be. It's pretty good Arvid. I wanted to make sure you knew about it."

He already knew the answer but he asked anyway. "Who wrote it, Noah? Any byline?"

"Sandy Marsh. You know him?"

"He's the guy you saw me talking to on Wednesday at the Organ Concert. Doggone it anyway. I didn't even think about anything like this."

"It's actually a good article. It's all about 'hope' and a guy who believes he has found it in a can of coffee."

"Thanks for letting me know. Guess I'd better go find a paper."

"Arvie, I've not known any famous people – at least until now. I'll be anxious to talk to you after you've read it."

"I'll call you tomorrow. Thanks, Noah."

* * * * * * * *

He headed to the gas station. It took him 30 seconds to find the rack, grab a paper, flip it over to view what was below the fold, saw the words "Coffee Brings Hope," paid at the counter and headed back to the car. Once inside, he gulped a deep breath, turned the paper over and began to read.

Coffee Brings Hope

By: Sandy Marsh

MINNEAPOLIS - He was brought into the police station by FBI agents at 2:18 Tuesday afternoon. He had been under surveillance since Saturday when he was observed conferring with a "person of interest" on a busy corner that was known to be a pick-up corner. In other words, if you have a need, you can get it there. He spent the rest of the afternoon in the police station under suspicion of dealing in illegal drugs. Compounding this confusion was a background check which went awry, placing him in several South American cities in the 70's and 80's, with direct ties to drug cartels in Bogota, Lima and Caracas. However, if you ask him, he has never been to South America. He has never had a passport. He has never been outside of the United States.

This is a human-interest story. This is a story about a good person attempting to do only good. Let's call him, "Samuel." Samuel will be 76 next month and is recently retired. He was sitting alone on a bench in a hallway. I sat down beside him and asked him what he was doing in a police station? The story he told me was one of love, compassion, mystery and hope. With hope, comes joy and who doesn't want both? Frankly, with what he told me, he could write a best seller.

I will tell you Samuel's story as briefly as I can. There is much detail which I will save for later. Samuel spent four days last week with three old college friends in a cabin up north. On his drive up, he bought coffee at a convenience store. The boys drank this coffee for the four days. By the end of their time together, they realized that each of them had been healed of something. Samuel said his acid reflux disappeared. Another said his psoriasis disappeared. Another had full range of motion in a knee that had been replaced years ago but had been stiff ever since. The 4th hadn't slept an entire night in years due to urgent bathroom needs and, by the 3rd night, did not get up once. We are not talking about healing cancer here or the Bubonic Plague. But who knows? If you can relate to acid reflux, psoriasis, a stiff knee, or the need for frequent bathroom breaks, wouldn't you be pleased if it just went away?

As we age, our bodies break down. When we reach retirement time, most all of us spend a large amount of our time in a doctor's office or driving to get to one. When seniors get together, their conversation time is spent almost entirely discussing health issues. Samuel invited me to attend an, "organ concert," Wednesday morning. Curious, I met him there. It was a Bible study at a church. Over 150 seniors were in attendance. There was no organ music but it did not take long to understand. As I wandered from table to table, every organ in the body was being discussed by someone. Doctors were compared. Hospital stays were discussed. Few spoke of the Vikings, but many discussed heart and lung trouble.

I must admit to not thinking about health issues I might face when I'm older. But this was a wake-up call. Today I scheduled a weekend trip to visit my parents. They are still living and I want to talk with them about what they are enduring at their age. I want to find out what happens with aging. How have they coped with it all?

As the four-day reunion drew to a close, the boys, realizing that there was something in the coffee, returned to the convenience store to buy more. It was a brand none of them had seen or heard of before. What they learned was that no coffee had ever been sold in that store. Yet Samuel had bought coffee there just a couple days prior. It was an old Native American gentleman who assisted Samuel with the coffee purchase. He was extremely old, wore thick glasses and a funny pork-pie hat and had difficulty breathing. However, when the boys asked about him, they were told that no old man had ever worked there, especially not one with thick glasses, a weird hat and breathing problems.

Here's where it gets good, friends: when walking out the front door, Samuel noticed several old newspaper clippings pinned to a small cork board. One of the clippings was an obituary with a picture of the old man in his pork-pie hat and the date on the clipping read 1963.

Samuel had purchased a shiny black can of coffee labeled, "Forever". The word Forever was printed in a bright red. There was no other printing on the can save for one line on the back side at the bottom, "A fine coffee product of Northern Minnesota." Samuel had purchased the coffee from a Native American who had been dead for 50 years and Northern Minnesota is not known to produce coffee beans.

Samuel doesn't know yet if the coffee he possesses is magical. He has reason to believe it heals disorders in the human body. He feels driven to pour this coffee for others in "need" and that's why he was seen on the wrong corner at the wrong time. He had noticed the same old man holding a sign on that corner for maybe two years. He was in need of funding to get to his mother's funeral. No matter the weather, he was on his corner. Samuel had decided the man needed a cup of good coffee. That's why he went there. He wanted to pour a cup for someone he didn't know because it might help.

I asked Samuel about his supply of this coffee; where does he buy it and how much does he have? He said that he did not know where to buy it, but it keeps coming to him. He found a case of 12 cans on his front porch when he came home last Saturday night. He walks into convenience stores and clerks fumble under the counter and pull up an old brown paper bag and give it to him. Of course, the sack contains a can of coffee. Samuel has asked these clerks how he can buy more and he's been told that "He will know when you have a need and he will get it to you." Sure enough, the cans keep coming.

Samuel believes the "He" is the old Native American who has been dead for 50 years. His name on the obituary was Jacob Whitefeather. There are many unanswered questions regarding the coffee and Samuel is aware of them all, but he is driven to take his "healing coffee" to the masses as best he can for as long as he has it. It has been a week since he returned home from the cabin and began his mission of hope. He says that there is still much to learn. He has faith that he will continue to receive the coffee and believes everyone, no matter their age, needs hope. He believes his coffee can provide this hope and he will continue to carry his canvas bag with three thermos bottles filled to the brim. He believes he has been sent on this mission by God. I, for one, believe him.

I asked him if he tells people that his coffee is magical. He says he does, especially the suspicious ones who don't know him and don't understand why he wants to give them a cup of coffee. Perhaps one day he will learn that his coffee is not magical. But until that day he will continue to provide friends and strangers alike with hope and possible healing through a mystical cup of coffee.

So be on the lookout. No matter where you are or what you are doing, should an older man walk up to you and offer you a cup of coffee, be prepared to accept his offer. There is reason to believe you

will be healed of something and will
experience first-hand what it is like to
possess Samuel's "HOPE".

* * * * * * * *

Arvie threw the paper into the passenger seat. His eyes were brimming with tears. One or two escaped, rolling down his cheeks. *Did this article make me out to be a stupid and mentally deficient old man? Is that the thought that grabbed me?* He sat back, closed his eyes attempting to clear his mind of emotion and feelings.

His name had not been mentioned. His story had been told in a straightforward manner, and did not seem to be slanted in any way. No. He did not feel that Sandy had made him out to be a stupid old fool. He reached for the paper and read the last paragraph again. He really did capture the theme of hope. He thought it was positive. Then his phone rang.

"This is Arvie."

"Hi Arvie. This is Sandy Marsh. I didn't hear from you last night so I went ahead with the story. Did it read ok to you this morning?"

"I just heard about it maybe 30 minutes ago from a friend. I'm sitting in the convenience store parking lot right now. I just bought the paper and read it."

"You mean you did not get my message last night?"

"No. Did you leave me one?"

"Sure did. I wasn't sure you would like the idea so I wanted to talk to you about it. You didn't have your phone on, right?"

"Yeah. I mean no. I'll go for days sometimes without turning on the damn thing."

"Well, I'm sure you've got my message in there somewhere. Anyway, I said that if I didn't hear back from you it would run this morning and it did. My boss thought it was good and wanted to run it on the front page as a human-interest story. What did you think of it?"

"That's why I'm still sitting here thinking. But I think I liked it."

"Well, let me tell you what happened right after the paper hit the streets. I got a phone call from the FDA. That's the Food and Drug Administration and they want to know what is in the coffee: the ingredients, where the beans come from and who manufactures the product. There is apparently an issue with using the coffee as a healing instrument unless it has been approved by them. I laughed out loud and said to the lady something like, 'You've got to be kidding. He brews a pot of coffee, puts it into a thermos and then carries it around to give to people. He's not going to people who are sick, promising cures.' She said, 'Nevertheless, the coffee needs to be analyzed and appropriately labeled by the distributor.' She then asked for your name and I told her that I do not have to provide her with that information."

"So, what happens now?"

"I'm not sure. I want to talk with my boss and tell him about this, but if I were to guess, he will want me to write a follow-up story about how silly this is. I'll let you know, and I will speak with you directly before anything further is done. Before I let you go, I want you to know that the phone has been ringing like crazy about this mornings' story. Oh, and, will it be ok if I attend the Organ Concert next Wednesday? I am anxious to hear if anyone's health has improved."

"Absolutely. I'll see you there, and call me if anything else happens."

"Thanks Arvie. Have a great evening."

He pulled away from the convenience store and pointed the old CRV towards home when the phone rang again.

"Hello."

"Hi Dad. It's Bren. Mom wanted me to call and let you know where we are. Gabby came running across the court after calling 911 this morning. Juan had a stroke – they think, and he was taken to Fairwood's Hospital. Gabby couldn't find the car keys so we brought her up here."

"Oh no. How's he doing?"

"Still too early to tell. All we know is they plan to transport him downtown to St. Mary's as soon as possible but we don't know when."

"So, you have been up there all day?"

"Sure. That's what friends are for."

"How's Gabby doing?"

"She's really scared."

"I'm on my way. I'll be there in 10 minutes. Did you see the morning Daily?"

"No. Why?"

"I'll show you when I get there."

Juan and Gabby had become good friends to Arvie and Hannah. They had come to the door on Arvie and Hannah's first night in the townhouse with a homemade Cherry pie and that began a close friendship. He pulled to the side of the road and at his first opportunity, made a U-turn and headed back towards the hospital."

* * * * * * * *

"Hi. Gabby. How are you doing? How's Juan?" Arvie pulled her into a gentle hug, patting her back as good friends do.

"They say he's doing as good as possible. But I don't know what that means. What did you do to your head. That looks painful."

"I blew up the grill last night and took a hit in the head when the top blew off. I've had a nice headache since."

"I'm so sorry. Ah, why does God let something like this happen to Juan, Arvie?"

'Oh Gabby. God wants only the best for each of us. He wants us to be happy. But the world is full of evil and He has told us that we will have our troubles. And we do. But we live not just for this world, one that we can see. We endure this world in order that we – through faith, will achieve the beautiful life we can't see. Jeremiah 29:11 says, 'I know what I'm planning for you. I have good plans for you, not plans to hurt you. I will give you hope and a good future.' Now we don't know what those plans are, we don't know what His time frame is, and we don't know what all we will have to endure in the meantime. All we can do is pray and keep the faith, remembering that He wants only good for us. Right now, we can't imagine any good coming of this but that's why we must remain faithful. Beyond that, Gabby, there is nothing else we can do."

"I believe that. It's just that we are so helpless at a time like this."

"I know. We'll keep on praying and we will keep the faith. Juan would want you to keep your spirits up and to stay close to Jesus.

Jesus gives us Hope, Gabby. He's always there for us. And if we remain faithful, He brings us joy. That's one thing we'll have for sure."

"He is always with us, isn't he?"

"And remember, we are just across the court and you are welcome any time. Please let us know how we can help you during these days. I'm sure Hannah is going to want to bring you a homemade cherry pie but she's not as good with pies as you are."

"Oh Goodness. Thank you. You are both so sweet and kind."

"I'd best go over there and talk to those two ladies for a moment."

"You go right ahead."

"Hi you two. Here Bren. Read this. Hi my dear. Do you need something to eat or are you doing ok?"

"We had a sandwich not long ago. I'm doing just fine. I'm so worried for Gabby."

"Yeah."

"Dad, did you know this was coming?"

"No."

"This is wonderful."

"What's wonderful?"

"Mom, look. This article in the newspaper."

"He tried to call me last night but of course I had turned off my phone."

"I think it's good. Here mom. Have a look. You were down at the hospital this morning Dad, right?"

"Yes. I had my meeting with Wilma and it went just fine – I think."

"You mean Wilda?"

"Yes. I do mean Wilda. I got confused on that this morning when I first got there. They do a background check. She'll call me in about a week. Remind me to ask you about 'fire halo's when we have some time."

"What?"

"Fire halos."

"I thought that's what you said."

"And, by the way, Sandy Marsh – the guy who wrote that article, received a phone call from a lady at the FDA today. She wants to investigate me because it's against the law to give to the public any product related to health unless its FDA approved – or something like that. Can you imagine? Is that all government agencies have to do these days: keep tabs on old guys running around trying to give coffee away because it might heal something? Anyway, he doesn't have to release any information on me. I am a protected source, don't you know."

"As well you should be. Where did you meet him? How did he get all the information?"

"He and I met at the police station yesterday and he gave me a ride up to my car."

"I see. Nice head, by the way. That's a very good look."

* * * * * * * *

Finally, the day came to an end. Arvie and Hannah had walked Bren and Gabby out to the car and watched them drive away. Gabby had left without receiving any indication regarding Juan's prognosis. They had told her that they should know about the severity of the stroke within the next 10-12 hours.

During their drive home, Arvie detailed his day for Hannah, including a synopsis of the halo of fire that he had seen on the wicked witch, the phone call from Noah, the purchase of the paper, and the call from Sandy Marsh. It had been a big day. He was thankful the headache was gone.

As Hannah warmed some soup and made sandwiches, Arvie took a dust pan and a broom out to the patio and cleaned up the debris from last nights' explosion. He knew the agents in the black car down the street were watching. For the first time, he thought of them watching last nights' activity and chuckled. *How did they report that to the boys downtown?* He looked at the black sedan, couldn't see anyone through the darkened windshield but waved a greeting anyway. Coffee. He'd brew a pot and take them some after supper.

While they ate their supper, Hannah re-read the newspaper article.

"My goodness. Did you ever think that you would make the first page of the Minneapolis Daily?"

"No. Never."

"It is a good article. I like the way he wrote it. Right in the middle of all the news of the day, here is an article about you and your coffee. I'll bet everyone will read that. It is totally different. It's about someone trying to do good. But Arvie, he called it a, "magic coffee that heals people." So, the secret is out.

There was a knock at the front door. Hannah asked the usual, "Wonder who that could be?" Arvie was on his way to find out. It was Gabby. She burst through the door as soon as he started to open it.

"He's awake and the doctor has said I should come. He's going to be fine. Apparently, it was a minor one or 911 got to him in time."

There were hugs all around and smiles of heartfelt happiness. "I had to tell you before I left."

"You are going back?"

"Yes. They said to come. He is weak but he is alert and I found the car keys."

"Please give him our love," said Hannah. "God is taking care of him."

"Yes. He surely is. Thanks for your help today. I'll see you later."

"Gabby, wait just a minute. I have something for you and Juan." He quickly went to the kitchen, opened the pantry and withdrew a can of Forever. He retraced his steps to Gabby.

"Here you are. This is a very special coffee. I will explain to both of you later, but please, when you make coffee, use this till it runs out. Ok?"

"Ok. Thank you. We will be anxious to hear about it. It's something special?"

"Trust me, it is special. Love to Juan. Bye-bye."

They had just settled down to finish their meal when there was another knock at the door. Through the window he saw the black sedan idling in the drive-way. "Agent Owens and Agent Settles. What can I do for you?"

"Sorry to bother you folks but we are here to take you to the station. We just got word from Special Agent Woodhull to pick you up. Please come with us now."

"Yes sir. Let me grab my jacket. I'll be right back. Hannah, they want me to go with them back to the police station. I don't know how long I'll be gone. Call Bren and Brooks and let them know."

"What can this be for?"

"I suppose more of the same foolishness. Say a prayer that it will all be straightened out. You and I and the good Lord know that I have done nothing wrong. I love you dear and I'll see you soon." There was a kiss and a hug.

They assisted him to the sedan's back door. Once underway, Arvie asked if they had any idea what this was about and they had responded that they did not. The 30-minute drive was a quiet one. Arvie put his head back, closed his eyes and relaxed. But not for long. *The picture. It must be the picture. Woodhull received the picture.*

* * * * * * * *

He was escorted inside and taken to Special Agent Woodhull's office. Woodhull, resplendently dressed even at this late hour, waved them in.

"Please, sit down Mr. Ellison. Understand you set off a device on your patio last evening that most of Minnesota could hear. Am I looking at the repercussions of that on your forehead?"

"Yes. I am afraid so. What did you need to see me about sir?"

"Let's begin with this." He slid a picture across the desk. Arvie picked it up and studied it carefully.

"How did you get this?" he asked.

"We have our ways. I had told you that a picture of you was coming via email. This was just received from Lima."

"Lima? As in Peru?"

"Yes. That's why we brought you in. That is you, isn't it? From quite a few years ago?"

"Yes. It is me. This picture was taken at Blackhawk State Park in the Quad Cities sometime around 1972 I think."

"What were you doing in the Quad Cities?"

"Well, we lived there for one thing, and secondly I was trying to get a job at a tv station and this was a promotional shot."

"Let's catch up here. You graduated from Southwest Texas State University in San Marcos, TX in 1960. Correct?"

"No sir. I graduated from Mount Holy Waters in Chicago in 1961. I was in the class of '60 but didn't have the credits to graduate. Didn't we have this conversation the other day?"

"Your degree was in Oil Exploration and Refining. Correct?"

"No sir. My degree from Mount Holy Waters was a B.A. with a Major in English and Minors in Communications and American Literature."

"So, after graduation, what did you do and where?"

"I was drafted. Basic training at Ft. Leonardwood, MO. Then to Ft. Carson, CO to the 5th Infantry Division Mechanized. All told, a two-year active duty Army commitment, plus four years in the reserves."

"Then what?"

"I went back home and got a job at a radio station."

"In the Quad Cities?"

"Yes."

"You traveled around a lot when you were growing up. Your dad was in the Navy."

"No sir. My dad was a carpenter. We lived in the Quad Cities."

"Didn't you graduate high school in Newport, RI?"

"No sir. Galesburg High School. Galesburg is a small town 45 minutes south of the Quad Cities. It was while I was in College that the folks moved to the Quad Cities. We visited Newport once when my sister's husband was in the Navy."

"What did you do after the radio."

"I had an opportunity with IBM."

"In the Quad Cities?"

"Yes sir."

"How long with IBM?"

"Six to seven years."

"And then what."

"Farmall. Worked on the line there for nearly 30 years."

"But you did do some moving around."

"No. After we had our two kids we bought a bigger place. But no, we didn't move much."

"Do you have any idea how the law in Peru just happened to have your picture? Do you have a twin brother?"

"Somebody in Lima got into a data base in the Quad Cities by mistake. Other than that, I have no idea and I have no twin brother."

"I was hoping when we got this picture it would eliminate you. Instead, until we figure how they could have your picture when you have never been there, I'm duty bound to hold you Arvie. I have no choice."

"Yes sir."

* * * * * * * *

"Hi, Arvie."

"Sandy. How'd you know I was here?"

"I've got my contacts. Woodhull tells me that you'll be here at least overnight. Ever spend a night in jail before?"

"75 years full of nights and this will be a first one in a jail."

"So, what have they got in order to hold you here?"

"Agent Woodhull has a picture of me, taken back in the 70's that the law in Peru emailed to him. I don't understand it. That picture was for a new job I was after at a tv station in the Quad Cities. How it would have ended up in South America I can't imagine."

"You don't have a twin brother?"

"He asked me the same thing. No, I don't. And even if I did, that picture was of me. I remember when it was taken and where, who took it and also what for. So that's their proof that I was there even though I've never been there? That's their proof that I'm in league with Henryk von Barstow and his drug business? What's going to happen to me? It suddenly dawns on me that even though I'm completely innocent of any involvement in this sordid business, they could get a conviction. Really? I wouldn't be the first innocent man put away for the rest of his natural life. I guess all things considered, that wouldn't be for too long."

"Don't get too far ahead of yourself here. There'll be a lot of water under the bridge before anything like that happens. Let me ask a couple of questions. Where were you born, and when?"

Over the next 45 minutes, Arvid Ellison poured out his life story and realized in the telling, how boring and dull it sounded. How could a life that common, dull, ordinary and boring, bring him to a jail cell in his 75th year?

* * * * * * * *

"That should do it." Sandy stated. "Thanks for that. Just so you know, I'm talking to my boss first thing in the morning because I want to do another story. If he goes along with my idea, it'll appear in the paper the day after tomorrow. And now that I got all these notes on your background, I'm going to spend some time checking you out. This is human interest at its best, Arvie. By the way, the story that came out this morning produced more of a reaction locally and even nationally than our paper has seen in many years, and that comes from old man Earhardt who's been around the Daily longer than anyone can remember."

"Really?" Arvie was astonished. "Why would people have an interest in magic coffee? No one believes that it heals anything except a few of us old men and from what I've seen so far, everyone who comes in contact with an old man attempting to pour coffee in the hope that something might get healed says, 'thanks a lot; tastes good,' and then asks the questions, 'what are you carrying around coffee for? Are you nuts or something? And, by the way, the police are on their way here to arrest you for setting up all the drug cartels in South America.'"

"And that reminds me of another thing. Corlis Unger Diddle of the FDA is coming here tomorrow to meet with you. She didn't know how to reach you until she found out through one of the DEA boys that you were going to be brought back in and might be spending a few days."

"Who's coming from the FDA?"

"Corlis Unger Diddle. The FDA is responsible for making sure that the food we eat and the pills we take are ok for us. They look

184

after us and for the most part, they do good work. Miss Diddle on the other hand, is the local rep, and she gets a little carried away now and then with her authority. She has a concern about you attempting to heal people with a coffee that they have not approved. I'm sure you'll be prosecuted for that too. I'm kidding on that one, but she is a real dandy. Anyway, I think she might play a major role in my next story – that is if she gets up on her soap box. Anyway, she will be here in the morning. What is so beautiful about her is that I've heard she signs everything using her initials - so it appears as 'C.U. Diddle.' I don't know about you Arvie, but that makes me chuckle. My contact will let me know when she arrives. So I will see you tomorrow. And now I've got to run. And by the way, my contact is on duty tonight and he will make sure you are safe. Sleep well."

"Thanks. I think."

Arvie was left alone in the small room. Woodhull had brought him here. Marsh had found him here. A totally barren room, save for a heavy metal table with very cheap and wobbly metal chairs on each side. *Am I going to sleep on the floor, the table, or would I be taken somewhere else? I don't have a clue.*

But there was much to think about. *Thank you, Jesus, for good news about Juan.* He folded his hands in his lap, bowed his head and prayed earnestly for his young friend.

After his 'Amen,' he began worrying about Hannah. This would be the first night they hadn't been together – well, since last week when he was up at the cabin with the boys. But other than that, when was the last time they didn't spend a night together except for those four days every July? It's been a very long time. He had left home rather suddenly when Owens and Settles had come for him. He hoped that she had talked with both kids. They have a calming effect on her, even more so since her anxiety diagnosis two years ago.

He stared at the barren walls in his little one room prison and wondered about tomorrow? What will that bring? *Why can't they figure out who I am? How can that be so difficult? Why, when they run a search using my name and Social Security number, do they get hung up in South America? How would my picture get down there? That's ridiculous. In their electronic search, they ended up in the wrong data-base which happened to be in the Quad Cities and they grabbed the picture of an Ellison in that data base? There's a bunch of Ellison's that live there. My folks were both Ellison's, also born and raised in the Quad Cities as were my two kids. There were two Ellison kids I went through school with and most likely others too. Somebody will figure out this mess, I hope. Maybe Sandy.*

Arvie's mind recalled a recent TV show titled "Convicted for all the Wrong Reasons." These things can happen. I wish my Uncle Cliff was still alive. He'd come rolling in here, bellowing like a constipated bull, and people would do most anything just to get him to shut up. He could get anything done and he did wonderful things for lots of people, and all because he could make more noise than anyone else. I suppose that's not true, but maybe I should make more noise. Maybe I shouldn't be Mr. Nice Guy, so proper and polite all the time. *Uncle Cliff, where are you when I need you? Why did you leave us so long ago?*

The door opened and a uniform walked in. "Mr. Ellison, if you'll come with me, I'll get you to your cell for the night."

Down a hall. They approached metal bars. A big key was inserted in a lock. The metal bars slid to the left. Once on the other side, the uniform clanged the door shut. A left turn and another set of metal bars. Another big key. Once on the other side, the uniform clanged the door shut. Arvie was aware that the same heavy metal bars lined the right and the left side of the hall for nearly the length of a football field. He thought of "The Green Mile." His stomach did an uncomfortable roll.

"Step right in here. Your home for tonight. I think you'll find everything you need. You get a space on a bench. You'll have to holler real loud if you need the bathroom." The uniform clanged the door shut behind him. Now he was locked in; locked in behind bars.

The cell was a 20 X 20-foot square. The back wall that he was facing was concrete block. It was painted a very light green; it was an ugly color. Nothing but bars around the other three walls. Along the front wall of bars there was no bench. The other three walls all had a bench. The benches were well occupied. He was standing just inside the sliding door of bars, making every effort to look casual and not concerned about his current environment at all. He was aware that there were nine sets of eyes focused on him. He was doing everything possible not to make eye contact with any of those eyes.

Yes. Nine cell-mates in all, mostly black, one Hispanic and one other Caucasian. Some were already asleep lying uncomfortably on the bench. Some were sitting on the bench staring off somewhere or asleep. An older black man was looking intently at Arvie. Their eyes met and with an almost imperceptible nod, the only greeting he would get was extended. All were older men except for the Hispanic and the Caucasian and another African American. The Hispanic was perhaps 18, shabbily dressed but clean in appearance. He was a nice looking young man and by the look on his face, extremely frightened. The Caucasian was slightly older, needed a shave and his clothes were a mess. He was perhaps 25. He appeared to be a physical specimen. He was a big boy. The expression on his face as well as his facial features were, well, frightening. He looked mad. No one was sitting within three feet of him on either side.

These men are lost, Arvie thought *but then, so am I right now.* He didn't know what to do so he just stood there feeling terribly out of place. *God, please help me.* The bench along the left side was mostly empty and he headed in that direction.

He was about to sit down when he heard a deep, gravelly voice say "Come. Sit down over here." It was the man who had nodded to him. "He is at least as old as I am," Arvie thought. At that moment, a most welcome sense of peace settled within him. He walked to the bench along the back wall and took a seat in reasonable proximity to the old man. His mind was whirling with thought. *Maybe I had missed something? Maybe I had been convicted and sentenced to life? Maybe I fell asleep and missed all that? Maybe I would never see a starry sky again? Maybe I'll never see Hannah again except for visitation days. Maybe the rest of my life would be spent with total strangers, these nine unhappy looking men, consumed on the inside with fear and panic. God, please help me.*

"First time to be in a place like this" came the question?

Arvie turned as much as his fused neck would allow to inspect at closer range, the face of the old man sitting next to him. It was a face that appeared to be much older than his. But the eyes, buried deep within caverns of bushy gray eye brows, were alive with life and, he wondered – love? His face was not smiling but his eyes were.

"Yes." He cleared his throat and said it again, "Yes." It came out better the second time.

A very black hand was extended towards Arvie. The warm voice spoke again – "I'm Henry Brannon. I'm a frequent visitor here."

"Arvie Ellison. I'm not a frequent visitor here."

"I gathered that. I get the feeling that you belong somewhere else? Are you from around here?"

"Up north, about 30 miles or so."

"Wife and family?"

"Umm, yes. My wife and a son and daughter."

"That's nice."

"How about you?"

"I have a wife and a son. What was your work? You look like you might be retired."

"Yeah. I retired recently. I've done several things over the years. Most related to the sale of something I guess. Doesn't sound like much when it's put that way, does it? How about you?"

"I've had a career in harvesting lost souls."

"Oh my. That sounds much more important and satisfying than selling something."

"Well, every work is important. Perhaps there are some more important than others. I guess it's all in how you look at it."

"You said you were a frequent visitor here. What does that mean?"

"I did. I'll spend two or three nights a week here. Some weeks, I'll spend more nights here than I do at home."

"Ummm. Does that mean you come and go as you please? How does your wife feel about you being in jail so many nights?"

"She understands. We are in this harvesting business together."

"So, do your visits here have something to do with – how did you say it, harvesting lost souls?"

"Very perceptible, Arvie. Yes, it does. I'll generally come later in the week. Weekends are really busy here and the field is very ripe for harvesting."

"So, you can come and go as you please?"

"Aahhhh. Yes. Perhaps I can do a better job of explaining. I've been a handyman for Jesus my entire life. My daddy taught me the business. He taught me how to make things, fix things and clean things. But he also taught me that working with the things of this world are not nearly as important as working on the road to eternity. When you are fixing some plumbing for someone, or cleaning out a garage, or washing windows, there are opportunities to talk about what Jesus has done for me and my family and what He can do for others. So, here in this place, I can always find someone who's in need of some fixin'. In Matthew 25:40, Jesus says, 'I tell you the truth, anything you did for even the least of my people here, you also did for me.' I do work every day for people at the bottom of the heap. I want to believe that what I do makes God happy. Yes, they let me come whenever I want to."

"That's a beautiful story. Your mission will never end, will it?"

"No. I think of it as job security. I usually find at least one or two every night - open to learnin' about somethin' better, learnin' that there is a better way to live in this world, and especially learnin' the message about forgiveness. So many are filled with regret and pain and hatred at somethin', anythin', everythin'. There are so many who aren't aware of God's peace and how to find it. There are so many willin' to accept a night or two in a place like this as being normal for them, not aware that life can be full of love, hope and joy. Some of our friends here tonight, I see most every time I come for a visit."

"So, you are not an ordained minister?"

"Me? Oh mercy, no. Schoolin was never the thing for me. Daddy told me school wasn't necessary to do what's really important: to help people; be of service to 'em. When you work with them like that, they're more open to listen and to hear."

"So, what kind of stuff do you do to help them?"

"In the middle of winter, they'll go two to three weeks without any heat. And then they'll think to knock on my door. Or they got no runnin' water. Toilets won't flush. Faucet won't turn on. Sometimes we help 'em with showers, keeping 'em clean, you know, that kind of stuff. Most every day we're fixin 'em meals because they don't know how to do that, or they physically or mentally can't do that.

And then there's those that can't remember anything like it's time for bed, or it's time to eat, or it's time to go to the bathroom."

"You're not serious. People forget when it's time to go to the bathroom?

"Oh, you wouldn't believe it."

"That can't be good."

"Trust me, it's not good. The clean-up is unbelievable."

"And why would anyone wait two to three weeks in the middle of winter with no heat?"

"'Cause they ain't got no money."

"And then you go fix it for 'em knowing full well you won't get paid?"

"You learn fast, don't you?"

"I'm starting to get the picture. Do you ever get paid for some of the work you do?"

"For some of the work I do, I do not ever get paid in money. Sometimes I get paid in other ways like when an old man I bin working with for 30 years asks me to kneel down with him and help him pray to the Lord for forgiveness. That's when I really get paid."

"I can understand that but rarely do you get paid in terms of money?"

"I may not get any money but I may walk home with a jar of strawberry jam, or a bag of week old potatoes that don't smell so good, or a used drying rack we can use in the kitchen to dry out dish rags, towels, and other washin'. And then once in a while, the pay is real good. My daddy used to tell me not to worry about gettin' paid. You keep helping people and one day you'll get paid real good."

"I understand that and I do believe it. But aren't there government agencies that provide for people with no money? Provide them with sustenance of some kind? Food stamps? A government check of some kind."

"Believe me, I did look into all that once. I could find no help whatsoever. I remember findin' a county agency once that I thought was gunna be of some help, but they were so overwhelmed they never got to any of my people. They promised they'd send out case workers and nobody ever showed up. I kept buggin those people month after month and nothin ever got started. Besides the county, I tried the Fed's and the State. I remember once sittin in a big state building for a 1 p.m. appointment. When it got to be 3:30 and I'm still sittin there, I got up and complained to the lady at the desk and all she could tell me was that she's sorry. When I got home, I found out one of my people drowned in a bathtub and I wasn't there. I ain't never gone back to that government building. Never will."

"That's not right. And then there are those nights when you come here to sit on this bench all night and talk with whoever happens to be here?

"I want my life to be spent serving people and that's what I do when I'm here. I don't serve anyone when I'm sittin and waitin for an appointment that never happens. Still makes me upset just thinkin about it. Anyway, yeah. Sometimes the nights are long. Most nights the benches are full of men sleeping it off or just sleeping. But some nights are very meaningful. See that young man over there, down on the end?"

"Yes."

"His name is Jesus Escobar. He's 18, 19. Parents are good people, Christian people. This one here's a fine young man. You notice he doesn't look at me. He knows me and he knows I know his momma and poppa. He also knows that if he doesn't have a talk with them as soon as he's outta here, I probably will. Does he look scared to you?"

"Sure does."

"Do you think he's scared cause of what some of these men might do to him? Or do you think he's more afraid of what his momma is going to do to him when he gets outta here?"

"Could be both but probably his momma."

"I'll be back in a few minutes."

Henry rose and stretched. He was taller than he looked and he was rail thin. He moved with a distinct limp and it had something to do with a fused knee, perhaps – maybe just arthritis. Arvie guessed Henry to be in his early to mid-80's. Henry walked slowly across the cell with his hands in his pockets to the open space next to the young Jesus. He paused before he sat down, saying something that Arvie could not make out. The young man nodded in the affirmative, and Henry sat down. Neither one spoke for several minutes and then

Henry leaned forward, placing his elbows carefully on his knees and his chin in his hands. The talk began; slowly at first, both of 'em staring at the floor. After a few minutes, the young man and Henry were immersed in conversation.

Arvie's eyes left them alone as he looked at the others around the square, bare, uninteresting enclosure. He didn't have his watch or phone or belt or anything, for that matter. Everything had been taken from him when the uniform had brought him here. He had put his name on the outside of a large 14 X 17 envelope, and his 'stuff' had gone inside the envelope. On the way down the hall, the uniform handed the envelope through an open space under some bars to another uniform that he could not see. He did not know what time it was, but from the looks of the others here, it was time to sleep. Three of them, Henry, the young Hispanic and himself, were the only inmates with open eyes.

Arvie closed his eyes but could not doze off. The bench was hard and the concrete block wall behind him felt like a hard, concrete block wall. He wondered if he would get any sleep this night.

Perhaps 30 minutes later, he heard Henry coming across the cold tile floor and he felt him drop onto the bench.

"How is our young friend?" Arvie asked without opening his eyes.

"He's scared to death and it has nothing to do with what the law is going to do to him. It's all because of what his mom and pop will do to him when they find out."

"What'd he do?"

"He says he tucked a tube of 85% lean ground beef into his jacket pocket and, of course, didn't have any money to pay for it. If what he told me was the truth, he'll get off with a warnin' and a wrist slap. He's probably in for a lot more than that from his folks. He's in his sophomore year at the Junior College north of St. Paul. He's a bright kid. He said his folks keep sayin' that he doesn't spend enough time with their church crowd, that they're a good bunch of kids. He didn't have any money because his part-time job ended two weeks ago and he hasn't taken any time to line up another one. That's #1 on his priority list now."

"It must be difficult for some of these young people to get their life started."

"It is. You see the big white kid at the end of the bench on our left? That kid's trouble. His name is Marcus Overstreet. He's been trouble since his mommy and daddy made him. He come outta the womb lookin for someone to beat up. He's in here every time I come, lookin like he just lost another fight. I don't try to get him outta here anymore. I did that for too long. I finally figured he ain't gonna learn anythin if I keep gettin' him off the hook. Jesus tells me that he's been tryin to get with his girl, a pretty little 17 – 18-year-old, like him – Hispanic. Jesus doesn't want to have anything to do with Marcus but he knows if this goes on, he's going to have to do somethin, which means he's gonna get hurt pretty good. He says he's not afraid of getting hurt, but he is very afraid of what Marcus might do to his girl. Now then: you haven't told me what you are doin' in here. You ain't the type I usually see."

"It's all screwed up. They think I'm somebody I'm not."

"That's what they all say."

"Hah. I suppose that's true." Now, he thought, I'm starting to sound like a real convict. "They caught me talking to a man suspected of having ties to some drug people in South America, or was it central America. I was pouring this guy a cup of coffee. I had seen him over and over again sitting on his lard bucket at this street corner week after week, month after month trying to pick up a few bucks from passing motorists. It's a long story."

"We got the rest of the night and I'm a good listener."

"Ok, then. This all began a week ago last Monday. Four of us old college friends get together for a few days every summer at a cabin up north. Well, on the drive up . . .."

"You stopped and bought coffee at a convenience store, took it to the cabin and discovered it heals all sorts of ailments. Then you all went back to try to find the place and there had never been an old guy with a pork pie hat selling coffee in there. And you saw a newspaper clipping on the wall which was the old guy's obit telling you that he had been dead for 50 years. Is that the story?"

"Yes. How'd you know?"

"I read all about it in the Daily this morning."

"I'd already forgotten that."

"So, you *are* that guy. That's a good story. Mary and I were readin' it this morning over breakfast and we were laughin and havens the best time with it. Well, then we started talking seriously about it and, well, what you are tryin to do is a really good thing. Hope is somethin there is far too little of any more. So many people, especially us older ones, are sufferin from too many things these days. You oughta come by sometime and I can show you some real sufferin just in my apartment buildin'. And then there's the threat of Social Security going away at any time. What in the world would we do if that was taken away? So many of our flock has got nothing: no money, no family, no clothes, no food, no place to live, and their health is awful. Can't go see a doctor cause there ain't no money. Even if they got a prescription there ain't no money to pay for it. Some that got a buck or two can't get out of the buildin to spend it because their mind is gone or they can't physically get up outa their chair. People starvin to death."

"How can you continue working like that day after day?"

"We love each one of 'em. Love's pretty strong."

"Oh, and here's something else I learned today. There is a lady from the FDA coming in to see me because I can't be selling or giving away coffee that has not been approved by them."

"Now how's she gonna to stop you from giving away coffee?"

"I don't know. She is supposed to be coming here sometime this morning. I wasn't looking for all this publicity."

"You feel like this is something you've been called to do?"

"Yes."

"How can you tell when someone is sufferin'?"

"I can't. That's why I've been trying to get to as many as I can. And here's the other part of it – I've come to believe that it can heal stuff even before it becomes a problem."

"How can you know that?"

"It's because of the Native Americans who have handed me a shiny black can. It's the way in which they talk of those 'who have a need.' They didn't say 'those who are sick.' See what I mean? We don't really know anything about this coffee. We haven't had it analyzed. We don't know what's in it. But drinking it for three or four days had a profound effect on all four of us. Something very real in each of us was healed. I know it sounds crazy. Aahhh…. I don't know? Still, what if? What if my acid reflux was healed? I haven't had a problem with it since that first cup. What if cancer had begun running around undiscovered yet, somewhere deep inside of me and it's been healed? What if? What if I am able to get more of it so I live until I'm 150? Will I have to say, 'what if' anymore?"

"I think, Arvid, that if you make it to 150, you will have proven your point. I have a friend who has a friend who works at 3M. He analyzes stuff. That's his job. You want to get it analyzed?"

"I do. No, I don't. Of course, I want to find in it some element that has never been seen before and we can then say – 'that's it. That's the magic.' But I know, well, I think I know that it is all natural. Since this coffee 'is a product of Northern Minnesota' where no coffee beans are grown, all it can be – is natural stuff: stuff that is found in the woods; grasses, weeds, tree bark, wild animal excrement, leaves, dead animal entrails, water, dead spiders and ants and whatever else can be found. Every element is from mother earth. Gitchi-Manitou has put it all together. There. I've said it. No. I don't want to know. Yes. I do. Can you give me your address? I will bring you a can."

"Sure. But we don't have any pencils in here, or paper for that matter. I'll be outta here at 7, when the shift turns over. I'll write it down and have the guys slip it into your envelope. You know – where you put all your stuff before they brought you down here. You'll get it all back when you leave."

"That's fine. I'll find you as soon as I can and I'll bring you a can of Forever."

"You haven't told me anything about your wife. Married long time?"

"52 years."

"That's a long time. What's she think about you runnin' around town givin' away coffee?"

"She understands. But there is one thing that bothers me. She was diagnosed with anxiety two years ago. It's a … it's an awful thing. Of course, we all have some of it and if all of us who have not been diagnosed with it went for a diagnosis, probably half of us would get a diagnosis too. Anyway, we're all pretty anxious people. Well, as soon as I got home I made a pot of coffee, you know, thinking it would heal her right up."

"What happened?"

"Near as I can tell, nothing. Nothing has changed."

"Healin' the mind is different than healin' the body?"

"I've wondered that. Maybe it just takes more time, forever maybe. I'm confusing myself."

"Forever?"

"Oh. Sorry. Forever is what this coffee is called. It comes to me in a shiny black can with that one word printed in a bright red. There is one other line on the back of the can, way down at the bottom that says, 'A fine coffee product of Northern Minnesota.'"

"Never heard of coffee beans growin' up there?"

"Yeah. Everybody who hears my story says that. Then one day I got a can labeled, Reunion and later a can labeled Mercy. And then I got a whole case of Forever. I keep wondering what the next can will be called? And I don't know if there is any difference in the coffee? But the names speak to me of Gitchi Manitou, God, Jesus, Christianity, being saved. The human search for happiness, hope, joy. That's another reason I think this stuff is special."

"Now that's interestin. I'd like to get it tested, see what's in there."

"Yeah. I guess I'm interested too. This room we are in right now – do they allow visitors to come in here?"

"No. If someone comes to see you, they'll come get you and take you to one of the visitin rooms. Why? You lookin for someone to come see you?"

"I'm just hoping, I guess. I really don't know."

"Here's a question. Do you know when someone has a need, is sick or somethin'?"

"No. Why?"

"Dunno. Just thinkin' since you're dealin' in healin', maybe you'd been given some kind of gift, so's you'd know who needs it and who doesn't."

It must have been the way Henry posed the question, because almost immediately, Arvie's mind was filled with the vision from his dream of the burning halo of fire. The wicked witch of this morning had a halo of fire. She was sick.

"That's it," he almost screamed as he jumped to his feet. It was loud enough that several sleeping prisoners stirred, changed positions, smacked their lips together, picked at their nose once or twice, and then faded away again.

"That's what?"

"My God, Henry." Arvie paced in a circle while rubbing the top of his head. "I had a very real dream several nights back. There was a lot of stuff but the first thing I remembered was that there was an explosion of sorts, and then I saw a circle of fire. I have thought of it as a halo of fire, and just this morning I saw it for the first time as I was walking away from a lady I had been talking with. I blew up my grill last night – that was the explosion. The explosion blew the lid off the grill and it hit me in the head, right here, and cut me and I had blood running down; saw that in the dream too. Hit me right here. And then there was a lady who touched my head and a voice said, 'She touched him and he understood.' I think I now understand that when I see someone whose head is wrapped in this halo of fire, I will know that that person is sick. The lady I was talking to this morning at the hospital was sick – is sick. Do I sound totally nuts, Henry?"

"Man. I'm startin to wonder," Henry said with a giggle. "A little bit anyway. That dream was real?"

"It sure was."

"What else was in that dream?"

"Well, there were some numbers. A 10 dash 10 dash 10. I haven't taken any time on that yet. Don't know what that might mean. And then there was a highway sign that read 'CR JW.' There was a dirt road with a wooden fence and a thick forest and then it seemed the road ended. And, I don't have my notes but I think there was something like the sound of many voices humming, or groaning or something like that. That was about all."

"If you received directions on how to determine when someone is sick or has a health issue, maybe the rest of it is also a set of directions. 10-10-10 could be a time frame, say October 10, at 10:00."

"Aaah yes, it could very well be that. And another thing; the 10-10-10 was surrounded by the brightness of a full moon."

"Then it's 10 at night on October 10. Some kind of a meetin awaits you at the end of that road, whatever it was, wherever it is. But who is it that will meet you there?"

"It sounds now as if we have the skills of Joseph; the ability to interpret dreams. But I would think that God helped him quite a lot during those bondage years in Egypt. Don't you think?"

"I agree. It sounds a little like you don't think God is helping you right now?"

"I hadn't thought of it like that. Maybe you're right. We know He works in mysterious ways and there is no reason we need to understand. We just need to do. But this all seems so weird. I wonder if I'll accomplish anything?"

"Seems to me that you believe God's involved in this. It also seems to me that we're both interested in doing the same thing – helpin those less fortunate. Here's something from Luke 6 that I like a lot: *'Give, and you will receive. You will be given much. Pressed down, shaken together, and runnin over, it will spill into your lap. The way you give to others is the way God will give to you.'* My daddy had me memorizin that one before I could walk. We're helpin others, Arvie. God likes that. So even when we feel that we ain't accomplishin' anythin, when we start to doubt and we're feelin kinda low, He's proud of us when we keep on givin."

Chapter 12

"If you're gonna be a success in this life you're gonna have to work 24/7. Don't be leanin on that ice chipper. Chip somethin. And you can do something else with your other arm.
That's called multi-tasking. Heh heh."
- *Ole*

"Give your worries to the Lord, and he will take care of you. He will never let good people down."
Psalm 55:22

7:00am. The sun had been up for a while. It was already hot and sticky. Henry could feel a storm coming. He could smell it. He stood on the crumbling concrete steps of the police station and surveyed his world. *It isn't much to look at,* he thought, shaking his head. The old vacant woolen mill occupied much of his view down the block. *If they don't take it down soon, burned out as it is, it'll fall down on its own.* Just beyond the mill, the Haptenstiel apartments didn't look much better. What rent they collected each month didn't seem to find its way back into any upkeep and maintenance. Old man Haptenstiel was a good man. He lived in the building too. He knew what needed to be done and he'd do it if his renters could pay. He was happy to get what he got. He wasn't about to run people out, 'cause he knew they had no where else to go. *It's a vicious circle when a good, well-meanin man owns a place in a neighborhood like this. There just isn't enough money to pay for it all.*

Next door to the Haptenstiel place was Nesterling's. *Old Lem Nesterling spends every minute of every day rentin his little one-room apartments. It's all he does. Every mornin he chases people out who can't pay. Every afternoon and evenin he stands on the sidewalk with a beer in one hand and his key-ring in the other, glad-handin every poor soul who's walkin by tryin to find someone who'll move in. Most all of 'em already lived there once or twice. And some of 'em will move back in, knowin they'll most likely be able to stay a week before Lem boots 'em out again. And sometimes in the winter, there might even be heat.*

A decent looking Honda Accord sat abandoned across the street on concrete blocks. The wheels were gone along with everything else. It was stripped right across the street from the police station, *Kinda like the kids are tellin the police if they want something, they'll take it.* Another car just down the street looked as if a howitzer shell landed in the front seat. Totally burned out: no paint, no glass. *People with nice cars don't come to this neighborhood. And to think when Mary and me came here, way back when, we thought we'd be a part of rebuildin it all,* Henry muttered to no one. *There used to be flowers too.*

He'd been to city hall more than once complaining about the condition of the neighborhood: totally neglected. The potholes in the streets were no worse than those in the sidewalks. The concrete continued to disintegrate. *Every day there are more pieces of concrete laying about that are the perfect size for bustin out windows in all the vacant buildings. There are worse things the kids could be doing. What's going to happen here?* He didn't think things were going to improve any time soon. The Irish Inn & Pub on the corner at the end of the block; nothing but a burned out old shell. That fire was two years ago. *Still smells burnt. More of these old buildins will be going the same way, especially those that have insurance.*

Henry knew it was going to be a hot one and hoped the fire department would come along that afternoon and open up a hydrant for the kids. As he walked along, he avoided most of the potholes, but his balance wasn't what it used to be and his knee just continued to deteriorate like the streets and sidewalks. Invariably, he stumbled over something. *One of these times I'm going down. I just know it. And that'll be the end of a hip and the end of helpin anybody.*

"Hi Mrs. Potts. How are you today? I think Mary's got your wash done. I'll be bringing it over in a little bit. It's gonna rain here pretty quick so don't be sitting out here once it begins, ok? Johnny doing ok? That's good. Real good. Still reading that Bible I gave you? God love's you Mrs. Potts. I'll see you later then."

Mrs. Potts hadn't been right for a long time. She couldn't talk anymore. Mary still did her wash even though she couldn't pay.

Years ago, she could. She had some disability money coming in and she and her kids gotten along ok. Her "old man" ran off not long after he brought them there. Both kids just disappeared one day. Some thought they died in the fire when the Rubenstein place went up, but there was no trace. Some folks didn't think the arson boys checked these places very well. *Everyone of these places that burns has got people livin in 'em. Mrs. Potts talks to Johnny and Marion all night, every night. She doesn't talk to any of us but she still talks to her kids. She's not doing good a'tall. Maybe them kids got stole.*

"Mornin Ms. Overstreet. How's Aurelius doin?"

"Mornin Henry. All things considered, he's ok. Little trouble getting him into his chair this morning. Think he just wanted to ly in bed all day. That ain't gonna do him no good."

"Naw, it ain't. Listen, you need help movin' him in the mornin's, or the evenin's too for that matter, come and get me. I'm happy to help."

"Oh, thank you Henry. Can you look at that old faucet one more time?"

"Still givin' ya trouble?"

"Oh, Marcus got mad at it t'other day. Gave it a yank and musta broke it. Don't work no more."

"I'll be over this afternoon."

"Thank you, Henry. I'll pay you soon's I can."

Henry raised a hand in farewell as he turned to continue his walk home. *That lady never complains about her arthritis, but she lives with a whole mess of pain. Strong lady, she is. And she has to live with that grandson of hers – that is, whenever he decides to come home and mooch off his grandparents. And Aurelius. Mercy me. How's he lived this long? Mind's still sharp but the body – well, ain't much left. Some lives are more difficult to live than others.*

Henry and Mary lived three blocks away from the police station. About half the buildings along that stretch weree vacant, yet people lived in all of 'em. Crack houses. Flop houses. Whatever you want to call 'em. It's the poorest of the poor that lived there. *The Lord keeps remindin us that it's not the buildin's that matter. It's the people in 'em. "Feed my starvin children," He says to us all.* That's what he and Mary had been trying to do. Hard to do when there was so little money.

"Hi there Ms. Koepke. Remember, I'll be over in a little bit to work on that toilet."

Mrs. Koepke waved a thank you to Henry. She was as deaf as a board and had no idea what Henry said but she waved anyway. The only reason she waved was because Henry touched her shoulder as she sat on the porch. She's couldn't see anything either.

He'd take his old tool box and get her toilet fixed, *even though nothin's wrong with it*, and she'd tell him that she'd pay him when her check arrived. Of course, her check would not arrive, which meant he'd not get paid. *There's nothin wrong with her toilet. she just can't remember how to flush it. Somebody has got to take care of these people. I'm trying, Jesus. I'm trying.*

His apartment building was like all the rest. He'd thought more than once that the steps up to the 2nd floor would fall in at most any time. He walked up the steps slowly, keeping as close to the wall as possible. The steps were the strongest right next to the wall. He sometimes remembered how he used to run those stairs, two and three at a time. *Not any more.* He reached 204, inserted the key and opened the door. Mary was dozing on the couch, still in her bathrobe. He thought she had lost more weight. Her face looked drawn and pale, especially in the morning light. She stirred, yawned, and tried to sit up. "Hi hon. How was your night."

He went and sat next to her, put his arm around her shoulders and kissed her lightly on her cheek. "It was a good night, thanks for askin. You'll never guess who I spent it with."

"Well, tell me."

"Member yesterday mornin? We were reading the paper about the old man and his coffee? Well, it was him: he spent the night with us and his real name is Arvie. Remember in the story that he was trying to give some coffee to a man the police believe is heavy into drugs? Well, right now they are convinced Arvie spent his life with the drug gangs in South America, and he says he's never been out of the country. This guy is plain as an old shoe. It'll all get straightened out here one day. But his story sure is interestin. I'll fill you in later. You got the wash all done?"

"Yeah. That in the corner is Ms. Koepke's. Next to it is Ottoman's, and the next basket is Mr. Elston and then Mrs. Potts. I sure hope someone can pay a little today."

"I do too, dear."

"I don't know what we'll do for food. There's only a little soup left. No bread. Nothing else."

"Do not worry my dear. Our God loves us and He has provided. I've got several dollars in my pocket. I ran into Morgan Hemmings on the way to the jail last night and he gave me four bucks for the work that I did for him last month. He says he'll get me the rest soon as he can and I know he'll try. We'll be fine. I'm gonna go fix Edna's toilet after I drop off the wash, flush Mrs. Koepke's toilet and then stop by Overstreets on that faucet again. I'll get some bread on the way back. Miss me?"

"Of course, I'll miss you. Be back soon."

"You bet. I love you." He grabbed the wash and his tool box and headed out the door. *Mary's in pain.* He could see it. She always said she was fine; didn't want to be a burden or cost them any money. *The tumor is getting bigger. I just know it is and it's all going to get so much worse and still, she keeps on smilin, and cleanin, and washin. What a lady. What'll I do?*

* * * * * * * *

Arvie awoke to a dandy stiff neck. Henry was gone and so was the Hispanic boy. The others are still sacked out except for the Overstreet kid. *Wonder if he slept at all?*

Arvie did the best he could to sit up straight, getting out the kinks a little at a time. It was a bit of a struggle but he managed. He yawned, rubbed his eyes, leaned forward and stared at the floor.

"Ellison. Come with me. The man wants to see you."

Arvie stood a little uncertain, stretched and moved towards the uniform. The cell door opened and he didn't look back.

He was taken to the office of Special Agent Woodhull. He entered the office and was told to take a seat. He said, "Thanks," and did as he was told.

A moment later, Woodhull entered carrying a cup of coffee – only one. Woodhull put a folder on his desk and then took a lengthy sip from the steaming cup. Arvie watched and could taste the Forever even though he didn't have any.

"How'd last night go for you?" asked the Special Agent.

"Went fine. Good company. Met Mr. Brannon."

"Good. Yes. He's a good man. I don't understand him, but he's surely dedicated to all the people around here. He's spends enough nights here." Woodhull took another sip, then continued, "That picture has got you in a bit of a bind. It ties you to South America. I've got my people looking into your background in the Quad Cities. If that picture was taken there as you say it was, how did it get to the law in Lima? What hospital were you born in?"

"Cottage Hospital in Galesburg."

"Is that one of the Quad Cities."

"No sir. It's about 45 minutes straight south. We lived there until I went away to college, and then the folks moved up there. Dad couldn't find work in Galesburg but he found work on the line at Farmall and for all those years he drove those 45 minutes both ways five days a week."

"What year were you born?"

"1938."

"And that happened in this Galesburg?"

"Yes. The folks moved to East Moline when I left home for College."

"Where did you go to school?"

"Mount Holy Waters College, Theological Seminary, Music School and Academy in Chicago."

"Play any sports?" Woodhull asked indifferently.

"Baseball, basketball and golf."

"Where did your dad work?"

"Farmall in East Moline."

"He worked there a long time?"

"Long time, over 35 years."

"What was his name?"

"Robert Lawrence Ellison."

"Your mothers name?"

"Elaine Margaret. Her maiden name was Siddyer. Two d's and a yer."

"That should be enough. I understand you've got a date with the Food and Drug Administration this morning?"

"That's what Sandy Marsh told me. Any idea when that might happen?"

"Whenever she arrives."

"Any idea when I might get out of here?"

"If I can verify your background, you'll be on your way right after your meeting with the FDA. But there's something wrong with your story. So, we'll see." There was a knock at the door and when it opened, "Yes Rosenius?"

"Mr. Ellison's son is here."

"We got a room open?"

"Yeah. Nobody in A."

"Let's put 'em in there. Mr. Ellison, go with Rosenius."

"Yes sir. A question if I may - is it ok to bring coffee into a jail cell?"

"No."

"That's not right."

* * * * * * * *

Woodhull led Arvie into 'A' and Arvie greeted Brooks with a heartfelt hug.

"What is going on?" asked Brooks with an irritated look on his face. Woodhull left the room and closed the door.

"Sit down. You're gonna love this" Arvie couldn't stifle a little giggle. "Based on the background check the DEA and the FBI did on me, I spent most of the 70's and 80's in South America working the drug thing in Bogota and Caracas and Lima, Peru. They caught me once in Peru and I was convicted, sentenced to 20 years or so, but I didn't even serve a week – or so they said. They don't believe that I've never been out of the states, and they don't believe that I've never had a passport. And here's the real curious part: the law down in Lima sent up a picture of me. Only problem was that it was taken in Blackhawk State Park in the Quad Cities and was part of my resume when I was trying to get into tv. How would anyone have ever found that picture, especially someone in Lima, Peru?

"I don't understand any of that but why did they pick you up in the first place?"

Arvie explained about meeting the pan handler on the street corner. When he finished, Brooks just shook his head.

"So, you gonna continue doing your coffee thing?" he asked.

"I sure am."

"Mom's fit to be tied. She's really scared, as you can imagine."

"I'm sure."

"So when can I take you home?"

"Don't know yet. I've got some lady from the FDA coming to see me. It has to do with me giving away unapproved coffee. They have to approve everything and make sure its ok for human consumption, ya know."

"What?"

"Yeah. That's what I think too."

"Now how they gonna stop you from giving coffee away?"

"That's what everybody asks. Anyway, I've got to meet with her. Agent Woodhull says that as soon as they can find a history of me – of us in the Quad Cities, he can release me."

"Well at 75, maybe its time you hang around the house and, what do they call it – putter? Sure, would make mom a lot happier and keep her from some worry. Don't you think?

"Right now, she'll worry no matter where I am or what I'm doing so I don't think it will make any difference. I am worried that I won't make the baptism tomorrow night. I'd like to be a fly on the wall in the church office on Monday morning when they review who showed up for baptism and who didn't. *"That Mr. Ellison didn't make it." "Oh. Didn't you hear? He's been in jail for days. They've been trying to catch him for years because he's spent his whole life running drugs from South America to the Twin Cities." "No, you can't be serious. Isn't he the man who volunteers in the bookstore? He seems so nice, smiles at everyone. Well, I guess he's one very bad dude."* Can't you just hear it? It really is funny."

"You don't suppose they'd already pronounce you guilty, would they? I guess people do it all the time."

"Sure, they do. It's human nature."

"So, you're really going to do the Baptism thing? You and mom both?"

"Yes, we are."

"Why do you think you need to be Baptized?

"Well, we really haven't been. They dropped some water on our heads when we were babies. That was more for the parents benefit than ours. I've wanted to do this ever since Bren did before she went on the Nicaragua mission trip. You need to think on that too. Both you and Kate."

The door opened and a young uniform walked in.

"Sorry to interrupt but we've got a lady waiting to speak with Arvid Ellison."

"That's me. Brooks, can you wait a bit out there? Have you got the time?"

"Sure. What's the guy's name who's got you in here?"

"Woodhull. Special Agent Woodhull."

"I'm going to have a little talk with him. Yes, I'll give mom a call too."

"Tell her I love her and this will all be over pretty soon."

"I'll tell her."

* * * * * * * *

"Ms. Diddle – right in here."

"Arvid Ellison?"

"Yes ma'am."

"My name is Corlis Diddle. I'm with the Food and Drug Administration."

"Yes ma'am. I heard you wanted to speak with me."

"I feel that I know you because of all the information about you in the paper. Do you know what we at the FDA are responsible for? I want to make sure you understand why I am here."

"Well, you look at food to make sure it's fit for human consumption. You are responsible for all the legislation to insure it's all right. You are also responsible for insuring that all the prescriptions are labeled properly: all the warnings are there and that all the drug companies are adhering to the laws of the land as well as all the Walgreens and the rest of 'em."

"Pretty good. It goes much deeper than that, but I think you've got the basic idea. First of all, I read in the paper that you believe this coffee healed you of something. How do you know that?"

"Well, before this coffee I had acid reflux. After drinking it for only one day, it was gone. No more pills."

"Do you suppose it is just in remission instead of really being gone?"

"All things are possible, ma'am."

"So, there is a chance that it is not gone?"

"Of course. But we are coming up on two weeks now."

"But you would agree that there is a chance nothing has been healed?"

"I suppose."

"Then I would expect that you wouldn't have a problem with not talking any more about how you have been healed of the acid reflux thing?"

"But I have."

"You just said a moment ago that there was a chance that it's not gone."

"Yeah, but until it returns, it is gone. Isn't it?"

"Hrmph. Now where do you get this coffee?"

"Mainly at convenience stores, although a case of it was delivered to our home."

"These convenience stores, part of a national chain?"

"I don't think so. They've all been different."

"Let's focus for a moment on the first store. Where was it located?"

"On 169, about 30 miles south of Mille Lacs, the lake."

"And what was the name of it?"

"I don't think there was a name. Just a little place. A couple of gas pumps outside. Pretty run down."

"Why in the world would you have stopped at a place like that?"

"Ummm, I'd been drinking coffee on my trip and I needed a little boys room."

"How much did you pay for the coffee?"

"Well, let's see. I bought two cans and I refilled my travel mug. I think it was around $14 or $15 bucks.

"And how big were the cans?"

"Same as that big can of Folgers we've seen for 100 years. You know, about this tall and about this big around. Looked like a standard size to me."

"The article said the name of the coffee was Forever. Is that correct?"

"Yes ma'am."

"And there was only one other line written on the can – what was that again?"

"A fine coffee product of Northern Minnesota."

"And the address? Where did it come from?"

"There was no address on the can."

"That's against Federal Law. How do people think they can get away with this? It violates every inter and intra state trade law in the world. I'm totally aghast. Now, then. The article said that you and your friends aaaahh … I've got the article right here … let me see … yes. You and your friends, after you realized that something had happened after drinking the coffee, went back to the store to see if you could buy some additional. But you couldn't find an additional supply there."

"That's correct."

"And they told you that the man you bought the coffee from, the man with the pork-pie hat had never worked there, nor had he ever been there, nor had they ever sold coffee there."

"Yes."

"And then you saw an obituary notice on a bulletin board that had his picture on it. The notice was announcing his death and upcoming services and the date on the obit was 50 years ago. Is that correct?"

"Yes. 1963."

"Well, what did you make of that piece of information?"

"I thought it was rather unusual. I had been there just two days earlier. Met the man. We talked. He sold me coffee. As I was leaving, he said to have a nice reunion. I wondered how he knew that was where I was going? And then I didn't think any more of it. But when we came back, he wasn't there and the young girl knew nothing about the old man that I described."

"Didn't you think that was a little strange, weird?"

"Sure, but she was rather young and I wasn't real sure that she was reliable and I thought ..."

"You must've thought that this man came back from the grave just to meet you at this run-down convenience store to sell you some coffee that he brought with him from the great beyond. Is that what you were thinking?"

"Well, frankly, yeah. I was thinking there was a greater purpose to all of what was happening, that Jesus, in all his glory, was sending me, Arvid Ellison, on a mission of hope. He had selected me to deliver hope to many and healing to some. I was frankly very humbled by the thought."

"Simple minded" she mumbled softly.

"I'm sorry?"

"Oh nothing. But you did buy more coffee. Where was that?"

"I did not buy more coffee. I've only bought coffee one time and that was on the first day when I bought two cans. When I was heading home after our time together, I looked for the same store again and I couldn't find it. It was gone. I needed gas so I stopped at the next one I saw. While my friend pumped the gas, I went inside to ask directions to that particular store. I thought maybe I had passed it or perhaps it was still further down the road. Well, when I came in, the man behind the counter looked me over and then ducked down behind the counter, fumbled around a little bit and then produced a well used brown paper sack with a can of coffee inside."

"And did you pay the same?"

"No. I didn't pay anything."

"You stole it?"

"No. The man gave me the sack and then walked out the back door and literally disappeared. I know because I walked after him, even went outside looking for him, but with no luck. He had just vanished into thin air. And, I suspect that after we drove away, that store disappeared as well."

"Oh, come now. There must have been some place he could have gone, or he got in his car and drove away?"

"There was no place he could have gone. There was no car in the parking lot except ours. He just vanished."

"Huumph. Well, then. It was the same coffee?"

"No. I mean the coffee may have been the same but the name on the outside was different. The first two were called, Forever. The third can was called, Reunion. It looked the same, but the name was different. The man I bought the first can from had said to me, 'Have a nice reunion and now I receive a can of coffee labeled, Reunion. What was I supposed to make of that?"

"When you had the coffee tested, did you find both cans to contain the same product?"

"I haven't had the coffee tested."

"So, you don't know what's in the coffee?"

"No ma'am. I have never had a can of coffee tested. It is not something I have ever thought of doing."

"But on a can of coffee, it tells you what is inside."

"Ma'am, I buy coffee to drink – to get my day started. I've never read the ingredients on a can of coffee in my life and I do not plan to start now. Do most people do that? Do most people buy a can of coffee and then run immediately to the "Coffee Testing Counter" to find out what's in there? I don't think so. My Walmart doesn't have such a counter."

"How'd you slice your head open?"

"I blew up my grill."

"Oh. I'm sorry."

"Yeah. So was I. It was really a good grill."

"So now you have three cans of coffee. Did you get more?"

"Yes, but why are you talking with me? What difference will any of this make? It seems to me that you are wasting taxpayer money by spending all this time on such a ridiculous subject. Is there not something more important you could be doing? Shouldn't you be at some pharmaceutical company checking out the newest cold cure or something? Why aren't you pushing someone to come up with a drug that will stop old men from having to pee all the time? Why are you not working to lower the cost of medicines so that seniors living on a fixed income can pay their energy bill?" Arvie felt his blood pressure rising dramatically. He continued anyway.

"Surely there is some way we can put a limit on the amount of money the CEO's of pharmaceutical companies make. Why do they need millions of dollars every year? Who needs that much? Why aren't you taking some of those millions and putting it towards defraying the cost of prescriptions? Or do you care that the cost of dearly needed medicine continues to escalate in order to pay those greedy exec's their exorbitant salaries? And do you know that 99% of all prescriptions don't do anything? I think its all graft and corruption. The government doesn't want medical science to find the cure for the common cold, or cancer, or anything else for that matter, because the government is getting kickbacks from all the pharmaceutical companies. You work for the government but your paycheck is really from the pharmaceuticals, it's just routed through the government."

"Well I never."

"How do I know that?"

"How do you know what?"

"That you never."

"Mr. Ellison, I can assure you that our agency, our government - there is no kickback, graft or corruption."

"And how can you know that? You work out here in the field, as it were. You have no idea what goes on in that Washington place. It's nothing but corruption and it's been that way since 1820."

"What? Where do you get your information? That's an absolute lie."

"I read the newspapers and I watch CNN and Fox News. I get the facts, and I'm instructed to 'decide for myself.'"

"You have decided incorrectly, sir."

"How would you know that? How can you say that? We're not either of us in that sorely tainted Washington. You can tell me I have decided incorrectly and another federal employee can tell me that but until some of this medicine actually does what it is supposed to do, and what your information tells me its supposed to do, I and many others choose to believe it is corruption at the highest levels. And then you people put all of the 'side-effects' on all the prescriptions. It's sick. It's all really sick. Do you know that on the prescription I picked up two days ago to help with sinus drip, I may experience hair growth on my elbows and knees? Not only that, I may experience trembling in my bowels that may lead to a urinary tract infection as well as constipation and colon cancer. And … I may experience temporary hearing loss, and … I may experience a lack of taste and … I may not be able to father a child and … I have four chances in two million of this giving me cancer of the urethra. Not only the colon but the urethra too. Now tell me why, after reading all that, would I ever want to take this pill? And it's the same for every pill. My wife reads all that stuff and starts to cry. Do you have any idea how many prescriptions she has? Do you have any idea how much crying goes on in our house? The founding fathers are throwing up all over themselves right now because of what you people do. Alas. I digress. I'm so sorry – you needed to know how many more cans of coffee I've received."

* * * * * * * *

Brooks hung up the phone after trying unsuccessfully to convince his mother that everything was going to be ok. His face was beet red and his fists were clenched. The more he thought about this entire circus, the more infuriated he became. He stopped the first uniform he saw and asked, "Where's this Agent Woodhull guy?"

"That's his office right there."

Brooks marched right in – completely oblivious to the fact that he didn't knock. "Are you Woodhull?"

"Excuse me. I'm in a meeting here."

"What kind of a horse-shit operation are you running here? You're unable to get intel that ties my dad into his life and instead you tie him into a life of drugs and into a place he's never been and can't even find on a map. You got a bunch of computer geeks doing your IT that haven't a clue what common sense is? My mom and dad were married in 1962 at the First Covenant Church of Minneapolis. I should think you could find a record of that marriage in the city of Minneapolis. Know where that is? Have you thought of looking for that? We lived in Galesburg until '58. I was born in Galesburg and my sister was too. Cottage Hospital. Your geeks can't find those records either? My folks were members of that Moline church for at least 30 years, but your intel can't find any of that either. I don't get any taxpayer dollars and don't have access to your so-called intel, but I can figure out that someone got into his file in the quad cities, stole his picture electronically as they could do in millions of files and passed it on to you saying that this is the guy. For your people to find him in South America is just plain ludicrous, stupid. My Dad wouldn't do anything against the law; lie, cheat, steal, hit another person – well, he hit me once because I was a little shit growing up and deserved it. He's an upstanding, law-abiding citizen who happens to be getting baptized tomorrow night because he is a Christian and believes in Jesus Christ, and has taught his family well over all these years. You've got a 75-year-old man in jail because you and your people are as incompetent as hell. Last week something happened to him and he believes that he must get this coffee to everyone because, as Jacob Whitefeather told him 'they will need it." So, he's out there carrying this stuff around because it will give people hope. There's so damn little of that in this world anymore. So then you come along, see him talking to a man and sipping coffee with him on a street corner and because you think this beggar on the corner is a drug peddler, you have my old man followed for days because he obviously is as bad as this other guy that you can't put away because you can't find anything that connects him to the drug world, but you can pick up my dad and put him in jail because he is tied to that guy that you've been trying to put away for years but can't because your intel sucks. Do you have any idea what you are doing here? Do you have any idea how incompetent you look? It's no wonder our country is in such a mess"

It was at this point in his diatribe that Brooks began pounding on Woodhull's desk out of frustration, "You can't find the bad guys because of incompetence so you waste the tax-payers' money by jailing the salt-of-the-earth, common, ordinary people who are doing nothing but trying to live a decent life, be kind to others and in the process of doing so, give them a little hope. Now … waste some more taxpayer money with this ridiculous meeting you're having here and now, another meeting which will accomplish nothing. But when you do have a free moment, you might want to better yourself by looking up the word 'intelligence'. I'm going to waste more of my time by hanging around here until my father is finished wasting his time with that lady in there who's wasting even more taxpayer money by trying to make him out to be a fool, much the same way you've been doing. Then, I'm going to take him home. If you don't like that plan, you'll have to put us both in jail. But let me invite you and your two agents who have been following him around for days to the baptism tomorrow. It's at 4:00 tomorrow afternoon at Dove Creek on 20th. You may even enjoy it though you probably wouldn't understand why my mother and father would do such a thing."

Once more, oblivious to the fact that every person in the entire building was listening, Brooks stormed out of the office, slamming the door shut behind him, rattling every pane of glass in the place. He began to pace back and forth in an effort to calm himself when he was stopped mid-stride by a hand taking his elbow.

"Excuse me. I couldn't help but overhear what you said in there. I thought you were wonderful. I'm Sandy Marsh. I write for the Minneapolis Daily. Can I have a few minutes of your time?"

* * * * * * * *

Arvie was still trying to answer the questions of Ms. C. U. Diddle. "I stopped for gas at another convenience store driving north on some street I can't remember the name of. Don't ask the name of the place. There was just a 'gas' sign. I'll bet that place doesn't exist any more. Anyway, I was looking for gum for my wife and there was a shiny black can labeled, Redeemed. That was last Saturday afternoon, and then when we came home from church Saturday night, we found a whole case sitting on our front porch. 12 cans. This was more of the Forever. That's all the coffee I've received. I would tell you about a friend of mine who lives out of state who was shopping in a Walmart one day when a Native American approached him with a wrinkled brown paper bag. It was a can of coffee, the same as what I've received here in Minnesota. We all assumed that he received it because his wife has been ill. I might also share that another friend was heading to California earlier this week and stopped for breakfast at a little place somewhere in South Dakota I think it was, and found a can waiting for him. I might also share that they just come to us. I think there is something very spiritual about the whole thing. But you know what? I'm not gonna share that stuff because you'd just have to waste more $'s exploring all that. However, back to the spiritual subject, have you heard of Gitchi Manitou?"

"No. So now you are telling me that this coffee is being transported into at least two other states."

"I said I *could* share that. In addition, I *could* say that there are still two more friends I haven't heard from but I'll bet they are receiving deliveries as well. That'll be two more states."

"We have to put a stop to this."

"I know nothing more than what I've told you. But I could tell you about the dream I had earlier this week. It told me how I can know when people are sick and have a need. It's a halo of fire. That came to me after I blew up my grill and the lid hit me in the head. Right here."

"I'll pass on that. Thanks just the same. I'm calling the home office on this. We need intra-state action here. It's hard to believe that all this lawlessness began with a simple purchase of a can of coffee somewhere in Minnesota, of all places. Who is responsible? Who planned all this?"

"Have you heard of Gitchi-Manitou?"

"I won't take any more of your time, Mr. Ellison. Thank you for meeting with me today. I want you to know that in my report I'll be filing with Washington, you will not be the target. The target will be whoever is providing you with the coffee, and I can assure you we will be conducting an in-depth investigation to find these people. In case I have further need of you, may I please get your phone number? You may get an invitation to appear before a sub-committee in Washington to tell your story and take a few questions." Ms. Diddle slid a piece of paper and pen across the table. "You can write your number down there."

"You mean I could get an all expense paid trip to Washington to talk about free coffee? That'd be nice. Let's see, a day to fly out there, two-three days of testimony and questions and then another day to fly home, that's a week. Tax dollars pay for all that, air fair, hotel, meals? I can get in a round of golf too one afternoon, maybe more. I've never played in Washington. Greens Fees there probably run another four hundred. What's the name of the Country Club the FDA Director is a member of? The FDA would spring for that too, wouldn't they?"

"I'm sensing some sarcasm in your tone, Mr. Ellison."

"You should come to our men's group at church. You think I'm sarcastic. You should hear how some of *them* talk about the government, the democrats, the graft and corruption, and all the government people in bed with all the pharmaceutical companies."

"Thank you for your time, Mr. Ellison."

"Yes ma'am. Thank you."

* * * * * * * *

Moments later, Sandy Marsh slid into "A".

"Arvie," said Sandy, "Woodhull's going to let you go home. You'll still see the black sedan in your rear-view mirror for awhile. Oh, and by the way, I happened to hear your son laying Woodhull out. Man, oh man, did he do a helluva job. It was beautiful. I talked with him for quite awhile afterwards and, yes, we'll have another article in the Daily in the morning. Tell me about C.U. Diddle. How did that go?"

"Did you ask her when she left?"

"Yeah. She said you told her she was being paid by pharmaceutical companies. You had said, 'It's a government check to you but it's kickback money from the drug companies. Everybody knows that.' She's never been so offended in her life. And she said you had told her the founding fathers were throwing up all over themselves because of all the corruption. Sounds like you did good."

"I started getting a little upset. I was wondering why she was spending all this time with me about a few cans of coffee that don't amount to anything. She really got bent out of shape when I told her that three of us, in three separate states, have received coffee from these people and that there are two more of us in two more states that I expect to hear from soon. 'Well, that coffee is going over state lines,' she said, 'and we can't have that.' I thought she was going to pass out or have an aneurism or something. She assured me there will be an in-depth investigation. Oh, and she said I might even get a call about coming to Washington to appear before a sub-committee. I asked if I could get in a round of golf out there at taxpayer expense too." Arvie couldn't repress a good chuckle.

"Hah hahaaaaa. Good one. I may have to write an article about that but right now, I'm going to get out of your way so you can go home."

"Sandy, do you know how I get all my stuff back?"

"Sure. Down that hall and turn left. You'll see the window. Tomorrow at 4:00 is Baptism, right?"

"Yes."

"I'll be there."

* * * * * * * *

He walked in the door and she was waiting for him with a big hug.

"That must've been a perfectly awful night for you."

"It wasn't all that bad and I made a very good friend. I have to tell you all about it. Let me make a pot of coffee and we'll sit down and I'll fill you in. His name is Henry. Henry Brannon, and he is the most unique man I've ever met. But, its time I got a good cup of coffee. Do you know how bad the coffee is in jail? Their priorities down there are sure screwed up. I'm going to have to start delivering there. Perhaps it will heal their intelligence illnesses? Hah."

They talked for hours. Hannah made some sandwiches and heated some soup. He told her about Henry, how he was harvesting souls for Jesus by helping people; fixing, cleaning, building, how he'd done this his entire life because his daddy had done it *his* entire life. His wife, Mary, washes clothes for people and cleans apartments. They get paid in cash – when they get paid. There is no Social Security coming in. Their trust is in the Lord because He provides. 'Always has and always will,' say's Henry. They talked about what a faith like that must feel like; to believe without a doubt that God will take care of their every need. How does a person develop that kind of faith and trust? How long must it take? What a wonderful life that would be. Not many personal possessions to have to take care of; no car, no phone, no tv. Henry had said, W*ho needs*

218

that stuff. None of it brings love, or that unmatched peace and joy that only He provides. You will meet Henry one day. I hope one day soon I'll meet Mary and maybe we can have them out for dinner some evening and just sit at the table and talk and drink coffee. That would be a wonderful evening." They agreed to do that as soon as possible.

He told her about the variety of people he'd met. He replayed his conversation with C.U. Diddle of the FDA and they enjoyed a good laugh about people in general and wished everyone could enjoy all the differences in individuals.

He told her about bumping into Sandy Marsh again and mentioned how Brooks had jumped all over Agent Woodhull about the stupidity of this whole circus. "Our family spent so much time in the Quad Cities and his IT people can't find a trace of us ever being there, but they can sure find me in South America, a place that I have never been." They laughed again.

It was a wonderful time. Hannah let him know how supportive the kids had been. She said she felt very fortunate. Before heading upstairs, he glanced out the window, just to insure they were still there. He decided that he'd take them coffee in the morning.

Chapter 13

"When you wake up, get up. Wash the sleep out of your eyes, put some clothes on and get to work. This is the day the Lord has made. Let us rejoice and get to work. Heh heh." - *Ole*

"Don't always think about what you will eat or what you will drink, and don't keep worrying. All the people in the world are trying to get these things, and your Father knows you need them. But seek God's kingdom first, and all the other things you need will be given to you."
Luke 12: 29-30

The day dawned a vivid orange. It was a brilliant start to the day of Baptism. He stopped on the patio to tie up the old white sneakers. He was wearing his favorite old golf shorts and his favorite old brown t-shirt from the Apostle islands and his favorite old brown Titliest golf cap. Shoes tied, he was off for a neighborhood walk. He couldn't help but think how much better this was as opposed to being in jail. And that thought put a smile on his face and a spring in his step. As he stepped off the patio he turned quickly and returned to the kitchen where he poured two big mugs of coffee. He closed the patio door with his foot and headed towards the black sedan parked down and across the street.

It was Settles and an agent he had not seen before. At his approach, the window was rolled down and he extended a jolly 'Good Morning' to them and handed the coffee through the window. Settles expressed his appreciation. The other agent didn't know what to do. After all, this man with the coffee was his mark, his target, his prey. And here he was, just outside the car handing him a cup of coffee. 'This duty is better than I thought' he thought.

Arvie said to them, "Enjoy the coffee and should your two-gallon jug on the floor in the back fill up, you are more than welcome to use our bathroom. Please, I am serious here."

Settles said, "Thank you, but we couldn't. It's against the rules."

"O come on now. Who was it that made up those rules anyway? How many stake-outs did they sit through? The offer stands, gentlemen, and who's going to know anyway?"

He took off down the street thinking that he began the day nicely. It hadn't been easy this morning. He had stood in front of the mirror for far too long. He stared at himself and it was not difficult to see why the most gorgeous girls in school always seemed to be at the dance with someone else. But back in the day, he had a wonderful, fun, and very outgoing personality. And it had saved him from a lifetime of being alone with no one but Numnum for companionship. Hannah and he had hit it off almost immediately during that year at Mt. Holy Waters. What a wonderful year that was. That's why finding the right one is so very special. And from that time forward, he had floated on a cloud because of her. Well, he thought, let's not get carried away here, but all things considered, he had been very lucky. He might have ended up with Gladys Munchumer. With that thought he let loose a happy guffaw. He then looked all around wondering if anyone had heard that.

It had been exactly one week to the day, that he had begun his list of ways to pour coffee. It wasn't until two or three days after that walk that he remembered that Brenda, as a nurse, worked in a hospital and, *duh, aren't there a lot of people there who could use a little healing?* That one and the senior Bible study on Wednesday mornings at church had moved to the top of the list. *That's enough,* he thought. Now if he got the call from the witch that his background check failed because they had learned about all those years in South America, well, he'd add back one of the others on the list. *I'm not going to fight the South America thing again. One time around with Woodhull was enough.*

A lot had happened since the previous Saturday. The guys in the ugly black sedan weren't around back then. Henryk. *What do you suppose has happened to Henryk? Can't believe I spent all that time in jail and never asked about him. I need to find out.*

He told himself to enjoy the walk. There was a time not too long ago as he sat on that bench with the boys in the cell, when the thought flashed through his mind that he may never again see the sky and the stars and the sun. *Here I am, out in nature again. Enjoy.*

He realized that he was concerned about the Baptism that evening. He had seen Baptisms on that stage before and it was always beautiful. *So, stop the worry. Bren is a part of the Baptism team and she'll be there and she'll take care of us. That's the right approach. Prepare to enjoy.*

What a morning. God is so good. He created all this for me to enjoy. Sniff the air. Watch the birds. The color of the leaves. Slow down. Take it in.

* * * * * * * *

Arvie came out his front door, with two "to-go" cups of coffee. He handed them to Brooks through the Prius window saying, "Hey. I sure appreciate this."

"No sweat. I got started on the yard work bright and early. Already worked up two good sweats and one super shower. I'm ready for a roady. You got the address?"

"Yeah. Right here. Hang on, got to grab one more thing."

"No sweat," Brooks said, enjoying a swig of Northern Minnesota brew. Arvie returned and buckled into the passenger seat.

"Is this Minneapolis?"

"Think so."

"I've been up here for 30 years now and I don't have a clue where this is. Ok, I've got it programmed in. Let's go find out. You got a tin of Forever?"

"Yup. Two cans – one for Henry and Mary and one for the testing. And some sammie's your mom insisted we bring."

"Good. Love her sammie's. Gonna be cool to see the results of the coffee analysis."

"Henry said he knows a guy named Bob who knows a guy named John who's got a son named Earl who works over at 3M. Earl does this kinda thing all the time. I'm still not sure I want to find out what's in it. There is something very comforting not knowing but hoping it's filled with miracles. What if we find out that it's nothing but a bunch of ground up oak leaves and some rabbit doo-doo?"

"How could leaves and rabbit doo-doo taste like coffee? Forever tastes like coffee. Do you suppose Native Americans can take elements produced by mother earth – excluding coffee beans, and end up with something that tastes like coffee?"

"I don't know. What do you think?"

"Beats me. But as far as the hope thing, can't you still have the hope if you find out its oak leaves and some kind of doo-doo?"

"Yes, you can" Arvie murmured.

"And I've been thinking about your friend Henry" continued Brooks. "He sounds like someone very special."

"Yeah he is. I hope you'll get a chance to meet him today. He spends a lot of time helping his neighbors with one thing or another so he may be out. Anyway, he says one or the other of them is always home so if we miss him, we'll both get to meet Mary. If she is anything like him, she'll be special too."

"GPS says we'll be there in 22 minutes."

* * * * * * * *

"Dad, this is a very dreary part of town."

"I'll say. Must be that building right there – 2nd from the corner."

"Think the car will be ok here?"

"Hah. Your guess is as good as mine. At least it's the middle of the day. Maybe that helps. And we'll pray for it. We've got to go up to 204."

"Steps are a little rickety."

"Yeah. Here it is."

(Knock, Knock)

--- --- ---

(Knock, Knock)

"Who is it?"

"Mary, my name is Arvie. I met Henry night before last."

"Just a moment. ... ... Well, Hi Arvie. I'm Mary. Henry told me all about you."

"Hi Mary. It is very nice to meet you. This is my son Brooks."

"Nice to meet you, Mrs. Brannon."

"Hi Brooks. Please call me Mary. So nice to meet you. Won't you please come in."

"Thank you, but just for a moment. We must be on our way. Here is the magic coffee, Mary. Henry said he could get it analyzed."

"Yes. He told me you would be by. He's over at Mrs. Mitchell's putting another bolt on her front door. She's got at least six by now."

"Oh my. Now Mary, I want you to feel comfortable keeping that second can for you and Henry. I would suggest both of you drink at least two or three cups first thing every morning. Henry told me you read the article in the paper the other day, so you know how I feel about this stuff. Matter of fact, you might want to make a pot right now."

"That sounds like a wonderful idea. Oh, and Henry said that he would have the results by the end of the day on Monday."

"Really? That soon?"

"Yes. So shall we plan on you stopping by early Monday evening, 6:00 or so?"

"Yes. Let's plan on that."

"We'll make another pot of coffee then."

"I'll look forward to that."

"Is it today you're getting baptized?"

"Yes. This afternoon at 4:00. Henry told you, huh?"

"He did. And he said how pleased he thought Jesus was going to be about that."

"I'm beginning to get a little nervous, you know? What do I do, how do I do it and when?"

"They'll lead you through it. My daddy used to say to people – 'you just come, I'll do the rest.' He was a preacher long time ago."

"I didn't know that."

"Yes he was. And your wife will be baptized with you?"

"Yes. We want to do this as a 'together' thing."

"Praise God. So next time I see you, you'll have been 'washed by the water'."

"Yes, indeed. Thank you so much, Mary. Say 'hi' to Henry. I'll see you Monday evening around six."

"It was so nice to meet both of you. God bless you."

* * * * * * * *

"Your car appears to be untouched."

"Thanks for that, although I must admit I'm surprised."

"What did you think of Mary?"

"Sure is a little thing but appears to be a very special lady. I had this feeling when we first saw her that she's sick. Did you feel that at all?"

"I'm going to tell you something I have not told your mother. I can tell when people are sick."

"What? How?"

"I can see a halo of fire around their head."

"You mean you can actually see fire burning around her head?"

"Yes. I did."

"When did all this happen?"

"Well it began with a dream. I … … …"

* * * * * * * *

"I can't believe that."

"Neither can I. But ever since that dream, I see the halos. That's not quite right – I had to get hit in the head with a grill lid to make it work. And you were there when I blew up the grill. It happened just like the dream: Boom. Pain. Blood. Apparently, the dream was telling me what was going to happen and it did. Ever since then I've seen the halos."

"Unbelievable. I've got to stop for gas. There's a Quik Stop at the next exit."

"Sure. You need anything from inside? I'm going in for gum for Hannah."

"No. I'm good."

* * * * * * * *

"That looks like a lot of gum."

"More'n gum. Here. Take a look."

"You got four black cans in here."

"Yes. And the name on the cans is ….?"

"Mercy. Where'd you find these in there?"

"I didn't. It found me. I got the gum and I'm at the counter ready to pay. The guy behind the counter is a Native American. He looks me up one side and down the other, takes the money for the gum, makes the change and then says, 'wait just one minute.' He goes under the counter and I can hear him fishing around for something, and then out comes the sack. I asked him where he got this and he said, 'They told me you would come today.' That's the same line I get every time this happens. And here's the question Brooks, how would anyone have known that I was going to be at this Quik Stop on this day, at this time? Huh? How would anyone have known? But, no. I am not surprised any more. And if you walk in there right now, I promise you that you will not see any Native American, and if you ask anyone in there if a Native American works there, you will get a negative response. So I am led to believe that I'm the only one who can see these people – they are invisible to all others. But they can make change and hand me a sack of coffee when they aren't really there. Are you starting to get the picture now?"

"Hold on – I gotta go see. How could I not after listening to that?" With that, Brooks sprang outta the car and dashed into the store. Meanwhile, Arvie made a mental note of the date and time and the fact that this was a Fast Stop on 32nd at Eastman so when Ms. Diddle did a follow-up, he'd have some information for her.

Brooks returned to the car with a side-ways smirk. He giggled, shook his head and said, "My God. This is really happening. And no, I did not see a Native American behind the counter. To be honest with you, Dad, I couldn't imagine that this magic coffee thing was really happening."

"So, you thought I'd gone a little nutso?"

"Well, yeah, I guess so. I'm sorry for that."

"Don't be. I've had the very same feelings. Every time I'm talking with someone about this I get the same feelings."

Digging out a can, Arvie proclaimed to Brooks "We now have four cans of Mercy."

"Have you received Mercy before?"

"Well, yes. But never in the form of coffee. And then, there is this." He held up a newspaper. "Page one. Again, just below the fold."

****

Coffee Man
Jailed

By: Sandy Marsh

MINNEAPOLIS – Much has happened in the two days since our first story about The Coffee Man, "Samuel," appeared in the Daily. That story appeared on Thursday, the same day that Samuel was hauled into the police station and held overnight because authorities in Lima, Peru had electronically sent a picture of the man who escaped from their custody some 35 years ago. A warrant for his arrest has remained in force for these many years.

There are usually, at least, two sides to every story and this story is a perfect example. The Law says the picture is of Samuel years ago. Back then, they say he was instrumental in the formation of the system, which remains to this day, of moving illegal drugs into the United States. On one of the hottest drug corners in our city last weekend, Samuel was seen drinking coffee and conversing with a person who also is under suspicion of playing an integral part in the same illegal activity.

Authorities say that their conversation was, "like two old friends who hadn't seen each other in years, laughing and having the best of times while sipping coffee."

Samuel says, "Yes, the picture is of me. I have told authorities when the picture was taken, where it was taken, and the purpose for which it was taken. Simply put, I was trying to get a job and the picture was to be part of my resume. Yes, I was talking to that man on that corner and we were drinking coffee that I had brought to the corner specifically for him. I have seen him there frequently

227

over the course of the past two years, in all kinds of weather, attempting to obtain money from passing motorists to get home for his mother's funeral. I simply thought I'd like for him to have good cup of coffee and one which will make him feel better, both mentally and physically and perhaps give him renewed hope.

"I have never been in South America. I have never been outside the United States. I have never had a passport and I am quite sure Government records will verify that fact. I have spent most of my life in the Quad Cities area, except for college and two years in the military. Both of our children were born there and went through school there. We were members of a church there. There are many ways in which to verify our residency in that area. How a picture of me taken in a state park there, for the purposes of my resume, got into the hands of the law in Lima, Peru, borders on the impossible."

Samuel spent one night in jail. The next morning, he endured an interview with the Food and Drug Administration because the coffee he carries with him is not "approved" by the FDA. If you read the first article, you'll remember that last week he had just returned from four days up north in a cabin with three of his old college friends. It was on his trip north that he stumbled into a new coffee in a convenience store and bought two large cans for the cabin stay. After drinking the coffee, the friends discovered they had all been healed of something; acid reflux, psoriasis and assorted other health issues.

Samuel felt that he had been called on a mission to take this healing coffee to as many people as he could reach. He said, "For us seniors, hope is something we have too little of." Samuel began his mission with a trip to this man he'd seen many times and in all kinds of weather, sitting on a street corner. Unfortunately, and unknown to Samuel, that was the "hot drug corner." He has also provided his coffee to a very large senior Bible study. He is doing his best to fulfill his mission.

An interview with Samuel's son provided this reporter with further insight regarding the family's home in the Quad Cities. "I fail to understand why it is so difficult to find records to validate where we lived for so many years," he stated. "My sister and I were born there. We went all the way through High School there. My Dad coached Little League Baseball for many years. He put in 35 years on the line at Farmall.

"One of two things must have happened: 1) The DEA, an arm of our Federal Government reeks of incompetency in gathering its intelligence and this is a case of stolen identity; or 2) The Government is involved in subversive activity and seeks to involve my father in something illegal while protecting someone else. Someone has an agenda and it involves convicting my Dad, an honest citizen of this country for 75 years, of something he has not done. He has never failed to pay his taxes. He has never violated any law. He has always done the right thing. He has always cared for his neighbor. I wonder how many times, every day, this type of government agency incompetence is occurring somewhere across our country? Why does this happen to good people? How can liberty and freedom be there one moment and taken away the next? This injustice is happening to good people. Is someone in a Washington office suggesting, 'Let's find someone out there to make the scapegoat for whatever the current problem might be? Let's indescriminately pin this mess on someone. So crank up the data base of honest citizens of the United States and pick one.' How else does something like this happen? What will it take to prove where our family lived for so long? Give me the job. I can sit down right here in this office at that computer over there and prove it. This whole thing is a farce and utterly ridiculous."

The intense "Saga of the Coffee Man" and his efforts to bring hope to the masses continues. In our city of so many people, this is but one story of a person just being a person, doing what people do. The world surrounding this person is unpredictable at best. No one knows what the outcome will be.

With all the uncertainty surrounding The Coffee Man, one important question remains: If they put him in jail and throw away the key, who will pour the coffee?

Stay tuned.

* * * * * * *

Brooks looked up from the paper. "Did I really say those things? I guess I must have. He had a tape recorder and everything, and he did tell me he needed the tape so that he could quote me correctly. Wow. I guess I was a little hot. Huh?"

"I guess so. I'm proud of you. You didn't pull any punches. You slugged away. Maybe you'll get a job outa that."

"Hah. Wouldn't that be something after what I said and the volume with which I said it. Seriously though, if this is some grand conspiracy, how did your name come up? I don't get it. Why not pick someone without family ties and a traceable history? It makes no sense."

* * * * * * *

"Thanks for driving and we'll see you at the 4:00 service," Arvie said, as he unbuckled his seat belt. Brooks responded, "You bet.

We'll be there." Arvie reached into the backseat and scooped up the paper sack with the four cans of Mercy, leaving one on the back seat. "I'm leaving you with a can of Mercy. Drink ye all of it."

"Rest assured, we will do just that" Brooks answered. "And thanks."

Once inside, Arvie found a very nervous and stressed out Hannah. She greeted him with "Arvie we have to be at church at 3:15. That means we have to leave here a few minutes before 3:00. We are running out of time. I don't think I can be ready."

"Now my dear, don't you worry. We have plenty of time. Did you have your breakfast?"

"Yes, I did."

"Good. Why don't we sit down and have our daily devotions right now? Then I can fix us a bite of something while you begin getting ready. It's all going to work out just fine. I keep thinking about how good we will feel inside when the service is over. Don't you think that will be a good feeling?"

"I know it will be. Ok, I like your plan."

They sat down at the dining room table. He read from <u>Jesus Calling</u> which they then briefly discussed. There were four Bible verses to look up. They both prayed, Hannah especially for help this afternoon at the baptism. The afternoon went well and at 2:55, they pulled out of the driveway. The black sedan pulled into the light Saturday afternoon traffic right behind them.

* * * * * * * *

At 3:15, Pastor Naylon met with all who were to be baptized in the front seats of the auditorium. The plan was discussed and everyone seemed comfortable, even Hannah. They were told that 72 had pre-registered and the expectation was that an additional 20 or so would make a spur-of-the-moment decision. In all, across the six campuses, a minimum of 940 would be Baptized this weekend at services today and tomorrow. Hannah and Arvie, like the others sitting at the front of the church at this moment, were prepared. All had packed a bag with what they needed. Those who did not come prepared would be taken care of as well. The church had packs filled with all the necessities to ensure that those who were not pre-registered would still be able to show their obedience by being baptized and being as comfortable as possible through the entire process. Pastor Naylon encouraged all to go immediately to the changing rooms and then return to this area of the sanctuary. During the service, they would be advised when to go backstage.

They rose and headed to the changing rooms. Arvie reassured Hannah every time they saw another baptism volunteer. "There are so many all around that if we have any questions, they will all help us. Don't forget that Bren is here as well. She'll be looking out for us." They moved to the hallway and as soon as they made the turn they saw her. She came to them with a big hug for each, her usual smile, and words of reassurance. They moved to the changing rooms confidently.

The service began. The music was exceptional. Pastor John's words were all about baptism, the meaning of it, the obedience. Beautiful passages from Matthew and Mark supported the decisions of all whose hearts were beating faster as the moment neared.

"All those who stand before others and say they believe in me, I will say before my Father in Heaven that they belong to me. But all who stand beforeothers and say they do not believe in me, I will say before my Father in Heaven that they do not belong to me." Matthew 10:32-33

"Anyone who believes and is baptized will be saved, but anyone who does not believe will be punished. Mark 16:16

The entire family had entered the conversation about whether baptism was necessary. It was made perfectly clear by Dove Creek that baptism was not necessary to enter the Kingdom of Heaven. Believing that Jesus is Savior *is* necessary. Both Arvie and Hannah had been baptized as infants. At that time, and in those churches, it was called baptism. In many current churches, baptism of infants was viewed to be more important for parents who were dedicating themselves to bringing up the child right and proper, taking responsibility for giving the child a foundation which would lead, one day, to that child making their own decision to be a follower of Jesus.

Both Hannah and Arvie liked the passage from Matthew 10. Tears welled up in their eyes when they thought of Jesus going before the Almighty and telling Him that, "These two are mine." Arvie shuddered as that verse was read. He couldn't stop the tears. "Amazing," he thought. Years ago, all wrapped up in his job, he hadn't a clue about crying. He was too busy with, "such important things back then."

And then the words, "Those who will be baptized can make their way backstage now." They rose as one and moved backstage. Then the sorting began. Singles would go first, followed by groups of two and three and then the full families or largest groups would be last. The line was formed. Bren was directing traffic. They would be the first couple. And then it was time, all was in order and the line began to move. They waited their turn watching those who preceded them. There were cheers from among the 2000 gathered to support their loved ones. There were cheers when they entered the pool, and even bigger cheers when they came up from the water. It was moving and emotional. Arvie felt the emotion building and then it was their turn. He would go first into the pool and Hannah would follow. It was up and over and then down into the warm water. He waited for her to join him, assisting her down the last steps. They moved arm in arm to Pastor John. He questioned them briefly. Arvie answered the questions in the affirmative. After joining arms, it was a quick backward drop under the water, a pause, and then they were brought back up. Assistant Pastor Brian was on Hannah's side, trained in matters such as this and he and Pastor John had no difficulty baptizing them. They talked later about how silent it all was as they came up from under the water. They had shared an immediate hug and kiss. Both Bren and Brooks told them later of the cheers that rocked the auditorium when they emerged from under the water. It seems that an elderly couple being baptized evokes the strongest support. There were many hugs, handshakes and tears exchanged with fellow baptizee's on the way back to the changing rooms.

The evening was completed at home with a delightful, tasty pizza. They sat at the dining room table long after, talking about the evening's experience. They discussed once again why they had felt the necessity to be baptized as adults. In watching the baptisms recently, both in the sanctuary and at the lake, they became convinced that they, as adults, needed to make the decision. Their parents had made the decision to baptize them as infants. Baptism is an act of obedience to let others know you believe in Him. To please Jesus and have him as the intermediary on our behalf is beautiful and means everything. Hannah said, "I'm so sorry that I was hesitant. Thank you for being patient with me. I'm so happy we did that together."

"I want you to know that I wouldn't have done it unless you were there with me."

"I know."

"There are many sick people in our church. I saw it tonight."

"You saw what?"

"Halo's of fire. After we had been baptized but before we left the pool, I happened to look out at the audience. You know how dark the sanctuary is kept during baptism. Well, the halos were everywhere. Hundreds and Hundreds. There is so much to do."

"I'm sorry. You know when people are sick?"

Arvie explained.

Chapter 14

"The grass grows on the weekend. The snow falls on the weekend.
The boilers get dirty on the weekend. On this job,
we don't take weekends off. Plan to be here bright and early
with a smile on your face. Heh heh."
- Ole

*"Then the Lord said to Moses; Make the Sabbath a holy day.
If anyone treats the Sabbath like any other day, that person must be
put to death; anyone who works on the Sabbath day must be cut off
from his people. There are six days for working, but the 7th
is a day of rest and is Holy to the Lord."*
Exodus 31:14

"What a beautiful, great, glorious and wonderful day this will be.
It's the weekend of the British Open. Golf all day beginning
bright and early and continuing almost until dinner.
Links golf – all day. Well, not quite all day. The Open
Championship starts early and ends early.
Hannah is excited because immediately following that Major
Championship, the LPGA tour takes over the flat screen until
bedtime. How does it get any better than that?"
- *Arvid Ellison*

Roles were reversed that day. As usual, he needed no alarm to begin the day. There was a difference that morning, however. Hannah was already on the couch with her clip board and pen poised to take copious notes to be discussed at great length throughout the course of the day. She had been watching it all since it began on Thursday morning. Arvie had seen it off and on, but, of course, jail time interfered. As he got to the bottom of the stairs, she gave him a brief wave, but her eyes could not be diverted from the action.

Arvie poured a cup and as he wandered past the patio doors, he paused, looked down the street to the west to ensure the presence of the black sedan. *How do those guys do it? All night in a car.* He took great pride in the fact that the law would spend the money to keep two special agents outside his door to ensure that he wouldn't escape.

Little do they know that I have been tunneling out from my basement to a creek bed, 200-feet to the north, bringing out the excess dirt in my pockets to spread it lightly across the lawn, undetected. They watch every day, and yet my covert activity appears to be so normal and acceptable, they do not suspect. He relished the fact that his advanced age didn't effect his ability to remain on the, "10 Most Wanted Yet Unable to Apprehend Because They're So Elusive List." *And they think they're gonna get me for this drug thing in South America. Hah. I've covered all the loose ends down there. I've killed all of them, those who might rat me out. There's been a river of blood, but I am safe now. They would never suspect Hannah of, somewhere north of, 30 murders in the jungles of the drug empires. Cold-blooded, she is. Ruthless. Providing the perfect cover for her is the diagnosis of anxiety, for which we basically bribed an Internist. That Internist will soon be eliminated. Hannah will go out through the tunnel, retrieve the silenced black Harley from the self-storage unit behind the strip mall, ride into town and eliminate our final burdens. And then-von Barstow. That should be the last, but in this business, we just never know. Hannah willl probably do 'em both tomorrow night. The cops can't find von Barstow, but the, "Black Widow," can. The picture from Lima, that she had inserted into his electronic file, had been a stroke of genius. Sandy, the reporter, was so easily coerced into writing that human-interest crap in the Daily. The public outcry has already been heard, "Free the old guy. He only wants to heal us – to bring us hope. He and his cohort in crime live as peaceful, law-abiding citizens in Minnesota dealing only in providing magic coffee to those in need. They've given him the vision of fire halos to enable him to not waste the magic stuff on those who don't need it."*

Yes, he was a master of the 'covert.' His tunnel, complete now. They'd not know until it was too late. How easily he'd sucked them in with his story about the old Native American and magic coffee. They even bought the line about selling it to him, but he had been dead for 50 years.

Genius. They think I'm nuts. The perfect cover. This 'hope,' thing, is so perfect. Everybody wants it and they'll believe it all because they want it so bad.

Yes, he was the master of delusion. He had learned over the years that the simplest BS works the best. His disguise was flawless: striped shirt, plaid bermuda shorts, white Keds with calf-high sweat socks; bald, skinny and weak (appearing). They believed him to be utterly helpless. *Hah.*

He sipped his coffee thinking that he'd read too many mysteries and watched too many movies. There was a roar from the gallery and a gasp from Hannah. He marched to the couch to begin his day.

Chapter 15

"When you get as old as me, you know death has been taken
care of. So, get back to work and stop talkin about it. You guys
waste more time analyzing insignificant stuff. That's the problem
with you college kids – you start thinkin you're smart and you got to
analyze everything. Stop with the analyzin. Just work. It's the sure
way to Heaven. Heh heh."   - *Ole*

*"When people sin, they earn what sin pays – death. But God gives us
a free gift – life forever in Christ Jesus our Lord."* Romans 6:23

Arvie poured himself a cup of Mercy, the newest coffee, received
the previous Saturday. He wonders again if the coffee was all the
same, no matter the name on the can. It tasted the same. If it was,
why would "They" waste time and money changing the name on the
can? *'Tis the same old mystery*. He decided he must be getting old
because he kept rehashing the same stuff. He had been preaching
acceptance to Hannah for such a long time, but it seemed his
preaching wasn't helping himself. It had gotten worse since he met
Jacob.

He stopped to look at the calendar and noticed it would be a
hectic day. Two appointments for Hannah; one with the Psychologist
and then other with the pool; water therapy, to be exact. Both
appointments required a lengthy drive so the boys in the black sedan
would have to be on their toes. They would start from home (30
miles north of St. Paul) and head to the south side of Minneapolis.
From there, they would head east to Stillwater which was east of St.
Paul, and then back home. *One giant circle.*

Arvie grabbed a pen and wrote, "Henry, 6pm" on the calendar.
He was anxious to find out the results of the analysis. *What if an
unknown substance is found? An element never before identified?
Wouldn't that intensify the intrigue?*

Through the front door he noticed Juan sitting on the front porch
in his bathrobe, sipping a cup of coffee. Out the door he went. They

talked for a half hour or so. Juan refilled both cups along the way. Juan said he was doing fine and how blessed he was; as if nothing had happened. They talked about the goodness of the Lord, coffee, and the British Open. Juan tied the three together nicely when he said, "I think God arranged this stroke thing for me because I have never had time to watch very much of it. But since I got home Friday morning, I haven't missed a shot. And it ties in so well with drinking coffee. Thanks, by the way."

"You bet. So, you saw Crawford's putt on 17?" Arvie asked.

Juan threw back his head. "Could you believe that? I had told Gabby that he'd be lucky to three-putt. How many breaks were there in that thing? Four? Five?"

"At least that many and those subtle little mounds? When that one went in, Hannah nearly broke a nail jumping off the couch. I love watching that tournament."

"Me too. So, big plans for today? It's another beautiful day."

"Yes, it is. Hannah's got some appointments today so we'll be heading out after breakfast. Won't get home till late afternoon. I am so happy for you. Glad you are doing so well. I'd better get back over there."

"Thanks for coming over. See you later."

* * * * * * * *

It was a 45-minute freeway drive to the south side of Minneapolis. The appointment was 45 minutes long and while Hannah talked with her counselor, Arvie would usually be consumed with reading his book - which wasn't very good. "Once you've read one story about covert ops within the government, you've read them all. When I write mine, the intrigue will be thick." He thought about the box under his desk; so many notes in there, reminders he'd been setting aside. *Maybe it's time for me to write it? Maybe I'd better wait till Woodhull is finished with me. Maybe I'd better hide that box. What if Woodhull comes to the house with a search warrant? I'm getting old. I'm getting complacent. There's that place in the tunnel. Perfect. I'll take care of that when we get home. I'm 478 pages into this book in my mind. Guess I'd better actually write it.*

Hannah woke him up when she came out to the waiting room. It was another 45 minutes across town heading east to Stillwater. The next appointment would take an hour and a half, including pool and shower time. They grabbed a bite on the way to the pool, hit the meat market for a few items and he picked up a few things at Walmart while Hannah was in the pool. Once therapy was complete, it was time for the sweet, 35- minute, drive home.

He wanted to get home. He had to get the box out of the house. The more he thought about it, the more paranoid he became that Woodhull would be waiting on the front porch when they arrived. *Maybe he's there now or they've broken in. After all, they've got the warrant. Stop it.*

Hannah was very interested in the upcoming appointment with Henry and getting the results of the coffee analysis. Her take on it was quite simple and very similar to his: The Native Americans don't grow coffee in northern Minnesota so there will be no coffee in it. It will be all natural and the flavor then comes from how much of each ingredient is blended in.

"You might be right with that. But I'm holding out hope for some ingredient that they can't identify. Wouldn't that be fun?"

"That would be interesting. Then we could all continue to believe that there was magic in the coffee, at least as long as we could point to some improving health concern within somebody somewhere. But wouldn't that make it illegal to give it out? Wouldn't that complicate everything with the DEA, the FDA, the POOPA, or quite possibly the WHIZY? I'm gonna hope it's all defined. We can still choose to believe in the magic," Hannah said.

"I keep waiting for the acid reflux to reappear. It's hard to believe that it's gone. Well, people sure believe me when I tell 'em that. And you know that lower back thing that I had going on? I've not had one twinge since that first cup."

"Isn't that wonderful. And I'm feeling so much stronger. I'll tell you, with the anxiety and the problem I had physically - the bursitis or whatever it was - I thought I was coming to the end of my rope. Now it seems that the water therapy has taken care of the hip – though maybe it was really the coffee, and I'm not having those emotional outbursts either. Maybe I'm coming to the end of this two-year roller-coaster. And could it be at least partially related to the coffee? I believe it could."

"That would be nice. Jacob Whitefeather would be thanking you for the complement."

"Jacob. Thank you so much."

"Hah. What a ride this has been. It's been two weeks now since it all began: having my first cup, Jacob and the magic coffee, the Hearty Boys all getting something cured, 'They will know when you need more and they will get it to you,' jail time, von Barstow and the drug issue, a picture of me taken in the QC's but filed away by the law in Peru, Juan's stroke, blowing up the grill and visions of halos. Yowza. Did I forget anything?"

"How 'bout newspaper articles and black sedans following us around and parked out front all night? That is a lot to pack into a couple of weeks," Hannah said.

"And I thought retirement was going to be boring. I'm sure we've forgetting some other stuff that could be added to that list…. like meeting Henry. I still can't believe him. I think we could learn a lot from him; from them."

"Let's do that dinner thing soon. I think it would be interesting to just sit around the table and listen to them talk."

"We've never known anyone like them, ever. They are the first people I've met who are totally unconnected with society and all the things of this world. They're connected to their own little society, those people in their neighborhood that they help. But think about it. No car. They don't go anywhere. They don't go to a movie. They don't drive to the store. They have no need to go shopping. They walk everywhere. He has to walk a mile roundtrip, I'll bet, to get to a hardware store to buy the necessities for his tool box now and then. How many vacations have we taken over the years? They've taken none. How much money have we socked away for retirement? Well, not enough, but they have socked away nothing. They don't even have a telephone or a tv. They live to help people. Can you believe people like that exist?"

"That's why I say I think we could learn a lot from them. Faith. Faith that you will eat another meal while not knowing how you'll get it or where it will come from. Trust. A trust that is so complete in the Heavenly Father that He will meet all your needs. I think we both want that. I think that's what we play at but just haven't taken the next step. It's been their mission to help people, just like Mother Teresa. Do you think the thousands that attend Dove Creek would be inspired by hearing their life's story?"

"Wow. Wouldn't *that* be something. I can see Pastor Wylie talking with Henry on camera, somewhere down in his neighborhood. I can't imagine what the reaction would be? Do you remember when he told the story about the mother whose young daughter was brutally murdered? The killer was found and convicted and put away and the mother realized that she needed to forgive him. She went to the prison and met with him. I don't remember now how many times she visited him, or for how many years it went on – 30 maybe? And then he brought the two of them out on the stage and they sat on stools and he interviewed them. I think we both sat there and cried as we tried to accept that level of forgiveness."

"I remember. That was so powerful. Maybe there will come a time when we'll have an opportunity to tell them about Henry and Mary. I wonder if Henry and Mary would even consider doing such a thing? What do you think?"

"I don't know if we know them well enough to even guess at an answer to that. I talked with him for several hours that night and Brooks and I met Mary only briefly. Perhaps their humbleness would not permit them to do something so public. Perhaps they wouldn't understand why they'd be asked since they are doing what God asks us all to do – help the poor, love all people, do unto others. Of course, it would be up to them, but I think it's something the church would very much want to do since they focus on those topics so frequently. They are inspiring. Let's just try to move forward with the idea to have them out for dinner."

"You could mention that to them tonight just to see if they'd like to do that. What time are you leaving?"

"5:30 or there abouts."

"When we get home, we'll have just enough time to make a sandwich before you leave."

As they pulled into their court, Arvie watched the ugly black Ford sedan slide into its usual place along the curb. Owens and

Settles were faithful to their mission. *The box. I must remove the box. No. Stop the paranoia.*

* * * * * * * *

As he headed south on the freeway, he thought about the report Henry would hand over that night. There was a brief feeling of panic that rolled through his stomach and nervous system which brought about a mild shudder. But immediately after, he felt quite peaceful. *After all, what difference will it make – really? I'm pouring hope for people. They don't know it but I do. For those who wear a halo of fire, I will share my story. I will tell them about what happened to me and the boys up at the cabin. One person at a time.*

In the rear-view mirror, he watched the black sedan. They knew that he knew he was being followed. There was no attempt to pretend. When he changed lanes, so did they. In a way, there was a feeling of comfort and safety knowing they were there.

There wasn't much traffic headed toward the cities at that hour. He was thankful to not be dealing with the rush hour traffic going the opposite direction. He flicked on the radio for a little company. He'd lost interest in music these days, so up came the only station he ever listened to: News, 24/7. A plane was missing in the Andes, feared to have gone down in a heavy fog with 97 on board. He then heard an update on a local Minneapolis story about a shooting earlier that day at the Gloria G. Hadley Middle School. "Three students have been shot... 911 had been called at 2:30 this afternoon... The shooter is believed to be barricaded in the gymnasium, though authorities concede that it's possible he could have gotten out of the building... The suspect is a white male, 5'11, approximately 190 pounds and was last seen wearing desert fatigues... No reason for the violence is known at this time... Police remain on the scene... Updates as they are received... Stay tuned."

More tragedy, he thought. *What makes people want to do such a thing: shoot innocent kids? Lord have mercy on the victims.* He turned off the radio.

Moments later he exited the freeway listening to Bonny talk through the required turns. He passed in front of the police station.

So Bonny was bringing him in a little differently than Brooks' GPS on Saturday. One final turn and he immediately recognized the apartment building. He pulled to the curb, checked the mirror yet again and watched the agents pull to a stop perhaps 50 feet behind. Out of the car, he locked the doors and gave the boys a wave. He rapped lightly on the door of 204, the three numbers were slightly askew.

Mary called from behind the door, "Who is it?"

"Arvie Ellison, Mary."

The door opened and he was shocked by her appearance. At that hour of the day, she was still in her bathrobe. Her halo was the brightest he had witnessed yet.

"Hi Mary. How are you?"

"I'm doing well, Arvie. And you?"

"Doing fine as well."

"Henry is upstairs in 306. He's up there with the Overstreets fixing something and he wants you to come up there."

"Thanks Mary. Take care of yourself and I'll see you again real soon."

She shut the door. He paused, wondering just how ill she might be. He would ask Henry about that. He turned to the stairway and headed up. When he arrived on the 3rd floor, he moved quickly to 306.

He rapped lightly. The door opened and he was face to face with Henry. They shook hands and Henry brought him inside the apartment. He immediately introduced Arvie to Aurelius and Phoebe Overstreet. If Henry was 80, this elderly couple was approaching 90 or perhaps even on the other side. They exchanged greetings. Aurelius extended his hand. Arvie took it gently. He wondered if there were any bones in the hand at all, and knew without a doubt that there was no strength. He also noted that Aurelius was in a wheel chair and had no legs. Henry pointed at two rickety, old, wooden chairs sitting opposite the Overstreets and invited Arvie to take a seat. Arvie headed towards the furthest chair and sat down carefully. The chair creaked at him as if saying, "Be careful please or we'll both be flat on the floor." Henry was explaining something to the Overstreets about the tangled bunch of plumbing laid out on the floor.

"I'm going to take this downstairs to my place where I've got a vice and a work bench. I'm gonna try to straighten this out and hope we can save a few bucks. I will be back up here tomorrow and either put this back in or I'll have to head to the hardware store and get new. One way or the other, we'll have this fixed tomorrow." Henry took the other rickety wooden chair.

Looking again at the Overstreets he asked, "What did you think of that coffee I brought you this morning?"

"Oh, it was very good, Henry," exclaimed Phoebe.

"Well, Arvie here is the man who brought it to us. There is a little magic in it that makes us feel better and I suggest you use the rest of what I left with you every day. Arvie might be able to get us a little ... ... "

The front door burst open. Arvie glimpsed a rather young, burly man but Henry blocked his view. Henry was off his chair immediately, springing up and walking toward the man saying,

"Hey Marcus. Is that a new g ...?"

BOOM. ... BOOM.

Henry was immediately propelled backwards into Arvie's lap. They went over backwards as the chair broke into little pieces. Arvie was flat on his back on the floor on top of those chair pieces, his head hurt and Henry was lying on his back directly on top of Arvie. Arvie felt something wet seeping inside his clothing and stinging sensations all over his upper chest, neck and his face. He didn't know what happened. He heard and felt Henry exhale and relax. And then he heard a sound he hadn't heard in years. It was the same sound he heard when he helped Grandpa clean his old shotgun; it was the sound of it opening – just what you would do to clean or - *reload* it. The sudden realization of what had just happened began to dawn on him. He could not see the man for all the liquid filling his eyes and Henry laying on top of him. Had Henry been shot? *Have I been shot? My God. Henry's been shot.* That reality shook him to the core.

BOOM. ... BOOM.

Is he shooting at me? Has he even seen me?

Again, that sound of the shotgun being opened. A rustling sound. The sound of the shotgun closing.

BOOM. … … BOOM.

Oh my God. I am going to die.

Then through the red glaze which covered his eyes, he saw the face. The young man, the one he had seen in the jail cell that night, peering around Henry directly at him, and the most terrifying aspect to it all was that the young man was grinning at him as if to say, "I'm coming for you."

The sound of the shotgun being opened. The rustling sound. The closing sound. Again, the grinning face peering at him. He watched as both barrels pressed up against the underside of the young man's chin and, "BOOM."

That must have been the sound of both barrels at the same time, Arvie thought. Matter of some kind or another rained down upon him as if dropping from the ceiling. Arvie was shaking. He was trembling uncontrollably. And then peace descended and darkness came over him.

* * * * * * * *

"Owens. It's up here."

"My God. What the hell happened here? Call 911."

"Will do. Pretty obvious these three are gone. You might check those two stacked on top of each other."

"Yes. Multiple homicide. We've got five bodies. Just happened. Address is . . .

"Hey, Arvie. Mr. Ellison. Are you ok? I got a pulse. Owens – a pulse. Tell 'em to hurry."

"We got a pulse here. You want to repeat that address for me? … Good. Tell 'em to hurry. Ambulance should be here in three, maybe four. I'm gettin on the radio with Woody – tell him about this."

"Good. You want to stand outside the door while you talk and not let anyone in here."

"Yeah. You need gloves. You got some?"

"I'm good."

* * * * * * * *

"Just got off the phone with Woody. He's on his way. Ambulance just pulled up along with everybody else."

* * * * * * * *

"Is this Brooks Ellison?"

"Yes. Who's calling?"

"Mr. Ellison, I'm agent John Settles with the DEA. I saw you at the station on Friday."

"The police station?" He stood. "What is this?"

"Yeah. You were there to get your dad out."

"So … how'd you get my number?"

"From your dad's phone. There has been an incident. Your dad is doing ok, we think. He's being taken to St. Luke's. I wanted to let the family know."

"St. Luke's. Can you give me any more information?"

"That's all I know."

"Is he awake? Is he talking?"

"He's unconscious. That's all I know. The ambulance just left."

"Oh. Thanks." Brooks hung up.

* * * * * * * * *

He dialed Bren and got the message. "Bren – where are you? Call me ASAP. Dad's been taken to St. Lukes. Some kind of an incident. That's all I know. Call me."

He was going to dial Mom, and then thought better of it. "Katy. Just got a call from the police. Dad's been taken to St. Lukes. I don't know any more. I've got to go get Mom and take her down there. You can't come 'cause Arnie isn't home yet – right?"

"No. I can't go. You go. Go. But call me as soon as you know. Your Mom needs you right now."

"Yeah."

* * * * * * * *

"Bren. Where are you?"

"Heading to my car to go to St. Lukes. Where are you?"

"Driving over to tell Mom and take her down there. Call me when you know something."

"Sure. Say a prayer."

* * * * * * * *

"Hi Mom."

"Well this is a nice surprise. What brings you over?"

"Where is Dad tonight?"

"Oh, he went down to see Henry and pick up the analysis on the coffee."

"Mom, let's sit down. I just got a phone call from … …"

* * * * * * * *

"Bren. What have you found out?"

"He's alive. He's in the OR right now – don't know yet what for? That's about all I know. Where are you?"

"Probably about 10 minutes away."

"How's Mom?"

"She's doing just fine. We'll see you in a few."

"Mom, Bren's there. Dad's in the OR right now, he's alive and that's all she knows."

Hannah turned back to the window, her lips moving in prayer, her hands wrapped around her Bible.

* * * * * * * *

"Hi Mom. Are you doing ok?"

"I'm doing ok. What do you know?"

"First, he has not been seriously injured, but he is in shock. I'll tell you the rest later."

"No. Tell me all of it now. And do we know anything about Henry?"

248

"Ok. The police don't know all the details, but what they do know is that a man came into the room where dad was visiting with three other people. The man had a shotgun. He shot the other three people and then he killed himself. Well, this is what they think happened. Dad was not harmed, but he witnessed the whole thing. He was found under the body of someone. He was drenched in blood and there were shotgun pellets found in his face, neck and chest area. There is a lot of detail we don't know and the police have all kinds of questions for him. The doctors are not allowing any visitors. They want him to be left alone until they've completed their assessment. They know I'm a nurse and they know you both are here and they will let us see him before anyone else. We just don't know how soon."

"Mom, do you understand all of that? He's going to be ok."

"Yes, son. Bren, tell me about the effect of trauma on a tender spirit."

* * * * * * * *

"Mr. Ellison, I'm Agent Settles. I'm the one who called you."

"I want to thank you for that."

"Listen, my partner and I have been following your dad around now for over a week. We followed him tonight. We heard the shots and found them and called 911. Because of all the blood, we couldn't tell if your dad had been shot. Anyway, we want you to know we're glad we were there."

"How much can you tell me about what you found?"

"I'm not supposed to say anything about what we found, at least not until the investigation has been completed. But, what would you like to know?

"We've been assuming that Henry Brannon was one of those killed. Can you just give me a yes or no on that? If it's a yes, we want to do what we can for his wife."

"Nobody has been id'd yet. But I'll give you a yes on Brannon, based on what I saw. But you didn't hear it from me."

"Thank you."

* * * * * * * *

"This must be the Ellison family. Hello Brooks."

"Sandy. Mom this is Sandy Marsh, the guy who wrote those articles in the Minneapolis Daily."

"How do you do Mr. Marsh. We really enjoyed your articles. Oh, and this is my daughter, Brenda."

"Brenda, it is nice to meet you. I'm sorry it's under these circumstances. Can any of you tell me what he was doing in that apartment tonight?"

"His friend Henry had gotten an analysis of his coffee. Dad had gone down there to get it from him. I wonder where that report went, what happened to Henry and also, where's Mary? Does she know what's happened?"

"I'm sorry – who is Mary?"

"Mary is Henry's wife. I just talked to Agent Settles five minutes ago. Mom, off the record, he believed that Henry was one of those killed. Maybe Settles is still here? Maybe he knows something about Mary. Be back in a minute."

* * * * * * * *

"Agent Settles – you're still here."

"Yes Mr. Ellison. What do you need?"

"We have a question about Henry's wife. Has she been told?"

"Yes. She's right over there. Agent Owens brought her here a few minutes ago. He stayed at the scene. I came here with the ambulance. Yes, she knows her husband was killed. Owens says she wanted to be with Mr. Ellison's wife and family tonight. I told Owens where you are and … …"

"Mr. Ellison." Mary was moving towards him, one very painful step at a time.

"Mary. We didn't know you were here."

Mary held out both arms to him, and, unable to stop the flow of her tears, wept into his shirt as they held each other. Brooks, while feeling her emotion deeply, felt his chest constricting as he tried to maintain control. This little lady had lost her husband earlier this evening and for some unknown reason, a reason known only to a killer, his father lives. He whispered 'Mary, I'm so sorry.'

She whispered 'Thank you. Now let's go meet your mom.'

She took his arm and he led her down the hall to the small waiting room where Hannah and Bren sat side by side, Bren holding her mother's hand and speaking softly to her. Brooks and Mary approached and it was Bren who noticed first. She said, "Mom, its Mary." Hannah's eyes opened wide and fixed on Mary as she rose to meet her. The two elderly women moved into a meaningful embrace and both were whispering words of comfort and love amid the tears.

Brooks took the chair next to Bren and said to his sister, "Would you look at that. They have never met before but in this moment, it doesn't matter."

Several minutes later, Hannah said, "Now Mary, you sit here." There was a corner table in between their two chairs. They sat, still holding hands, still conversing, eyes focused on one another.

"Have you received any word yet?" Brooks asked his sister.

"Nothing yet. If I knew any details regarding what happened, I'd have a much better idea what is happening now."

"Does it usually take this long before ya find out something?"

"Sometimes it does. It all depends."

"Are you worried that it's taking so long?"

"Yes. If they had all the answers they needed, they would have been out here already. I worked in the ER for a while a long time ago so I don't know the current protocol, but back then it was a priority to get information to family as soon as possible. I'm guessing there is something they don't know yet."

* * * * * * * *

Brooks and Sandy fetched coffee and donuts for all. Brooks had introduced Bren and Sandy to Mary. All five shared in conversation. None of them knew what had transpired in that room. Why did it happen? No one would ever know the reason it happened. The "Coffee Guy" had been there, but at the moment, he was not talking.

A light knock on the door; a man in a white coat entered. "Mrs. Ellison?"

"I am she," replied Hannah. "This is my son and daughter, and these is our friends, Mary Brannan and Sandy Marsh."

"Hi. I'm Dr. Ari Niro. We still don't have all the answers. I will tell you what we know. He suffered a Subdural Hematoma, brought about by a blow to the back of the head. He was covered in blood when he arrived. We were expecting more serious injuries when we first saw him. We removed, perhaps, two dozen pellets from his face, neck and upper chest. These were all surface wounds, which was surprising. The pellets must have passed through something before they struck your husband. He is unconscious at the moment and is unresponsive. His vital signs are good. You may see him if you like, though not for long. Remember, that he is not responsive. Severe trauma could be present here. We don't know what he may have witnessed. We will be watching him very closely for the next 48 to 72 hours and he will be moved to a private room before morning. Nurse Jensen will take you to see him now if you like."

Hannah took Mary by the arm and followed Brooks and Bren, with Sandy bringing up the rear, writing furiously in his notebook.

There were police everywhere as they moved down the hallway. Three were positioned around the elevators, and both stairwell doors were guarded by two uniforms each. Three were standing in a cluster talking with a man in a suit – 'Woodhull.' Brooks muttered under his breath. As the procession drew closer, the uniforms fanned out, two positioning themselves on each side of a door and the third stationed directly opposite that door. Woodhull, hands in pockets, kind of 'hung out' in the middle of the hallway. Sandy zeroed in on Woodhull and picked up the pace, reaching him before the others arrived. They immediately engaged in conversation, Sandy still scribbling furiously in his little notebook.

Nurse Jensen opened the door and stepped aside to allow the others to enter. Mary stepped back saying to Hannah, "You take your children. I'll wait right here."

Arvie's face was covered with little bandages. There was a large gauze and tape bandage on the back of his head. Other than the array of bandages and a pale pallor, he looked like he always looked. Hannah took his hand in hers, patted it gently, and leaned down to kiss him on the forehead. She made nice contact with a bandage. She whispered something, then stood up and backed away. Brooks was on one side of the bed with Brenda on the other. They both shared a moment with their Dad. Mary watched the proceedings through the window. Sandy Marsh was still scribbling frantically in his notebook when the Ellison's returned to the hallway.

All except Brooks returned to the waiting room. On her way, Brenda introduced herself to Nurse Jensen and fired a barrage of questions. "We don't know – yet," came the reply. That one answer sufficed for all the questions Bren had asked. "All we can do is wait."

Brooks hung out in the hall, waiting for Sandy. Woodhull left him in the middle of the hall, still writing. As Woodhull approached Brooks he paused and said, "Sorry about your dad. We are anxious to talk to him as I'm sure you are. Since we don't know who is responsible, we are providing police protection – as you can see." He moved towards the elevators.

Sandy ambled over to Brooks in a careful, very controlled manner, still writing as he ambled. "There," he muttered, looking up at Brooks. "Did you learn anything from Woodhull?"

"Nothing, except that they want to talk to dad and they're providing police protection."

"Yeah. He would only give me some sketchy stuff, but they believe the shooter was the grandson of the Overstreet's, the people who lived in that apartment."

"A grandson murdered his grandparents?"

"Seems that way. They are retrieving his teeth from all over the apartment –or what's left of them. Hopefully, they can positively identify him that way because he had burned the fingerprints off all 10 fingers somehow."

"What?"

"Yeah. Can you imagine doing that to yourself? Woodhull's mystified about the motive. Why did the kid do it? Pumping rounds from a shotgun into two helpless people? And not one round, but two into each one. He's pretty much convinced he was either crazy or totally whacked out on something, or most likely both. Did you hear about the school shooting today?"

"Heard one report on the radio. They think it was this guy?"

"They think so. The school report made it sound like the uniform was the same. Why all this happened will never be known. Henry Brannon. He was a good man. I got to know him a little when he would spend time at the jail. It's tragic that it had to be him."

"Yeah. My dad was so impressed with him."

"His wife appears to be taking it well."

"Appearances are very deceiving. Dad believes she is very sick."

"Is it the halo of fire?"

"Oh, so you know about that?"

"Yeah. He told me."

"Dad and I went to Henry and Mary's place on Saturday morning. Henry apparently knew someone out at 3M who could analyze the coffee. We didn't see Henry, but Mary was home. Dad said he was really worried about her because the 'halo' was so bright."

"Interesting. You're familiar with the name Henryk Von Barstow?"

"Yeah. The guy on the drug corner."

"That's him. He was in the hospital and supposedly very sick. He had a guard positioned just outside his door. Well, he got the guard to come into his room, somehow bopped him over the head, traded clothes with him and walked out. He's gone. They don't know where to. Woodhull is really pissed. Have I got your phone number?"

"Yup. You got it that day at the jail."

"Good. What are your plans for tomorrow? Spend the day here, or wait for word at home?"

"I don't think Mom will be satisfied waiting at home. She'll want to be here."

"I'll be here too. Lots of people want to find out what your dad saw tonight. By the way, I'll have another story in the morning paper. Since this has now turned into a news story, it'll for sure be on Page one. I'll see you tomorrow."

"You bet. Thanks Sandy."

* * * * * * * *

254

Back in the waiting room, the discussion about heading for home was underway. It was nearly 10 pm and there was no reason to think Arvie would be doing anything other than sleeping through the night. Brooks asked Mary if they could take her home since they would be going right by her place in order to pick up Arvie's car. That was most agreeable to Mary.

Once in the car and underway, Hannah asked if Mary would be ok being alone that night and thought that maybe, both of them, could use each other for company. Hannah invited Mary to come spend the night at her place. Mary declined. "Tuesday mornings are very busy. I have two places to clean and wash to deliver."

"But Mary, after what you've been through tonight, I should think people would understand."

"Yes, they would. But I would feel as if I had let them down. I feel so responsible for my little flock and most of them are so elderly and crippled they are all but helpless. Thank you so much for your offer. It is so nice of you. And, you know, I haven't had time to have my talk with Henry since it all happened. For 61 years we been havin a conversation every night before bedtime. And tonight, especially tonight, we need our time together. I'm probably goin to get a whole lot of cryin out the way too."

"Oh, Mary my dear. I do understand. I'll be thinking of you."

They said their good-bye as Brooks pulled to the curb in front of the old apartment building, just behind the Ellison family car. Brooks watched in the rear view mirror as the ugly black Ford sedan slid to the curb. "So now they are tailing the family" he muttered to himself. He opened Mary's door and offered her his hand. With a difficulty which brought concern to Brooks, Mary was able to exit the car while pulling mightily on his arm. He walked her to her front door. Mary thanked him for his kindness and said good night. They hugged. As Mary pulled away, Brooks saw the tears brimming in her eyes. Last night she had Henry. This night, she does not.

Hannah was preparing to drive the family car home, when they heard a car door slam. Agent Settles walked up to Hannah and Brooks standing outside the driver's side door, and said, "Excuse me folks. If you'd be looking for a driver, I'd be happy to assist. Hannah reached out her hand and Agent Settles took it as she said, "Thank you, ever so much." Agent Settles responded, "You are very welcome, ma'am."

The freeway was not busy this Monday night at 10:30. Brooks led the way, followed by Agent Settles and then Agent Owens in the black Ford sedan. 35 minutes later, they pulled into the townhouse driveway. Agent Settles opened the door and handed the keys to Brooks. The two of them shook hands and Agent Settles walked down the drive towards the Black Sedan, now parked in its familiar position at the curb just down the street.

"Mom, I'm not working tomorrow so when you want to go to the hospital, I'll be glad to pick you up."

"Thank you honey. Mid-morning, I suppose. I'll call you first thing. I don't know when that will be. I don't know how well I'll sleep or even if I can sleep. Thanks, Honey. I'll be fine now. You go on home to Katy and the kids."

"Ok, Mom. Talk to you in the morning." Brooks couldn't help being thankful when he saw the black sedan down the street. He found comfort knowing his mom was being protected.

Chapter 16

"Some things happen in this world that even I can't explain. Heh heh." - *Ole*

"I trust in God. I will not be afraid.
What can people do to me?"
Psalm 56:11

Coffee Man
Spared in Killing Spree
By: Sandy Marsh

MINNEAPOLIS – There are heavy hearts this morning as friends and neighbors mourn the loss of four persons killed last night in what appears to be a murder-suicide on the Minneapolis lower north side.

This article is focused on The Coffee Man who was in the apartment, but somehow was spared in the bloody carnage. We named him "Samuel" in articles written last week. Samuel possesses a magic coffee that he believes capable of healing a variety of human ailments. He is on a mission to bring this healing coffee to as many people as possible.

We found his mission to be a refreshing human-interest story and based on the response of many readers, that belief has been substantiated. Why Samuel was spared is but one of the questions yet unanswered. The shotgun and a duffle full of shells were recovered at the scene. The weapon however, was clean, meaning no prints were found.

Authorities stated the end of all 10 of the shooters fingers had been severely burned, and all prints were unrecognizable. Because of how he died, no visual identification of the shooter could be made. Identification through dental records is thought to be nearly impossible since the shooter's teeth were disintegrated by the self-inflicted shotgun blast.

Additional information on the above incident as well as the shooting incident earlier yesterday afternoon at the Helen G. Hadley middle school will be found in a separate article in today's Daily. Authorities believe the two incidents may be related. Our focus here is to continue the story of Samuel.

We reported in an earlier article that for the past week or so Samuel has been followed by DEA agents wherever he has gone. They have been staked out every night at the curb just outside his townhome, watching, because the DEA believes this 75-year-old senior citizen is somehow connected to drug cartels in South America. The agents followed Samuel downtown last evening and were the first on the scene, responding to the sound of the shotgun blasts, of which there were at least eight.

The police report states that apparently the shooter entered the apartment and immediately unloaded both barrels into a male victim. Names of the victims have not yet been released. First responders indicated that apparently the first victim was blown backwards, landing on Samuel who was seated. Samuel's chair went over backwards, shattering under the weight of two bodies. The first victim landed on top of Samuel. In the process, Samuel banged his head on the floor causing a concussion and a laceration which required eight stitches. It is also believed that his life was saved because he was under the body of victim one. The suppositions continue: after shooting victim one, the shooter then turned his attention to an elderly couple, believed to be in their early 90's. Blast #3 killed the male, knocking him from his wheel chair to the floor. Blast #4 killed the female as she sat on the couch. Blast #5 was into the back of the male, and blast #6 was into the back of the female's head and neck. Blasts seven and eight were fired simultaneously into the shooter's head apparently from a position just under the chin.

First responders, upon entering the apartment, believed all five to be dead. Samuel was covered in blood and unresponsive because of the blow to his head. But a pulse was found and he was rushed to St. Luke's Hospital.

Samuel remained unconscious into the night, surrounded by his wife, son and daughter. Many questions remain unanswered, some relating to the safety of Samuel. Was the shooter operating alone? If Samuel is in some way connected to drug trafficking, was he the primary target? Did the first responders arrive so quickly that the killers mission was interrupted? Did the first victim, being blown backwards on top of Samuel, save his life? When Samuel emerges from unconsciousness, will he remember what happened and be able to provide answers? Police guard the entrance to his hospital room and the elevator and stairwells opening onto his floor.

Authorities are investigating information alleging that the shooter may be the great-grandson of the slain elderly couple who had resided in the apartment for a time. We may never know the identification of the shooter.

Samuel brings hope to many through his healing coffee. We now must hope and pray for healing for Samuel.
Again, Stay tuned.

* * * * * * * *

Bren was pacing back and forth in the hall when they walked in. She had a concerned look on her face. She greeted each of them with a hug. "He's still the same."

"What have they told you?" asked Hannah.

"A blow to the head is unpredictable. It's not unusual for someone to be unconscious for 24 hours, perhaps longer. They are concerned about psychological effects of trauma, having no idea yet what he experienced. That's the unknown right now. Vital signs are still good. Nothing to do but wait."

* * * * * * * *

It was supper time when Dr. Niro entered the waiting room. "He's awake. However, he's not speaking. His vital signs continue to be good and it is not unusual that after a blow to the head and/or psychological trauma the patient doesn't speak. In this case, it's not surprising because of the events he may have witnessed last night. It might mean something to him if you spent a few minutes with him."

"Sure," said Brooks, getting to his feet as did they all. Hannah was a bundle of anxiety as she trundled down the hall. Bren had trouble keeping up and Brooks asked her, "What does it mean if he can't speak?"

"Not sure. I suppose it depends on the severity of the blow to the head. No one seems to have learned much about the effects of psychological trauma on communication skills but in the journals I've read, all seem to believe there is a relationship." Dr. Niro opened the door and they entered.

It was a strange sensation as they entered the room. Hannah, then Bren followed by Brooks, leaned over their father, hugged him, kissed him, talked to him. There was no response. His eyes followed them but he said nothing, he didn't move a muscle. His lips did not kiss back. There was no connection between his eyes and feelings or emotions; a total disconnect. The family looked at each other with unspoken questions, unsure if he could hear and understand, just unable to respond? Hannah moved to the chair sitting near the bed and sat down heavily.

Bren decided quickly that she would go on as if he were responsive. She talked with him as she patted up his pillow. She patted his shoulder while continuing to ask questions she knew would go unanswered. She told him all about Sophie's volleyball game of two nights ago, the weather, what she was having for supper tonight. His eyes followed her as if saying, "Keep talking to me. I'm hearing every word." And so, she did.

* * * * * * * *

Arvie thought it very strange. He saw them enter his room. He felt that he knew them somehow, yet he couldn't be certain. Their voices sounded hollow as if the reverb was turned up too high; shadowy figures, their backs to a blazing sun. There were moments where lips were moving but he heard nothing. He wanted to ask if the volume could be turned up or to stop talking through the pillow. He thought he should know what they were talking about – at least those parts he could hear. Deep inside somewhere, he could feel something of a concern, yet he wasn't sure what that feeling meant. All he could do was look at them; it was all disjointed somehow. His eyes moved from one to another. He couldn't move his head. If they were standing in front of him, he watched them. His eyes were the only sign of life.

* * * * * * * *

Katy and the kids came to visit as did Juan and Gabby, and Sandy Marsh. Noah Sayles and Moggy came in the early evening. Hannah did the best she could but her mind could not stay away from her husband down the hall in that room, eyes open and looking, but unresponsive. She couldn't stand it. She was continually down the hall peering in the small window. Each time, his eyes found her. Several times she entered and walked to his side, reminding him that she was here and she was waiting for him. She told him she was going to visit Marci tonight, that her depression was serious again and that she may spend the night with her. She didn't want her to be alone. She hoped he might respond to that since the three of them had been acquainted for so long. But there was no response.

She told him about all who had come to visit. Noah had come to his room and prayed with him. Noah told him about George Hopkins from the senior Bible study who, for some unknown reason was not going to need his surgery. Noah asked Arvie if he had any idea how that miracle could have happened. He assured him, also, that he would pour the Forever for everyone in the morning at the organ concert and he would appreciate his help again once he was back on his feet.

It was after 8:00 when Hannah, Bren and Brooks said goodnight to him, assured him that they would be back in the morning and headed for home. He watched them walk away. There was something vaguely familiar about them.

Chapter 17

"When you're walking into a stiff wind, pull your hat down tight,
bend at the waist and get after it. Heh heh." - *Ole*

*"For David said this about him: I keep the Lord before me always.
Because he is close by my side, I will not be hurt. So, I am glad and I
rejoice. Even my body has hope, because you will not leave me in the
grave. You will not let your Holy One rot. You will teach me how to
live a holy life. Being with you will fill me with joy."*
Acts 2:25-28

Hannah arrived bright and early and made her way to the nurse's
station. Nurse Jensen and Dr. Niro were talking in the middle of the
hall. Nurse Jensen saw Hannah enter and motioned her to join them.

Dr. Niro turned as she approached. "Good morning. Well, all of a
sudden he's back and he's asking for you. It happened just a few
minutes ago. I was about to call you."

"That's wonderful. Is he kind of ... well ... you know, normal?"

"He seems a little agitated, but other than that, yes. Are you
ready?"

"Yes."

"One thing to keep in mind – he seems to have blocked out
Monday night. He may not remember. He may not want to
remember. We don't want to force Monday night on him. We need
to be gentle right now to see where he is, what he remembers and
what he doesn't. In other words, we don't want that whole incident
to come crashing in all at once. Do you understand? I believe he is
going to remember Monday up to a point. It would help us to know
where that point is?"

"I understand."

Nurse Jensen opened the door and Hannah hesitantly entered.

"Hannah. Where have you been?"

"Good morning, sleeping beauty. Nice of you to join us once
again. I've been right here. Where have *you* been?"

"I don't know. The nurse and I had that talk a few minutes ago and I guess I missed a couple of days. She said it's Wednesday."

"Yes, it is. You missed all of yesterday. What do you remember? Anything? How is your head?"

"My head? I guess I bumped it, or something. I've got a little headache and the nurse told me eight stitches too."

"Everybody is so anxious to talk to you about Monday night. Do you remember any of what happened?"

(Silence). "Aahh … I remember driving the car a lot. That was Monday, wasn't it?"

"You scared us bad, Arvid Ellison. Here, I need a kiss and a hug. … Well, that's much better. I've kissed you several times over the past several days and your lips weren't working. I like it much better when your lips are working."

"Pull the chair over and sit down. Where did we go Monday?"

"Ok. First, I had an appointment with Dr. Blower and you drove me there, all the way to Edina. Do you remember that?"

"No. Then what?"

"Well, then we headed for Stillwater for my therapy in the pool. We stopped for lunch on the way. We both had the Spinach salad … "

"At Walts."

"That's right. Good. And then we stopped at the meat market and got a few things and then you dropped me off at the pool."

"And while you were doing that, did I go down the street to Walmart with a short shopping list?"

"Yes, you did. And when I was finished, what did we do next?"

"We drove home."

"Right. Do you remember what we talked about when we were driving home?"

"No. What?"

"We talked about inviting Henry and Mary over for dinner some night."

"Henry. Henry. Henry? No. I don't remember." His eyes were closed, his head shaking back and forth.

Hannah reached for his hand. It was shaking. She stood, moved closer, sliding her other hand under his neck. Her face moved close

264

to his. She buried her nose into his cheek and felt his entire body tremble. "It's all going to be ok" she whispered. "It's all ok. I love you."

* * * * * * * *

Sandy approached Brooks as he entered the hospital. "Good morning Brooks. How's your dad doing?"

"Don't know yet. Just got here myself. I think Mom's upstairs with him now."

"I'll walk with you. Just came from the police station. A body was found this morning – believed to be a henchman of Von Barstow. Slain the way it's done in the drug worlds of South America: wrists bound behind the back and his throat slashed. They have a name for this killer down there, 'The Black Widow of the Jungle.' Someone caught a glimpse one night and said it's a woman and she's blonde. Of course, she wears all black and I doubt she, if it is a she, would be out doing her thing with her blonde hair flowing in the breeze. Interesting thing is, everything about this killing, matches up perfectly with the 30 or 40 down there attributed to the Black Widow. Don't think they're going to try to pin this on your dad. He's got a pretty good alibi for last night. He also doesn't have long blonde hair. Am I right?"

"Good grief. Have they found Von Barstow yet?"

"No. He's vanished. Maybe he made it home for his Mom's funeral? I've got to make a stop at the front desk. I'll be by to see how things are going in a few minutes."

"Sure. Hey, any idea when the Black Widow did her last thing down there in the jungle? Is she still working down there?"

"Oh, I don't know. Why?"

"Just curious, I guess. Sounds like a good book, if you like that sort of thing. See you in a few."

* * * * * * * *

Brooks headed to his dad's room. As he approached the Nurse's station, Nurse Jensen called to him, "Mr. Ellison, your mother is in with your father at the moment."

"Thank you." He noted the police still positioned at the entrances to this area, as well as at the elevator, and three guarding the door to his Dad's room. Pacing up and down the hallway in his immaculate and freshly pressed black pin-striped suit was Special Agent Woodhull. Upon seeing Brooks, he moved quickly to him. "Mr. Ellison, how is your father doing?"

"He is doing as well as can be expected. I'm really not up to speed. I just got here."

"I understand he's speaking now. I'm waiting for the doctor because I want to know when I will be able to question him. What do you think? Is he ready yet?"

"I don't know. I didn't know he was speaking yet. But Mom is with him now. She'll know more than I do."

"It's imperative that I speak to him. We have just found another body and it's being ID'd as we speak. We need to learn what happened on Monday night."

"I can understand that but you must talk with Dr. Niro first. Here he comes now."

"Are you Agent Woodhull?"

"Yes."

"And you want to question Mr. Ellison, is that correct?"

"Yes, again."

"His wife is with him now and I'll want to talk to her first. If you'll be patient for a moment, I'll get right back with you."

"Ok."

Dr. Niro headed to Arvie's room.

* * * * * * * *

Brooks sat impatiently in the small seating area outside the ICU. Sandy Marsh arrived in a rush saying, "Brooks, listen to this. I've just been talking with my contact at the Police station. They've just found another body and they think its Von Barstow. Just like the other one, the hands were tied behind his back and his throat was slashed. The Black Widow has been busy."

"Good Lord."

"I just saw Woodhull. I'll bet he's real anxious to get some answers."

"I'll say. Mom's in with Dad now and Dr. Niro just headed in, so we'll probably find out something pretty quick. Dr. Niro said yesterday that we'll, in no way, subject him to any questioning until we are certain he is ready."

"What does that mean?"

"I think it means that Dad's got to have dealt with everything that happened Monday night in his own mind, that he's faced the reality of it all, especially losing a good friend to such horrible brutality."

* * * * * * * *

Dr. Niro followed by Hannah came into the hall from Arvie's room. They moved away from the door and then huddled up. Brooks ambled over listening in. Woodhull, at the far end of the hallway, moved slowly towards the huddle and then changed his mind, standing in a position of attention in the middle of the hallway, watching carefully. Sandy Marsh had just entered. He leaned against a wall in a more casual position and waited also.

"Hannah, I have just completed a check of everything physical, and he is doing well. The mind is most important. You've been talking with him. Tell me about your conversation."

"We were having a good conversation, catching up, and he asked about what we did on Monday. So I started with the appointments and he didn't seem to remember at first, but by the time I got to the second one, he jumped in and pretty much told me the rest of the day. Here's where it all changed: I asked him if he remembered what we talked about on our way home. He said he didn't and I reminded him it was about inviting Henry and Mary over for dinner. He said Henry's name three times and then started trembling all over. I just held him until he seemed to calm down. I didn't dare bring it up again. What do you think that means?"

"I'm quite certain that means he's not ready yet. I doubt very much if he has begun to process anything that happened Monday night. Every one of these situations is different so I can't be sure, but my guess is that when he begins that, we'll know about it. So, here is how we'll approach it: you and I will talk several times every day to discuss progress, more frequently if we need to. Both of us, when we have the opening, will gently bring up Monday night, Henry, Mary, very subtly of course. And should he begin to talk about it, it will be very important for us to quietly take a chair and just listen. He may pour it all out from start to finish. He may let it go in pieces, but once he begins, it should not be difficult to gently prompt him to continue. Let's leave it at that for now. We'll adjust as we need to. Now, I will go speak with the Special Agent and let him know that it will not be today."

* * * * * * * *

It was late afternoon when Bren arrived. Mom, Dad and the two kids sat around Arvie's bed and laughed for what seemed like hours. How the time flies when recounting the early years of one's own family. When Arvie's supper was served, Hannah and Bren decided they would go down to the Cafeteria and find a meal. Brooks gave his dad a hug and said he was going to head home for supper and that he would be back tomorrow. Arvie enjoyed his meat loaf swimming in tomato paste, a bowl of vegetable soup, a glass of milk and a cup of coffee. The coffee wasn't as good as what he was used to, but it helped to wash down a square of tasteless, nondescript cake. He decided he'd have Hannah bring a can of coffee tomorrow and that he would have a talk with Nurse Jensen or Dr. Niro about getting the hospital to brew some good stuff. After all, he had some healing to do.

After supper, Hannah and Bren returned to Arvie's room. Hannah announced that she was going to head for home - she was in need of a good nights sleep. She said she and Marci had been up most of last night in conversation. Bren would stay with Arvie for awhile longer. Hannah and Arvie said some endearing words to each other and then she headed home.

Chapter 18

"Us guys are not as smart as we think we are. But … one thing we know: there are things we just gotta stand up for and tackle head-on. And so we do. Heh heh." - *Ole*

"Since we have been made right with God by our faith, we have peace with God. This happened through our Lord Jesus Christ, who has brought us into that blessing of God's grace that we now enjoy. And we are happy because of the hope we have of sharing God's glory. We also have joy with our troubles, because we know that these troubles produce patience. And patience produces character, and character produces hope. And this hope will never disappoint us, because God has poured out his love to fill our hearts. He gave us his love through the Holy Spirit, whom God has given to us." Romans 5:1-5

Arvie was at the far end of the hall when Hannah arrived. He was staring out the window, watching the cars moving like little minions, marching in unison towards the next stop-sign, where they would stop almost as one. The brief pause allowed a minion to cross in front of them. And then the next, and the next, and the next. He thought it a snapshot of life. Everyone is trying to get somewhere. Many don't know completely where they're heading, but they are on their way, stopping and starting as if to indicate their uncertainty.

She put an arm around his shoulder. He turned to her and they hugged for a long moment. She was about to speak to him when she saw his face. It was tear stained and appeared to be the face of one who has fought the good fight and emerged victorious but emotionally spent. "Your eyes," said Hannah. "They are very much alive but your face looks like it was a struggle."

"Yes. Yes, it was."

"Oh, my dear. You've had a difficult night. I brought the coffee you wanted."

"Thanks, and yes. I have had a difficult but a very interesting night. I spent most it thinking about and talking through Monday night. There was a voice in my head telling me to deal with it, that it would be ok, and then suddenly a door opened and I saw Henry smiling at me. His smile said that he was in a good place and I knew I would be ok. It was emotional and I cried a lot because I do not fully understand, but I can talk about it. I know I have to do that."

"It must have been so hard for you."

"There were some scenes that I didn't need to see again. But like those cars down there – see them stop and then they start up again? Like life, they must stop to allow other things to happen and then they begin again. I have had to do the same thing over the last several days. I've been at a stop sign waiting. It's time to start up again. What time do you think Brooks and Bren will be here?"

"I don't know. Would you like me to call them and find out?"

"Would you please?"

They went into Arvie's room and Hannah made the calls.

"I talked to Dr. Niro just before you arrived. I told him I was ready to get this over with. He asked me numerous questions and I passed his test. So … when the kids get here, I also want Special Agent Woodhull and Sandy Marsh. I want to go through this once, tell my side once, so if we can get everyone in the room at the same time, it will be easier. It's going to be emotional again. I can't help it. Will you help me do this?"

"Sure. With the kids help we'll get it done."

* * * * * * * *

It was a little after 10 when Brooks and Bren arrived. It was close to 11 before all were assembled. Arvie was standing. Standing makes it easier to pace. Special Agent Woodhull elected to stand, not wanting to muss his perfectly creased trousers, his notebook at the ready.

"I guess we can do this. Anything before I begin?"

Sandy raised his hand and asked, "Arvie, are you ok if I record you? If it's ok, then Agent Woodhull can use that for your statement."

"That's fine."

"Sandy mumbled into the tape recorder 'this is the statement of Arvid Ellison regarding the events of Monday evening, July 29. Ok, Arvie. We're ready when you are."

"Ok. Here we go. (Pause) Monday night I went to visit my friend Henry Brannon at his home. I had met Henry the night I was in Jail which was Thursday night, July 25. Henry had a friend who had a friend who worked at 3M and could analyze a can of coffee to determine the elements contained therein. This was the night Henry would have the report. I left home around 5:20 and I arrived at Henry's place shortly before 6:00. I knocked on his door and his wife Mary told me that he was upstairs in 306 helping the Overstreet's with something. I went to 306. Henry introduced me to the Overstreet's. He had some plumbing laid out on the floor and was telling them that he would take it down to his apartment tonight because he had a vice there and he hoped he could get it fixed and reinstalled by sometime tomorrow. The Overstreet's were very elderly. He was in a wheel chair. I noticed he had no legs. His wife was seated on the couch. There were two other chairs in the room. I took the chair furthest away from the Overstreets and Henry took the chair that was closer to them. He was asking them if they enjoyed the coffee he had given them earlier in the day when the front door burst open. Henry reacted immediately. He was on his feet and was moving towards the person who had entered and he said, 'Marcus, is that a new sh.' That's when the first two shots were fired. It could have been one shot, but it sounded louder than that. Henry was between me and the person who entered."

"Sandy with the Daily. So Arvie, you did not get a clear look at the shooter, is that correct?"

"I only caught a brief glimpse."

"Do you think he could have seen you?"

"Since I got a glimpse of him, I suppose he could have caught a glimpse of me."

"Thank you. Did you see any weapon?"

"I did not."

"Thanks Arvie. What happened next?" Sandy prompted.

"This is the hardest part. I think there were two shots fired almost simultaneously. I can only assume they both were fired at Henry since he was on his feet and moving towards Marcus."

"Please excuse me again. You called the shooter, 'Marcus.' Did you know him at all? Had you ever seen him before?"

"I had seen him once before, the previous Thursday night in the jail cell. Henry had pointed him out and had indicated that he was not one to mess with. I think his exact words were 'That one's trouble.' I never met him."

Agent Woodhull had been scribbling furiously. He slipped a note to Sandy.

"A question from Agent Woodhull, Arvie. Do you remember the exact words that Henry said as he moved towards the shooter? If not, what do you think he was asking?"

"As near as I can remember, his words were 'Marcus, is that a new sh…?' The gun went off before he finished the sentence. I think he was asking him about the gun he was carrying.

"I had wondered if Henry had thought of what he would do if he ever faced a situation such as this. He was up and moving so quickly it was as if he was prepared. Perhaps the thought was that if he was immediately moving towards someone with a gun he just might catch him unprepared. That's just a guess. Anyway … two shots, fired almost simultaneously, and Henry was suddenly in my lap. We crashed through the little chair I was sitting in. I'm on the floor on my back and Henry is on his back laying on top of me. I could … feel his … blood seeping … into my … clothes. I could feel his … blood … very warm, running into … my eyes, my mouth. I felt stinging sensations all over my face and my chest. Dr. Niro said they extracted between two and three dozen pellets from me. I'm guessing again, but … … the only … … way they … could have got to me … … was … through Henry."

Bren was on her feet pouring water into his cup. "Here Dad. Drink some water."

"Thank you. I remember being deafened by the sound and it was very quiet. The only sounds I could hear were those of the gun being opened, the shuffle of a shell inserted and the gun closed. I remembered the sounds because I used to watch my grandpa clean his old shotgun. A woman was crying and sniffling. Mrs. Overstreet, I guess. As soon as the gun snapped shut, there were two more blasts. I assume one was aimed at Mr. Overstreet and the other at Mrs. Overstreet. The sounds of the reloading again. The gun snapped shut and two more blasts, fired again, I guess, at the two old people. The sound of reloading again. I remember feeling sick. I remember thinking 'now it's my turn. And then from under Henry I saw him peering around Henry directly at me. And then I saw the gun barrel being placed under his jaw and then he must have pulled the trigger on both barrels at the same time. And that's all I remember. If you have any other questions, I will try to help."

There were none.

* * * * * * * *

Sandy had been the first one to offer his hand and say a 'thank you.' Woodhull, recognized Arvie with a nod before heading out the door. Sandy followed him out the door.

"Are you all right, my dear?" Hannah asked Arvie.

Arvie was standing at the head of the bed, his back against the wall, studying his hands. They were still shaking. "I'm just fine. I'm very glad to have that behind me. By the way, have we heard anything about Mary?"

There was no response. Then Brooks spoke up, "I'm sorry Dad. I could have thought to check on her. I'll stop by on my way home. Did any of us tell you that she was here Monday night?"

"No. She was? I'm glad to hear that. How did she seem?"

"She seemed unbelievably strong," said Hannah. After what she had just learned about Henry, well, I can't imagine being that strong. She was certainly continuing to think of others before herself. We took her home that night and I asked if she would consider coming home with me to spend the night. She said, 'For over 60 years, Henry and I have ended every day talking to each other. Tonight, especially, I need to have that talk with him.' Something like that. Yes. She is very strong."

"How interesting. Thanks, Brooks, for checking on her. I feel a sense of responsibility for her."

There was a knock at the door and Arvie's lunch rolled in. He decided he would eat sitting in the chair by the bed. The nurse who brought the food said, "I hope you enjoy your dinner Mr. Ellison."

"I know that I will. Thanks so much. Oh, and by the way, could you see if they could make me another cup of coffee using this?" He handed her the shiny black can.

"Well, I don't know but I'll ask."

"Before you ask, could you make me a cup first so I could get at least one? I'm sorry. I don't want to get you into trouble. Thank you. I really appreciate you looking into that for me."

"Would you be ok honey, if I went home for a nap?" asked Hannah. "I woke up tired this morning. It was a long night with Marci. And now, after listening to your story, I'm exhausted."

"I'm going to eat this lunch and then I'm going to take a nap as well, so I'm not going to be much company this afternoon. That would be fine with me. And, thanks to all of you for being here for this. I got to tell it one time and now I'm hoping that I'll be able to forget it very soon. I doubt that'll happen though."

"Ok dad. I'll take off too. You did good today. I'll be happy when you don't look like a measle's patient any more." Bren leaned over, patting his shoulder and giving him a kiss on an un-bandaged area of his forehead.

"And I'll go check on Mary and I'll let you know" added Brooks.

"That's great. Thanks again – for being here."

* * * * * * * *

Arvie felt like he had just closed his eyes moments before. But as he looked around and saw Brooks in his doorway, he realized he'd actually been asleep.

Brooks said, "Good. You're awake."

"Your back awfully soon."

"Dad, I had to call 911 for Mary. She's not good at all. She's downstairs in Emergency. When I got there, I found a Mrs. Koepke with her, sitting by her bed, holding her hand. I think they both were waiting for Mary to take her last breath. They don't know if she'll make it. She's terribly weak. I should've thought to check on her earlier. I'm so sorry."

"Be thankful you got there when you did. Remember, your priorities are your family, Kate and the kids. To take care of them, you must tend to your job. I've been the distraction here, so don't beat yourself up."

"I'm going back down there. I'll come back when I know something."

"Thanks, son. You do that and I'll do some praying. If you have a moment, you might call your mother and let her know. She'll want to pray too. Have I lost my phone through all of this?"

"I called her on the way back here. Bren too. Mom was going to call her small group and get the prayer chain started. By now, many requests have already been sent upstairs for Mary. Your phone is laying over here."

* * * * * * * *

"Knock – Knock."

"Noah. Please come in."

"Arvie, I couldn't help but overhear your prayer request. Who's Mary, and can I help?"

"Yes, indeed you can. Mary is Henry's wife. Henry is the man I met in Jail one week ago tonight. The only reason I'm alive is because Henry took both blasts from a double-barreled shotgun to protect me Monday night. Mary may be gone by now. She's downstairs in the ER. Would you walk with me down there?"

"Certainly."

* * * * * * * *

"Dad. You're out and about?"

"Noah, this is my son Brooks. Brooks, Pastor Noah Sayles from church." They shook hands and greeted each other. "Have you heard anything Brooks?" Arvie asked.

"No. There has been a steady stream of white coats in and out of that room. No report yet."

"Noah, she's got to be in her early 80's, and just a little thing. She and Henry have given their lives to work with the poor. Henry said he learned the business from his father. When you help people with something, there is plenty of time to talk about Jesus. Henry did whatever needed to be done around somebody's apartment, while Mary took in wash, and cleaned apartments. From what I learned, they hardly ever got paid. But they trusted the Lord, Noah, for their next dime, or meal or anything. I can't believe faith like that. A lifetime of living like that."

"A faith like that humbles us all."

"Who brought in Mary Brannan?"

"It was me."

"Are you a family member?"

"No. There is no family."

"So, family friend, then?"

"Yes."

"Mary is a very sick lady. We don't have time to list everything that needs attention but we suspect a very large tumor in her chest cavity which is pressuring several vital organs. We haven't done the definitive test for that yet, but we are quite certain. That tumor must come out. We've got her on fluids now and we'll be getting her some IV nutrition which should help build her up for surgery, but I'm not sure she's going to give us enough time. We want to do more tests but not until tomorrow. Until then, she is going to rest and soak up all the liquids and nourishment we can get into her. That's where we are. She's sleeping now and we're going to keep her isolated for a good long while."

"Do you think we might be able to talk to her this evening?"

"There is a possibility, but we won't know until we get there."

"Thank you, Doctor."

* * * * * * * *

Arvie, Noah and Brooks headed upstairs together, walking Arvie back to his room. Brooks said, "Dad, I volunteered to help that Mrs. Koepke with a couple of things in her apartment on Saturday. Any idea yet when they're going to turn you loose?"

"Dr. Niro said it could be tomorrow."

"Well, if you are out of here and you feel like it, you want to come along?"

"I'd love to. Noah, you can see the effect that Henry and Mary have had on my family."

"And you met Henry in jail?" Noah asked.

"Yes. He had an arrangement with the jail that he could spend a night whenever he wanted to. He was harvesting lost souls any way he could."

"I see. He was not in there because they put him in there. He was there because he wanted to be in there."

"Exactly. Three or four nights a week."

"Wow. And I thought my schedule was demanding."

"Dad, I need to get home. Will you be able to get down there to check on Mary later this evening?"

"I sure will. You go ahead. Say hi to Katy and the kids. And thanks for being here."

"You bet Dad" They shared a hug. "Noah, it was nice to meet you."

"Same here, Brooks.

As Brooks was leaving, the nurse reappeared carrying a burden that appeared very much like a pot of coffee.

She looked at Arvie, winked noticeably, and said, "I thought I'd bring you some coffee. I just happened to find some in the kitchen. It was an unopened can and so fresh. My, doesn't it smell good? And if you tell anybody, I'll be hung on a garage door somewhere." She put the pot and two cups down, and with a big smile for Arvie, she turned and left the room, closing the door quietly behind her.

"Well, Noah. What do you think we can do to a fresh pot of Forever?"

"I've always enjoyed a good challenge."

* * * * * * * *

Noah had just left when Hannah came into Arvie's room.

"Hannah, come in. I've got a little Forever left in this pot the nice nurse brought. Want some?"

"Maybe half a cup."

"How's Mary?"

"It was a one-sided conversation," Hannah began, "but it was a chance for me to say some things that were on my heart. I don't know that she heard me, but I want to believe she did."

"Noah was here; we prayed for you and Mary."

"Thank you."

"You drove down here by yourself?"

"After Brooks called, I knew I had to come—my fears and other feelings just didn't seem so important. Sitting there with her, I sensed she was smiling, that she was seeing Henry, and that she was being welcomed home. I felt a moment of such joy. Then the Doctor and some nurses came in, and they asked me to leave. So I came up here." She dabbed at her eyes. Arvie reached an arm around her, and she leaned into him. They sat that way for a long time.

Chapter 19

"Life can be really brutal and tough to deal with. I can't imagine anyone having an easy life. This earth is a tough place to be, and the devil can be so mean when he's passing out the sin. He's learned not to mess with me." - *Ole*

*"I tried to understand all that happens on earth.
I saw how busy people are, working day and night
and hardly ever sleeping. I also saw all that God has done.
Nobody can understand what God does here on earth. No matter
how hard people try to understand it, they cannot. Even if wise
people say they understand, they cannot; no one can really
understand it."* Ecclesiastes 8:16-17

It was 6:16. He saw it on his phone on his way back to bed. He had made his usual 'sun-coming-up-trip' to the little boy's room. He made his way to the window where the view of his world was from above the trees. His hospital room faced mainly south and just a little east. It was going to be a pretty day, and he had no plans.

He'd be a guest of the hospital for most of the day. Dr. Niro had said he would be released by mid-afternoon. He was happy that he had recovered so well from what happened last Monday evening, yet he was overflowing with sorrow over the loss of Henry. As he peered out at his beautiful view, his thought was that Henry never woke up to such a broad and spectacular vista. His view was one of sorrow, broken dreams and spirits, pain and suffering. But he did not look at it in that way. May God bless his memory and fill his cup to overflowing as he basks in the brilliant presence of his lord and master. Lord, please enclose Mary in your love as her journey to You continues. *And as for me, breakfast will be in any minute now.*

He remembered the earlier days when his mind was filled with his dreams of a bigger house, a lake cabin, a new car, but most of all enough in the bank to pay the ever-increasing amount of his bills; the objects of this world that he was striving to possess. That's why he worked so hard, trying to be successful in his work. More and more hours on the job and less and less time allowed for thanking God for what he had; his wife and children, the roof over their heads, and food to eat. How he longed to be able to return to those days and years, to revisit his shortsightedness. At this time in his life, his heart-felt prayers were for forgiveness. He could not go back and change it all. He was thankful for a forgiving Lord that, when he confessed his sins and asked to be forgiven, cast his sins away; as far as the east is from the west, forgave them and forgot them. He wished the pain he felt could go away but he knew it never would. God made him this way so he would be continually reminded that he is forgiven and he can live life with a thankful heart. *What mercy.*

The door opened as he was pulling up the sheets and lying back on his freshly patted pillows.

"Good morning" she sung with beautiful musicality in her voice. "Aren't we up early today."

Arvie quickly realized it was the same nurse that brought him the Forever the night before. "Breakfast will arrive shortly, but in the meantime, I have brought you another pot of that free coffee I found last night. And ... a copy of today's Minneapolis Daily. A very nice newspaperman gave this to me just a few minutes ago and asked that I make sure it was hand delivered to Mr. Ellison. And here you are sir." She handed him the paper. "May I pour your first cup of the day?"

"You certainly may. Thank you so much."

"It's going to be another beautiful day. Aren't we the lucky people? God is so good to us. I hear you will be leaving us this afternoon."

"Yes. I've been told as long as I take it easy for a few more days I may as well be at home."

"Well good for you. Just so you know, you will be missed."

"Oh sure. I'll bet you say that to all the old men."

"No ... I, definitely, do not. Only the ones who have a sunny disposition like yours. Oh, I nearly forgot. The newspaperman said to tell you to 'begin reading on the first page.' I couldn't help but look. That's you, isn't it?"

Just below the fold on the first page, another chapter in the saga of the coffee guy. "Yeah. That's me." The badge on her uniform identified her as Alex.

"I think it's wonderful what you are trying to do. All of us here do. Your breakfast should be ready. I'll be back in a few minutes."

"Thanks again Alex." He sipped on the Forever and relished its goodness. He began to read.

Coffee Man
Tells Brutal Story
By: Sandy Marsh

MINNEAPOLIS – Four were killed and one was spared in a shooting that took place Monday evening in a run-down apartment building on the city's near-north side. Because of the ongoing investigation into this multiple homicide, I cannot reveal the details as explicitly as was related by The Coffee Guy.

In our first story about the him, we named him Samuel. Samuel and three of his college buddies from the Mount Holy Waters University Class of 1960, spent four days together in a cabin in Northern Minnesota two weeks ago. On his way to the cabin, Samuel stopped at a convenience store to use the facilities and was sold two cans of coffee. In a subsequent visit to that same convenience store, Samuel learned that the Native American who sold him the coffee had been dead for 50 years (don't begin to analyze this information until you have completed the reading). You might say to yourself, "This sounds a bit different," or "What a unique thing to have happened." Nevertheless, it happened.

Samuel took the coffee to the cabin and the four friends drank many pots of it over the course of the four days. They realized that health issues had been suddenly eradicated in each one of them over the four days and the only conclusion that could be reached was that the healing was caused by the coffee. They returned immediately to the convenience store to purchase more. It was then that they discovered the gentleman who had sold the coffee had been dead for all those years. Not only that, he had never worked in that convenience store and no coffee had ever been sold out of that convenience store – ever. If you were Samuel, how might you feel upon learning that information?

Samuel, undaunted, returned home planning to pour this coffee for anyone and everyone. He wanted to bring hope to everyone who was suffering from one ailment or another. You see, Samuel just turned 76 and his crowd is aging and illness abounds as the human body continues to, "waste away" – as it says in the Bible.

I first met Samuel at a local police station. Samuel had been brought in because he had been seen standing on a street corner giving away coffee to a suspected drug dealer. Samuel had gone to that corner to give that man a cup of coffee because he had seen him working that corner for months. He also could tell that the man was older than he was. Samuel was trying to do a nice thing because every senior citizen has ailments.

So, the authorities arrested Samuel and he spent a night in jail. The authorities' intelligence information indicated that Samuel had spent many years back in the 70's and 80's in South America assisting the drug cartels in setting up their distribution channels into North America.

Samuel reported that he had never had a passport or been outside the United States. He was born and raised in a Midwest community southeast of the Twin

Cities. He, like his father before him, lived most of his life in that community. He was married to his college sweetheart in that town and they worked and raised their family there. Samuel and his wife moved to the Twin Cities area a few years ago because both of their children lived in the area. They moved here for their retirement years. Samuel, seen giving coffee to a 'bad guy,' was taken to jail.

During his night of incarceration, Samuel met a man older than himself – we shall call him, "Henry," who came to the jail three or four nights a week to, as he put it, 'harvest souls for Jesus.' This was a man who had given his life to those living on the near-north side of Minneapolis. He learned the business from his father: helping neighbors fix things around the house meant there was plenty of time to talk of Jesus. While Henry was fixing things, his wife, "Mary" was taking in washing and doing apartment cleaning. They were rarely paid. They lived in poverty, yet they were doing what God asked them to do; what God asks all of us to do. We can all remember the story of Mother Teresa.

This man, Henry, was slain last Monday evening. Perhaps he was the first of the four to be killed.

Henry knew someone who could analyze Samuel's coffee and provide a report of what the ingredients were. This is not a coffee that can be bought at a local grocery store. The name on the can is, "Forever." Samuel was in that apartment Monday evening to get the results of the analysis. He did not get those results.

Following the shootings, Samuel was unconscious for 36 hours and could not speak for an additional 24 hours. Trauma can do that to a person.

Samuel has a name for meetings where senior's come together. These gatherings are known as Organ Concerts because the conversation revolves around this organ or that one, and the concert can go on for hours. One of these concerts occurs every Wednesday morning; a Bible study at a local church attended by over 150 Seniors. Samuel is usually there insuring every attendee receives his or her coffee.

It would be very easy to say that Samuel and his friend are short on intelligence. Why would Samuel give away a magic coffee and Henry work for people who can't pay? Many in today's society would laugh at them both, believing their work to be foolish and inconsequential.

Henry is dead and Henry's wife is near death in a local hospital today. Samuel remains hospitalized, with his integrity greatly challenged by false allegations.

Henry was the poorest of the poor. Or was he? His work did not bring he and his wife anything in terms of worldly benefits, including Social Security.

Henry, Samuel's friend, lived according to words in the Bible, found in Luke 12 and Matthew 25, and he might have set aside more treasures than all the rest of us put together.

"Don't always think about what you will eat or what you will drink, and don't keep worrying. All the people in the world are trying to get these things, and your Father knows you need them. But seek God's kingdom, and all the other things you need will be given to you." Luke 12:29-31

"I was hungry and you gave Me food; I was thirsty and you gave Me drink; I was a stranger and you took Me in; I was naked and you clothed Me; I was sick and you visited Me; I was in prison and you came to Me.

Then the righteous will answer him saying, Lord, when did we see you hungry and feed you, or thirsty and give you drink? When did we see you a stranger and take you in, or naked and we clothed you? And when did we see you sick, or in prison, and come to you? And the King will answer and say to them, "Assuredly, I say to you, inasmuch as you did it to one of the least of these, My Brethren, you did it to Me." Matthew 25:35-40

Since I met Samuel, and learned of his friend Henry, I've been seriously re-thinking my line of work.

* * * * * * * *

Arvie re-read the last line. *Well,* he thought, *perhaps some good will come of this after all. Maybe this can be an important story to some people. But there are so many out there who are lost in this world, captivated by it and its toys, missing what really matters. Maybe Henry and Mary will continue to influence people even after...*

Alex returned with his breakfast. "Crispy bacon and eggs over medium, just as you like them. Whole wheat toast – 2 buttered slices with honey on the side. A bowl of oatmeal with a packet of brown sugar. A glass of milk and of course, you already have your coffee. Did I forget anything?"

"You've got it all. I thank you very much."

"After I finish serving breakfast, may I come back and talk with you for a moment?"

"I'd enjoy that. Please do."

"Thank you. I'll be back then."

What a delightful young woman, he thought. Then, it was all about consuming bacon and eggs, oatmeal and toast, and enjoying more Forever.

* * * * * * * *

Arvie had long ago finished his breakfast and had nearly completed his reading of the newspaper when Alexandra returned. Her head came in first "Is this a good time?"

"Sure, it is. Come in." The rest of her followed her head through the door. "Now what is it you wanted to speak to me about?" He pointed to the chair on the right side of the bed. "Please. Sit down. Is this your morning break?"

"Yes. I have 15 minutes. Ummm … I've read the articles about you and hope and coffee, you know, in the paper, and I've seen you with your Bible several times over the past couple of days. I moved to Minneapolis four months ago. I had just graduated from nursing school and I was offered a position here. I'm from Milwaukee. My folks are over there and, well, I'm over here and I need some advice."

"Why wouldn't you get on the phone and call Mom and Dad?"

"I know what they'd say. I want to see if someone else would give the same answer."

"Ok. I can understand that. What's the question?"

"I want to get married to my boyfriend, but even before that I want to move in with him. Isn't that ok? Most all my friends have done that."

"Oh, my. That's a big question. I don't know if we've got enough time in what's left of your 15 minutes to tackle that one."

"Well, what's wrong with that? We know we're in love."

"May I ask how old you are, Alex?"

"I'm 25."

"Ok. How old is your boyfriend?"

"He's 28."

"And how long have you known him?"

"Almost three months now," she said with a smile from ear to ear.

"I see. Do you think three months has allowed you enough time to really get to know him?"

"Oh, Yes. He's the one I've been dreaming of, and he says I'm the one he's been dreaming of. Isn't that the way it should be?"

"Yes. Very much so. I'm guessing that you've not been married before."

"Oh no. He got married right after high school. He says they made a mistake and should have waited. They got divorced two years ago."

"I see. Have you asked him why his marriage didn't work out? Has he told you why it didn't last until death as they both promised it would?"

"He's said they were too young and they weren't ready for that kind of commitment."

"Has he told you how old he thinks he should be to take on that kind of commitment?"

"Well, no."

"Alex, you and I don't really know each other, so I'm going to talk with you as I would to my own daughter. I love her very much and I wouldn't want her to make a mistake with a decision as important as this one. I wouldn't want you to do that either, because this is one of the most important decisions you'll make in your whole life. You make the wrong decision here and you may very well live with a lot of regret for the rest of your life."

"You're making it sound overly dramatic, aren't you?"

"No. I don't think so," he responded with a serious tone in his voice.

"I don't even know if you're married. Are you?" she asked.

"I'll say. 52 years."

"Well, you obviously found the right one. I guess I have seen her in here with you."

"I think we made the right decision. But if you and I were having this conversation 51 years ago, I doubt very much if either my wife or I would have thought so then. There was so much fighting going on. I didn't know how to live with another person, nor did she. All the little things about the other person irritated us terribly. She didn't have a clue how to stack the dishwasher properly. I didn't know how to fold a bath towel. I put seasoning salt on a piece of meat before grilling it. She said that's all wrong, that the seasoning is put on after it's grilled, depending on what it tastes like. She'd take the socks out of the dryer and stuff one inside the other. I thought that was wrong because that would stretch the sock that got stuffed. And we paid good money for that sock. On and on it went. All these little insignificant things piled up on top of each other made for a big mess. We loved each other, at least we thought we did, but we couldn't stand living with each other. Know what we did?"

"No. What?"

"We threw away the key. We had vowed in front of God and family and friends to love each other until death. The marriage door was locked. Divorce was not an option on the table. So, we had to figure out what we were going to do. We had to go to work. If you think marriage is sitting at the kitchen table dreamily staring into each other's eyes is what it's all about, you are sadly mistaken. And then about the time you figure out how to live together, peacefully at least some of the time, here comes the kids. Do you think we had spent any time talking about how to raise kids? So, there was more conflict. We then had to figure out how to raise kids together. Here's the question to ask your young man – 'Why didn't you and your wife battle together to save your marriage?' And then you might add, 'because when I get married, it will be forever.' See what he says to that."

"You're taking all the fun out of it."

"Aahhh, perhaps so, but please remember that the really good things in life don't come to us until we've done some very good work. I feel very blessed at this stage in life but it wasn't always that way. Life on this earth isn't easy. God doesn't promise us an easy road. To be honest Alex, life is a lot of work. Marriage is a lot of work. When I got married, I thought to myself, ok I got that job done. Next, I've got to be successful at my work. Guess what I found out? I put 120% of me into my job. And guess what? My life sucked because I was not putting 120% of me into my marriage too. I learned that each area of my life had to have that much of me. So here come the kids and there goes another 120% of me. And that's what it takes. We only have 100% to invest in our life. But I needed 360% of me to invest, and that didn't include moving closer to God on a daily basis, and it also didn't include an involvement with keeping up my health."

"Where is the romance in all of that?"

"Good question. That's something else to work at. See what I'm getting at? Marriage is a lot of work. It's a serious commitment and not one to be taken lightly. Matter of fact, have you looked into marriage counseling? Most people enter into marriage totally unaware of what to expect. Most of them fail. It helps to have some idea. Ask him to go to marriage counseling with you."

"Oh."

"You know that 50% of all marriages fail, right?"

"I've heard that."

"Guess how many 2nd marriages fail?"

"I have no idea."

"75%. So why would you think 2nd marriages fail more than 1st marriages? Any idea?"

"No. Why?"

"Because those who failed in marriage #1, failed to understand why. They didn't work at it. They thought it was all going to be peaches and cream. It wasn't and they did nothing about it. So, did they then do a better job of preparing themselves for marriage #2? No. They changed nothing, expecting the roses again, and wanting the other person to make it work. Guess what? It doesn't work that way. Marriage is a lot more than rolling in the hay. Marriage takes work. And it helps if you marry the right person."

"And how do you do that?"

"Well, for starters, date someone who is a Christian and goes to your church."

"Why does he have to be a Christian?"

"If you are a Christian, it will be so much easier if he is one too. It's important to go to church together, to worship together, to have the same beliefs. It's important for your children to be in church with you because they need to see that it is important to mom and dad. It's easiest if it becomes an every-Sunday thing. A harmony is developed that way. I, for some reason, sense you are a Christian?"

"I was brought up that way. I have slipped away since I left home for school."

"We all desire a life that is happy and is filled with joy. But as we read in Jeremiah, in this world we will always have troubles. This is far from being a perfect world because sin is all around us. But, if we can eliminate as many troubles as possible, life can be less stressful and more satisfying. Remember that this world cannot promise peace but Jesus already has. And we need that in our lives. Now I'm going to rain on your parade some more. You mentioned moving in together before you marry. I'll tell you in no uncertain terms, don't do that. You want to be pure when you marry. You don't want to take any guilt over previous relationships into your marriage. Keep yourself free of that. It says very clearly in the New Testament to stay away from that. It's the best thing you can do to prepare yourself for that one right relationship."

At that moment, there was a brief knock on the door and then it opened. Hannah walked in, followed by Brenda.

"Alex, I'm pleased to introduce you to my wife of 52 years. This is Hannah. Hannah, this is Alex. I have known her since I rejoined the world two days ago. She's my favorite nurse because she brews me a pot of Forever now and then." The Ellison women shook hands and exchanged the usual pleasantries. "And, this is my daughter of 46 years, Brenda. Brenda this is Alex my favorite nurse, and you know why."

"From the outside looking in," said Hannah, "this looked to be a very serious conversation that we just interrupted."

"Yes, it was – is," said Arvie. "I'm glad you are both here. You can help me. Alex asked if she could ask me a very important question. She said she had read about me in the paper and thought I might give her a good answer. She's from Milwaukee and her folks are over there. Alex, please don't be embarrassed, but Hannah, what would be your advice to a young 25-year-old who is pondering moving in with a boyfriend."

"Oh, my goodness. This *has* been a serious time. Well, Alex, my dear, I have three words for you: don't do it. There will be a time in your life, perhaps many of them when the shame will be overwhelming. Save yourself from that and I promise you, you will be glad you did."

"May I say something here?" asked Bren. "Have you been dating this man for at least a year?"

"No. Only three months."

"Please. You have your whole life ahead of you. I know that sounds trite, but it's true. Do you go to church together?"

"No."

"Do you want your husband to go to church with you? Is that important?"

"I don't know."

"There's your answer, Alex. You need to settle a few things in your mind; what do you want out of a husband and your marriage? We have a wonderful marriage counseling program at our church. I can line you up for that if you would like. Let me give you one of my cards. You call me anytime. I am not married, but I was once, for two weeks. And then I had it annulled. I have some experience in this area, and I'm happy to share it if you would like."

"You're a nurse too," she exclaimed, looking at Bren's card.

"Yes. Over 20 years now, though I find that hard to believe."

"Would you have another moment for another question or two?"

"Sure. Let's go find a place to talk and we'll leave these two alone."

Before they got to the door, Alex turned back to Arvie and said, "Thank you. You should meet my dad. I'm sure the two of you would get along great."

"I'd look forward to that. They're checking me out of here sometime this afternoon. If I don't see you again, I'll be thinking of you and praying for you."

"Thank you." Alex and Bren closed the door behind them.

"That was interesting," said Hannah. "And just how many pretty, young nurses have been sitting at your bedside soaking up your wonderfulness when I'm not around?"

"Gosh, dear, there have been, wait, I'm counting – one. And by the way, I'm glad you showed up when you did. I was traveling down an uncomfortable road there. Thanks for the help."

"Sounded like you were doing just fine."

"Well, Dad's perspective to a young lady is one thing. Mom's perspective is also one thing. A young lady needs to hear both."

* * * * * * * *

Shortly after lunch, Nurse Jensen came in to shoo everyone out. "Time for some final tests," she said. "If we're going to get you out of here sometime this afternoon, we got some work to do." Just then two more nurses rolled in two pieces of 'testing' equipment. The three of them rolled up his sleeves and began to hook him up. "Whatever it takes" he chuckled. "I'm yours."

* * * * * * * *

It was nearly 4:15 when Nurse Jensen and Alex came to send him on his way. Arvie, having already packed away his stuff in his gym bag now sitting on the chair by the bed, was looking out the window. The ebb and flow of the traffic down below was intriguing to him.

"Packed and ready I see. I hope the next time I see you it won't be in one of my hospital rooms. You'll be happy to know," she said with a wry smile, "that Dr. Niro has given you a clean bill of health. He does advise you, however, to refrain from hitting yourself in the head again."

Arvie could not keep himself from letting loose a loud "Hah." He then went on to exclaim, "I will take the good doctor's advice seriously, and thank you for everything." He shook hands with both Nurse Jensen and Nurse Alex. For the latter, he included a brief hug and with a serious look in his eye said, "I wish you the very best."

Hannah had been holding the door open, waiting for him. He picked up his duffle to depart, and after taking two steps towards the door, felt a firm hand on his upper arm. Nurse Jensen said, "And where do you think you're going? You'll not be walking out of this room, Mr. Ellison. You will ride in this chair out the front door of the hospital to your car." Nurse Alex rolled the wheel chair up behind him.

"But that's not necessary."

"Tut, tut, my dear sir. Do you want me to lose my job?"

"No, I don't want that."

"Then please be seated."

He did as he was told.

Nurse Alexandra said proudly, "I will do the honors."

* * * * * * * *

Once at the curb, Nurse Alexandra released him from the bondage of the hospital wheel chair, and he walked the few steps remaining to the front seat of his car. Bren held open the door to the front seat for him, and the back door for her mother. Once both were settled and the doors closed, she shared a brief hug with Alex along with a few words, then proceeded to the driver's side and climbed in behind the wheel. Arvie and Hannah both waved to Alex as they departed.

"Well, we've survived another very interesting chapter in our lives" murmured Hannah.

"Yes, we have," said Arvie. "And what's for dinner tonight? I'm hungry for some home cooking."

"I've got all the stuff in the trunk for some of my special spaghetti. Will that work for you?"

"Boy, I'll say."

"Good. I also bought a nice bottle of Pinot Noir for our welcome home celebration."

"Nice. By the way, how did you get along with our young friend Alex?"

"We got along nicely but we did not have enough time. So, she and I are meeting for lunch tomorrow. I invited her to the 4:00 service and she accepted. Can we sit together as usual?"

"Absolutely. Well done."

Chapter 20

"You boys better figure out what you want to do, what your life's work is to be. There's nothing worse than to float listlessly from one thing to another your whole life. When you come to the end, you feel that you wasted your time. Fortunately, I don't have that problem."
- Ole

"All who make themselves great will be made humble, but those who make themselves humble will be made great."
Luke 14:11

On Saturday morning, Brooks picked up his dad and the two of them headed down 35W to keep the appointment with Mrs. Koepke. They talked primarily about yesterday's article in the newspaper and what they might expect to find with Mrs. Koepke today. Arvie told Brooks about the conversation with his young nurse.

"Why do you think she picked you as the audience for her story, her questions?"

"I don't know. Maybe she looked at me and saw a very wise man, capable of providing sage advice."

"I'm sure that's it."

* * * * * * * *

They pulled up in front of the apartment building. Yes, Henry and Mary's apartment building. They both stared at the building. Arvie said quietly, "It all happened here, five days ago. Henry is gone, and Mary continues her brave struggle. But life goes on." He turned to look at Brooks. Brooks was looking at him and said, "Are you ready for this? Are you ready for what's next?"

Arvie said, "Yes I am. Let's go help Mrs. Koepke. Let's do what Henry did for all those years."

Mrs. Koepke lived in 210, just down the hall from 204. 204 was where the Brannon's had lived and served for so many years. That era was now over. Arvie stood looking at the door and he felt himself filling up with emotion, but now was not the time to mourn. There was work to be done.

They knocked on a fragile looking door. According to the numbers on the door jam, it was apartment 21. The '0' was nowhere to be seen.

Many seconds later, Mrs. Koepke opened the door. If Mary was 80, Mrs. Koepke was 90. She was so tiny and frail and hunched over, but Arvie saw no, halo of fire. Brooks said hello to Mrs. Koepke and asked if she remembered he was going to come by today.

"What?"

Brooks asked his question again, a little louder this time.

"Oh, yes. Of course." She stepped slowly away from the door saying, "Please … come in. Thank you … for coming. If you'll … follow me please." With great effort, she turned and began her struggle to walk. As she slowly led them down the narrow hallway, Brooks turned and looked back at Arvie with an expression on his face of "how can people live like *this*?"

The three of them reached the little bathroom. It was obvious the stool needed plunging, but she said, "The drain in my sink is … plugged. Can you unplug … it for me? Henry has always done … it for me but I can't seem to find … him, this week."

Brooks took over. "Yes ma'am," he said. "We'll fix that up for you in a jiffy." He dropped quickly to his knees, put his bucket underneath and began to unscrew the trap.

One face towel hung on the only towel rod. No wash cloth or bath towel was visible. There was no way she could ever take a bath any way. She would not be able to climb in the tub. Arvie's eyes found the plunger. It was not difficult to find in the barren room. He reached behind the toilet bowl to retrieve it.

Mrs. Koepke asked, "Oh, what is that? I don't remember … too well."

"Don't worry about a thing, Mrs. Koepke," Arvie said. "I'll take care of this for you."

"How's that?"

"I SAID," a little LOUDER this time, "WE'LL TAKE OF THIS FOR YOU."

It was obvious that the stool had not been flushed for quite some time. Arvie had learned that the first thing to do with a stopped up toilet is to flush it, and see how bad it really is. He hesitated to do that, as high as the water lever was. He eyed the water shut off under the tank, and then flushed it to see what would happen. He didn't want to overflow this one. It would have created a real mess. But it flushed. Perfectly. After it filled again, he flushed it again. It worked perfectly again. And then it struck him – she has forgotten to flush her toilet – for at least a week? Perhaps she has forgotten *how* to flush her toilet.

"Mrs. Koepke," Arvie said gently, "remember now to flush every time you use the toilet."

"What?"

Louder this time, he repeated "REMEMBER TO FLUSH THE TOILET EVERY TIME YOU USE IT."

"Oh, yes. I guess … I've … forgot how to … do that. Can you show … me?"

"SURE. THIS IS THE HANDLE RIGHT HERE, AND YOU PUSH IT DOWN LIKE THIS. SEE HOW THAT WORKS? LET'S LET IT FILL BACK UP." (Wait)

"NOW YOU TRY."

She reached down for the handle. Her hand fluttered around in the air. She couldn't see the handle. "HERE, LET ME SHOW YOU." Arvie took her hand and moved it to the handle. "HERE'S THE HANDLE. NOW JUST PUSH IT DOWN."

"Oh, I didn't know." She flushed. "Oh, I see. Isn't that nice. I'll try to remember to do that."

Oh, dear Lord Arvie mumbled to himself *she is both blind and deaf.*

By this time, Brooks had cleaned out the trap and put it all back together again and was running the water to check for leaks. "IT'S ALL WORKING JUST FINE, MRS. KOEPKE, SEE?"

"Oh, that's so … nice. Thank you so much."

"YOU ARE WELCOME. IS THERE ANYTHING ELSE WE CAN HELP YOU WITH?"

"No. That's all. I can't thank …you enough. I won't be able to … give you anything until next week."

"THERE IS NO CHARGE FOR WHAT WE DID TODAY. CAN I GIVE YOU MY PHONE SO THAT YOU CAN CALL IF YOU NEED ANYTHING?"

"I don't have a … phone."

"OK. WILL IT BE OK IF I COME BY NEXT SATURDAY TO SEE IF YOU NEED ANYTHING?"

"That would … be so nice. Would you … please? Henry usually … does that for me."

"I WILL SEE YOU NEXT SATURDAY. YOU TAKE CARE OF YOURSELF. OK?"

"Yes … I will."

"GOODBYE THEN."

"Goodbye."

She led them back down the hallway to the door, supporting herself with the walls as she felt her way long. The two rooms they saw off the hall had no furniture except for one folding chair sitting by a window in one room. On the floor of the second room were two blankets strewn haphazardly in a corner. No pillow, no bed, no dresser, no chair, no mirror, closet door open revealing two dresses, each hanging on a hook. They did not see the kitchen.

Brooks opened the door and they stepped out into the hallway.

* * * * * * * *

After Arvie pulled the door closed, Brooks looked at him and said, "Oh my God. Dad, I've only been doing Henry's job for 15 minutes and already I want to cry. People actually live like this? You know what had clogged the sink? Toilet paper."

Arvie could only shake his head. "She's blind, Brooks." He didn't want to think about it. They turned towards the stairs, and noticed a young man leaning up against a wall near the stairway. He was a handsome lad, tall, maybe 6'3" or 6'4", very slender and quite young. There was a hint of Henry in his looks. It was as if he was waiting for them.

Arvie walked over to him and said, "I feel like I know you. Have we met?"

"No sir. I don't believe so. I live here. Judging by the tool box, you were doing some work for Mrs. Koepke."

"Yes, we were."

"Was it her bathroom sink and toilet again?" he asked with a slight smile.

"It was indeed." Arvie noticed for the first time the tool box near the young man's feet. "I take it that you are also familiar with her sink and toilet."

"Yes, I am. I stop by at least once a week to check on her. She doesn't remember very much from one week to the next."

"So, then, you ... flush her toilet?"

"Yes, I do. And then I show her again how to do it."

"And you live in this building?"

"Yes sir, I do."

"Then you knew my friend. Henry? Henry Brannon?"

"Yes sir, I did. Very well."

All of a sudden, a very warm feeling rushed over Arvie. "I'm sorry. Please forgive me. My name is Arvie Ellison, and this is my son Brooks."

"I'm very pleased to meet you both." And then to Arvie "You are the Coffee Guy. Right?"

"I guess some people have called me that."

"Henry did. He told me all about you. I've been reading the Sandy Marsh columns in the paper. Hope is a wonderful thing, Mr. Ellison. I'm very impressed that you would be doing what you are doing. As you have seen after visiting Mrs. Koepke, there isn't much hope around here, especially if you are old and you can't read any more because you can't see any more. The Bible is only a memory if no one is around to read it to you. And if someone is around to read it to you, like Henry or me, it's all forgotten five minutes later because the memory is gone. How is it possible to have any hope when you can't read the Bible and there is no one around to remind you of Jesus. Children and grandchildren have moved away, and any other relative in town doesn't come to visit anymore. All the old friends are gone or are as equally helpless and can't get out. In the end, no one comes to visit anymore and in reality, life is over. But it continues on, and on and the helplessness only gets worse. I try to help with the hope thing too," - he pulled a small Bible from his hip pocket, "but around here there are too many who have quit, given up. What happened upstairs last Monday evening is what happens when someone can't see the point in living any more and therefore has no hope. Most don't use a shotgun. Most just quit and wait for death. Oh, my name is Colby Billings. I should have introduced myself earlier."

"Colby Billings. It is a pleasure to meet you," said Arvie. They shook hands.

"Hi, Colby. I'm Brooks." They shook hands also.

"So, Colby, how did you come to know Henry?" asked Arvie.

"Eight years ago, I'm on the streets. I was 14. It was a very cold winter night. I had given away my jacket to a little girl. She was on the streets too, and she had no coat. I fell asleep in an alley that night hugging her. I woke up the next morning on Henry's couch. They found me. They did not find the little girl. They took me in. I lived with Henry and Mary for several years. Henry got me back in school. Where they got the money, I don't know, but they fed me, put clothes on my back. I never knew what love was until I met them. Three years ago, Henry got me my own place to stay. It doesn't cost me anything and now I have a part-time job so I can pay for my books and stuff and what I need in my tool box. I never learned what happened to that little girl," he said sadly.

Brooks said, "I've got to ask. Where are you living for nothing?"

"Let me show you." He turned and headed down the stairs. They went down two flights, into the basement. Over by the furnace was an old metal army cot with sheets, pillows and blankets.

"Henry talked to the landlord and arranged this for me. I study here some, but mostly at the school library. Henry found me that little bookcase and there is a big wash tub over there I use. Mary always brought me a clean wash cloth and towel every week and she'd wash my clothes now and then. I clean up around the building on a regular basis: sweep the halls, wash windows, shovel snow, paint and do other stuff. I've learned how to take care of the furnace. So for what I do the owner of the building, Mr. Nash lets me stay down here. And, he pays me a few bucks every month. Thanks to Henry, of course."

"What about your family, Colby?"

"I don't have any. As I understand it, my dad ran off before I was born. When I was 13, one day my mom just left too."

"Do you have any transportation?"

"No sir. I walk, or I run, wherever I need to go."

"So where do you eat?"

"Right here. I've got a little hotplate under my bed. I've got everything I need, again thanks to Henry and Mary. I used to go up and eat with them more often than I should have because they rarely had enough for one of them, to say nothing about feeding three. I was always invited and I'm sure they always ate less than they should have."

"What are your plans for the future? What do you want to do?"

"I want to take over Henry's business. I want to be a man like him."

"So, what is the schooling for? What will that do for you if you want to be like him?"

"There is something inside that keeps me wanting to learn. I know I want to help people. I ate too many dinners of thinned soup and crackers with the two of them, sitting around their little table listening to the passages in the Bible all about serving people. It made sense to me. 'Unto the least of these…' I love that."

"Henry didn't make any money, Colby. Aren't you interested in making money?"

"No sir."

"Did you have plans to help some people today?" Arvie was pointing down towards the tool box at his feet.

"Yes sir. Saturday is my favorite day. I have a full plate all day."

"Would you mind if we tagged along? Perhaps there is something we can help with?"

"I'd sure appreciate that. Let's go next door to Mr. Elston's." They headed up the stairs to the second floor. They passed Mrs. Koepke's door and stopped at the next one.

Colby rapped on the door. There was no answer. He knocked again, but still no answer. He opened the door and entered. The door was not locked. "Mr. Elston," he called. "Mr. Elston, it's Colby. Follow me," he said, quietly, and quickly walked through a small

300

empty room to an open door on the right. Colby entered the room quickly saying, "There you are Mr. Elston. Let me give you a hand there." Brooks and Arvie peered into the little room, discovering it to be a bathroom.

It was a very small bathroom with only a sink and a toilet. Mr. Elston was seated on the toilet. He looked at them distantly, emptiness in his eyes.

"Can't get up" he mumbled softly.

"Have you wiped yourself?" Colby asked.

"Huh?"

"Do you want to do that or do you want some help?"

"I could use some help."

"All right then." Colby reached for the toilet paper, taking the last little bit on the roll. He had obviously done this before. He was fast and expert, yet his actions were kind and gentle. There we are. All done. Now, where is your underwear, Mr. Elston? Did you forget to put some on today? Remember that we talked about underwear helping to keep you warm. Remember?"

"Oh yeah."

"You wait right here. I'll get it."

"Ok."

Colby retraced his steps towards the front door but turned left into a little room. Arvie stood in the middle of the empty living room grasping for an understanding of what he'd just witnessed. Brooks followed Colby down the short hallway. They moved quickly to a small closet with no door. On the floor, was an undershirt and a pair of underpants in a pile. Colby quickly retrieved them, conducted a quick inspection of the garments, gave Brooks a quick smile and returned to Mr. Elston. Brooks looked around the room that was obviously Mr. Elston's bedroom. A small cot with a thin mattress and two blankets left askew on top. There was a small pillow, but no pillow case. No other furniture. Perhaps two changes of clothing hanging from hooks in the closet. A pair of worn shoes on the floor.

Brooks stopped to look into the kitchen. He could hear Colby assisting Mr. Elston get dressed. He saw a very small stove and refrigerator on one wall with cupboards above. Brooks opened the refrigerator door. He saw half a quart of milk. Nothing else. Opening all the cupboards revealed one box of Cheerios and two cans of chicken noodle soup. On the stove in a sauce pan was one tablespoon. There was nothing else in the kitchen, save for a very small drop-leaf table in the corner and one rickety metal chair. He closed all the cupboard doors and drawers and left the room.

Colby got Mr. Elston dressed, including the underwear, a pair of pants and a shirt, socks, and the pair of shoes from the bedroom. The entire time Colby was dressing him, Mr. Elston stood staring directly at him, his arms hanging limply down his sides. There were times when trying to put on his shirt that Colby had to take an arm and hold it a certain way in order to get it in a sleeve. And then it was the same with the other arm. His arms appeared to be totally useless.

Before leaving Mr. Elston, Colby reminded him he'd be back to fix his lunch. "A bowl of soup would be good," he said. Mr. Elston nodded. Colby walked to him and hugged him and said, "I love you man. Keep it going. I'll see you soon."

Colby looked at Arvie and Brooks, nodded almost imperceptibly towards the door. Brooks turned to Mr. Elston and said, "Good bye Mr. Elston. You have a nice day." Arvie waved and said, "Bye."

Once outside, Brooks asked, "Colby, how do you do that?"

"You mean, cleaning him as I did?"

"Yes."

"Henry taught me. The first time I came to see Mr. Elston, I didn't know what to do. Henry had told me that his arms didn't work, that he had no strength; something to do with pinched nerves. I learned that the VA had done back and neck surgery several times and they wanted to do it again but in a different location. Mr. Elston had said no, never again. That first time I entered his apartment, the smell was so bad, and it was all over the apartment. Henry and I cleaned and cleaned. Mary had to wash all his clothes. We used a disinfectant everywhere. It was then Henry told me that at least once a day we needed to visit Mr. Elston for the purposes of keeping him clean."

"He is very sick," said Arvie, quietly.

"Why do you say that, Dad?" asked Brooks.

"I could see the halo. It was very bright."

"I'm sorry – what's a halo?" asked Colby.

"Dad can tell when people are sick because he sees a halo of fire around their heads."

"Oh, yes. I read about that. That's a God thing, isn't it? Will you come with me to see Jim Schilling?"

"Sure. Where does he live?"

"Right next door. Right here."

Colby knocked on the door.

"Jim. It's Colby. Let me in."

"Go away. I don't need nothing."

"Come on Jim, open this door – right now."

There was a scraping sound that came through the door. A moment later, another. Then, another.

"He's coming," said Colby, smiling softly. "Jim is one of my challenges."

The door opened slowly, with a distinct squeak of the hinges.

"Jim, I'm checking toilets and water faucets today. I won't be a minute. These are friends of mine – this is Arvie and this is Brooks. They'll wait for me right here, just inside your door. They won't let Bertil out."

"Better not. Been awful today. Mean. Hurry up, then. Get your crap done and get out."

"I'll only be a minute, Jim. Have you heard from Emily recently?"

"She came by last night with her two daughters and we had a nice chat. They brought me a birthday cake. Chocolate, just like I like."

"Well that was nice. Last time I was here, you told me you had spoken with Sonja and that she was planning to take you north to the cabin for a couple of weeks. Did you get that on the calendar?"

"She hasn't got back to me on the dates yet."

Colby returned from the bathroom and was heading for the small kitchen located at the far end of the main room. "All good in the bathroom, Jim. You'll be sure to let me know those dates, won't you?"

"What are you? My mother? Yeah, I'll let you know." He jumped up from his wooden chair, held his left hand over his right eye and screamed "BERTIL. YOU'D BETTER QUIT THAT OR

I'LL TELL ON YOU. I MEAN IT. QUIT IT." He then sat back down.

Arvie and Brooks felt their blood racing as their blood pressure skyrocketed. They both glanced at the door to make sure it was still in the same place in case they had to make a hasty retreat. Colby, in the meantime, hadn't reacted to the "Bertil" outburst at all, continuing to work with the kitchen sink.

"Yesterday was Friday Jim. Did Mary Nell get you to see Dr. Goodschell for your meds?"

"Yeah, and she took me to Panera's for a salad, too."

"You've still got a way with the women, Jim."

"If you got it, you got it."

Jim Schilling jumped to his feet again, covering his right eye with his left hand and screamed "BERTIL, JUST KEEP IT UP. DO YOU WANT ME TO HIT YOU A GOOD ONE?"

There was a soft little girl's voice that came from somewhere "No."

"THEN STOP IT RIGHT NOW."

"K."

Jim sat down.

"All done, Jim. Everything looks good. You going out for lunch today?"

"No. I'm eatin in."

"Good to see you Jim. Be back tomorrow. Ok?"

"Yeah. You can see the trouble with Bertil?"

"Yeah. I'll say. Tell him the story of the Prodigal Son again. Be good, Jim."

Both Brooks and Arvie offered a "Bye, Jim" almost in unison.

Jim glared back at them.

Back in the hallway, Brooks asked, "What was that?"

"That's Jim being Jim. He's got a whole family of imaginary people. I learned from Henry that it's the only way to have any kind of relationship with him. I don't even use the same names every time I use whatever name pops into my mind and he responds. It was a very bad automobile accident many years ago. He never leave's his apartment and he's always the same. You should hear him tell Bertil the story of the Prodigal Son. Hard to imagine but he tells it so beautifully, and most times, he's crying at the end. I don't know what his relationship was with his father. He won't talk about it. Bertil is his best friend. How did you like Bertil's voice?"

Brooks asked, "Was that him?"

"Yes."

"Dad, did you see a halo?"

"No. He's physically good."

"Colby," said Brooks, "we've got to be going. But next time we come, we'll take more time. Now we realize what it takes, after watching you today. Do you go door to door like this every day?"

"Every day. Most every apartment in this building. There are other buildings next door and down the street. I'm in most all of them every day for one thing or another. Thanks for coming this morning. It was nice to meet you." Colby shook hands with both of them.

Arvie had one last question. "Colby, how do you begin every day? What do you do to prepare yourself for what we just saw?"

"I start with God, prayer, and the Bible. I don't understand how anyone can begin a day without that. Philippians 2:7 is a good place to prepare. *"But he gave up his place with God and made himself nothing. He was born to be a man and became like a servant."* That verse gets me in the right mind-set."

"May He bless you Colby. Stay strong."

Colby raised a hand in farewell.

* * * * * * * *

Arvie and Brooks headed to the stairs and out the front door. Once outside, Arvie inquired, "What do you make of that?"

"Well, Dad, I didn't know Henry. What do *you* make of that? To me, based on what I've heard of Henry, finding Colby there and listening to him talk, doesn't surprise me at all. You?"

"No. It's exactly what I *should* have expected. Nice looking young man, isn't he?"

"Yes. Can you believe how he helped Mr. what-was-his name?"

"Elston. Yes. Wasn't that sad. It was some beautiful too, wasn't it?"

"Yes. Yes, it was. Isn't there anything that can be done in a case like that? Like all three of them we saw today?"

"Maybe we should make it our business to find out the answer to that question. What services might be available to these people. What county are we in down here?"

"We'll find ..."

"Stop. Stop the car."

"What?"

"Look there."

"Where?"

"Right there. Tacked up on that telephone pole."

"Ok. It's a placard with a picture of someone with the word "Tribute" at the top and some writing underneath."

"That's Henry. I'll be right back."

Arvie headed to the pole, reached up and pulled it down. He was reading it as he walked back to the car.

"At the top is the word *Tribute*. Then Henry's picture, and then the words...

Did you know Henry and his wife Mary? If they meant anything to you, if they helped you in any way, light a candle in your front window at 11 pm on October 11. Let's light up this part of town to show we care for their memory and thank them for their loving service. Thank You.

"Who do you suppose would head up something like this?"

"It'd be nice to find out, wouldn't it?" Brooks hinted.

"Maybe Colby would know. Let's go back."

Brooks pulled a U-turn and they again headed to the 2nd floor. They found Colby still in the 2nd floor hallway, on his knees looking for something in his tool box.

"Colby. We just saw this flyer. Do you know anything about this?"

"Yes sir. Me and a couple of men got together and we wanted to do something. This is the best idea we could come up with. We watched them for so many years giving themselves to all these people, doing everything for them at all hours of the day and night, and coming away empty handed. They had no money for anything, not even medical attention when one or both were sick. They gave and gave and even when I thought there was nothing left to give, well, they gave some more. It's all they knew – giving; serving others. No one outside this neighborhood knows anything about them, what they did, the dedication. They weren't after any kind of recognition. I can't tell you how many people within a one-mile radius of this apartment building they helped one way or another. It was unending. I tried to tell them about several people they were giving themselves to that were just taking advantage of them. They couldn't see that. They could only see helpless people in need and as such, they had to be there for them. It was as if being taken advantage of made their serving those very people even more important and meaningful."

"Did you get upset when you saw what was happening?"

"I saw purpose in what they were doing. In some cases, it took me longer to understand than in others. They never sought so much as a thank-you. By the world's standard, they ranked at the very bottom. And yet, they had their flock as they called them, they had each other, and they had their God. It was all so simple for them and that's what I loved about them. For some, having everything money can buy still is not enough. Henry and Mary not only had happiness, they had joy – real joy. And they had joy because they had Jesus. Jesus gave them the peace that passes all understanding, and the promise of eternity, long after all the things of this world have rusted away. That's what made sense to me. That joy, that peace. That is what I am after."

"You are very adult for someone so young."

"That's what Henry said."

"So, what you are asking is that all the people that knew them light a candle in their front window at 11 pm on that date – what was it again?"

"10 – 11."

"Ok. That's weeks away yet. How many of those placards have you put out so far?"

"Nearly 500. One of the guys who is in on this with me is providing all the materials and the printing services for free. It seems that Henry and Mary helped not only this man's parents but his grandparents as well. Both sets lived in the neighborhood. He wants the Brannon's to get a sense of payback even though there is no money involved."

"So, if you have thousands that light a candle at that time on that night, what will that accomplish? You'll see it, I'll see it - but Henry is gone. Mary may be gone too by then."

"I believe what we do will be seen by the two of them. There are so many here who owe their lives to them who were totally unable to thank them appropriately while they were living. Now all it takes is a candle to express a lifetime of thanks. I have promised to provide candles to any who might need them. There is another gentleman I have met who owes the Brannon's a 'huge debt.' I don't know what that might be. But in that gentleman, I have found another friend who is helping me finance this tribute."

"If there is anything we can do to help, will you please let us know?" Arvie was fumbling in his back jeans pocket for his billfold. "I'm another one that owes them both a sincere debt of gratitude." He pulled out every bit of folding money he had. He found a $5 bill mixed in the bills, extracted that and stuffed in his pants pocket. The rest he handed to Colby. "Take this Colby, for whatever you need it for."

"I'm not looking for money."

"I know. But maybe a few dollars will help you in your work. Please take it – it'll make me feel better."

"Ok. I will do that. We want this tribute to be a show of thanksgiving from those who knew them and appreciated them for what they did, for what they gave. I truly believe that if all who knew them will light a candle, this whole area of the city will glow like downtown Minneapolis over the Christmas holidays."

"I want to see that."

"I know, I just know that the line waiting for them up there (he pointed up) will be extremely long when they arrive. Well, Henry's already experienced that. Mary's moment is still to come. I'm hopeful that lighting these candles in their memory will sooth the souls – in some way, of those who remain here."

"You are very young to feel so deeply about someone, and have such an understanding of what their lives meant to so many."

"They showed me what love was all about. No one had done that before, ever. I want to love the way they did. How do you repay someone for giving that to you? Because of them, I have hope; both for me and for all the others."

"Are you sure you're not related to Henry?"

"I don't believe so," he sad with a giggle, "I never knew my dad. Henry and Mary's son ran away at a very young age. They never knew what happened to him. I really never knew my mom either. She left me with different women all the time, day and night. I have been to every hospital searching for my birth records. I can't find any. Unless mom or dad shows up some day, I doubt I'll ever find any family history."

"You remind me so much of him."

"I'll take that as a compliment."

"Colby, Brooks has a wife, children, and a job. I am retired and I have much more time available. We plan to be around here to help when we can. If you need one or both of us for any reason, here is my phone number. Please call."

Brooks took the note and added his number. And he added, "Please Colby. We want to help."

"Thank you. Thank you for being interested. There are many Mrs. Koepke's here. The building is full of them. The next building down the street and the next one too."

"By for now Colby."

"Have a safe trip."

* * * * * * * *

Neither of them spoke, both lost in their thoughts, reliving the morning's experience.

"Dad, do you begin your day with God and the Bible?"

"I do now. Your mom and I began that a couple of years ago. Now we can't go a day without it. We've heard that often from the pulpit at church too. I think it was Pastor Wylie who asked how anyone could start their day without it. He said he wants God to be a part of his day and he invites him in every morning. He said, 'If I don't do that, it's too easy for me to start making decisions on my own'. He said that he needs God's help every minute of every day.

As for me, well, I've made way too many decisions over my life all on my own. I don't know that very many of them were good ones. And I do regret that."

"You don't miss church ever, do you?"

"No. I believe that's a part of living the Christian life. This world will drain you over the course of a week. You gotta get back to church to fill yourself up again. You've been missing a few lately, I've noticed."

"Trust me, I'll not miss any more. I've learned my lesson."

"Do you keep the kids with you in Church?"

"Yeah. Why?"

"Given the age they are, you should drop 'em off for the kids programming. You know that one Saturday night a month when we're in the bookstore?"

"Yeah."

"There is a get together out in front of the Info Center when we arrive for all the volunteers. I've never counted but I suppose there are always 60 or 70 of us. They always have the people from the kids-areas talk about what they are doing that day, and I've been impressed. It might be a good idea to take advantage of that for Arnold and Sophie. You might want to look into that. I remember when you kids were growing up. You went to Children's Church – that's what they called it back then. Remember?"

"I do."

"What do you remember about those times?"

"Not much, I guess."

"Yeah. I think Dove Creek's got a better idea. I'm sorry, I gotta call Noah. I gotta tell him what you and I just witnessed. Give me a couple of minutes."

"Sure. I met Noah the other night at the hospital."

Arvie hit the speed dial for Noah. He answered on the third ring.

"Arvie. We're talking so much these days my phone now tells me it's you calling. What's up?"

"Where are you Noah?" Are you at home?"

"I'm on my way home. Grandpa Bros. Coffee is about five minutes in front of me."

"Let me buy you a cup. Can we meet you there in say, 10 minutes?"

"Absolutely. I'll get us a table. It sounds like there is more than one of you?"

"Yeah. My son Brooks is with me. We're on our way home from Henry's building. I've got to tell you what we just witnessed."

"I'll be waiting for you."

"Thanks. Be right there."

* * * * * * * *

"Where's your coffee, Noah?"

"I decided I'd had enough for the day."

Brooks and Noah greeted each other."

Arvie began. "Noah, I wish I'd had a tape recorder a little while ago. Colby, the 22-year-old protégé of Henry's, was telling us about the situation he faces every day in trying to help all the people in the flock that is now his. I must tell you this, and Brooks can help too. We were with Colby as he dealt with three of the most pathetic situations you can imagine. We were standing in the hallway and I can't say it as good as he did but - it had to do with helpless seniors, crippled with old age and decaying minds and bodies. He said something like . . ."

Arvie's eyes had been closed as he tried to summarize Colby's recent words. When he finished, his head dropped almost to his chest. Arvie opened his eyes and looked across the table at Noah. Noah was staring right back at him. They sat there. Finally, Noah shook his head. "I think that's the most disturbing sequence of words I've ever heard uttered. Helpless and hopeless. Is that what you saw today?"

"Yes. I've never dealt with anything like this before in my life. Maybe that describes normal life for some folks. I don't know."

"Arvie, that's not typical. That's tragic. What can I do?"

"I don't know. I felt like I had to tell somebody from the church. I think Brooks and I will feel better knowing that you know and maybe if more people know, something can be done to put an end to all the misery. There must be a solution."

"I'll think on it, and I'll pray about it as I know you will also. I keep thinking that there is something Dove Creek might be able to do. There are a lot of resources there. But now, I've got to be getting home. Moggy's sister and brother-in-law are coming to supper. Let's stay in touch. I believe we can find an answer. Keep the faith."

Noah stood to leave, shook hands with Arvie and Brooks and departed.

* * * * * * * *

Brooks dropped his dad off outside his townhouse. They both leaned against the car and talked briefly about the dilemma.

"Dad, all I know to do is to keep going, one day at a time."

"Me too. Something is going to come along. There is something that can be done. We just can't see it yet. Brooks, do me a favor, will you?"

"Sure, Dad. What?"

"Pray about this every morning and every night and as many times during the day as possible. I'm going to be doing that. Will you do it too?"

"Yes. Good. I'm glad we're in this together."

"Me too."

* * * * * * * *

"Honey, I'm Home. Guess who I almost invited to dinner tonight?"

"If it was going to be Marlon Brando I'd be divorcing you Monday morning."

"Well, then it's a good thing it wasn't Marlon Brando. Would you divorce me if I told you his name was Colby Billings? He's very young and he is much better looking than Marlon Brando?"

"Well, if he's that good looking, maybe I would. Who, pray tell, is what's-his-name again?"

"Colby Billings. We bumped into him down at Henry's building. If I had surprised you and brought him home, what would you have prepared for us?"

"I've been craving Chateaubriand with a Béarnaise sauce, a wealth of butter-fried asparagus flowerets in a horseradish marinade, and we'd finish it off with a flaming Banana's Foster for desert. There would also have been a very expensive bottle of Pinot Noir – maybe even a $12 bottle. Would that have worked for you?"

"Gee, I would have liked that," he said slowly and with a big smile.

"How about we order a pizza? I think that'd be good since that's what the kids will be looking for."

"I suppose you're right. Could we at least do the Banana's Foster after the pizza?"

"Hah. And yet again, Hah."

"Does that mean no?"

"You continue to be not as smart as you look. So who is what's his name and how would you know that he loves Banana's Foster?"

"Well, let me tell you how we came to meet Mr. Billings. We had just finished flushing Mrs. Koepke's toilet when . . . ."

* * * * * * * *

Prior to leaving for church, Arvie was clearing the dining room table of all his stuff so there would be room for the pizza eaters. All his notes were piled there, notes regarding the serving of coffee at the hospital, and the Organ Concerts. Henryk Von Barstow. The newspaper articles. He collected all the loose paper lying there, shuffled it all together and was about to stack the pile on top of his notebook when a word on the top note caught his eye. The word was "BOOM." He picked up the note.

It read "BOOM. She touched me and I looked at her and I understood. But as I (coffee stain) into the star filled night sky, the mirror above the sink reflected '10-10-10' encircled in flames. There was a full, very bright moon. A winding road. A barbed wire fence. A thick forest of pine and birch, walnut and oak. A heartbeat. A faint, distant heart beat. The wind moaned through the trees. No. Someone was groaning. Singing? There were many."

The dream. He had forgotten. He had to review those notes. What's today's date? August something. We're still in August. I've got plenty of time to figure this all out. In the jail cell that night, it was Henry who suggested that the 10 – 10 - 10 was a time and date for a meeting, maybe? Where is the rest of it? There was something about a county road J with a W after it? Wasn't there? Yes. He was sure of that. He went through the stack of notes and paged through his notebook. He could find nothing further.

* * * * * * * *

He and Hannah had watched as Brooks and Katy checked Arnie and Sophie into the kids programming prior to church. While they were waiting, Brenda and Alex walked over and joined them. After Alex was introduced to Brooks and Katy, they headed into the sanctuary to their usual section. On the way, Brooks turned to Alex and asked, "Didn't we meet the day before yesterday at the hospital?"

Alex replied with a smile, "Yes, we did."

"I thought so."

The kids programming during the church service was a real topic of conversation over pizza. The kids loved it. They played games, broke up into small groups, learned a lesson about the Good Samaritan and being kind to others. Arvie leaned over to Brooks as the discussion continued and said, "Sounds like they had a great time."

"Yeah. They haven't stopped talking about it yet. Good idea, Dad."

Alex accepted hesitantly the invitation to the family pizza time. Bren had sealed the deal with her comment that she needed some time with a family. She quickly became Arnie and Sophie's newest best friend.

All through church and pizza with the family, Arvie was distracted by the memory of his dream and the unknown destination for the meeting – if that's what it is? One thing he did know; he'll be somewhere at 10 on October 10. But where? It's got to be up 169 probably close to Mille Lacs somewhere. He closed his mind to any further thought on the matter and returned in earnest to the family time.

It was a memorable evening. After the pizza debris had been disposed of, the domino's hit the table. The seven of them plus Alex entered into some spirited competition. Alex sat with Arnie on her right and Sophie on her left. Arvie was entranced with how the kids had taken to her. They discussed every move with her, and she helped them count points. She had a way with kids of this age. Later, as she was leaving, Arvie made sure to let her know she had a special talent in that area. She blushed as she said, "Thank you, and thank you so much for letting me tag along tonight. It was so good to be in church and then to spend this evening with your family. I can't thank you enough."

"Please join us any Saturday at the 4:00 service. You have an open invitation."

"I will take you up on that. Thanks again."

"Come on," said Bren. "I'll walk you to your car."

Once they had left, Hannah said, "I think being with us all tonight was good for her."

"I agree," added Arvie. "And the way she took to the kids. That was special."

Later, as Arvie and Hannah were heading upstairs. "How about you and me going for a ride tomorrow?" he asked.

"What? Where?"

"Do you remember that very vivid dream I had a week or two ago, the one that had 10 – 10 - 10 on a mirror surrounded by a ring of fire?"

"Vaguely, I guess. What about it?"

"I have to go find County Road J, west. That's all the direction I was given. I am guessing that because it has to do with the coffee thing, the Native Americans and all that, it's up 169, close to the big lake. That's a guess. I'm supposed to be somewhere on October 10th at 10 pm. At 10 pm it's dark and I don't want to be trying to find this road in the dark, so I have to go find it some day during daylight hours. I'm gonna meet people at the big bonfire that night, and there will be dancing and chanting and we'll smoke the pipe and hum songs to Mother Earth. Maybe I'll even find out how they make the coffee and how they know when I need more. I'd really like to know how a total stranger can walk up to me in a store somewhere and say to me 'They told me I would know you and I'm supposed to give you this sack of coffee' and then he walks off into a cloud of smoke never to be seen again. How can that happen? So, what do you think? Wanna go for a ride, little girl?"

"You are cute when you talk like that, but no. I'd rather stay home and re-do my sock drawer. And tomorrow is my day to sort trash, you know. And I do need to polish our Sterling. I don't seem to get much help on any of the household projects lately. Yeah. Tomorrow is a big day for me. Plus, I want to watch golf."

"Oh, yeah. Golf."

"Don't give me that 'Oh, yeah. Golf' stuff. It's the Bridgestone this week, and the PGA next week. This is one of the best times of the year for Golf and you want to run around the northwoods looking for some hidden valley somewhere where you and Glitchi Maritime can meet to discuss the ingredients in coffee. You and this coffee thing, and helping people all over the place is starting to get in the way of watching golf. Where are your priorities, anyway? DON'T answer that. But anyway, if you do have some time tomorrow, perhaps you could spend a little time with golf and me. What d'ya think?"

"I'll see what I can do. Interestingly enough, I have no plans to get in the way. I'll take that little trip one day next week. So, who is doing what? Any guys on my team doing anything? I can't believe I've watched so little golf this year. And by the way," he chuckled, "it's not Glitchi Maritime. It's Gitchi Manitou."

"Is there a difference?" she asked.

Their conversation was interrupted by the ringing of Hannah's phone. She didn't recognize the number and thought of not answering. But for some reason, she answered anyway and pushed the speaker button.

"Hello. This is Hannah."

"I'm sorry to bother you, but I believe you called us yesterday regarding Mary Brannon. This is Mary Kay Brunnella at St. Lukes."

"Yes. I called yesterday. What can I do for you?"

"I'm afraid I have bad news. Mrs. Brannon passed a few minutes ago without regaining consciousness. It was very peaceful."

"Oh. I think we knew that we would hear that news one day soon."

"Yes. She was very ill. I'm sorry to be so blunt, but do I talk to you about what to do with her remains?"

"Yes, you can speak with me. The Brannon's have a niche at Lakewood. She is to be cremated and her ash's will be put there."

"Very good. We'll contact Lakewood and arrange for transportation. I'm sorry for the bad news."

"Thank you so much for calling."

"Thank you for your help."

The phone went dead.

"I stand here listening to you," said Arvie, "and I realize that I don't know what happened to Henry?"

"You were going through that rough time at the hospital where you weren't communicating. I had your phone with me and received a similar call. I had no idea what to do, but I did make a decision because I wasn't aware there was anyone else to decide anything. From what you had told me, it was only the two of them and there was no mention of children in the picture at all. I told them to do the same thing with Henry. And then I called Lakewood and purchased a niche right above ours. I'm sorry I forgot to tell you any of that. I don't know why?"

"No matter. That was the perfect decision. Thank you for that. I like the idea of Henry and Mary being right above us. That's beautiful."

"I wished we could have talked about it, but I thought you'd approve."

"I do. And thank you."

"I expect we'll get a bill for the transportation and the cremation of both, plus the cost of the niche. How will we handle that?"

"We'll find a way. It was the right thing to do."

"Just so you know, I prayed about it. Afterwards, it just seemed so right. I thought I had received approval. I got a message that 'at a time like this, do not be concerned with money.' And so I made the call. It will be several months before they do the names on the front. They will be in touch prior to verify how we would like it."

"Well done, my dear."

Chapter 21

"Two old men were out on a beach early in the morning. The tide
had gone out and there were thousands of Starfish dying.
One old man picked up a Starfish in each hand, walked out to the
waters edge and put them in the water. The second man said,
'There are thousands of them here. You can't save them all.'
The first replied, 'Maybe not, but I just saved those two.'
He picked up two more and turned towards the water."
- Ole

*"Instead, when you give a feast, invite the poor, the crippled, the
lame, and the blind. Then you will be blessed, because they have
nothing and cannot pay you back."*
Luke 14:13-14

Another warm day. The morning walk was satisfying, surprising
since his sleep the night before had been fitful. He couldn't slow
down his mind; it wouldn't allow him to forget the tragic scenes he
had witnessed: Mrs. Koepke, Mr. Elston and Jim Schilling. Very
unfortunate people, but people, nonetheless. *They are people very
much alone, seemingly without friends and family. To us looking in,
it seems all wrong that people should have to live the way they do.
After all, God loves them too.*

Arvie and Brooks visited three apartments with Colby the day
before. There must have been at least 50 more in that building alone,
if not more. Colby had said that Henry's ministry extended for as
much as a mile in all directions. *How many more might there be? A
total of several hundred or a few thousand? Several Thousand? If
Colby has known Henry and Mary for the last eight of his 22 years,
chances are he knows of many more deplorable situations like we
saw yesterday.*

Arvie didn't know how to fix this mess. He was almost certain it
couldn't be fixed. There would always be those less fortunate. As
long as there are people, the unfortunate ones will always be there.

Maybe he couldn't fix all of it, but he was determined to try to make life easier and more pleasant for some.

He was so transfixed by the problem whirling around in his head, he failed to see Hannah standing in the patio doors across the street waving her arms at him. She slid the door open and literally screamed, "ARVID." That got his attention. He looked up, saw her waving him in, and headed across the street towards the patio doors.

"What's up?" he asked from several steps off the patio.

"Telephone."

"This early?"

"It's Noah. I told him you were walking the neighborhood. He said he'd wait."

"Thanks dear." He picked up the phone.

"Noah. You're up early."

"Well, it seems not as early as you."

"What's going on this early on a Sunday?"

"Tomorrow is the first Monday of the month. As such, the Dove Creek Board meets at 8:00 at the Church offices. I apologize. I should have remembered this when we talked yesterday. In any event, I spoke with Hedrick Gordon last night at church, he's the President of the Board, about the burden on your heart. He approached Wylie about it. They talked for five or six minutes, and then he waved me over, and said, "We would like to address this subject. The board wants you to be there tomorrow morning to bring this to their attention. If you can be there, I'll introduce you.""

"I'll be there, but I'm not prepared to make any kind of a presentation, Noah."

"No presentation needed, Arvie. You stand up and talk about what you have learned, just like you did to me yesterday. Look at it as a fact-finding meeting. You tell them something that you think they need to hear. They'll take it under consideration. If they should want more information, more detail, whatever, they'll call you back in at another meeting. They may even want to see what you are describing, and a field trip will be in order. This is the first step, Arvie. I'll be there and there will be other familiar faces. Do it, Arvie. This may be the answer to our prayers for those people."

Arvie took a deep breath and said quietly, "I'll be there Noah. Please pray."

"I will. You too."

Arvie hit the red disconnect button and put the phone on the table. Hannah looked over and asked, "So what was that all about?"

"I've got to be at the church offices in the morning at 8:00 to present the story about these suffering people. Board meeting. I'll be addressing the Board of Dove Creek."

"Oh my. … … You'll do fine. Let's talk about it over breakfast."

* * * * * * * *

They talked it out over breakfast. They prayed about it and then they relaxed in front of the TV for an afternoon of golf: the Bridgestone. It was an exciting tournament to watch. There were moments when Arvie actually paid attention, but his mind was forming a script for his presentation at the morning meeting.

Chapter 22

"I always have loved the toughest situations. That's when I have done my best work. You *cannot* screw up the tough situations. If you can't handle 'em, what good are you anyway?" - *Ole*

"So don't worry, because I am with you. Don't be afraid, because I am your God. I will make you strong and will help you; I will support you with my right hand that saves you."
Isaiah 41:10

Arvie was too nervous to eat a breakfast. "Maybe afterwards," he thought. "I could stop for something then."

He was ready to go well in advance. That was his custom. Get ready early so there can be some good quality time spent pacing around the house. That time of subtle panic helps to build more nervousness, thinking about all the things that can, and probably will go wrong. Arvie quickly corrected his thinking. *Positiveness. I have an opportunity this morning. This is the first step towards fixing the problem. Perhaps something can come out of this that will put Mrs. Koepke, Mr. Elston, Mr. Schilling and Bertil in a better place. Be friendly, concerned, and down to earth.* He took a final sip of Forever, loaded his bag with the three thermoses and left the house.

* * * * * * * *

The parking lot was nearly full. Arvie took the last parking space available, located in the most remote corner of the lot. He had never been in this office building before. He would have to ask at the reception desk, assuming he would find one, where the Board is meeting. He looked up to see Noah standing just outside the door, most likely waiting for him. Noah looked in his direction and they gave each other a wave.

They shook hands and Noah led him inside and down a long hallway to the back of the building and the board room. There were others milling about, most with the usual white styrofoam cup in hand, signifying "I'm about to go into a meeting but I've time enough to sip on a little more coffee." Arvie noticed the usual early morning banter being traded back and forth among folks who perhaps hadn't seen one another in a while. Noah suggested they get a cup and steered him toward two steaming pots on a small table just outside the door to the board room.

Arvie was accepting his cup from Noah when another hand was extended towards him. He looked up and saw an unfamiliar, smiling face. "Morning Arvie. I'm Hedrick Gordon and I'm pleased to meet you. I've read all of Marsh's articles about you. I'm very sorry for your loss last week, but I'm very happy that you are here today. I'm looking forward to hearing what you have to say. Is this coffee as good as Forever?"

"No sir. It doesn't come close. I'll have to get you a cup soon. Thanks for having me today. Oh, here's an idea – can I provide the coffee for your board meetings?"

"I for one would love that. Noah mentioned that your subject today just recently came to your attention."

"Yes sir. I have begun to meet members of Henry's flock. It's staggering to me what he did for so many years."

"Noah said something about 'many who have fallen through the cracks, the poorest of the poor. Have you an idea yet how many there are?'"

"Not really. I feel assured there are at least several hundred. But I've just scratched the surface so far. Henry had been working this neighborhood for nearly 70 years. Quite possibly, there could be several thousand."

"I'm looking forward to this, Arvie. I think what you've been doing is quite remarkable also. Hope is difficult to hang on to sometimes. You are doing a great work."

"It overwhelms me. I don't know how I'm supposed to keep up with it."

"Maybe help is just around the corner. God is always with us. Isn't he? Good to talk with you Arvie. I've got to get in there and get this meeting started or we'll be here till sometime tonight. Glad you're here."

"Thank you."

Hedrick Gordon, walked into the board room, and most of the others trailed in behind him.

"Arvie," said Noah, "you'll stay out here and I'll come get you when it's your turn. Ok?"

"Thanks, Noah. I'll be right here."

"You got some ice broken with Hedrick. He knows who you are. That's great." Noah punched Arvie in the shoulder on his way into the room.

The door closed and he was left alone. He had supposed that there would be others presenting possibilities for the church to consider but, it appeared, he was to be the only one. He wondered if that was a good thing? Perhaps so. He bowed his head and prayed that God would be close by, giving him the words and the right spirit to truly present this crisis. "And then it's up to you, Lord. I leave it in your hands. Your will be done. Amen." He kept his eyes closed and focused on Romans 8:26: *"Also, the Spirit helps us with our weakness. We do not know how to pray as we should. But the Spirit himself speaks to God for us, even begs God for us with deep feelings that words cannot explain."*

He thought that verse more comforting now than it had been on previous occasions. The Holy Spirit is working with me and for me, and then he felt a hand on his shoulder. It was Noah. Arvie hadn't heard his entry back into the room.

"Still a couple minutes, Arvie. Did I wake you up?"

"No. I was meditating on Romans 8:26, for the Holy Spirit to be with me today, and, if at all possible, to communicate with God for us on this."

"What's the verse?"

"Romans 8:26. The Spirit pleading with God on our behalf."

"Aahh, yes. That is comforting, and very appropriate for your mission today."

"I think the best place to begin is with Henry, his people, his flock, for his whole life and then some particulars, as Colby talked about. Brooks and I saw some of that on Saturday. I've prayed for the words to bring it to these people as well as I can."

"I'm sure you are going to do it justice. Remember, this is the beginning today. You won't be closing a sale in there, your goal today is awareness."

The door to the boardroom opened and Mr. Gordon appeared. "Gentlemen, please come in."

Arvie entered the room. Noah made his way to his place down the left side of the table. Without counting, Arvie guessed 15-16 people, as many women as men. Mr. Gordon led Arvie to the head table, and introduced him to The Board.

"I'd like for you all to meet Arvid Ellison. Because we all read the paper, we know Arvid as Samuel, the Coffee Guy." Around the table Arvie heard a general murmuring including one female voice say "Really? This is him?"

"Yes, really," said Mr. Gordon, with a pleasant smile.

A familiar male voice to Arvie's right began, "Arvie, I know you have something on your heart you wish to share with us and I don't want to get you side-tracked, but before you leave today, I really want some detail about your coffee."

Arvie looked to his right and realized that the familiar voice belonged to Senior Pastor Wylie Hoyt. "Yes sir," Arvie responded. "I'll be glad to do that."

Dove Creek, largely because of this man, had grown to become one of the largest churches in America. This is the man who has the faith of a mountain. He has given this church to God to lead and as he's said many times from up front, "We are just tagging along, doing His work."

Noah had yet to take a seat, still standing behind his chair. "If I may jump in very quickly here. I received a phone call from Arvie quite recently. I would call it a frantic phone call. I have had several frantic phone calls over the years, but none quite like this one. Arvie and I met for coffee and he told me what we've asked him to tell all of you. Arvie, it's all yours."

"Thank you, Noah." The thought crossed his mind that these next few minutes are the most important minutes of his life. For a moment, he could feel his heart rate rapidly increasing. He took a deep breath, forced himself to smile and regained control.

"One week ago, last Thursday, I was taken from my home and jailed on a variety of drug related suspicions. I spent the night in a jail cell. One of my cell-mates was an older man named Henry. Meeting him that night was, definitely, a God thing. Whereas I had been brought in by DEA and FBI agents for my night in jail, Henry had come of his own accord. He had an arrangement with the police that allowed him to come for a night anytime he wanted. He said when it was busy, particularly on weekend nights, there were always opportunities to help people in trouble, and talk about Jesus. In the course of our conversation, I learned that he and his wife Mary had spent their lives 'harvesting souls for Jesus' – as he put it. He said he learned the job from his daddy who spent his entire life working for Jesus, doing odd jobs for his neighbors. He said his daddy told him that when building something for somebody, or fixin something, or cleaning something, you have a lot of time to talk with them about Jesus. Mary, his wife, took in washing every day, and took it upon herself to clean neighborhood apartments when they got especially bad. Henry and Mary have been doing this work for nearly 70 years, living in poverty, rarely being paid for work done and trusting the Lord for every scrap of food. He told me that the Lord had been especially good to them both.

"One week ago, tonight, Henry was murdered in an apartment just above his own. Perhaps you read something about that in the Minneapolis Daily. Two nights ago, Mary passed in a hospital room at St. Lukes. She had been ill for some time but no one knew of it because she had her wash to do and cleaning … for those in her flock. She just … kept going." He paused for a deep breath and a swallow, hoping it would help the lump in his throat. He was filling up with emotion and yet felt surprisingly calm.

"My son and I have talked about who will carry on the work that they have been doing? We have since learned that their flock consisted of perhaps hundreds of seniors who lived in close proximity to them. Remember, they did not have a car, a phone, a radio, a TV or anything else you and I might take for granted. Every day they made their rounds. Personal contact. Being there with as many as they could get to. Seven days a week. 24 hours a day. Think of it. I don't know about any of you, but now and then, I really enjoy doing what I want to do because I'm full of selfishness. Henry and Mary wouldn't have known anything about that because they served the needs of the less fortunate. They wanted to do nothing but *that.*

"This past Saturday my son and I went down to help some folks in that apartment building. We met a 22-year-old, young man, who has taken up Henry's cause. Henry and Mary had found him on the streets some eight years ago, middle of winter, and no coat. They took him in. He had no family whatsoever. I'll not go into further detail regarding this young man, Colby, except to tell you that he not only told us what Henry did every day for 70 years, he showed us. We followed him into several apartments; we tried to help him, but mostly we just watched.

"I want to tell you what we witnessed in three apartments. The first is the story of Mrs. Koepke. She must be in her 90's. My son had learned that she was having trouble with her toilet and her bathroom sink. The two of us knocked on her door. When she opened the door, she didn't seem to remember my son who had told her we were coming. Finally, because she thought we were Henry, she led us down the hallway to her bathroom. She could barely walk and used both hands on the wall to support herself. The two of us looked at each other wondering how this lady could be living alone.

"In the bathroom, we found the stool in desperate need, totally full of everything you might imagine. My son went to work on clearing the drain in the sink, and I went to work on the toilet. My first thought was to try flushing the toilet. I saw the water turn-off near the floor, just in case. I flushed the toilet. It worked perfectly. I looked at Mrs. Koepke as it was re-filling, and the look in her eyes told me she didn't know what she was seeing. It dawned on me then that she doesn't see anything. I said, "Mrs. Koepke, remember to flush the toilet every time you use it." She said "What?" I repeated myself, this time a lot louder, to which she responded, "I think Henry told me to do that too." She had forgotten how to flush the toilet.

"I asked her to practice, to go ahead and flush the toilet. She didn't know how to. I showed her the handle and demonstrated what to do. 'Can you do that?' I asked. She said she would try. The toilet refilled again, and I said, 'Try now, Mrs. Koepke.' She reached out and couldn't find the handle. I knew then she was totally blind. I took her hand and showed her how to feel the top of the toilet and find the handle down the left side. Once she got her hand on it, she operated it perfectly. She is not reminded to flush by what she sees, because she can't see. Henry had told her many times I'm sure to flush every time. Not only can't she see, she can't remember.

"My son had finished clearing the blockage in the p-trap of the sink. It was operating perfectly. He showed me later that the bucket he used to catch the water from the p-trap was filled with used toilet paper. Mrs. Koepke washed her toilet paper down the sink.

"Mrs. Koepke doesn't know what she is doing. The lady barely has enough strength to stand up. She can't see. She is deaf. Her mind has failed. She doesn't remember. She lives alone. She has one dress other than the one she is wearing. She has one old wooden chair in her living room and an old arm chair in the bedroom that she sleeps in because there is no bed.

"The two of us thanked Mrs. Koepke for her time. She promised to pay us something when she had some money. We told her that would not be necessary. We told her we would be back soon. When we closed the door, we both wanted to cry. We talked briefly about her living there alone. How can that be? In a society like ours, how can it be?

"It was then we noticed the tall young black man standing by the stairway leaning against the wall, hands shoved deep into his jean pockets with a tool box at his feet. We introduced ourselves to Colby, only 22 years old and taking over Henry and Mary's flock.

"He asked if we had been helping Mrs. Koepke with her stool and her sink. When we asked him how he knew, he said that he does it almost daily for her. He said that Henry had trained him and then thanked us for helping because it meant one less task for him. He then invited us to visit Mr. Elston who lived next door.

"Colby knocked several times with no reply. He tried the door and it was unlocked. He opened it and marched purposefully to the bathroom. We followed. An elderly man was sitting on the toilet. We learned that he had no use of his arms due to nerve damage of some kind. Colby asked him if he needed help or if he could do it himself. He said he needed help. Colby wiped him, expertly and efficiently. He had obviously done that many times before. We asked him about it afterwards and he said Henry had trained him. Henry had told him that it will take time to get to know the people and what services they need and how often they need it.

"Colby then washed and dressed Mr. Elston. He goes back at noon every day to heat a can of soup or make a sandwich for Mr. Elston and feed him. Mr. Elston's apartment, like Mrs. Koepke's, void of any furniture. Mr. Elston slept with two blankets on the floor. Mr. Elston gets along unbelievably given his arms do not work. Still, Colby must visit him two or three times every day because he can't go to the bathroom alone, heat a can of soup or make a sandwich.

"Next, we went to see Mr. Schilling, just next door to Mr. Elston. Colby knocked on Mr. Schilling's door. We heard a man's voice inside telling us to get away from his door. Colby talked him into opening the door. Mr. Schilling asked why he was being bothered, and Colby apologized but stated that he was doing a check up on plumbing in the kitchen and bathrooms in every apartment, and he would be only a moment. Colby said afterwards that he tells Mr. Schilling the same story every day in order to get him to open his door. Mr. Schilling doesn't remember that he hears that story every day. Colby went about his business, which we learned later was just an excuse to get him inside. He talked with Mr. Schilling about a variety of people coming to visit, bringing him meds, and several other things. In the middle of that conversation, Mr. Schilling screamed to 'Bertil' to stop what he was doing or he would have to hit him a good one. Bertil is his imaginary friend. Mr. Schilling had to chastise his friend for a second time later, while we were still there. We found it particularly interesting when his imaginary friend answered him in a little girl's voice.

"Mr. Schilling, we learned when we were back in the hallway, had received a serious head injury years ago in an auto accident. All the names Colby used in his conversation with Mr. Schilling were bogus; made up. Colby said he could use any names and it didn't matter. Mr. Schilling would answer all the questions, making up the answers without any problem. Colby said the man is virtually helpless and does nothing all day, every day, except sit in his one chair and talk with Bertil. His mind is gone.

"My son and I, once back in the hallway, wanted to cry again. We had been in three apartments and witnessed devastating situations, seniors living in untenable circumstances.

"Colby stood in the hallway with his young face reflecting enormous empathy for us; so much so that his eyes watered as well. And then he spoke what I am going to read to you. When he had finished, I had wished I'd had a tape recorder for it. His words captured all the emotion we were feeling. It had to do with helpless seniors, crippled with old age and decaying minds. When I got home, I tried to write what Colby had so eloquently said."

Arvie opened the folder in front of him. He withdrew one piece of paper.

"What we saw with Mrs. Koepke, Mr. Elston and Mr. Schilling, is that people still live when there is nothing to live for and when there is no hope left. This is what can be found in nearly every apartment in this building; this neighborhood. How can a human maintain hope when so old and feeble, especially when body and mind are both failing or have already failed? The Bible means nothing anymore, unless someone is there to read it to them. But there never is anyone, except the Henrys and the Marys who carry a Bible with them, at all times. Children and grandchildren have moved away and don't come to visit anymore. Frankly, no one comes to visit. Too many of these human beings are able to do nothing for themselves. If their minds were functioning, they would want life over and done with but it doesn't end; it continues, on and on, relentlessly. Imagine another day with nothing – all day, with nothing. They can't go anywhere because they aren't physically and mentally able and … they have no money. They can't remember where they would go even if they were able, and had both transportation and money. What's the purpose of living another day? They sit alone for another day, and then another. They sold their bed to buy a box of mac'n cheese. They sleep on the floor not remembering ever sleeping in a bed. Loneliness and hopelessness is what the devil loves. He preys on the lonely, the lost. I feel that society has given up these people to the Devil. I try to provide hope as did the Brannon's but it is too late for people like these. What happened to Henry Monday night is just one example of what can happen when all hope is lost. (Arvie folded the paper and returned it to the folder.)

"There are retirement homes for independent seniors, where all forms of assistance can be called in to provide help, even hospice. There are nursing homes for those who cannot live alone any longer. There are places for people suffering with Alzheimers, memory care. There are wonderful retirement centers where a continuum of care is provided, from independent living to nursing home and finally to hospice. It would sound like everything has been provided for our aging society. But, to go to those places, money is required. These people here, that Henry and Mary took care of for so many years, have no money, so they must wait for it all to end, but continue to live in the manner that I have described." Arvie was ready to cry, so filled with emotion but knowing he must press on.

"I hope I have not taken up too much of your time. I'm sure you have many things to discuss. I will wait out there until you are finished, should you want to ask me anything further. Thank you for giving me the time to bring this to your attention. And please, when you sit down for supper tonight with your family, remember Mrs. Koepke, Mr. Elston and Mr. Schilling. Pray for them please, and all the others. The tragedy in all of this is these people have no hope. They don't know what it is anymore, and without hope, there can be no joy, no happiness – only an ongoing despair. Thank you." Arvie picked up his folder and turned to leave.

"Mr. Ellison, may I ask you a question before you leave?" It was Pastor Hoyt.

"Yes sir. Of course."

"Am I correct, that all of what you just told us began because you wanted to pour your coffee for a man begging on a street corner?"

"Well, I guess you could put it that way, yes."

"That's what got you a night in jail, where you met Henry."

"Yes sir."

"How old are you, Mr. Ellison?"

"I'm 75, sir."

"The story I read in the paper talked of all the ways you were going to try to give out your coffee, including opening a coffee shoppe. Have you had time to look into that one yet?"

"No sir. I continue to think about it, but I'm afraid that idea is a bit out of my price range."

"It occurs to me that your idea about getting your coffee to everyone is a good one. It's beautiful, I think. How is your acid reflux?"

"It's really good, because it's gone."

"Amazing. We should have thought to ask you to bring some coffee with you. We sell a lot of coffee before services at church, you know."

"Yes sir, I know. I have a cup every Saturday during the 4:00 service. Oh, I almost forgot; I have three thermos bottles in the car, sir. I'd be happy to bring them in."

"Really?"

"Yes sir."

"Let's take a 10-minute break, everybody. Thanks, Arvie. I would love for us to try some – what is the name – Forgiven?"

"No sir. Forever. I also can brew Redeemed, Reunion and Mercy."

"Wait. You have coffee named Forever, Redeemed, Reunion and Mercy? I love those names."

"I do too. Let me get my coffee. I'll be right back."

* * * * * * * *

Arvie returned with his bag slung over his right shoulder. He was invited to come back into the board room where Pastor Hoyt had set out two stacks of Styrofoam cups. Four of the sixteen requested a half-cup. Arvie thought he would have enough Forever to go around. The cups were of the usual small styrofoam style.

Everyone served, the conversation began. The five minutes left in the 10-minute break went by as did another 15 or 20. Arvie answered a barrage of questions regarding how he happened to find this coffee, how could the Native American have been dead for 50 years, how did he know the acid reflux had disappeared, what doesn't the coffee heal, and how much does it cost?

Finally, Hedrick Gordon called out, "Breaks over. Let's get back to work." As the board members began to re-seat themselves, Mr.

Gordon asked Arvie for his phone number. He said he had an idea that he wanted to discuss and asked if he could give him a call. Mr. Gordon said he would be in the meeting for the rest of the day and asked if it would be ok to call the next day. Arvie said he would look forward to it.

As he was packing up his bag with the thermos bottles, two ladies of the board came by to thank him for his presentation. Their name tags identified them as Charly and Marion. They said he had opened up their eyes to a whole new world of opportunity for the Lord's work. Just then, Noah leaned in and said, "You're going to get a call about coming back for a special meeting. I just know it."

"And when that happens," one of the ladies added, "it's all good. Thanks again."

They scurried around the corner of the tables to find their places. Arvie picked up his freshly packed bag and headed out the door of the board room, but not before both Pastor Hoyt and Mr. Gordon shook his hand and thanked him for what he had brought to the table. Pastor Hoyt asked if he would provide the coffee for all the services at all the campuses and could he provide a written proposal for consideration.

"Well, Pastor, the coffee costs me nothing. I am assuming they—whoever they are—know my need and will provide enough. It will cost the church nothing."

Pastor Hoyt's face screwed up into a funny looking grin. "Seriously? It heals us and we get it for free? We'll talk again. Oh, and would you have any more?" He slid his empty cup in Arvie's direction. Arvie fished a thermos out of his bag and filled the cup.

As Arvie was heading towards the door, Mr. Gordon leaned back in his chair and asked, "Is the Forever all gone?" Arvie thought it would surely be emptied out by now, but one of the bottles still had some coffee sloshing around inside. Arvie poured him a full cup, emptying the thermos.

As the boardroom door closed behind him, Arvie started thinking … *Sixteen cups on the table when I walked in … two more for Charly and Marion, then another one for Noah … another one for the pastor … one for Hedrick Gordon … twenty-one cups in all. Did my three thermos bottles really hold that much?*

There were some cups stacked by the coffee pots in the waiting area; they were the same size as those being used in the board room. Arvie took one to the sink, filled it with water, opened up a now-empty thermos and poured it in. Three more cups nearly filled it to the brim.

So ... four cups fill a thermos. I have three thermos bottles. That means I had a total of 12 cups with me when I walked in here today. And I just poured twenty-one cups ...

Arvie decided he needed to go home. It was still early, but he was pretty sure he needed to lie down. As he walked to the parking lot all he could think about were loaves and fishes.

* * * * * * * *

Arvie was about to exit the building when he heard his name called. It was Debra, moving towards him at a brisk pace.

"You didn't think you could get out of here without seeing me, did you?"

Arvie put down his bag. They shared a hug.

"It's good to see you," he said. Deb was the manager of the church bookstore at the campus where he and Hannah volunteered. They had become good friends.

"Are you alright?" she asked. "You were in the hospital for several days I know. You lost a dear friend and what you had to endure. I read the story in the paper. That must've been just awful."

"It was a week ago tonight that it happened. I'm still getting over it. Maybe I never will."

"I'm so sorry. All of us here have been praying for you. Had I known you were going to be here today, I'd have baked a cake, or something. But seriously, I just heard you brought something very important to the Board today."

"Yes. I feel good about that. It seemed that it was received well."

"I'm so glad to hear that. How's Hannah?"

"She's doing well thanks."

"Well, please say hi to her for me."

"I will. So, tell me, how are you doing? How are the feet? It looks like you are walking better than you were the last time I saw you."

"Much better. The therapy has been good. But sometimes I wonder if I'll ever walk right again."

"Sure, you will. I wish I had thought to save you a cup of my magic coffee. I don't know yet if it heals the feet, but it'd be worth a try."

"Is it really magic, Arvie?"

"I don't know, Deb. But what I *do* know is that it put a stop to my acid reflux. I'm happy about that. It's still been such a short time since this all began, I must admit I don't know what else it has done. But I do have hope. There is one thing: we poured Forever last week at the Wednesday morning Bible study, over at the Deerwood campus for the seniors, and I heard just yesterday that a rather serious surgery had been called off. Who knows? Maybe because they had a cup or two of Forever."

"Oh, Arvie. Wouldn't that be something?"

"I'll say. We all need hope, especially as we get older. Well, I'd better let you get back to work or they won't ever invite me back again."

"It's so good to see you."

"You too. You take care."

Arvie watched her walk away. Yes. She was walking better. Almost a year ago, she had suffered a horrendous fall and seriously injured both feet. He didn't know every detail regarding her fall, but he was reminded how many bones there are in feet. Injure only one, and many others will be affected somehow. A foot is intricately constructed. Almost a year of therapy and she still walks hesitantly. But he saw no halo, so her health is good – it's only the injury. He remembered how he felt after his neck surgery several years ago; sometimes it takes a year to recover from a serious surgery or an accident like hers. Well, perhaps she needs a little longer.

* * * * * * * *

Arvie had just started his car and rolled down the windows, when his phone went off. He loved the ring because it sounded like the horn of his first ford way back when. He had installed – he called it, the old 'a-ooogaah' horn. Now his cell phone sounds that way every time he gets a call. So, he answers with the usual "This is Arvie" but what he really loves is the remembrance of the good old days and his favorite car of all time, the '53 Ford Convertible, red and white, with the heater that didn't work. And then he heard a familiar 'screech.'

"Good morning Arvie. This is Wilda Maring down at the hospital. It took a little longer to get the results of your background check, but no problem, we are ready to go. When would you like to begin? Oh, and before you answer that, I got boss approval to use your coffee the days you are here. I told her all about it. Sound good?"

"That's great. I was hoping for that. Let me think for a minute. How about I come in every Monday, starting next Monday?"

"That's good with me. I've got you down on the calendar. Give me a rough idea of what you are thinking for hours because I want to be here to get you set up your first day. You know, show you the kitchen where you'll brew your good stuff, and all that."

"I'm thinking bright and early, Wilda. How about we plan on 7:00 – 2:00 on Monday, and we'll go from there?"

"Sounds great. I'll look forward to seeing you then at 7:00 next Monday morning."

"Thanks, Wilda. I'll see you then."

"How's your head, by the way? Last time I saw you, you had taken a hit the night before. Something about a mad grill, or something?"

"Hah. Good one. I sure had a headache that day. But now all is well. I think I'm going to have a lovely little forehead scar that all the babes will think is real sexy."

"Can't wait to see that. Next Monday, right?"

"Next Monday it is, and thanks." He touched his 'off' button.

"Well, here we go and I get to use my coffee" he thought. "Wonder if on Monday she'll still be wearing her halo? Jesus, forgive me for having negative thoughts about her, and all that. I didn't know she was so sick and I'm sorry. I would like to pray for healing for her. Thank you, Jesus. And perhaps I'll see some evidence of healing before Monday morning. Thanks again."

* * * * * * * *

Arvie called Hannah to check in.

"Hello."

"Good morning. I'm heading home. Anything you need?"

"How did it go?"

"I thought it went quite well. I'll give you the detail when I get there."

"Ok. Good. What else do you have lined up for today?"

"Nothing. Not one thing. I was thinking about taking a walk. Want to walk with me? It's a beautiful day."

"I'd be honored."

"Good. So back to question #1: anything you need me to bring home?"

"I'm out of gum."

"I'll get you some. But you know, every time I stop to get you gum, I find another can of Forever. I guess that would be good. All right then. I'll be home in 20 minutes. Lace up your walking shoes. Oh, and one more thing. I'd love for the kids to come over tonight. I want you and them to help me work through a miracle. Do you have time to call and invite them – that is if they're not busy of course?""Yes I have time and I'll see what I can do. See you soon and I can't wait to hear about today – and now I learn of a miracle of some kind. And to think I thought life with you might be boring."

* * * * * * * *

"I'm home."

Hannah responded from upstairs, "Did you find more coffee?"

"No. I guess he thinks I've got enough. But I did find gum."

"Good. I think you've got some emails you'd better look at. And the kids had nothing pressing tonight so they'll be over – both anxious about the miracle."

"Ok, good. Hah. Can't wait to talk about that. I'll check the emails. You ready for your walk?"

"Five minutes."

"Good. When you come down, bring down my croc's please."

"You going to walk in those?"

"Absolutely."

"Ok."

Arvie sat down in front of his laptop on the dining room table and pulled up his email. Most of it he immediately trashed. But he found an email from Freddie. He needs coffee. He's not received a single can. Arvie hit reply and said he'd have a can in the mail today. Next up: an email from Dweebs with a line stating his wife canceled her most recent doctor's appointment and stated he received a second and third can of coffee, both Mercy. Arvie sent a reply and thanked him for the good news.

Arvie had found boxes at a packaging store two days ago, the perfect size for a can of coffee. He went to the cupboard, pulled down two cans, opened up the boxes put in the cans and sealed them both. He had Freddie's address stored in his phone. He'd run the two boxes to the post office after the walk.

The last coffee Arvie had received was the case of Forever left on the front porch over a week earlier. That was the day of the Baptism. *Maybe it's running out? Maybe he knows we don't have a need just now? But what if it is running out? Not now – not after today's conversation with Pastor Wylie about pouring coffee at all campuses?*

"Hi. I'm ready."

"Good. Let's go."

"Here's your croc's."

"How'd I get along for 75 years without croc's?"

"Well, you did."

"I can't imagine how unhappy my feet were for all those years. Unhappy appendages just hanging at the bottom end of my legs, waiting. Ok. Ready. Don't you look nice."

"Oh, my. A compliment? It must have gone very well."

"Come on. I'll tell you about it."

* * * * * * * *

Once on the sidewalk and the walk was underway, he asked if she was interested in the long version, or the abbreviated one. When Hannah said she wanted the whole story, he started at the beginning.

* * * * * * * *

That evening, when the kids arrived, Sophie and Arnie were situated on the living room floor with a game they enjoyed, and the five adults sat down around the table. On the table was a white styrofoam cup and a thermos bottle.

"Brooks," Arvie said, "I'd like for you and Bren to do a little experiment for me. This white cup is the size of the cups used this morning at the board meeting. Would the two of you take the cup and the thermos to the sink and determine how many cups this thermos will hold, please?"

They did so without saying a word. Two minutes later they returned to the table.

"And the results?"

"This thermos will pour four of these white cups full, plus an additional 1/3 cup," Brooks said.

"Now Brenda, if I pour 4 1/3 cups from one thermos, how many cups can I pour with three?"

It took Bren a few seconds and then she responded, "Thirteen, unless this is a trick question."

"No tricks," replied Arvie through a very large smile. Thank you very much for your kind assistance."

"So, Paul Harvey," Bren said looking at her father, "how about the rest of the story?"

Arvie told them about his presentation to the church board that morning and then pouring coffee for all 16 members. "From these three thermos bottles, I poured a total of twenty-one full cups of coffee."

Puzzled looks from all around the table.

"How is that possible, dear?" Hannah asked.

"A very appropriate question. So far, I've only been able to come up with one explanation—excluding the possibility that I'm lying about pouring twenty-one cups, which I'm not."

"Dad … are you saying that Jacob Whitefeather - or Jesus - manufactured a coffee-pouring miracle this morning?" Brooks asked.

"That was the only explanation I could come up with."

Brooks folded his hands on the table and stared at them. Bren, with eyes closed, massaged her temples. Hannah just looked at Arvie with her, "you're nuts" facial expression. The only noise came from Sophie and Arnie on the living room floor, arguing vociferously over their game.

Several questions were asked having to do with some extra coffee somehow finding its way into a thermos or two. Arvie just shook his head answering simply "impossible."

How do people in this day in time accept learning that a real-life miracle happened that very day to a member of their family? Four of the people at the table kept working on possible solutions to the mystery while Arvie's face gleamed with his silly grin.

* * * * * * * *

Hannah served a plate of sandwiches and Arvie poured fresh Forever for all.

"So," asked Hannah, "what do you think the result of this morning's presentation will be? Any idea what they might want to do?"

"I really have no idea, except that Pastor Noah said that he was betting I'd be getting a call for a return visit. The two ladies talking to me at the end said, 'If that happens, it's all good.' But I don't know what to think yet. These people lead a very large church that is committed to serving the Lord, serving His people, getting the message out to every corner of the twin cities, saving and baptizing, and doing it all with as much wisdom as they can muster, following the Lord wherever He leads. I fear, that for some reason, they might not be able to do anything, or perhaps nothing can be done just now. But maybe, just maybe - they'll want to do something. I'm praying for the latter, of course. Oh, and Noah also said that they may want to take a field trip and see the situation first hand."

"I'll bet that's the next step" guessed Brooks.

"Why do you think Mr. Gordon is going to call you?" asked Brenda.

"If I knew more about him, I'd be in a better position to answer that question. I was thinking about that on the way home. He may want to talk more about Henry's flock and all of that, but for some reason, I think he wants to talk about coffee. He asked for my number at the very end of the meeting, and the last thing we did was pour Forever for everyone. Wylie Hoyt asked me several questions about the coffee. That's what led me to go get the bag out of the car. Oh, and he asked if I could provide the coffee for all the services at all locations? What do you think of that? It's almost too much to comprehend. We'll find out tomorrow what Mr. Gordon has on his mind."

The family meeting ended with the usual hugs and kisses, the kids obviously proud for their father. When they had left for home, Hannah announced she was going to call Marci. "She left me a message before I was up this morning. She didn't sound good."

"You do that. I'm going to lay down on the couch with Wylie's new book. I haven't had much of a chance lately to get very far with it. Plus, I didn't sleep very good last night."

"So, you might as well say you're going to squeeze in a little nap. Huh?"

"Well, yeah. That might happen too."

Chapter 23

"Once a guy told me to go see so-and-so about investing in something. 'Double your money over-night,' he said. So, I invested $100 and the next morning it was gone. I learned to take advice from a smarter guy than that guy. Bottom line: you need to know who you are listening to.
- *Ole*

"Trust in the Lord with all your heart, and don't depend on your own understanding. Remember the Lord in all you do, and he will give you success."
Proverbs 3:5-6

Arvie awoke before dawn. "Good," he thought, very pleased with himself for getting up instead of rolling over. He'd get to see the dawn, and it will be worth seeing today. The dark was just beginning its turn to a dark gray and the stars were fading into the increasing light. "Clear morning. It's going to be a beautiful sunrise."

On his way to the coffee pot, he stopped at the dining room table and picked up his Bible. It seemed his Bible always opened to Proverbs without assistance. It seemed to know he had an affection for King Solomon's wisdom, especially the third chapter, verses five and six. *"Trust in the Lord with all your heart, and don't depend on your own understanding. Remember the Lord in all you do, and he will give you success."*

When he awoke, these words had been bouncing around in his mind. He had fallen asleep last night thinking of all the negatives that the board members were mulling over. *This is going to be a project that is too big, there are too many in need. It will cost too much money. Yes, we need to serve people such as these, but this is just too much. We will need to pay for buildings, and nurses, and doctors, and janitors. Food services? Who's going to be in charge of all the volunteers? What are the regulations – local, county, state, and Federal that we'd have to adhere to with all the nursing and drugs and food service? Do we really want to be involved with all that?* He woke up with a headache.

Trust the Lord. That's what I must do, and take my mind, my understanding out of this whole picture. And he bowed his head immediately and prayed.

"Oh, God. I don't know how any of this can work. But I don't need to know. The leaders of this church follow you faithfully, whenever and wherever you lead. So I'm praying for you to feel the same way about Henry and Mary's flock as I do. Please help them. Help our church find a way. These lost souls exist in many places throughout the Twin Cities community. Someone must lead the way. Why not us? You have told us over and over to help those who are lost, find the lost sheep, bring home the prodigal. Help us to help those who cannot help themselves. Lead us in setting the example for others to follow. I'm praying for your help in doing what's right: feed the hungry; clothe the naked, and do unto the least of these. Your will be done, dear Jesus. If something monumental cannot be done, help us then continue Henry and Mary's work, one poor soul at a time. Perhaps you know of others who want to serve as they did. If this is Your will, bring those people who wish to serve the poor and the helpless to our church or direct them to Colby who is fully invested in this need. Bless him and keep him strong. Wait. Why have I not contacted Sandy Marsh about all this? He can energize a multitude with his reach. Please open his heart to this cause. He has been interested in the healing of people through coffee. I should think that perhaps I can ask him and his paper to take up this challenge. Please be with me as I call him this morning. Continue to speak to me Lord and the church leaders and board members. Take all of us to higher levels of faith. Make us more anxious to follow your leadings and open to all challenges. There must be a way. And why Lord, why did you put me in the middle of this? I'm an old retired guy who didn't really do anything noteworthy with my life. I feel much more comfortable with a coffee pot in both hands than I do being involved with Henry's people. But I am so blessed to serve in any way you can use me. The president of the board said he was going to call me today, for what reason I don't know. Please be with me when that call comes. Doggone it anyway, Lord. We've just got to be able to do something here for all these people who suffer so. Mrs. Koepke, Mr. Elston and Mr. Schilling, just to mention the first three that I've met. Make us all Henrys and Marys: willing to serve these people. I remember your words very clearly "and the least shall become the greatest." Thank you for loving us. Thank you, Jesus for your sacrifice. Bless us this day. I pray all this in Jesus precious and holy name – Amen.

During his prayer, Arvie had paced the length of his front room, through the dining area and into the kitchen and then back around again. Midway through, he had taken a seat at the dining room table. When he finished, he felt physically spent. He continued to sit with eyes closed, head bowed and hands folded on the table. He felt tears trickle down his cheeks. Never before, in his life, had he felt so passionate about anything. Every time he thought of those people, he felt physically and mentally sick. And then he felt Hannah's arms encircle his neck from behind as she laid her cheek on the top of his head.

"Arvid Ellison. I love you more now than ever. That was as heartfelt a prayer as I've ever heard from you."

"I didn't know I said any of that outloud."

"In that case, I want you to know that I heard it and it was beautiful. Arvie reached up, placing his hands upon her arms. They just swayed back and forth, left, right, and back again.

Hannah continued. "I thought I loved you so much back at Mt. Holy Waters when you asked me to be your date to Ties & Heels. I couldn't contain myself because I thought I loved you so much then. But that was kid stuff compared to this moment. I always knew," she murmured, "that I wanted to marry someone who loved Jesus, and I remember being some disappointed in how much I thought you loved Him back then. Well, I think I picked right. I couldn't ask for any more in a husband and the love of my life than what I just heard in that prayer. Did you know that I think you are very special? Did you know that?"

"Maybe not as much as I do right now. I feel so overwhelmed and so completely helpless. Maybe it is times like this when Jesus can do his best work in us – when we admit our helplessness?"

She slid around the corner of the table, pulled out the end chair, and sat down. "Look out there," she said, looking past him, through the sliding glass patio doors. The reds and the pinks were creeping in. The sunrise was almost upon them.

"I can think of nothing more wonderful to do right now than to take you for a walk out there. Can we be ready in five minutes?"

"Yes, we can. Let's go."

* * * * * * * *

They made their way to the little playground in the neighborhood park. They picked out two swings and began to gently swing back and forth, unsure if they would hold the weight of mature adults.

They were facing west as they swung. The little park was surrounded with big oak, birch and pine trees. The trees were filled with birds, all singing their happy 'good mornings' to each other. Mr. and Mrs. Wren were sitting on the back of a bench perhaps 15 feet in front of them. They were singing 'good morning' to Arvie and Hannah. Anyone listening would not have been able to understand as all four of them began talking back and forth: Grandparents trying to talk to little wrens, and vice versa.

The tops of the tallest trees to the west were beginning to show the reddish hue of the sunrise. The air was still. A little gray squirrel sat off to the left and a little in front of them, looking in the same direction, so still, as if mesmerized with this picture of nature unveiling itself. Arvie and Hannah were swinging slowly now, watching just like the squirrel. Mr. and Mrs. Wren still stood on the bench back, looking at them, and probably thinking that these two large creatures might make good friends.

Arvie stopped his swing and pointed up. Hannah looked up and when she realized why Arvie was pointing, she stopped her swing as well. Almost directly above them were two Eagles soaring lazily in the red sky. From this distance, Arvie and Hannah could only assume they were Eagles. They had watched Eagles many times from the bluffs along the St. Croix river, just a few miles east of their current perch atop children's swings in the middle of a little neighborhood playground. There was no wind stirring through the playground, but there must have been something moving way up there. With wings not moving at all, they floated this way and glided back that way. They drifted in circles, sometimes darting towards the ground a little, and then with a flap of their wings they would soar even higher. The freedom they must feel up there.

"Think they can see us down here?" Hannah asked.

"With all they can see from way up there, why would they want to look at us little creatures way down here?" There were times, playing up there in the sun-drenched sky, that their color changed radically. There were moments when they were mostly black spots, and then a flash of red as one moved a certain way. "Can you see a white head now and then?" he asked.

"I think so. But I wonder if I see it only because I know its there."

"Yeah. I think I could sit here all day and watch them, wishing all the while I could be up there with them."

"Look now. There they go. They are going towards the river. Why, I wonder?"

Arvie hazarded a guess, "Probably heading home to write some checks and pay some bills. Even Eagles have responsibilities, you know."

"I'd think that Eagles would be doing the automatic bill paying thing. If I was one of them, I wouldn't want to be bothered with writing checks and all that. They'd have to buy stamps too."

"I wonder if they'd only buy the stamps with pictures of Eagles on them?"

"Arvie, I've loved the sunrise this morning. Why haven't we done this every morning this summer?"

"Good question. We've got the rest of the summer, you know."

"Let's think about that over a cup of Forever. Huh?"

"Good idea."

They left the swings then and hand in hand trekked through the dewy grass towards the path that would lead them home. Mr. and Mrs. Wren decided it was time for coffee as well, and the little gray squirrel turned to watch everyone depart the playground.

* * * * * * * *

Arvie and Hannah readied themselves for the day and met in the kitchen to prepare a breakfast. Hard boiled eggs with whole wheat, high fiber toast and honey would be the fare this morning. It was cool at that hour of the day and a refreshing breeze was stirring. They opened the doors and the windows and breathed in the sweet-smelling wonderfulness of this new day.

Arvie had forgotten about his expected phone call but his phone rang anyway and he felt immediate panic followed quickly by a surprising sense of calm.

He closed his eyes before saying, "Hi. This is Arvie."

"Good morning Arvie. This is Rick Gordon calling as promised." There was a joy in his voice that Arvie took as a positive.

"Yes sir. You are up early."

"It's the old early bird thing, I guess. I'll only keep you a minute, Arvie. Have you got time to meet with me sometime today?"

"Sure. I'm flexible these days. What time and where and what's the subject?"

"I consider you to be an expert on coffee and that's the subject. How about 10 this morning? Is that an ok time for you?"

"That works for me. Where do you want me to be?"

"204 Lake Street, Forest Lake, Minnesota. I think that's probably just around the corner from you. Park in the back lot and come in the back door. I'll be there."

"Well, sure. That's close by. I'll see you at 10."

"Thanks, Arvie. I'm looking forward to it." The line went dead.

"Well, isn't that interesting," mumbled Arvie.

"Your meeting today?" asked Hannah.

"Yeah."

"I heard the '10' part of it. What didn't I hear?"

"Well, coffee is to be the subject, and we are meeting at 204 Lake Street, downtown Forest Lake. I'm trying to picture 204."

"204," Hannah repeated. "Let's see ... That first block just north of the roundabout is a long one. All the businesses there back up to that big parking lot on the lake. Well, between the businesses and the city park that's on the lake. So, I'd guess 204 is almost at the end of that long block. Am I right on that?"

"I think you are. He said to park in back. Yeah, I'll bet so. Well, that's a different location from where I expected to be meeting with him."

"Why? What were you expecting?"

"I know nothing about the man, so keep that in mind. He's President of the Board at Dove Creek, and I suspect that means that he is a very successful business man. That's an assumption on my part, but I can't understand why he wants to meet with *me*, some old retired guy."

"And you said he wants to talk to you about coffee."

"Yup."

"Well, if you think about it, who knows any more about coffee in the Twin Cities than Samuel, the coffee guy?"

"Huh" Arvie breathed. "Maybe that's it. But still, why meet in that location? Moving on - I've got to call Sandy Marsh."

"You've got 40 minutes between now and your meeting" reminded Hannah. "This would be a good time."

"Yes, it would." Arvie reached for his phone, looked for Marsh's number and hit dial. On the fourth ring, it went to the message system.

"Morning Sandy. This is Arvie Ellison. I wanted to speak with you today if possible. You've got my number; please call when you have a moment. Thanks. Have a good one." Arvie hung up. "Do you think that's why Mr. Gordon wants to talk to me because of my magic coffee?"

"I don't know. But you were featured in two or three columns that made the first page of the Minneapolis Daily. That's a lot of exposure in the upper Midwest, you know. So, yeah. Maybe it's because you are kind of a cult hero, or something like that."

"Huh. I don't get it. I guess I'll find out real soon."

"Finish your breakfast. I'll freshen up that coffee."

* * * * * * * *

Arvie was pulling on his old, faded Mount Holy Waters University golf shirt when his phone rang. He saw it was Sandy and he reached for it quickly.

"Hi Sandy. Thanks for returning my call."

"I have a note I scribbled last night to call you today. What's on *your* mind?"

"I'm on my way to a church appointment at the moment, but I wanted to talk to you some more about the people Henry and Mary spent their lives working for. I've begun to get involved a little bit and it is the saddest story you could ever imagine. I know I have to try to do something, but I don't know what it should be. I want to tell you about it and see what you think?"

"Sure. Want to meet somewhere midway between Forest Lake and Minneapolis this afternoon or what were you thinking?"

"That'd be fine. You know of a place?"

"Yeah. Coming down from the north get off at the Mississippi exit, take a right at the light and you'll see a Caribuck's on your right maybe a half a block away. Lemme see, aaahhh, how about 1:00, 1:15 or thereabouts?"

"That's great. Thanks Sandy. I'll see you then."

He put the phone down and looked at himself in the mirror questioning his choice of attire for this meeting with Mr. Gordon. *It's a good look, perhaps as good as I can do these days.*

* * * * * * * *

Arvie turned right at the roundabout and where the street dead-ended at the city park, he turned left into the parking lot that was behind the business that fronted onto Lake Street. He liked that area. The park included several covered structures that could be used for picnics on rainy days. There was a large bandstand, two pavilions for larger groups, and four smaller pagodas placed throughout the grassy space.

There was a large public boat launch and dock at the far end, well away from the beach. Throughout the summer, boaters would tie up to the dock and take advantage of the lakeside eatery's and ice cream establishments.

It was the place to be every summer holiday evening, especially the 4th of July. There were several local bands that would fill the bandstand to overflowing. The music was fun, lively, patriotic, and all through the afternoon and evening it was not uncommon to see dancing break out anywhere throughout the park. Later in the eveing, just after dusk, the fireworks display was always awesome. They were launched from a barge located in the lake, perhaps out 100 yards beyond the beach area. Brooks and Kate hosted the family for the cook-out on the 4th, and then the pontoon ride into position; the fireworks exploding nearly directly above them. What a display of color and excitement.

Forest Lake was not just a large hole in the ground filled with water. It was shaped like a figure eight with a third circle on top. Narrow channels connected the three. Cabins and homes filled every inch of the lakefront. On those summer holidays, the water of the lake was covered with watercraft of every size and shape. Fun times for everyone on warm summer days.

Forest Lake was not only used during the summer, but during the winter as well. Hearty souls would place their ice fishing houses carefully, to take full advantage of their favorite fishing hole throughout the cold months. The village-on-ice scenario is not unusual. Friends gathered together to enjoy the frigid, wintry blasts while dropping a line through six to twelve inches of ice. Not much cold was felt thanks to consumption of adult beverages. There was nothing like a golf tournament played in January on a foot of frozen ice.

All of this rushed through Arvie's mind as he navigated the parking lot in an effort to find 204. *There's 200. There. 204.* He found it. He slid into one of the many available parking places, exited the vehicle, and made his way in the door that had a sloppily painted 204 in white paint on the shabby looking, poorly painted black door.

Hesitantly, he entered, having no idea what to expect. He stood just inside the door for a moment allowing his eyes to adjust to a very dim interior. Shabby. He would have chosen that word to describe what he saw, along with old and run-down.

"Arvie" came the sound of a big voice ricocheting off the walls. "Up here."

Arvie looked up as high as his neck would allow and saw Mr. Gordon leaning over a railing and waving at him. Arvie waved back as Mr. Gordon waved at him to "come on up."

Arvie walked towards the far end of the building, carefully avoiding piles of swept up dust, dirt and trash. Someone had begun some clean-up in here. From the dank smell of the place, he knew it had been a long time since it had been opened to some clean Minnesota air. It had the stale aroma of too many years of cigarette smoke and a lot of spilled Hamm's and Schmidt. If he was here to have a talk about coffee, why would they be meeting in this dingy dump?

He climbed the flight of stairs and was greeted at the top with "Good to see you Arvie. Thanks for coming." They shook hands. "Well, what do you think of this place?"

Arvie said what he felt, "Needs a good cleaning and it sure could be aired out. After that, maybe we could see what else needs to be done."

"Good man. You don't beat around the bush. You say it without pause and deliberation, and you are right. The place is a dump. But … but … what *might* it become? That's the question I've had ever since I first saw it. I'd been just north of here, in Wyoming, on a business matter and I was coming down 61 heading for home. We used to come through here on our way to Duluth, back when I was little. My dad always talked about this row of buildings along here. He wanted to open a hardware store in one of these places, or a popcorn shop. For some reason that day, I thought of that and so I drove along here, kind of down memory lane.

"I parked the car across the street and just walked along these store fronts, looking in windows and wondering what could be done here. As I'm sure you've noticed, there are several empties along here. And then a God-thing happened. A man walked up to me and asked if I was interested in property along here and I told him I was. He said he was the realtor for one of these storefronts and asked if I'd like to see it. 'Sure,' I said, and we walked to the front door of this place. As we were walking, he asked what I'd do with a place along here and I said I was hoping I could figure that out once I'd seen the space.

"Arvie, I'm a very lucky man. My father left me with a lot of money and for some reason, unknown to me, I've been very good with money my whole life, at least so far. To be very truthful, I've talked to God about every opportunity I've stumbled into. Together, He and I have a knack of turning a piece of property into something that returns a lot of money. Well, I saw this place and I knew I had to have it. Wasn't sure right then what I was going to do with it but yesterday, after listening to something you said, it hit me. On the way home last night after the meeting, I prayed about it. This morning I knew what I needed to do."

"So, before I left the meeting yesterday and you said you wanted to call me today, you still didn't know for sure?" asked Arvie.

"I'd had a thought, but I needed to pray about it and if it made sense to Him, get His blessing."

"I see. So, you bought the building this morning?"

"Hah-hah. No, no. I bought the building the first day I saw it. That's over a year ago now. What I was praying about was whether I should open a coffee shop here? I knew when I woke up this morning that the answer was a resounding yes."

"What if the answer had been a no?"

"Well, then I would have called you to meet me at the Caribuck's at 96 and 35E, not only to have a cup of coffee, but so I could have let you know that the Executive Committee of the Board voted unanimously last night to move forward with your proposal."

Arvie looked puzzled. "Did I make a proposal?"

"Not officially. But there was no doubt in anyone's mind what you were driving toward: that the church get involved with its resources and people to find a resolution to the misery and the hopelessness of Henry's flock. We voted to take the next step. We appointed a team of three to visit the people you would want us to see, perhaps the same three you talked about yesterday, or as many as you would like. The committee will bring back a report to the board. I'll be heading up that committee. Miles Dillard and Signe Goethe will be the other two members."

"I ... don't know ... what to say." Arvie leaned back against a wall, put his head back and while looking up at a ceiling filled with dirt and cobwebs, whispered "thank you, Jesus." His throat was tightening with emotion. He stood up straight, looked into the eyes of Mr. Hedrick Gordon and whispered, "Thank you, Rick." Rick stuck out his hand. Arvie took it and found himself pulling Mr. Gordon into a manly shoulder bump.

A moment later, Arvie fumbled for his handkerchief, wiped his eyes and blew his nose.

Rick continued: "I don't know if you realized at the time the impact your story had on us yesterday. It was very powerful, Arvie."

"How soon do you want to make that visit?"

"As soon as possible. The three of us can be ready at a moments notice. We assumed that you would need a few days. Here's my card. Call me when you are ready, and we'll meet you there."

"Thank you. I'll work on that this afternoon and hopefully get back to you before the end of the day."

"And now – would you like to help me put a coffee shop in this dirt and filth?"

"Yes sir. I would," Arvie chuckled.

"Oh, there is something else, Arvie. If that's what this becomes, I want to serve only Forever or Mercy or Forgiveness or whatever the current name of your coffee is. I would also like you to spend a good deal of time here talking with people and pouring. I was thinking that the name we would put out front would be something like "Samuel's Coffee House, For the Brew that Heals", or something like that. I am envisioning these coffee houses scattered through the lakes country; initially in Minnesota, and later, into Wisconsin and Michigan. I'm not talking about the coffee shops that you find on every corner these days. I'm talking about a building that is three stories tall, where every table looks out upon a lake or something spectacular. I'm talking about having heavy north woods type furniture throughout, a meeting room to seat 15 on each level and little hideaways for singles or a couple that requires perfect solitude to work on a project. Every place we put one of these would be a place where senior citizens can be bussed to on the 4th of July for the best view of the fireworks over the lake. Our marketing studies show that people will drive 30 minutes to get to place like this. So, draw a circle with a 30-mile radius around this place and count all the prospects. It's going to be big, Arvie. At least, I think so. You want to do this with me?

I'll make it worth your while. You think about it. We'll do some paperwork after we get started with this one. I want you to be a part of this."

"I don't know what to say – again," said Arvie, a smile radiating from ear to ear.

Rick had a brilliant light in his eyes as he spoke. "You don't have to say anything right now, just walk with me, Arvie. I'd like your ideas on a few things. First, we'll tear out all the ceilings up to the roof to open it all up. Picture one big room, three stories tall, a rough dark wood finish throughout with several open fire places down there, on that lower level. Tables scattered around both the 2nd and 3rd level balconies. Picture that huge window, three stories high, looking out over the lake. The lake can be seen from virtually any table here. Then, have I got an idea for this – we'll ....''

* * * * * * *

After an hour with Rick, Arvie was spent. He was emotionally drained. He was so filled to the top with coffee house ideas he was near exploding. When they parted, Arvie thanked Rick for all he had learned today and said he would be in touch as soon as possible to schedule the visit to Henry's neighborhood.

Once outside, he leaned up against the building, closed his eyes and listened to the sounds of children at play. They were laughing and playing in the park and laughing and splashing in the water at the beach. Moms watched dutifully, sitting on park benches, blankets on the grass or at a picnic table. There were two seniors, men his age, backing a bass boat down the ramp and into the water. He wondered if those men were as happy, at this moment, as he.

He retrieved his phone from his shirt pocket to check the time. 12:25. He called Hannah.

"I've been waiting for this phone call all my life. What happened?" she asked with a smile in her voice.

"I can't tell you on the phone, but it is so good – I think, and I can hardly believe it. Not one total surprise, but two."

"Two? What two?"

"I'm coming home and I'll tell you. I have been this happy only once before in my life."

"Was that the day you shot the 68 in the city tournament at Soangetaha so many years ago?"

"I was pretty happy that day, but not this happy. I'll be home in five or 10. I'll pick up lunch. I gotta call Brooks." He pushed the off button, pocketed the phone, and moved towards his car. He opened the car door but stood there for an extra moment listening to the beautiful sound of children playing in the warm summer sun. He retrieved the phone and dialed Brooks.

"Hi. You've reached the voice mail of Brooks Ellison. Please leave me a message and I'll get back to you soon. Thanks for calling." Arvie waited for the beep. "BEEP."

"Brooks. It's me. I just learned that the church board appointed a team to investigate the situation with the seniors down in Henry's building. I'm going down there this afternoon to talk to Colby and set a time for that appointment. I hope you can be there with me. It could be as soon as tomorrow. I wanted you to know. Call me tonight. We'll talk."

* * * * * * * *

He stopped at Oleson's Deli and picked up two ham-and-swiss on rye. He walked next door and entered the floral shop, bought a dozen long-stemmed red roses, wrote a note on the little card and then returned to his car. Five minutes later he pulled into the garage of the townhouse.

Hannah was waiting just inside the door. "Ok, start talking. I've just got to hear."

"These are for you." He handed her the roses and she was speechless. Arvie hadn't done much of this over the years. He felt their relationship had always been rock solid and it wasn't necessary to bring her flowers. He also knew that he didn't know for sure how she felt about it because he had never asked her.

"By the way, the happiest day I've ever had was the day you said, 'yes,' nearly 54 years ago. I remember that moment like it just happened."

"You expect me to believe that? You forget that I know all about your memory. But, thank you for these. They are beautiful. And I just want you to know that it's ok if that 68-day was really the day. My, but it must have been special morning for you, huh?"

He held up a finger, "First: the church board formed a task force of three members to do an on-site visit to the people I told them about. Mr. Gordon is the head of the task force and the other two are Miles Dillard and Signe Goethe. I don't think I met them yesterday. But I am to pick the day and the time and they will be there. I left a message for Brooks to call me because I'd like for him to be able to get off work for that. That may be asking too much of him.

"Were you expecting to hear any of that?"

"No. Mr. Gordon said that they came to that decision last evening, so it must've been a long board meeting."

"That's wonderful, hon. I'm thrilled for you. You must've been very convincing."

"I guess I did ok."

"So, what's number two?"

"Rick is going to open a coffee shop on Lake, just past the roundabout, and he wants me to assist him, and he wants to use my coffee. We met in this old ….."

"Wait. Did you just call him Rick?"

"We're suddenly old buddies. Yeah. He said to call him Rick."

"Interesting. Go ahead."

Arvie excitedly reviewed the conversation. He paced back and forth as he talked, obviously fired up. When he had finished, he sat down at the dining room table, motioned for her to join him and opened up the sandwich bag.

"Wow. And he even brought me a deli sandwich. I'm a lucky woman."

They both dug into their ham and swiss on rye with a passion. "We don't have anything tonight, do we?" he asked with a full cheek.

"Not a thing. Why?" she asked while dabbing at a corner of her mouth with a napkin.

"I'm meeting Sandy down 35W halfway to Minneapolis at 2:00. Then I'm thinking I'll go ahead down to Henry's building and find

Colby and set up a day for these board members to visit. I told Rick I'd call him ASAP. I'd like to do that no later than tonight. Will that work? I don't want to mess up supper, but as long as I'm that far down 35, I might as well go the rest of the way."

"No problem. I made a salad for tonight. And, if I say so myself, it's a good-looking salad. So, if I get hungry for it before you get home, I'll go ahead, and you can eat when you get here. How's that?"

"That's perfect. Thank you dear."

"What do expect to accomplish with Mr. Marsh?"

"I don't know, but I haven't seen him since the hospital stay. He has been very kind to me with those articles in the paper and all and I'd like to keep him for a friend. I want to tell him about what Colby is doing and the plight of those poor people I saw. Wat I don't know is how many more of them there are. Why don't we eat these sandwiches more often, by the way?"

"All you have to do is bring 'em home."

* * * * * * * *

Arvie pulled into Caribuck's parking lot. All the way there, he thought about nothing but the conversation this morning with Mr. Gordon. Now, it was time to focus on something else. After he shut the CRV down, he reached over to insure his wastebasket full of Forever was still secure. He would need that later when he met with Colby.

Sandy Marsh had arrived early, had selected a corner table and had a large latte halfway consumed by the time Arvie joined him. They exchanged greetings warmly, and before they had even sat down, the reporter was asking questions: "How are you feeling? "Have you recovered fully from that night?' 'Are you going to be at the Church pouring tomorrow morning?" "Are you still getting coffee?"

All those questions finally answered, plus a few more, Arvie proceeded to tell Sandy about meeting and getting to know Colby, what had transpired yesterday at the Dove Creek board meeting, and the results of that presentation learned this morning.

"You mean there are people living there who can't even take care of themselves?"

"Absolutely. I thought the seniors were pretty well taken care of these days, and then I realized that maybe most of them are, but there are many who are not. Perhaps these people are hidden away somewhere and have to be sought out. Obviously no one cares about all of those hiding in plain sight in that apartment building."

"So, you are trying to bring this issue to the attention of the church to hopefully accomplish what?"

"I'm not sure I know. They do have a lot more resources available to them than I do, and I think it's possible there may be something that can be done."

"Good Lord," said Sandy, looking confused. "I've always thought our society was quite civilized in most areas, but this? I've never heard of anything like this but I shouldn't be surprised. Do you remember back in the late 70's - it must have been, when they shut down all of the mental hospitals across the country?"

"I do. There was a large one in East Moline where we lived and when it closed there was a big hoopla about where all the patients were going to go, to say nothing about all the doctors and nurses, and the staff. It was a big deal."

"Yeah, it really was," said Sandy. "I was in College up in Detroit. We protested about all of that, sit-downs, stopping traffic, doing our best to call attention to what we thought was so wrong. That was a long time ago. It would stand to reason that perhaps a lot of those people could be in their 80's and 90's by now. What a story that could be. So what's next?"

"I'm going down to Henry's building in a few minutes to find Colby and set a time for those board members to come down and meet his people. That meeting could occur as soon as tomorrow."

"Will you be coming down for that too?"

"Yes, and Brooks too, I hope."

"I don't suppose it would be right for me to be there?" Sandy asked.

"I don't think so. I wanted you to know what was going on, because if the church decided they could take action, you could be a critical piece in getting the word out; perhaps calling more churches to get involved in some way."

"How many of these lost seniors are there? Any idea?"

"That's a question I was going to ask Colby. He spent several years working with Henry."

"This young Colby is an important player in all of this, isn't he?"

"Yes, he is."

"Can I follow you down there and sit in on your conversation with Colby?"

"Of course, you can. I'd like that," said Arvie.

"I'm ready any time you are."

"Let's go."

* * * * * * * *

They parked immediately in front of the building. Arvie waited at the curb for Sandy to join him.

"Wow," exclaimed Sandy. "I've never been in this part of town before. These buildings are decrepit to say the very least. Look at them. All along here."

"Yeah," responded Arvie. "That's the same reaction I had my first time here. Follow me. Let's go find Colby."

Moments later, they were heading down the basement stairs. "Colby," called Arvie, to announce their arrival. There was no answer. They had just turned back towards the stairs when Colby came bounding down to them.

"Boy, am I glad to see you. Can you grab that bucket there, fill it with water from the faucet over there, and pick up that jug of vinegar? He headed to a small spindly looking wooden drying rack near the furnace, grabbed towels that were draped there and then picked up a stack of towels folded neatly on the concrete floor. "I don't know you," he said, looking at Sandy as he handed Arvie the towels. "Please bring these." He moved quickly to a small plastic box under his cot, threw it on top of the cot, opened it and grabbed a set of underwear and then picked up his old wooden folding chair. "It's Mr. Elston, Arvie. He's done it again."

Colby headed up the stairs two at a time. Arvie and Sandy followed as quickly as they were able.

Outside Mr. Elston's door, Colby turned to them and said, "Take a deep breath and enjoy it." He opened the door. They entered. Virtually everywhere they looked, they saw feces. The one chair in the room, a trail of it on the floor to the kitchen sink, to the bathroom and back again. Mr. Elston was covered with it.

Colby took him by the elbow and led him to the kitchen sink. He undressed him and began to clean him with soap and water. He looked to Arvie and Sandy standing just inside the door holding their cleaning materials, and with a look and a nod to them, he indicated "if you can start cleaning, it would be much appreciated."

Colby washed and dried Mr. Elston, then helped him into clean clothing. He opened up the little folding chair, helped Mr. Elston sit down, and then, patting the old man on the shoulder, lovingly said, "We'll have you back to normal in no time. You relax right there and I'm sorry I did not get here earlier." Colby had just indicated that this was his fault, not wanting Mr. Elston to burden himself with guilt. He picked up Mr. Elston's only chair and carried it to the front door where he balanced it on his hip with one hand and opened the door with the other. He set it outside in the hallway. He quickly opened the windows in both the living room and the bedroom.

Meanwhile Arvie had begun in the bathroom, while Sandy was tackling the floors. They were using both sinks to rinse towels and sharing the vinegar and water solution in the bucket, and they were making progress. With Colby's help, the remainder of the task was soon completed.

As they were leaving, Colby explained to Mr. Elston that he would return in 30 minutes or so to close the windows, but he wouldn't be able to return his chair until later today. Mr. Elston opened his mouth to respond and the sound that emerged was a combination sob and cry of agony. Colby responded, "you bet, you are welcome and I'll be back to see you in a little bit." They departed the little room and met at the little arm chair in the hallway.

Arvie quickly introduced Sandy to Colby and the latter thanked them both for their assistance.

"So, you are the guy who wrote those articles about Samuel in the paper. I enjoyed every one of them."

"Thank you. I loved writing those, but Colby, how often does this happen?" He nodded towards Mr. Elston's apartment.

"It happens frequently, I'm afraid. It all depends on when he has the urge to go. I have it timed so that I'm here at the usual time every morning, but when I've got to be somewhere else because of some other troubles, like this morning, well, this can happen."

"What is his problem?" Sandy asked as gently as possible.

"He has no use of his arms."

"Good lord. So, he is a regular stop for you every day?"

"Yes sir. I learned how to take care of him by watching Henry. We'll head downstairs now."

Colby hoisted the chair. Arvie carried the bucket, now emptied of the vinegar solution but now full of soiled towels. Sandy carried a towel wrapped around Mr. Elston's soiled clothing.

Once in the basement, Colby filled his wash tub, added a small amount of soap, and put in the soiled items. "I'll have to do this two or three times," he said, mostly to himself. With a clean towel, he wiped down Mr. Elston's chair, took the cushion to the faucet, hosed it down as best he could and then dropped in into the tub, submerging it below the surface of the soapy water.

He offered a bottle of hand soap to his guests, and the three of them gathered around the faucet, scrubbing their hands with the soap and cold water.

After drying their hands thoroughly, Colby looked at Arvie and with a smile asked, "and to what do I owe the pleasure of your visit today?"

Arvie explained about the board meeting yesterday and what he had heard from Mr. Gordon this morning and that he wanted to learn from Colby a good time for them to come to see first hand.

"Wow," said Colby. "You mean that something really good could happen for these people? That would be unbelievable."

"Colby, you had said once that Henry had people he helped within a one-mile circle around here. Do you have any idea how many people that might be?"

Colby turned and walked to his little bookcase, pulled a small box from the upper shelf, opened it up and extracted a small zip drive which he handed to Arvie. "All the names and addresses I know of are here. There are probably more because Henry kept track of all this in his mind. He had nothing written down, so he could have overlooked a few. We'd go to someone's apartment and I would write down the information. I do updates almost every day at school on a computer. Unlike Henry, *I* can't keep track of them all without writing them down. I think there are 160 some names there. I'm actively involved with 90 of them, some more than others."

"That many?"

"Yeah. Occasionally I'll have some time now and then to seek out others, you know, when I'm in some other building out there somewhere. There is a constant ebb and flow to this; people go from one of these apartments to the homeless category and a month later they show up back here somewhere. I can't really help any more than I'm working with now because I need to get to most all of them several times a week, and some of them every day. Really, I have too many now to do it right, but without me, they would have no one. I feel it important to find all of them I can. On that stick, you'll find two lists: Henry's people – well mine now, are the first list. The second list is those people I've found that I can't help but there is at least some record of them. Maybe I've been building these lists for this church thing you are working on. I just didn't know it."

Sandy the reporter, always looking for a story, said, "Colby, it's unknown what will come of this church interest, you know, what they might do. Let's say all these people can be put somewhere where they will have daily assistance; more help than you, alone, can provide. Won't that take you out of your job, so to speak?" he asked.

With a slight smile, Colby replied, "No. It would be nice to think that, but should these people go to a better place, more will float in. It's like water. They will always be with us. I'll always be able to serve the less fortunate, and at least in my lifetime, right here." As usual, Sandy was busily writing in his little notebook. He knew he had found another human-interest story.

"One more question." Reporters always have 'one more question.' "Out of these 160 names, are there others as helpless as Mr. Elston, for one reason or another? And if so, how many?"

Colby thought for a moment. "I don't know for sure. Out of the 90 that I work with, there are probably 30 to 40 that are severely handicapped; mentally, physically or both."

"You're familiar with nursing facilities and the care that is offered?"

"Yes sir."

"How many of the 160 need the nursing home level of care?"

"Probably 130. I should give some thought to that. I should update that stick to include categories broken down like that. I'll do that. Looking at it the other way, I think I can say that there are 25-30 who could survive in independent living with a bit of help called in.

"How old are you Colby?" Sandy asked, his eyes never leaving his notebook.

"22."

Sandy sat down on the edge of Colby's cot, his pencil jotting away furiously.

"Not to interrupt here," said Arvie to Colby, "but is it ok with you if we plan on Thursday for this team to visit?"

"That's fine with me. You pick whatever time is convenient for those people. I'll be here all day on Thursday, doing my work."

"Ok, then. I will call Mr. Gordon tonight and have him talk with his committee to decide the time. I'll be at the Bible study tomorrow morning and into the early afternoon, so I'll come down tomorrow afternoon to let you know the time. Are you generally in this building Wednesday afternoons?"

"No. I'm here in the mornings, but there is another building down at the end of this block." He took a piece of paper, jotted down the address, and handed it to Arvie. "I'll be there tomorrow afternoon. Come see me there. I'll introduce you to a few more customers."

"Thank you."

"I sure want to thank you both for lending a hand today. I need to get upstairs and look in on Carolyn Hasterlitch. Arvie, you've met

Mrs. Koepke. Ms. Caroline is much the same. Thanks again to you both." Handshakes all around.

Before parting, Sandy, still with pencil and notebook at the ready, asked, "Colby, may I come back sometime to help you for a day, half-day, or something?"

"You're welcome to come anytime. I'd enjoy that."

"Oh," said Arvie, "before I forget, Brooks and I were talking last night about your candle lighting event for Henry. Is all that progressing well?"

"Yes, it really is."

"Good. If there is any way we can help you that night, we'd be glad to. Just let us know. We've got that night blocked out. Hey, you mentioned a couple of men who are helping you with the financing part of it. I remember you said one of them owed Henry a great deal because he had helped parents *and* grandparents. I ask only because perhaps he would want to partner with or share insights with the church for whatever is to come on that front."

"I've met him several times. He'd come to find Henry and he would give him money every time. Since Henry isn't here now, he stopped in day before yesterday to talk to me. He gave me a couple of his cards. I put them right there, on top of the bookcase. Here, let me give you one. He also gave me $100 bucks. I will use that for the expenses related to the folks. I spend everything I get suppies for them ... ... the list is a long one. I think he's a wealthy man. I heard him tell Henry once that he lived in Minnetonka, out west of here somewhere."

Arvie and Sandy shared a glance, and Arvie said, "Minnetonka is an up-scale community here. It's thought of as a well-to-do community, but that doesn't necessarily mean that every resident is well-to-do. Perhaps, I or someone from the church can reach out to him once the church has a plan in place.

"Just one more question, Colby. I was thinking about this when I woke up this morning. When one of your flock passes away, what happens when there is no family?"

"Well, it's like the law of the jungle goes into effect. Whoever discovers the body calls 911. They come and take the body. It's the same thing as with a homeless person. I don't know where they are taken and what is done. I don't want to know. There have been many times when Henry and I would walk in someone's apartment and we'd find the body. We'd go to whoever was responsible for that building and let them know. They'd call 911."

"Don't you feel more of a responsibility for them than that?" asked Sandy.

"Sure. Can't get away from that. But they are in God's hands then. My responsibility is to continue with those who are living. I can't serve them anymore. I watched Henry many times after he found one of his people dead, stand up straight and tall and offer a prayer to God to welcome this person into the kingdom and then he'd shed some tears. Then he'd cover the body best he could, and he'd move to the next apartment."

Arvie looked at the floor for several moments before raising his eyes to meet those of his young friend. "God bless you Colby. We'll leave you now and I'll see you tomorrow afternoon."

* * * * * * * *

Arvie and Sandy shook hands at the curb. "Looks like you've found another human-interest story, Sandy."

"I'll say," replied Sandy. "What we saw in there was what Henry did for 70 years or so."

"Yup."

"I can't imagine. And for no pay."

"Well, virtually nothing," said Arvie quietly.

"I find it truly amazing that a man and wife could live their lives in that manner, serving others and receiving nothing for it."

"Don't forget Sandy, they were on a mission, doing what they believed God called them to do."

"I find that amazing too." Sandy was quiet for several seconds. He continued, "Ever since I met you, I have been thinking thoughts that are so new to me, I must admit to being a little afraid."

"Don't be afraid of learning something new. Welcome those thoughts. Perhaps one day soon we can talk about them, if you'd like."

"Maybe so. I'll think about that. ... Now, after you bring those board members here, will you call me and let me know what happened? I'd like to be here but I doubt that would be appropriate."

"Probably not. But I will give you a call. Might not be much to report since they'll take their findings back to the board for discussion. But I'll keep you posted."

"And can I pry into that candle-lighting thing? What was that all about?"

Arvie told Sandy all he knew about the candle-lighting event. Sandy filled up several more pages in his notebook. "I suppose it wouldn't be a good idea for you to put anything in the paper right now, I mean about any of this."

"Arvie, I wouldn't do that, I promise you." He looked up from his notebook to add emphasis to his words. "Where is that Bible passage about serving the least of these?"

"That's in Matthew chapter 25, verse 40, if I remember correctly."

"Could be a heck of a story." Looking at Arvie, Sandy added "I want you to know, I *am* going to begin to build an article about all of this, because if the church does make something happen with those people like Mr. Elston and the others, I hope you'll give me the first chance to print the story."

"You've got my promise on that, as much as I can promise it anyway. Right now, I have the ear of the President of the Board and I'll do what I can."

"Great. Oh, one more thing ... I bumped into Woodhull this morning."

"Uh-oh."

"Yeah, he was really hopped up. He asked if I'd seen you recently and I said no. He said he still thinks your story about wanting to give people a cup of your coffee is suspect. He told me you were seen sneaking into the back of an abandoned building on Lake Street in Forest Lake in broad daylight."

"He saw that? Well, sure he did. Owens and Settles were on our tail but I don't remember noticing them." I told Sandy the story about Rick Gordon and his coffee shop idea.

"Fascinating. Well, Woodhull asked me what I thought you were doing and I told him you were probably still getting your coffee to people. He kind of sneered and told me that no matter what, he was going to get to the bottom of all this. Said maybe you could pull the wool over my eyes, but he was smarter than that."

"You're kidding me, right?"

"No, I'm not, Arvie," he said very seriously. "Have you seen any of those sedans behind you recently?"

"I haven't seen a one."

"Well, keep an eye out. I still don't get what makes Woodhull tick, but I do know he is not one to mess with. Watch your step. He's still looking for whoever played the Black Widow and killed von Barstow and that other guy last week."

"Sandy, I'm not going to worry about Woodhull. If I see a black sedan in my rear-view mirror, I'll let you know. Now, come on. Let's go find Colby."

"That's good enough for me." They shook hands warmly.

* * * * * * * *

Once in his car, he reached for his phone and called Mr. Gordon. On the fourth ring, he got Mr. Gordon's secretary. "Good afternoon. Mr. Gordon's phone. I'm Maria, his secretary. How may I help you?"

"Hi Maria. My name is Arvie Ellison and I'm working with Mr. Gordon on a project over at the Dove Creek Church."

"Yes. He's told me to expect a call from you. He's in a meeting, at the moment. I'll be happy to tell him you are on the line."

"Thank you very much."

"Hold please."

Arvie's mind flashed to the scene in Mr. Elston's apartment. The smell of it returned to him in a flash. He closed his eyes and offered a short prayer for Mr. Elston, made even shorter when Mr. Gordon picked up the phone.

"Arvie, glad you called. What did you find out?"

"Let's plan on Thursday, the day after tomorrow. I'll let you and the other members of the committee determine the time. Colby said any time will be ok with him."

"I will check with them and I will call you back no later than tomorrow morning. Arvie, I'm so pleased with our meeting this morning. I'm going to have some plans for us to look at in about 10 days. I've found a property on Lake Calhoun to look at and another on Lake Harriet. There are two on Lake Minnetonka and three more to study on the river road, two on the east side and another on the west. I hear the views at all of these locations take your breath away. But you know how realtors talk. I can imagine though that the views could be just what we're looking for. I'm going to check 'em out before the week is over and then you and I can spend some time next week looking around. How's that sound?"

"Goodness. It sounds like way too much fun."

"That's just what I've been thinking. But first, let's tend to the business at hand. I'll call you with the time for our Thursday visit tomorrow morning and at that time you can give me the address where we'll meet. Right?"

"Yes, that's good."

"Arvie, I don't know where this will end up. I don't know what the church will decide to do. But I feel confident, it will be at least something. I've had talks today with four other board members who have called with questions about how this could be handled, so there is a lot of interest. And, listen to this, I've learned of a substantive amount of related expertise that's available to us in the church should we vote to take action. That's a good sign. Thanks, Arvie. I'll call you in the morning. Bye."

All the way home, Arvie could think of nothing but coffee houses on the East and West River Roads, Lakes Calhoun, Harriet and Minnetonka. *Good grief,* he thought. *My life is full of excitement, fun things going on and the church isue that really matters. Thank you, God. For some reason, you have put me in the middle of so much. My head is swimming with so many ideas. Keep me grounded, Lord. Help me to remember that I am still Arvie Ellison. Nothing more. Nothing less. I'm still Arvid, and you know what? I'm happy being me. Be with me tomorrow morning as I serve coffee to your flock of seniors. Oh, and I could use some more coffee. Would you please let Jacob know that I have a need? It could be very soon that I might have a very big Coffee House need. Tell Jacob, just in case he wants to call in extra help to get it all blended and roasted. Bless my family, Lord. Keep them safe. Amen.*

* * * * * * * *

Brooks' car was parked in the driveway. "Good" he thought. "We need to talk about Thursday."

"Honey, I'm home. Anybody else home?"

"We're out on the patio, dad."

"There's ice tea in the pitcher."

"Got it. Thank you dear."

He poured himself a full glass, and headed to the patio. "Brooks, glad you're here. We've got to talk."

"I guess so. Mom's been telling me about the board meeting yesterday and this morning's meeting with Mr. Gordon. How many things you got goin on now?"

"Oh, mercy. I just came from Henry's – aahhh, Colby's place. I had to give him a heads up on all of this and to set a time for Mr. Gordon's explorative committee to visit down there. It's going to be on Thursday, and I'm hopeful you can make it."

"I wouldn't miss it. I'll juggle everything. Have you got a time?"

"Not yet. Colby said anytime that day is good so I called Mr. Gordon on the way home and told him the time would be up to him and his people. He said he'd call me in the morning with that, so I'll let you know – most likely mid-morning."

"I'm tempted to want to change to the other subject because it sounds like great fun, but I don't want to leave this one because this is the important one. I think Mom covered it well, so let's not go back over that, but given what you know, what are your expectations?"

"I honestly don't know. He's made it clear that there are a lot of resources available. I don't know what they are at this point, and it's not important that I know. I do know that this visit is critical. They will report back to the board and then they'll try to figure out what's to be done, what can be done, what resource's can we call upon to come in and explain various options – I really don't know how something like this works."

"Is this Mr. Gordon someone you feel will give you the straight scoop as this unfolds?"

"Gosh, I just met the guy yesterday. I can't believe it's only been 24 hours. So much has happened. But after this morning's conversation, I want to answer your question with a strong yes. But you both have to help me with this. You know how many times I've been duped before. You know how I trust people when I shouldn't. So tell me when I'm going off the tracks. I don't want to take another hit in the head, to say nothing about another one to the heart and to the wallet."

"Now, honey," began Hannah, "trust is a beautiful thing. You have this wonderful way of throwing trust out to everyone who comes your way. Remember, trust must be earned. We've learned that, haven't we?"

"I'll say, but I feel better when I trust everybody."

"Please call me tomorrow as soon as you find out the time. Now, tell me about this coffee house business. Where did that come from? And downtown Forest Lake?"

Arvie smiled. "Yeah. Well, this is all something he's wanted to do for a long time. He told me that he's been watching the revenue streams of the leading coffee house chains across the country, just to see if they can maintain their share of the business. In general, he says, it appears that those shares are dropping. He thinks he's got an idea that will work better than what they are doing. He wants to put up bigger houses to begin with and then locate them strategically where they've actually got a view. In other words, in our little community here, where would you want to put a coffee house - on the corner of an intersection downtown? Adjacent to a freeway exit, off of 35? Or perhaps where there is an awesome view of the lake? Given the time frequent visitors spend in one of these places, he believes people will travel a few extra miles to get to a place 'with a view', rather than go to the usual, easy to get to location at the corner of a busy freeway exit. He said, 'We must remember, above all else, that people want to be entertained these days and a beautiful view out a window is entertainment at its very best.' I wish there was a place for a coffee house up in Taylor's Falls with a view of the river going through the steep rock- walled gorge. It's reminiscent of the Grand Canyon in that respect. Beautiful. People could sit there for hours watching the St. Croix bubbling rapidly south."

"Interesting. So, what's the location here in Forest Lake?"

"It's downtown Forest Lake, on Lake Street just north of the roundabout. It's an old building that is right now a real dump. It's been vacant for a number of years. Rick showed me this morning that there could be a three-story tall window in the back of the building that could look out over the parking lot, the city park, the beach, and the lake itself. He's talking about taking out the 2nd and 3rd levels, opening up the interior into one huge rustic room with several open fireplaces on the first level, and balconies surrounding the 2nd and 3rd levels, but every table in the place will have a view of the water. He talked of building up elevation levels on the first floor from the window at the front all the way to the back so that every lower level table would have an unobstructed view. The 2nd and 3rd levels would look like a movie theater or an opera hall with tables around three sides but every table will be open to the water. He talked of residents on the east side of the Mississippi that still take Route 61 north to Duluth just because they always have. They like the old way up north and not cruising up 35 at 80 miles an hour. He mentioned other possible locations around the Twin Cities that are currently available; Lake Calhoun, Lake Harriet, Lake Minnetonka, and along the Mississippi on both the West and East River Parkways. And, he's going to investigate all those locations. He's convinced the coffee business is about to change."

"How about drive through business there?" asked Brooks. "That's still important, isn't it?"

"Oh yes. He's got that figured out too. The building next door used to be an old meat market. Long and narrow. He's bought that building too. It'll be torn down and the drive up will run through there."

"Is he made of money? Is it coming out of his ears?"

"Well," chuckled Arvie, "he told me that his daddy had been very successful in business and he had been left with a lot of it, and he also has been quite successful in his own right. He's going to begin here in the Twin Cities, and then expand into Wisconsin, north and south along the west side of Lake Michigan, and then into Michigan, on the shore on the other side of the lake. After that, he said, who knows?"

"And he's talking to you about this because he wants to use your coffee as an additional boost to marketing?"

"Yeah. That's right."

Brooks thought for a minute and then asked sheepishly, "Do you think he might be taking advantage of you?"

"Maybe, a little. There will be no promotion of 'magic coffee' or 'healing properties' in the coffee or anything like that. He had initially thought of that but there could very likely be some liability involved if someone didn't get healed of something. That could get expensive."

"That makes sense. I imagine he has his own legal counsel."

"He indicated as much, but he would like to use the names of the coffee like Forever, Mercy, Redeemed and any other name that comes along. All coffee sold would come through me. He likes the idea of selling hope, so if there are those people who recognize the coffee names from the newspaper stories, they may buy it because of the hope thing. And if they don't know anything about any of that, perhaps they'll get healed of something anyway. All the fancy coffees like lattes, expresso, cappuccino and the like would be made using Forever, Mercy or whatever the name. Those drinkers will have a chance of getting healed too. The menu on the wall would show those coffee names as well, in the small, medium, and large, and the coffee sold from the rack in the one-pound bags – the same."

"It sounds good, doesn't it? Well, I think he's got an interesting idea there. I'd need to study the numbers he's looking at to at least offer an intelligent opinion, but it sounds as if he's got an interesting take on it. Besides the coffee, what else does he have in mind for you?"

Arvie continued, "He talked about me visiting the various locations on occasion, and being on hand for new store openings and things like that. He said that on special occasions, he'd like to see people circulating throughout the store carrying a couple of pots of steaming coffee – free refills, perhaps."

"How much of that can be done and still manage a profit margin?"

"He told me that I can charge him whatever for the coffee and he'll still make a profit."

"If you are able to get the coffee for nothing will you charge him for it?"

"No."

"So, will you receive a monetary benefit from all of this?"

"He said he, 'will make it worth my while.'"

"Any details on that?"

"No. He said the coffee house progress is secondary to the more important church issue, that of finding a way to help Henry's people. 'First things first,' he said."

"Dad, I know you want to believe that this man is trustworthy. I want to believe the same thing. But, I know you've been taken to the cleaners a couple of times along the way, and I don't want to see that happen again. May I ask a favor, that you keep me posted on any coffee house progress, and will you use me as a sounding board? Can we work together through any negotiations that might occur? I do this kind of work frequently, and I can help you. Ok?"

"Yes, my son. You and I will go down the path together. Where were you back then, when I needed you? Oh yes. You hadn't been born yet."

"Mom, help me on this. This could be the little nest-egg that you guys don't have right now. I don't want to sound like a money-grubber or anything like that at all, but there are people out there that will do all they can to take advantage of a situation like this. If dad forgets to call me, will you?"

"I won't let him forget to call. Trust me on that. We have already had that conversation on trust."

"Good," Brooks said, slapping his hands on the patio table, causing the iced tea glasses to jump and clink and rattle around. "I've got to be getting along home. Dad, you call me with the time of Thursday's meeting. I wouldn't miss that for anything. Thanks for the iced tea, Mom."

"Bye honey. Thanks for coming over. Hi to Kate and the kids."

* * * * * * * *

Arvie and Hannah sat at the dining room table enjoying a light supper. They had cleared away some of his clutter, electing to sit at the table tonight instead of turning on the tv and eating off of the coffee table. Over the course of the past month or so, tv had taken a backseat.

"So much has happened since I headed to the cabin – what, three weeks ago yesterday? I can remember feeling so free that day going off to see the boys. And then I made the mistake of stopping for a bathroom break and seeking more coffee for the travel mug. Coffee, Jacob, things healing at the cabin, black cans arriving, taking coffee to a drug dealing beggar on a corner, getting picked up and spending a night in jail – think of it. Of course, it was that night in jail that I met Henry. He knew someone who could analyze coffee and the night I go to get the report from him, Henry and two others were killed. What ever happened to the analysis by the way? The authorities believe that I spent years in the jungle of South America and I'm followed all over by black sedans. Sandy Marsh and those articles. Then we meet some of Henry's flock and realize the severe helplessness of so many people. The board meeting, Rick Gordon and his ideas, and now, maybe, something good might happen because the church may get involved."

"What if they don't? Then what will you do?"

"The only thing I know will work."

"What is that?"

"I'm going to the Democrats."

"Huh?"

"I'm serious. They want to grow the government. They want to provide more services so they can create more departments in order to support those services. That means they get to hire more people. Grow the government. They build buildings all over the country to house these forgotten seniors, and they must hire more people to staff the buildings. That will create a lot of additional jobs, more departments, more payroll, more taxes for us to pay. With the increased hiring, the unemployment numbers will go down and then their ratings will go up. They'll be happy because it's all a positive gain for them. That will also give the president the opportunity to ram a few more of his pet projects through without legislative approval and no one will care because his overall ratings are at an all-time high. Once those bills are signed, there will be more construction, more hiring, reduced unemployment, and more positive ratings for the president and his party. The government would have to borrow more money to pay for all this since it is broke, so what's several more trillion added to the national debt? It's just another reason why the forefathers of our country are rolling around in their graves. This entire idea makes me want to vomit. But if I thought for one moment that it could work, and Mrs. Koepke and all those like her would have a place to live with someone to look in on them once in a while, make sure they have two meals a day, some heat in their apartment, running water, some hot water even, a bar of soap, a towel and a wash cloth, a toilet that works, some clothes, and a staff of people on hand to remind them how to flush. No tubs, dammit. These people can't get into a tub and don't put showers in tubs either. If they can't get in a tub to take a bath, how can they get in a tub to take a shower? There is no end to this. But still, if some one could make something like this happen, even the democrats, I guess I could live with it. I may even stop thinking so negatively about them."

"Oh, come now. You have always gotten such pleasure with your rants against the democrats. Have you ever thought that maybe you're wrong about all that stuff?"

"Sure. All the time. And then I don't like the feeling of not being right, so I disregard that feeling because it's so enjoyable to go off on a good rant now and then."

"I hope the church comes through. I'm not sure I'm comfortable with you making that pitch to the democrats."

"Yeah. I know. But I'm going to remember that rant for next year at the cabin. Most of those preachers are democrats and it'll sure get 'em going. It'll be fun."

Chapter 24

"I've had lots and lots of dreams over the years. Never understood a one of 'em. Nothing but garble and gibberish. There was one time when we had a lady in our church who could interpret dreams. Went to her once. She said my dreams were nothing but garble and gibberish. Cost me $10 bucks to learn that. Heh-heh."
- Ole

"You will teach me how to live a holy life. Being with you will fill me with joy; at your right hand, I will find pleasure forever."
Psalm 16:11

Following the morning's Bible study and organ concert, Arvie and Hannah picked up their favorite sandwiches at the Deli on Lake Street, drove to the park, sat at a picnic table and enjoyed their lunch. Arvie pointed out the backside of 204 Lake to Hannah.

"What are you thinking?" she asked.

"Couple things. First, at this morning's Bible study, Jan's list of our fellow seniors that are suffering with old age. Her list seems to get longer and longer every week. I sure am hoping that our coffee can make a difference. And second, I find myself thinking about Rick's philosophy on coffee houses and wondering if he might be right."

"He called you this morning. Did he have a time for the field trip?"

"Yes. Tomorrow morning at 10. I gave him the address so it's all set. When we are done here, I'm going to drop you off at home and then I've got to run down there and let Colby know. I shouldn't be long."

"I'll be prepared if you're a little late coming home, just in case Mr. Elston has another surprise for you."

"Hah. Let's hope there is not another one of those," he said with a smile.

"You were sure making the rounds of the tables this morning. Hear anything interesting?"

"There were a few comments about some minor things like arthritis, sinus and allergies. Most of that could be changes in the weather, of course. It was interesting listening in to the table where George Hopkins sits. Noah had told me recently that George had a surgery cancelled because whatever the problem was disappeared. I kept waiting to hear some detail and finally I leaned in and asked what it was, and he pointed to his head and said, 'tumor.' I asked him what had happened and all he said was that he had prayed about it and Jesus had taken it away. A miracle."

"Do you think the coffee could have had anything to do with that?"

"I want to think so. But who knows?"

"Whatever happened, it certainly was good news for him."

"I'll say. How about you? Did you hear anything from anyone?"

"I didn't hear anything, but Moggy had heard Earlene Fleeting talking about shoulder pain that had been awful for a month. Monday morning it was totally gone. She has been rejoicing ever since and loving life again. That could be something, huh?"

"I guess it could be. It's something to put in our notes when we get home."

"Is it worth taking a look in the back window of 204?"

"I don't think we can see a thing but let's try."

With lunch completed, they dropped the trash in the green receptacle and made their way towards the back of 204. Besides the window in the backdoor, there was only one other window and it was rather small.

As they approached, he said, "This window reminds me of the windows in my grandparents' place years ago. You don't see windows this small any more." He peered through the dirty glass, into the gloom. "Can't see much."

Hannah cupped her hands on both sides of her head to eliminate reflection. "No. You sure can't."

Arvie stood back and looked up at the back outside wall. There were two more small windows on both the 2nd and 3rd floors. He tried to picture what this would look like if it were all glass. What he did notice was the width of the building. It seemed wider than he remembered.

Hannah was looking up too. "You said this back wall was going to be all glass. Wow. That could be really something."

"That's just what I was thinking. Maybe if Rick and I meet over here again, you can come with me. Might be a good idea to get some feminine input."

"Oh, I'd like that."

They turned around to look at the view. "It's pretty from here, isn't it?" she asked.

"It is. Don't they shoot the fireworks from about right out there?" He pointed in the general direction of where he thought the barge usually floated.

"I think that's about right."

"If that's right, then Rick is right. Every table in there would have a perfect view."

"I'd better get going, hon. Marcy is going to call me and I left my phone at home."

"C'mon dear, your carriage awaits. Oh, give me a quick minute. I've got to call Brooks and tell him about the time for tomorrow." He got Brooks' voice mail and left the message.

* * * * * * * *

By the time he brewed his Mercy, filled his three thermos bottles, packed them in their usual place and drove down the driveway, it was 1:45. When he was strapping in the coffee, he happened to notice a stack of styrofoam cups sitting with some extra pots and pans on a shelf. He realized that there was room in the bag for them. Every time he visited Colby he needed cups for coffee for every resident. He mentally kicked himself for not thinking of this before.

* * * * * * * *

Arvie reached inside the cover of his notebook and retrieved the address Colby had given him. He would be visiting a different apartment building, "Just down the street," Colby had said.

Arvie found it easily, even though one of the four numbers was missing. As he retrieved his coffee bag from the passenger seat, he studied the building for a moment. This is another old one and in desperate need of maintenance. The paint, what's left of it, looks as if it will be gone with the next rain. This one is a wood frame, and is four stories instead of three. It also is considerably narrower. He was curious to see the apartments.

The inside décor was far worse than the outside. Everything needed work. He walked down the long hallway not wanting to touch anything. Midway down the hall, he came first to the stairway leading down to the basement. Just ahead of him was the stairway leading up to the 2nd floor. He stood still, listening. Colby spoke with a strong voice. Arvie was sure he would be able to hear him talking to someone. He moved forward and stood by the stairway leading up. He heard nothing. Continuing down the hall, he was nearing the back door when he heard Colby's voice coming from behind the last door on the right. He stood outside and listened.

Colby was talking about Henry. He was explaining what had happened to Henry. He was explaining that he would be taking Henry's place. And then Arvie didn't hear anything. He knocked gently on the door. Almost immediately, Colby opened the door and invited him in.

Arvie was shocked and he had difficulty not showing it. This was like no apartment he had seen in the other building. He had grown used to seeing apartments without furniture. This apartment had way too much of everything. Wall to wall furniture of every color, size and shape. Tables. Table lamps and floor lamps. Paintings filled every square inch of wall space that could be seen; bizarre paintings with wild, loud and crazy colors. A huge wooden chandelier hung over a wooden drop leaf table against the far wall. The size of the furniture, the amount of furniture, and the gaudy paintings, were overpowering in this small space.

Tucked into a stuffed arm chair sitting next to the huge drop leaf table underneath the monstrous wooden chandelier, was a very little old lady. She couldn't have weighed 60 pounds. The fiery halo around her head was as bright as Arvie had ever seen. The hair on her head, what he could see of it, protruded straight out in all

378

directions. Her make up was thick. Arvie was trying to take all of it in, when he realized that Colby was introducing him. He snapped back to the present, put on his best smile, and responded cordially. The lady opened her mouth to speak but though her mouth moved, no sound was heard. Colby had introduced her as Beulah. Beulah Goyanovitch.

Arvie recovered quickly. He took the bag off his shoulder and asked Beulah if she would like a cup of good hot coffee. She looked first at Colby and when he nodded yes, Beulah nodded yes. Arvie filled up three Styrofoam cups and handed them out. Her tiny hand shook as if she had Parkinson's. She had to use both hands to steady the cup.

Arvie's gaze immediately went back to Beulah's face. The size of her eyes was changing with every pulsation of the blazing halo. Surely Colby could see this. Arvie glanced in his direction and realized that he was continuing his conversation with her. His face was so filled with love and caring as he talked to her. Beulah's eyes were fixed on him. She was enamored by him, and yet she must have been in her late 90's. Arvie couldn't hear what Colby was saying. He stood there mute, looking back and forth, watching their lips move.

His eyes fell on the red and black life-sized painting of a showgirl that nearly filled the back wall above the dropleaf. It was her. It must be her. But she is dying. She's dying. Right now, she is breathing her last. The halo is so bright. Unbelievably bright. Arvie felt fear. He couldn't breathe.

He excused himself and left the room, needing a moment to compose himself. Colby noticed that something was not quite right and with a look of concern, quietly asked, "Is anything wrong?"

"I'll be right back. I just need a moment" Arvie whispered.

He slipped into the hallway, leaned against the wall, took off his glasses and rubbed his eyes as if clearing his mind of what he had seen. He had grown used to seeing the halos over the past several days, but that was because they had been common, ordinary, like halos would be for nasal congestion or an arthritic elbow. Beulah's halo had to indicate stage five cancer of every major organ or something equally terrible. "Oh, Jesus. Please be with this lady," he prayed. He sucked in two very deep breath's, stood up straight, and re-entered Beulah's apartment.

* * * * * * * *

Five minutes later, having said good-bye to Beulah, they were back in the hallway.

"Colby, how sick is she?"

"She's lost nearly 60 pounds. It must be cancer or something equally as bad. Sometimes when I'm walking down this hall, I can hear her screaming in pain."

"I couldn't even hear her talk. What do you mean when you say, 'it must be cancer?' Don't you know?"

"No. She won't go to a doctor and she won't allow me to take her."

"So, she's going to sit there until she dies."

"Yeah. Arvie, you need to know that in situations like we are dealing with here, this isn't uncommon. With nothing to live for, and the opportunity to get to Heaven, why not die?"

"How old is she?"

"I don't know. Ignatius, who lives right next door here, believes she is 98. They've been friends for a long, long time. Let me introduce you to him. Glad you brought the coffee. That's a good idea."

Colby knocked on the door and called out, "Ignatius. It's Colby." There was no answer. He called out again, "Ignatius?" Again, no answer.

He tried the door but found it locked. With a very concerned look on his face, he reached for his wallet. He extracted a thin sheet of metal, about the size of a credit card. He stuck it between the door and the door jam, fumbled with the door knob for moment and opened the door. He mumbled to Arvie "another trick I learned from Henry."

They entered the apartment and found him laying beside his sleeping bag near the stove. "Oh no."

Colby knelt beside him and reached for the nearest wrist, feeling for a pulse. "Nothing" he whispered. He put his hand around the front of his neck hoping his finger tips would feel a pulse. He paused for a moment looking into the wrinkled face of the old man.

Arvie was also looking into the face of the old man, but what he was watching was a vanishing halo. It had been faint when they entered the apartment. There were no bright flaming reds. Quiet colors remained now.

"Arvie, you asked the other day what is done when someone is found dead. Well, now you get to see first hand."

The old and yellowed eyes of Ignatius Garballo remained partially open. Colby gently closed them. "He must have died just minutes ago. He's still warm." He stood up and made his way to the bathroom and returned with two towels which he used to cover the body as best he could. He motioned to move alongside, then folded his hands, closed his eyes and bowed his head. Arvie was watching as the last remnants of the halo died away.

"Sweet Jesus, please welcome Ignatius, a humble servant of Yours into Your presence. I wish I knew more about him. But over the last few years, I have found him to be a humble and caring man. We have prayed together several times. I have seen him care for his neighbor as best he was able. I know he has loved You, Lord, in spite of his tough exterior and I know he has been waiting every day to come home. Please let him know that there are those of us here who will miss him. Thank you, Jesus, for loving us so much that You would take the nails for us so that our sins would be forgiven and eternity with You would be our reward one day. Bless this gentle and good spirit. In Your precious and holy name, we pray, Amen. Follow me, Arvie."

Colby led the way to the steps leading down to the basement. Once at the bottom, he led the way towards the front of the building along the gray, cold and dusty concrete floor. More apartments lined this lower level as well. Apartment doors were much closer to each other on this level. Arvie realized that the doors were perhaps 14 or 15 feet apart. Smaller apartments mean more renters. Colby stopped and knocked at a door with the number "14" tacked to the door jam close to the door knob.

A big man opened the door. For his size, his deep, gravelly voice was surprisingly soft and gentle. "Colby. What can I do for you?"

"It's Ignatius, Micah. He's gone. We just found him."

"I'm sorry to hear that. I'll make the call."

"Thanks. We'll wait upstairs."

The door closed slowly. Colby led the way back upstairs. "And now we wait. What's our appointment time for tomorrow?"

"10:00, or thereabouts."

"You'll find me somewhere on the first floor. You'll meet some new friends tomorrow."

"Colby, a life has just ended. It seems so cold. It's over and it seems almost cruel to move along so quickly."

"Yes, it does. We get to know more about some than others. Many of these people don't talk much about themselves. A lot of them don't have a good memory of what their life has been. Henry said we don't have the time to sit down with people and really get acquainted, but what we can do is spend a few minutes with them, to let them know there is someone who cares about them. Some people don't talk at all. Those I don't know much about, but I help them the best I can anyway. The main thing I remember at a time like this is Ignatius has gone to a better place but there are many still here who need to see me today. Can we sit on the steps and have another cup of that coffee?"

"You bet." Arvie poured two cups while Colby dusted off the second step.

"As soon as they've taken Ignatius, we'll look in on Louise Roush. Louise and her sister Maizee live together, though Maizee doesn't spend much time here. She pretty much lives on the streets and sells herself most every night. She's usually here once a day, and she is very faithful about bringing Louise something to eat. I usually try to get to Louise most every day as close to noon as I can because she needs help putting together her lunch."

"How long does it usually take to get an ambulance here?"

"Sometimes it can take awhile. When the call gets made, they know they're coming for a dead body, so there is no rush. It can slip down the priority list pretty far some days. Ah, here they come now. I've seen these guys before."

Colby stood, motioning for them. He opened the apartment door as the rolling stretcher made its way down the hall. Colby exchanged greetings with them both. While no names were used, it was clear that they had met before.

Ignatius was lifted, situated and an ambulance blanket was spread over him. "Any known next of kin?" Colby was asked as a clipboard was unceremoniously handed over.

"No." Colby signed on the bottom line and passed the clipboard and the pen back. "No."

Ignatius Gradollo rolled hurriedly down the hall and out the door. Colby and Arvie followed them as far as the front porch. They watched the process of loading and securing and closing the rear door. Colby raised his hand in farewell as the ambulance drove away. "And just like that, a life is over," he said. He watched it disappear around the corner. His eyes were wet. A large tear-drop fell to the warped, weathered wooden porch floor, and disappeared as soon as it splashed down. "He was a beaten up, emotionally spent old guy. Underneath all of his built-up armor, his spirit was beautiful. I saw it once. That's what I'll remember."

* * * * * * * *

Colby knocked on the door. Centered on the door was a business card piece of white paper, scotch taped in place. Written with a shaky hand was the name "Louise." "Louise always wants a name plate on her door. Maizee does this for her."

A rolling sound was heard approaching the door. A voice from the other side of the door uttered unintelligible sounds. Arvie looked at Colby, wanting to ask the question "What was that?" But Colby was saying, "Yes Louise. It's me." Then followed several moments of something sounding like a dog scratching at the door. "What's going on?" Arvie asked. "You'll see," responded Colby.

Finally, an unlocking sound was heard and the door slowly opened. She was another little thing seated in what was a home-made wheelchair of sorts: a kitchen chair with small rollers at the bottom of the wooden chair legs. There was a seat belt, of sorts, that she had wrapped around her hips and upper legs. There was not an ounce of fat on her. In that respect, she and Beulah had a lot in common. But this lady was much younger. There was a bigger look to her. Her face was long and narrow. It was twisted in such a way that it appeared she wore a perpetual smile. Arvie was happy to see her halo was dull and did not shimmer. Her arms were twisted about in an uncontrolled manner, as were her legs. And then more unintelligible sounds, to which Colby laughed out loud, bending down to give her a hug, while she literally threw her arms up and around his neck. He said, "Yes, yes, yes," to her.

After a moment, she let him loose and uttered a few more unintelligible sounds to which Colby responded, "Yes. I've got it right here." With that, Louise unbuckled her seat belt, Colby picked her up and placed her in an armchair. He then took her wheelchair, turned it upside down and placed it over the edge of the chrome kitchen table. Out of his tool box, he extracted cans of, '3 in 1 oil' and compressed air.

"She can go for about a week with these little rollers, and then they get all bound up with dust and grit. I clean them up and oil 'em and then she just flies around this place." Louise bellowed out an unintelligible guffaw and added a few unintelligible words besides, to which Colby responded, "Yes you do. You just fly around this place."

More unintelligible sounds followed by a series of grunts. "I'll say," he responded. "Let's not let that happen again. That scared me when I came in that day and found you."

Colby explained "Her chair fell over one day because she was going too fast and hit something. She laid there until I found her the next day." Raucous unintelligible guffaws filled the air.

"Yes, you did, too," he said.

Arvie interpreted her next communication as a question. He was correct.

"Yes, we were just there a few moments ago." Colby blew another blast of compressed air into one of the wheels, put down the can, and turned to look directly at Louise. "Louise," he said softly, "I'm afraid I have some bad news. He passed this morning."

There was moment of absolute silence as she let that message sink in. And then there erupted a sound of whining the likes of which Arvie had never heard before. Colby knelt in front of her, gently took both flailing hands into his own and carefully massaged them, waiting for the outburst to subside. He took a clean handkerchief from his pocket and dried her cheeks and dried her upper lip of the residue resulting from a running nose. Quietly, she made some more sounds, to which he responded, "Yes, he was ready to go."

"I'll get your lunch started now and then I'll finish your chair." He opened a cupboard door and pulled out a can of soup, half of which he poured into a sauce pan on the stove. He turned on the electric heat. Out of the little frig, he took out a partial loaf of bread and a container of lunch meat. Today it was bologna. There was also a small jar of yellow mustard. He washed his hands with a small bar of soap on the sink, dried them with a clean bar rag from his tool box, and then finished making the sandwich. He finished cleaning all four wheels on the chair, and then dripped some oil into the ball bearings in the wheels, spun them all several times and placed the chair on the floor. He rolled it over to Louise, gently picked her up and moved her back into the chair. He quickly snapped on her seat belt to which she responded with a short unintelligible grunt. Colby said, "You are very welcome." He rolled her to the little kitchen table, poured the soup into a small bowl and placed it in front of her along with a soup spoon. And then the sandwich. He opened a drawer and pulled out a bright red bib which he quickly tied around her neck. He then laid a hand towel across her lap.

While Louise was eating, he opened a closet door and retrieved a small hand operated carpet vacuum which he placed near the kitchen table.

He went down the short hallway to the bathroom with Arvie following along. He checked the sink drain and the toilet by running the water. Both appeared to be functioning properly.

"What's the vacuum for?" Arvie asked.

Colby chuckled "You'll see." They returned to the kitchen table.

A disaster. Most of the sandwich was on the floor. The soup was mostly into the bib, or the towel across her lap. Colby asked, "had enough?"

There was heard some low pitched unintelligible grunt, followed by an easily recognizable belch. "Good," he said. "Let me fix you up here."

She let him wash and dry her face, neck and hands. He then untied the bib and laid it in the sink. Ran some warm water into the sink, put the stopper in place, shook out the towel in the small waste basket under the sink, and then dropped both the towel and the bib into the soapy water. He sloshed them around a little bit, dried his hands and reached for the vacuum.

By this time Louise had rolled away from the table, enjoying her ease of travel. Colby vacuumed the lunch off the linoleum floor. He then cleaned the vacuum thoroughly, dropping the contents into the small waste basket. He made sure to wash and wipe dry the insides of the vacuum just in case any liquid had been vacuumed up.

Everything in order, he knelt in front of her and the hug was re-enacted once again. He said good-by to her and assured her he would be back at noon tomorrow. Arvie heard her sounds and felt sure she said a thank you in there somewhere.

* * * * * * * *

Once out in the hall, Arvie asked Colby to tell him about Louise.

"Well, she has MS, Multiple Sclerosis, which is a disease of the central nervous system. I don't know what all that means, but Henry explained it as a problem where all the wires are not hooked up correctly. Nerves, muscles, and the brain aren't in sync. Everything operates independently. She needs to be in a nursing home but she has no money. Years ago, after they moved in here, Maizee stayed home to take care of Louise."

"So what happened? No money?"

"Yeah. They have no money coming in. Maizee sacrifices herself every day for her sister. It's another example of great love. That's what Henry told me. Maizee is a few years younger than Louise, but she has taken care of her since their parents ran off and left them when they were quite young. I don't think Maizee is very well. I don't have any idea where she sleeps every night or what she eats or really, anything at all about her. She's not here very much. I can count the number of times I have seen her on one hand."

"You think Maizee would quit the life she's leading if she had money coming in? You know, to stay home and take care of her sister?"

"Louise has been very positive about that, but they have no hope for that happening."

"And you can have a conversation with her. I think that's wonderful."

"Being around her a little bit most every day makes a big difference. Can I ask you a question about tomorrow?"

"Sure."

"What do you think I should do? Should I do anything different from what we've done today?"

"No. I've told them about Mrs. Koepke, Mr. Elston and Mr. Schilling so we should really see some others. The three we saw today for instance were perfect examples of needing daily care. I'm sure you have three or four more in your own building who can communicate the same need. A couple of hours tomorrow are all that's required. I don't know what the 'next steps' will be *after* tomorrow, so let's not start supposing anything. Whatever is to come, rest assured I will let you know what's happening."

"What are the names of the people?"

"Mr. Gordon is the President of the Board. The two others are Mr. Dillard and Mrs. Goethe. I addressed the Board the one time and I found everyone to be very interested in this area of need. I want you to feel like you can be yourself. You just plan on being Colby. Show them the love you have for these people as you have shown me. The five of us, including Brooks, will be here to accompany you on your rounds. And if you think that's too many people, Brooks and I can wait in the halls. You let us know if we need to do that. Any other questions?"

"I'm going to pray about tomorrow morning. Will you too?"

"I plan on doing that, for sure. I want Jesus walking with us all morning."

"Me too. I wish Henry was gonna be with us."

"I think we can depend on him walking with us too."

"Yeah. I'm sure you're right."

"I've got to be going, Colby. I'm so anxious for tomorrow I can hardly stand it. Hannah tells me that I'm lacking faith. She says I've given Him this so I can be assured He's going to make it work, or He's not. It all depends on His plan, His time. Those are the details we'll never know."

"We are just people, Arvie. Henry told me years ago that if I pray, all the day long, it fortifies my faith. The closer we are, the stronger our faith. Sometimes what I do every day gets me down. My sadness for these people weighs me down and it's hard to knock on the next door. But if I'm in prayer all day, I see Him in the face of Mr. Elston and Mrs. Koepke and Ignatius and Louise. When the spirit has hold of you, it's all good."

Arvie picked up his bag and looped the strap over his shoulder. They shook hands and shared a hug. "God bless you" Arvie whispered.

"And you as well. See you in the morning."

Arvie walked the decrepit hallway towards the front door. Before opening the door, he turned to look back. Colby was holding his head in his hands.

* * * * * * * *

Arvie was on his way to the freeway, but his mind was not on his driving. He was wrapped up in tomorrow morning. What would be the message taken back to the board? Only time will tell. "And I'm not going to waste the rest of this day worrying over it", he thought. "I'm going to Walmart to get my new grill. That'll be fun. On the way, I can drive by the "Samuel's Coffee House" and imagine that for awhile. That'll be fun too." By now Hannah and Gabby were at their massage and wouldn't be home until six. He's got plenty of time.

As he approached the freeway entrance ramp, he noticed that traffic out there was at a standstill. He made a quick decision to keep going north and take 36 east up ahead. He was driving by one old apartment building after another. He wondered if each building had a Henry or a Colby? Did churches sponsor an apartment building or two and send in volunteers? Maybe the American Legion? He had to admit he had no idea. Perhaps if he stopped his car and walked into any of these buildings right now he'd find a person helping those who could not help themselves.

He took the 36E ramp, was merging into traffic when his phone rang. Bren. "Hey. How are you?"

"I'm fine dad. How are you? Are you at home?"

"No. I'm coming home. I've been down at Henry's building making plans with Colby for tomorrow's meeting with the Dove Creek Board members."

"Is this the field trip you were hoping would happen?"

"Yeah. I'm a little nervous."

"Well, I've got a question for you. Some of us were talking today and we'd like to help out. There could be as many as six nurses and at least one, maybe two, doctors. We could work on finding at least a half day every week when we'd come over and talk to people, the doctors could prescribe medicines and we'd figure out a way to get them at a reduced price somehow or we'd all chip in. Would something like that be of help?"

"Oh, gosh. It would be like a miracle."

"What time is the field trip tomorrow?"

"10 in the morning."

"Can I come and see what it's all about? My boss wants me to take a field trip too and report back."

"Oh, yes. Absolutely. Let me give you the address. Ready?"

Arvie rattled off the address and thanked his daughter profusely. He said he'd be looking for her in the morning.

"Ok, good. Are you on 35? I just heard a report on the radio that there's been a bad accident and traffic isn't moving."

"I was about to get on when I happened to notice nothing was moving, so I'm taking 36 east at the moment."

"I want to tell you the latest news about Alex. She's going back to Milwaukee this weekend. We've had supper together Sunday night and again last night. We must be an impressive family because she says she wants to get back to hers. After being with us Saturday night she has decided she wants to go home."

"So, what does that mean regarding that man in her life?"

"All over with. She told him last night. She told him she was not ready to get married; she definitely wasn't ready to move in with him, and that she's resigned her position at the hospital and is leaving town."

"Wow."

"Yeah. Know what he said?"

"What?"

"He said, 'I'm very disappointed. I wish we could have had a chance.' And then he got up and walked away."

"She said she was glad it was over but terribly upset that she meant no more than that to him. She is very thankful to our family dad, especially you. You're the one that shook her up a little with your first conversation. Mom helped with her comments, and I served up the dessert. She thinks we're a good team and she wants to ensure that one day that she'll be a part of a good team too. She's going to take your advice and find someone at church and she's going to take my advice about getting acquainted for a minimum of two years."

"Isn't that wonderful."

"She's anxious to get home on Saturday to tell her folks how this all came about."

"And what about her job?"

"She's not worried. There are many nursing jobs in Milwaukee. She came over here to get away from her parents for awhile. Now she can't wait to get back to them."

"That's great news. Thank you for your part in that, Bren."

"All this has been a good reminder that I've got the best family in the world and I'm not about to trade you and mom in for a different model."

"Well, I'm sure glad to hear that."

"Love you dad. See you tomorrow morning."

"Love you too, my dear. Thanks for the good news, all of it."

He slipped the phone back into his shirt pocket and at the same time realized where he was; he had missed two opportunities to head north because of Bren's phone call. Just cruised right by them. He was almost to Stillwater which meant he would take Manning Road north. So he was taking the long way home. That was ok. Manning was a paved two-lane road that wound through the beautiful countryside just west of the St. Croix.

Milk and bananas. Hannah had said not to forget. He almost had. Luckily, the Fast Break Convenience was still ahead of him, just past Highway 97.

The apprehension about tomorrow's meeting was offset by Bren's good news, tomorrow's field trip and that about Alexandra. For several minutes, he thought about life being that way, at least it seemed it always had been. Life is like a roller coaster, full of ups and downs. He slowed and turned into The Fast Break, parked and went inside.

He saw the 'dairy' sign and headed in that direction. He picked up a gallon of 1% and then found a beautiful bunch of eight bananas. He waited at the counter for a little old lady, also buying bananas. After she talked about the weather for way too long, she finally took her bananas and left. Arvie stepped up to the counter and noticed a cane hanging on the ledge. He grabbed it and asked the cashier at the same time, "Hers?"

"Oh my, yes."

Arvie walked off after her calling "Ma'am. Ma'am." He noticed she wasn't walking in a straight line and her left leg appeared to be much shorter than her right. He caught up with her as she was reaching out for the door handle.

"Ma'am" He bellowed.

"You don't have to raise your voice," she said, turning rather slowly to face him.

"I'm sorry, but you forgot your cane."

"So, I did. Thank you very much, young man." She took the cane, opened the door, and hobbled towards several parked cars.

"I think she just paid me a compliment" he thought as he turned back to the counter where there was now a line of four people. He went to the end of the line.

Finally reaching the counter, he plopped down the milk and bananas. Watching the cash register, he handed across a five-dollar bill to pay the $4.37 charge.

The man-made change, and asked, "Does the CRV just outside the front door belong to you?"

"Yes," he said slowly. "Yes, it does." He thought he knew what was coming next.

"I've got something for you," the man said. Please come around back with me."

Arvie was more than a little apprehensive. This was unusual behavior by a clerk at a convenience store. He had become used to watching as the person fumbled beneath the counter for something, but he'd never been invited out back before.

He followed the man out the door and around the building. Once around back he noticed at the far end a shed that looked to be a white frame 12 X 12. The man had been twirling a ring of keys all the way around the building. He now selected one, unlocked the padlock and swung open both doors. "These are yours. They told me you'd be stopping today."

He was pointing at a stack of cardboard, 12 boxes high. He'd seen this box before on his front porch one week ago last Saturday night. Coffee.

"Thank you very much."

The man grabbed a two-wheeler, expertly maneuvered it under the lowest box, pulled the two wheeler back and said, "I'll help you with these."

"Thanks. I appreciate that. Who delivered these today?"

"I came on duty at 2:00. When I walked in the guy I replaced was leaving. He passed me this note that the truck driver had given him, a license plate number. He said, 'There are 12 boxes in the shed for that plate number and there is no charge.' That's all I was told."

Four boxes fit in the back. Six filled the back seat. The last two went in the front passenger seat.

* * * * * * * *

"Honey, I'm home. Anybody here?"

"Yes. Me."

"How was your massage and look what I've got."

"It's a cardboard box that looks vaguely familiar."

"It's the very same that we found on our front porch not too long ago."

"And which handy-dandy little convenience store handed you this?"

"But there is more."

"More what?"

"More boxes. Come help. There are 12 in all. Let's stack these 11 on the work bench."

"So today you add 144 cans of coffee to your inventory."

"That's right. You were a math major at Mount Holy Waters. I had forgotten."

"You and your short memory."

"Thanks for the help. Let's go open up that case inside. I'm anxious to see what kind we got this time."

He grabbed his handy dandy box cutter and quickly sliced through the tape. The top open, he pulled out a can labeled, Joy.

"Look at that. It's Joy. So now the list reads Forever, Reunion, Redeemed, Mercy and now Joy. Don't you wonder why he sent us 144 cans of Joy? Do you think he knows something big is going to happen like pouring all the coffee at all church locations? Let me count here … six locations and four services a weekend. That's 24 services each weekend – for a potential of how many cups total each weekend – 20,000 or so? Or is he telling us that we need to entertain more?"

"*That's* not going to happen," Hannah dramatically announced.

"Oh, that reminds me - Alex. Have you talked with Bren today?"

"No. You have, I take it?"

"Yes. Alex is going back to Milwaukee. Bren had her over Sunday night and last night. She is done with this guy and Friday will be her last day to work."

"So, Bren did good."

"Yes, and according to Bren, so did you and I. Matter of fact, that's why she is going back to Milwaukee. After being with our family, she made up her mind to get back to her own. Being alone in a strange city isn't as wonderful as she thought it would be."

"I'm really glad to hear she's going home. She seemed so nice. But didn't she make that decision rather quickly?"

"Maybe she knew what she needed to do all along and just wanted confirmation that it was the right thing. Maybe she got that confirmation being with all of us on Saturday night or maybe it was talking with Bren a couple of times. And on a different subject, remind me to tell you about Beulah, Ignatius, Louise and Maizee sometime. Four more members of Henry and Mary's flock. Interesting and unbelievable. There's not much to say about Ignatius except to say that we found his body today. I watched as his halo slowly disappeared. It was sad to see a life flicker away like that."

"Were you there when he died?"

"No. He was gone when we found him."

"I hadn't even thought of that. I suppose the likelihood of that happening is obvious, given the health of people so old."

"Yeah. I followed Colby to the apartment of the building manager. Colby told him what had happened and he made the 911 call. We were there when they took him away. Colby prayed over him when we first found him. He said Henry had taught him."

"I want to say that's too bad, but I'm not sure that's the right thing to say."

"I know what you mean."

"Here's a question. Given the health of so many in Henry's flock, would he have prayed that their health be restored? Wouldn't that be hard to do? So, they would continue living on? I wonder how many times he would've prayed 'please take them Lord.' Wouldn't you pray for that if you loved them?"

"It is very hard for us to think that way because we are not used to it. We are accustomed to praying for restored health for those we know and love. But after what I've seen down there, I would believe that Henry prayed for the Lord to take them. That's the most merciful thing he could do. Darn it. I was going to buy a new grill today. I forgot."

"There's no rush on that. Are you nervous about tomorrow morning?"

"Oh my, yes. We're meeting them there at 10. Mr. Gordon, Mr. Dillard and Mrs. Goethe. I wonder what they are like? Well, Mr. Dillard and Mrs. Goethe. Wouldn't you think that they would have been selected for this because of some expertise in health matters? Senior health matters, perhaps? It would make reporting back to the board much easier, I should think."

"That would make sense to me, but I've never been on a board of directors. I wouldn't know much about that kind of decision making. I'll surely be anxious to hear about it. How long do you think it will take?"

I suppose we'll be a couple of hours. I'll call you when I'm leaving to head home."

"I'll be praying until you call."

"One other thing that will please you. I got a call from Bren on the way home. She was wondering if a group of nurses and a couple of doctors could be of help one afternoon a week at Henry's place? She had been talking to some of the people she works with and they want to help. Isn't that something?"

"How wonderful. Oh, I *am* proud of our daughter."

"Yeah. So am I. She is going to meet us tomorrow down there for a field trip of her own and report back. We might accomplish a lot tomorrow. So, now – what culinary delight have you in mind for our pleasure this night?"

"I had been thinking about a ham and swiss on pumpernickel but we have no pumpernickel. Then I thought of tomato soup, but alas, there is none of that in the pantry. Thirdly, I thought we might have some Chinese delivered. Which one of those three sound the best to you?"

"Well, it's a tough choice, but I'll go with number three."

"Good choice. I'll put in the call."

Chapter 25

"I can remember when I had to make a presentation to the boss.
We needed a new boiler to heat Old Main, Wilson Hall and the
White Field House. I worked for weeks on that pitch.
In the end, I walked in and said, 'We need a new boiler to heat Old
Main, Wilson Hall and the White Field House.' He said, 'Ok.'
Sometimes you're smart to tell it like it is."
- Ole

*"Whoever wants to become first among you must serve the rest of
you like a slave."*
Matthew 20:27

Arvie didn't sleep very well. He was awake, over and over again, wrestling with the bed covers, in a state of total agitation – it seemed to him, all night. Doubts had crept into his mind. It seemed to be the same doubts that kept coming back. "You're not the right one to be leading the charge into this battle. You're not strong enough. You don't know enough. You shouldn't have put yourself into this position in the first place. There are so many people better qualified than you. Who do you think you are anyway? Get out now. Call in sick. You're an old man. They'll understand. Get out."

He threw the bedcovers aside and went to his knees. He silently called out the name of Jesus, again and again, until the shadows had disappeared. He felt clarity returning to his mind. *It's those moments just before awakening, when in those shadows I'm the weakest,* he reminded himself. *It's the evil one wanting to plant the seeds of doubt to stop me. But he can't defeat Jesus.* He stood up in the darkness, steadied himself, and made his way to the closet for his robe and slippers.

A cup of Joy helped a lot. His first cup of Joy. *Isn't that a great name?* He stood in front of his sliding patio doors smelling and sipping, looking out at the pitch black of 3:30 in the early morning. He tried to make out the black sedan parked down the street before he remembered it was no longer a part of his life. His mind was racing.

Why do I have all that going on in my mind this morning? Wasn't my faith strong enough? Could that be what it was? No, not a lack of faith. It was doubt. I didn't know what was going to happen after exposing three people from church to the reality of Henry's world; Colby's world. I only know what I wanted to happen. Ok Arvie, put it into words. What do you want to happen?

I want these people to be put in a nursing home where people are available to help them 24 hours a day. I want them to receive the care they need even though they can't pay for any of it. I want people or organizations that have the money to pay the bill. I don't know who those people or organizations are but that's what I want. I want the people who can't physically help themselves to be helped. I want the people who can't mentally help themselves to be helped. I don't want these people suffering any longer. I don't want these people dying alone. I want someone reading the Bible to them every day, whether or not they can comprehend what is being read. I want them given every opportunity to find hope again; to feel it every second I want them to feel some bit of happiness every day whether they know what they are feeling or not. I don't want them to be alone in an empty room. I don't want them sitting on a stool confused about what they should do next, or wondering how to take care of completing their business. If they must talk to their imaginary friends, I want someone there to be the voice of their pretend friend. I could go on. Is that enough? Does that give you some idea what I'm looking for?

That's fine, Arvie, but who's going to pay the bill? he asked himself.

The Democrats will provide all the money that is needed. They'll just print more of it if they need it. They do it all the time, but if that's what is required to meet the needs of these people, then so be it. Grow the government some more. Build some more departments to provide the services required. Hire more people. Raise taxes, even. God Bless the Democrats.

Why don't you put your faith in God, Arvie? He promises to answer prayer. Can't you just say, 'God, my faith is in you, my trust is in you. I am going to give all this to you. Your will be done. If I can play any part in this, let me know what it is.' How many times in your life have you done that already? So why can't you just say that and stop all this doubting nonsense? Huh?

Yes, I can say that. That's exactly what I mean to say.

So why don't you say that, Arvie?

I'm a human. I'm weak. Some moments I'm strong, others I'm not. I want this so much, too much. He put his chin in his hands, his elbows on the table.

* * * * * * * *

Hannah found him with his head laying on an arm, sound asleep at the dining room table. She woke him gently but firmly saying, "Arvie. You'd better wake up and get moving or you're going to be late."

She refilled his coffee cup, heated it in the microwave and put it under his nose.

"What time is it?" he asked.

"It's 8:15. You said you wanted to leave at 9:15."

"I'm getting in the shower. Thanks." He got off the chair stiffly and headed toward the stairs.

* * * * * * * *

As Arvie turned onto Henry's street, his pulse quickened with the flashing of red lights in front of him. Two ambulances, a fire truck and a police car were all gathered in front of the apartment building next to Henry's – Colby's. He pulled to the curb well down the block from the building. So transfixed was he by all the activity in front of him, he failed to notice Brooks pulling to a stop behind his car. "Hey dad. What's going on?"

"Hey Brooks. I didn't see you. Must've been a 911 call."

"All these people show up when 911 is called?"

"Yes. SOP. Standard Operating Procedure."

"Even a hook and ladder?"

"I think that's because it's a multi-story apartment building."

398

"Is Colby involved in that building?"

"He's not mentioned it, but I wouldn't be surprised."

The sound of three car doors slamming shut behind them caused them to look back. "Ah," said Arvie. "Rick, Mr. Dillard and Mrs. Goethe."

"Arvie. Good morning," said Rick with a puzzled expression on his face. "What's all this about?"

"Good morning Rick. We don't know yet."

"I believe introductions are in order." Rick introduced the two board members and Arvie introduced Brooks. Hand shakes and greetings were exchanged. The attention shifted back to the flashing lights as they walked slowly down the middle of the street towards them.

Mrs. Goethe appeared to Arvie to be 'matronly.' He guessed her age at 60. She was a big lady, tall and very strong in appearance. Dressed nicely but not as stylish as Mr. Dillard. It was obvious at a glance that Mr. Dillard belonged in the board room, not in the middle of a street in *this* neighborhood. He was a small, yet very dignified middle aged man, and he was dressed to 'the nines.' To Arvie, Mrs. Goethe appeared at first glance to be very personable while Mr. Dillard was either very shy, intimidated by his present surroundings, or stand-offish. Perhaps all three.

They left the street in favor of the sidewalk as Bren came around the back of the hook and ladder. Arvie halted the procession and introduced his daughter. Bren looked very professional in her blue scrubs. Arvie explained to all her purpose in being with them today.

He also explained that the building they were heading for was the one on the other side of this one, where all the activity was taking place. Mr. Dillard quietly asked something about the fire truck. Arvie wasn't sure what the question was, but Mrs. Goethe responded with a quick, "Yes."

EMT's burst through the front door with a rolling stretcher. The stretcher was carried down the front steps and rolled down the front walk to the street. A small body lay under the blanket with a very pale face exposed above it. A woman's face with eyes closed.

As one stretcher was being loaded, two more EMT's emerged through the front door with another body. As the stretcher rolled by, all six of the sidewalk observers mumbled about 'the same body again.' "*Yes*," thought Arvie. "*Identical*."

And then Colby emerged. Even from this distance it was obvious that he was drenched in perspiration. He was wearing jean shorts and a blue T-shirt with the words "Love Everyone" on the front. Grasping his arm bravely was a very old man, hunched over at the waist, fearful of taking the next step.

Arvie said, "That's Colby," just loud enough for the group to hear. At that moment, the firemen emerged from the building, made their way to the Hook and Ladder and climbed aboard. The big truck slowly pulled away and moved down the street.

As Colby and the old man approached the steps, Colby bent down to the old man and said, "Now Hjalmar, I'm going to pick you up and carry you down. Are you ready?" Hjalmar continued looking down and said nothing. Colby, with his usual care and gentleness, picked up the old man easily and slowly descended the stairs. He carried him to the ambulance. He paid no attention to the six visitors as he walked by with his burden, focusing only on the broken concrete of the walkway.

The EMT's took Hjalmar from Colby's arms and placed him inside the ambulance. Quickly then, the doors were shut. Colby shared something with the EMT's and the vehicles moved away. The police car was the last to leave but only after Colby thanked them for coming. Colby stood in the middle of the street watching the convoy of emergency vehicles departing. His chin dropped to his chest and Arvie knew he was praying.

They stood there in silence watching the tall young man in the middle of the street. He straightened up quickly then and turned to face them. Arvie stepped forward, shaking hands with Colby, and then introducing him to Rick, Mr. Dillard and Mrs. Goethe and daughter Brenda.

It was Mrs. Goethe who asked, "Colby, what just happened here?"

"That was Hjalmar Bjorkman and his two twin sisters. Hjalmar is 92. His sisters are 89. Food poisoning, I think."

"Oh dear," said Mrs. Goethe.

"Yes. It was not pretty. I haven't stopped to see them in several days. I should have been there."

"How many do you work with?" asked Mrs. Goethe.

"Between 90 and 100. Some more than others."

"How can you do that?"

"It's what I do every day."

"How often do you see them?"

"There are over 30 that I see every day."

"Why?"

"There are many reasons. Some can't make a sandwich or heat a can of soup. Some need help going to the bathroom. Some need to be cleaned up every day. Some I have to dress. There are toilets to plunge, drains to clear. Washing to be done. The list is lengthy."

"There is no one to help you? No family members?"

"No ma'am. These are Henry and Mary's people. Henry was killed a week ago last Monday. Mary passed at the end of the week. There is only one family member that I see, ever. She comes to see her sister and bring her food. And then she returns to the streets for more money."

"Oh dear."

"Yes ma'am."

It was quiet for a moment. It was Rick who said, "We came to see some of your people, Colby. I guess we've seen three already."

"Yes sir. If you'll please follow me. I didn't intend to introduce you to Mr. Elston, but because I didn't get to him earlier, I do need to stop there first. But before that, I need a moment to run upstairs and get my tool box. I'll be right back." He moved quickly up the steps and into the building.

"I'm already getting the picture," said Mrs. Goethe.

"I'm not comfortable with this" mumbled Mr. Dillard, a frown on his face.

Colby was out the door and down the steps. They made their way next door and up to the second floor. Colby moved quickly to Mr. Elston's door and knocked lightly. "Mr. Elston." It's Colby." He looked knowingly at Arvie, then opened the door and moved quickly towards the bathroom. The entourage followed him down the short hallway. Mr. Elston was exactly where he was expected to be, sitting

401

with his arms hanging down his sides, the loose fitting sweat pants puddled at his feet.

"Sorry I'm late Mr. Elston. I had planned to be here earlier. Are you finished?"

Mr. Elston grunted something and nodded in the affirmative.

"Can you wipe today?"

He grunted something else.

"All right then. We'll get you fixed up in just a moment." And again, Colby did his job, quickly, gently and very efficiently.

"There we are," he said as he pulled Mr. Elston to his feet, "all fixed up." Colby reached down and pulled up Mr. Elston's pants. Mr. Elston stared down at the floor, looking helpless, embarrassed and sad."

"I'll be back at lunchtime. Ok?"

Mr. Elston looked up at him. A lone tear streaked down his cheek. Colby wiped it away with his thumb. "Love ya, man." He led the contingent down the hall and let them out the door. "I'll be right back."

Leaving the door open, Colby went back to the kitchen area and opened several cupboard doors, obviously looking for something. He opened and then closed the small refrigerator. They watched him from the hallway, and then he rejoined them. "I was checking for food. There is none so I'll bring some from the basement.

Rick asked, "He has no food in his apartment?"

"No sir. He never leaves his apartment. He really can't."

"So, there is extra food in the basement?"

"My food is in the basement. I share my food with him."

"How many of them do you share your food with?"

"There are several, sir."

"Where do you get money to buy the food if you are working with these people every day?"

"I have a part time job, three hours, four nights a week. I make enough for the food."

Mr. Dillard asked, "What is Mr. Elston's difficulty?"

"It's nerve damage sir. I don't know the whole story but things got messed up years ago that a couple of surgeries couldn't help. His arms are useless. He's one I must see at least several times every day

– food and bathroom needs. While we are here, I'd like to look in on Mrs. Koepke." He knocked on her door. Mrs. Goethe, Mr. Dillard and now Brenda were making entries in their notebooks.

Colby knocked a second time. There was a faint rustling sound behind the door. "Is that you Henry?"

"Yes Mrs. Koepke. It's me."

The door opened slowly. Mrs. Koepke was not wearing any clothes. Mrs. Goethe inhaled deeply and at the same time whispered "Oh no."

"Hi Mrs. Koepke," said Colby as he walked past her and headed for her bedroom. He returned quickly with a dress. He very politely and considerately dropped the dress over her head, straightened it nicely on her shoulders. Brenda stepped up to button the front. "There you are. Don't you look nice today," she said.

"Thank you, Henry. My bathroom is right here." She began to make her way down the hallway, feeling her way along the wall. "Here it is."

"I'll have this fixed for you in no time." Colby flushed the toilet. He removed the p-trap from the sink and cleaned it out in his bucket. After replacing and tightening, he announced "all is fixed, Mrs. Koepke. I'll see you again tomorrow."

She turned as Colby headed down the hall, and bumped the side of her face into the door jam. He immediately turned and retraced his steps to her. He gently rubbed the side of her face. "I'm so sorry. Did that hurt?"

"No."

"It'll be better now. See you tomorrow. Don't forget your supper."

"Yes."

Back in the hall, there were the questions about flushing the toilet, a discussion about her sight, her memory.

Mrs. Goethe asked, "What was that business in the bathroom?"

"She doesn't remember how to flush her toilet, nor does she remember that used toilet paper goes in the toilet. She washes it down the sink. So every day I visit her to do both tasks. That's why she led me her bathroom automatically. She does remember that."

"Does she usually forget to dress herself?"

"Not usually but often."

"How sad. Does she have anyone? Besides you, who visits her?"

"No ma'am. There is no one else."

"She never leaves that apartment?"

"Yes ma'am. She's left several times. Sometimes we find her quickly. On other occasions, it has taken up to several days. Henry didn't find her once for a week. Fortunately, it was summer time. She's not the only one. I spend way too much time searching for people who have just walked away. That presents me with a crisis, especially when it's cold. Most of these people don't have a coat. Many don't know the purpose of a coat."

"Has Mrs. Koepke been diagnosed with Alzheimers, or dementia?"

"There has never been a diagnosis."

"You mean she has never seen a doctor?"

"Yes ma'am. Exactly."

"And why is that?"

"There is no money for a medical appointment, nor is there anyone to take her."

"So, taking these people to see a doctor is not something you do?"

"No ma'am. How would I do that? I have no transportation nor do I have money to pay some one for it. I also don't have the time. Henry said there is no time for that. We have too many people to serve. But ... how nice it would be if there was a steady stream of money flowing in and I had a large enough team of people to do that. We would be filling up the waiting rooms of many doctors: medical, Psychologists, Psychiatrists and more. There is no money for prescriptions. These people can't afford any of that."

Arvie and Brenda shared a quick eye-to-eye moment of contact.

"So, these people have no hope?" Mrs. Goethe asked.

"No ma'am. Well, I shouldn't say that because I really don't know. There are those who wear a permanent smile and giggle and laugh a lot. But they don't necessarily know why."

"I see. Thank you. Who will we see next?"

"We'll go up to the 3rd floor and visit Sigurd Borndahl. Just to give you a little background, he is an albino and as such was abused in every way by family members when he was young and of course was considered a freak by many as he grew older. I don't know the details but Henry did say that he spent several years in a carnival freak show. I can't imagine. Sigurd is … well, you'll see."

They climbed the creaky old oak stairs, using the wobbly hand rail gingerly. Halfway to the 3rd floor, there was the sound of a door slamming and a man's deep voice screaming out "Colby."

Colby stopped and yelled out "I'm here."

"Come quickly" the voice screamed back. "Next door."

"Micah?"

"Yes. Hurry."

"It's the building next door. Please come," Colby said as he raced down the stairs.

"Follow me," said Arvie quickly. They did an about-face and headed down the stairs as quickly as they could.

Arvie led them down to the main floor and out the front door. There was no sign of Colby. He had already raced up the stairs and into the building. He was in this building yesterday. He had met Beulah and Louise. Well, Ignatius too, in a way.

Inside the front door, they were met with the sound of Colby screaming in agony "No, No." Then the sound of his uncontrollable sobbing. They moved hurriedly down the hall. Micah Branch was in the hallway, his back against the wall: the end of the hallway; on the right. His head was in his hands, his body was shaking.

Oh no. It's Louise, Arvie said to himself. He raced ahead of the others, as rapidly as his 75-year-old body could move. Brooks and Bren kept up with their father, the others followed at a respectful distance.

Colby was on all fours in the middle of the living room floor, cradling the bloody head of Louise. Arvie and Brooks stood just inside the door as if in a trance. But Brenda quickly dropped to a knee next to the body being held in Colby's arms and reached for a bloody wrist for a pulse. Colby's tears were flowing down onto his friend's face. Louise was staring into his eyes, and then an unintelligible sound emerged from her throat.

"Yes. I'm here. Why did you do this? Why?"

She blinked once. There was the sound of a small exhale. Her eyes froze then, open, in death. The last picture she had of her life on this earth was that of Colby's face and his grief. Bren's head dropped in despair, her bloodied left hand, placed on the floor, steadied her.

He closed Louise's eyes. With tears still flowing, he unbuckled her seat belt and slid the chair away from her. Sitting next to her, he lifted her up, pressed her head into his neck, cradled her lifeless body and rocked back and forth. "Louise" he whispered. "Louise."

Micah was heard choking back emotion in the hallway. Hedrick Gordon, Mr. Dillard and Mrs. Goethe were frozen in place, standing in the doorway, staring at the painful scene in front of them. Brooks was bent over, his hands on his knees, tears flowing down his face. Arvie had gone to his knees and was slumped over, his handkerchief to his eyes. This was the little lady he had met just yesterday who could make no intelligible sound, her arms flailing all around, strapped into a rolling kitchen chair with a seatbelt. With her pencil thin arms dangling down on each side of Colby, Arvie saw the ugly gashes across her wrist, the last of her blood slipping slowly from her finger tips to the floor.

Yesterday the floor had been covered with the tracks of her rolling chair. Arvie had seen Colby clean and oil the little rollers, and watched Louise race about with such happiness and abandon, her arms flailing around and the guttural laughter and chatter that only Colby could decipher.

It was quiet in the room now. It was over. Louise was gone. Arvie went down the hallway to her little bedroom and pulled the top sheet from her bed. He walked back to Colby's side and waited.

A few moments later, Colby slowly and lovingly laid Louise on the floor, folding her arms over her chest. Her glasses were several feet away. He retrieved them and slid them into place. And then he stood next to Arvie and yesterday's prayer over Ignatius, in the apartment next door, was re-lived in this moment.

Colby's emotion was evident throughout his haltingly sweet prayer. "Sweet Jesus, please welcome Louis, a humble servant … of Yours into Your presence … into Your Kingdom. I loved her. … … She was as sweet a soul as any one of your children. But … the life she was forced to live, was so … … terribly hard. She loved You, …

Jesus. ... In our talks about You, she knew ... You ... very well. I know she loved You and talked with You every moment in every one of her ... ... lonely days. We have prayed together many times. She knew You loved her. She thanked You for creating her ... as ... you did. I know she has been longing for relief from her earthly struggle. Thank You for taking her this day. I wish I could have been here for her, but I know she was tired. Please remind her of my love for her and her sister's love for her as well. Thank you, Jesus, for loving us so much that You would take the nails for us so that our sins would be forgiven and eternity with You would be our reward one day. Bless this gentle and good spirit. She deserves a special place, a special robe. In Your precious and holy name we pray, Amen."

As Colby spread the sheet over her, the sounds of seven human souls sniffling, blowing noses and stifling heaving hearts was heard. The young man, standing so straight and tall above his friend, with eyes closed continued with silent prayer. Mrs. Goethe was heard to whisper "That was as beautiful as anything I have ever heard." Mr. Dillard had whispered in response "Yes. Yes, it was."

Arvie had turned to Brooks and they embraced. Brenda, who was as new to this as the team from the church came to her father and brother and joined in the embrace with tears streaming, not concerned about the blood on her hand.

Micah had entered the room and approached Colby. When Colby's eyes opened, Micah said softly, "If you are ready, I'll make the call." Colby looked down at the sheet for a moment, and then nodded his approval. Micah made his way downstairs to his apartment to dial 911.

Arvie approached Colby. "I'm so sorry." The young man's sobs had subsided but not the tears. Arvie pulled him into a hug. Arvie whispered "She said something to you just before – what did she say?"

Colby, still hugging Arvie said, "She said ... Colby ... I love you."

Hedrick Gordon approached and asked, "I'm sorry, but what was her name?"

Colby straightened, wiped some fresh tears from his face, and answered "Her name was Louise. She lived with MS since birth. It's an awful thing. Henry made this chair for her, with the rollers. She could move around here very nicely. Just yesterday I cleaned the wheels of dust and dirt and oiled them. She was so happy. She could slide around with her arms flailing all around her, and for a few moments she was free."

"Did she live here alone?"

"Basically yes. She has a sister named Maizee. Maizee sells herself on the streets to pay the rent and to put some food on the table. The two of them were all they had in this world. I don't know how to find Maizee, to tell her."

Upon hearing this, Mrs. Goethe closed her eyes and whispered, "Oh no."

"Why do you think she did this?" asked Mr. Dillard.

After a moment's hesitation, Colby said, "At least partially because she was sick and very tired of her life. But I would think she was thinking primarily of her sister. She wanted Maizee to be able to stop what she was doing and knew that if she was gone, Maizee could and would give it up."

Mrs. Goethe entered into the conversation, "Colby, what happens now – I mean funeral plans and all?"

"Nothing, Mrs. Goethe. There will be no funeral. There is no money for that and there is no one, except her sister and me who would be there anyway. The EMT's will be here in a few minutes and they will take her away. And life here will continue on."

"But there are costs. Who pays for the EMT's? Who pays for the 911 call? Who pays for the burial plot or cremation?"

"I don't know. Henry told me not to worry about any of that, that we have more important things to do, more people to serve. Just keep moving, he told me. Get on to helping the next one."

Colby had blood all over him. It was on the floor, on the walls, her table. He did not want to think about how she was able to grasp a razor blade and do what she did to herself. The bloody razor blade was on the floor, to the left of where she must have been sitting in her chair. He found a box of medical gloves in his tool box. He quickly slipped them on. He carefully picked up the razor blade, washed it off, wrapped it in a paper towel and put it in his toolbox to be disposed of later. He took the wash cloth from the sink, soaked it in water, and began to clean the blood off the floor. Brooks and Bren grabbed gloves and soaked towels and began on the walls.

Arvie was explaining to the others what he had seen in the apartment next door just yesterday, about waiting for the EMT's and the removal of the body. "So now, we'll wait for them to arrive."

"How many more must we see today, Arvie?" asked Hedrick Gordon.

"I believe it's up to the three of you, Rick. Colby continues until exhaustion sends him to the basement. It's up to you, Rick."

"What do you mean when you say, 'sends him to the basement?'"

"That's where he lives. He has a cot next to the furnace."

"I'll be in the hall, pacing," stated Mr. Gordon.

"I'll join you," said Mrs. Goethe. Mr. Dillard followed them into the hallway.

Colby, Brooks, Bren and Arvie continued to clean the apartment. They didn't have to clean up but they felt the needed to do so. Each of them paused now and then to look over at the small form under the blanket. How quiet she was. How peaceful.

Moments later, the EMT's arrived. Louise was lifted easily and positioned on the rolling stretcher. The sheet was cast aside and the blanket they brought with them was placed over her. They passed the clipboard to Colby. He scratched his signature and handed it back to them. He shook hands with both of them and thanked them. They rolled Louise from the room and she was gone.

Colby took a deep breath. "I've been thinking. There must be a phone number around here somewhere. I'm guessing that Maizee would have wanted Louise to be able to get to her if there was an emergency. He began opening drawers and cupboard doors, searching for a phone number written somewhere, or a small piece of paper.

"I'll look in the bedroom," said Brooks. He was gone for only several moments before returning. "There is so little in there that it didn't take long. I found nothing."

"Nothing here either" added Colby, with obvious frustration in his voice. "It's time we get back to Sigurd."

The three of them left Louise's apartment, Colby closing the door and then looking at it for a moment before turning and walking away. They collected the other three who were talking near the front door. As they were about to descend the front steps, Colby muttered "Maizee." He hurried down the steps.

Maizee was perhaps on the other side of middle aged, but very attractive and dressed very nicely. She and Colby shared a hug. It was obvious she had been crying because her eye shadow had run to places where it shouldn't have been. She had obviously seen the EMT's leaving with someone. She had asked them to look under the blanket. "Micah called me," she told Colby. "He had my number. We had a system."

She turned abruptly and walked away. Colby said later that she was coming back tonight for a talk. They would meet by the furnace.

They walked back to Colby's building. On the front porch, Colby reminded everyone that they were going to see Sigurd. Mrs. Goethe, Mr. Dillard and Bren continued to write in their notebooks.

When they reached the third floor, Arvie saw the door to the Overstreet's apartment and was stopped in his tracks. He wasn't prepared for this moment. The yellow police tape was still draped around the apartment door. This was where it all happened one week ago last Monday night. Arvie stopped so quickly that Brooks, following closely behind, bumped into him. Then he too, realized what his dad had seen.

"Dad. Is this where ....?"

"Yes" he whispered.

He didn't want to look, but he approached the door anyway. He reached around the tape and tried the door. It opened easily. He pushed it open.

By this time, the others realized that Arvie, Brooks and Bren were not with them. Colby, looking back, seeing them at that door, knew immediately. He said to his three guests, "You may not want to see this, but we must go where they are." He led them back to the crime scene, explaining what had happened in that apartment.

Arvie had by now pulled away the police tape and had entered the apartment with Brooks right behind him. "My God" he whispered. "All this blood. I can't do this." He turned quickly and retraced his steps back to the hall, bumping into Colby on the way out. He closed his eyes and backed into the wall for support.

"Are you ok, Arvie?" Colby asked.

"No," Arvie replied. He was visibly trembling.

Bren had taken only a brief look inside before going to her father and holding him tightly.

Colby entered the apartment and stood beside Brooks. They looked at the bloodstained wall, the blood-soaked couch, the bloodstained ceiling, the bloodstained floor. "Arvie and Henry must've been over there" Colby mumbled, looking at the floor.

The members of the Dove Creek investigative team had gathered outside the door and were peering inside the apartment. Hedrick Gordon took one look and then moved to Arvie's side.

"I'm so sorry Arvie. Can I do something for you?"

"No. I'll be ok in a minute. I didn't know we'd be right here. I wasn't prepared. The memories."

"I understand."

Both Mr. Dillard and Mrs. Goethe backed away from the door. One glance was enough. It led to more writing in their notebooks.

* * * * * * * *

Colby knocked on the door of Sigurd Borndahl. "Sigurd. It's Colby. I must come in for a moment."

"OH, ALL RIGHT. COME IN."

Colby opened the door and led everyone in, introducing each of them as they entered. Sigurd repeated everyone's name and then laughed while saying, "THIS IS WONDERFUL." It didn't take long for everyone to understand that Sigurd Borndahl was, among other things, very deaf.

"SIGURD, THIS IS ARVIE, THE COFFEE GUY."

"HAH HAH. THIS IS WONDERFUL."

"AND THIS IS HIS SON BROOKS."

"HAH HAH. THIS IS WONDERFUL."

It continued that way through Hedrick Gordon, Mrs. Goethe, Mr. Dillard and Brenda. Once everyone was in the room, Sigurd walked lightly to the door and gently closed it. Then he turned and walked to a movie poster of Marilyn Monroe, turned to the group while pointing at Marilyn and asked,

"SHOULD THE MONET BE PUT ON THIS WALL," he asked as he pointed to the wall behind him on which there was a golfing picture of the three stooges, "OR SHOULD THE KLIMT GO THERE AND THE MONET AT THIS END OF THE SAME WALL?" He walked to the far end of the same wall. "I HAD THOUGHT OF THE CEZANNE HERE, WITH THE DEGAS NEXT TO IT HERE, BUT I'M WONDERING THEN, WHERE WOULD I PUT THE KAHLO? I'M TERRIBLY CONFUSED." He walked the room, stopping to look at every wall directly opposite where he was standing. He moved back where he started, standing directly in front of Marilyn. "BUT, I DO HAVE THAT PORTRAIT OF JACK LEMMON I PAINTED WHILE ON THE SET OF 'SOME LIKE IT HOT." He then pointed at Marilyn, "YES, MY DEAR MARILYN, YOU WERE THERE. OH, HOW I WISH I HAD PAINTED YOU IN OILS INSTEAD OF BLACK AND WHITE FILM."

He, again, looked at the people gathered just inside his door. "WHO ARE YOU PEOPLE? ARE YOU WAITING FOR THE SHOW TO BEGIN? WHY ARE YOU HERE? THE MESSIAH? THAT'S DOWN THE STREET AT 150 PARK PLACE ACROSS FROM THE RIVIERA. FRANK ALWAYS HAD HIS CONCERTS THERE WHEN HE WAS IN SINGAPORE.

"MOM IS FINE, THANK YOU FOR ASKING. YES, SHE STILL PLAYS OBOE FOR THE PEORIA SYMPHONY. DAD STILL RUNS HIS TRAINS. OH, THIS IS WONDERFUL. BEEF STROGANOFF ON MONDAYS.

"NO. A THOUSAND TIMES NO. I WAS SIX AT THE TIME. OH, ISN'T THIS WONDERFUL. I'VE PUT YOUR SUITCASE IN THE TRASH. DID YOU SEE HIM IN 'STAGECOACH WEST?' I JUST LOVED YOUR BOA."

"CARAVAGGIO IS MY ABSOLUTE FAVORITE." He pointed at the three stooges in their golf attire. "SWEDISH PAINTINGS?

YOU CAN'T BE SERIOUS? GRAND CENTRAL STATION. OH, THIS IS WONDERFUL. THE ZEPHYR ISN'T LATE. I MUST SAY IT IS ADORABLE. I THINK THAT CORNER. NO, OVER THERE BY THE SEASHORE."

As Sigurd took in a breath, Colby interrupted, "SIGURD, YOUR TOILET IS WORKING NOW AND WE MUST BE LEAVING."

"DID YOU SAY I WAS WORKING? THIS IS WONDERFUL. ISN'T THIS JUST WONDERFUL."

Colby walked up to Sigurd, put a hand on his arm to get his attention, and while standing directly in front of him said, "SIGURED, YOUR TOILET IS WORKING NOW AND WE MUST BE LEAVING."

Sigurd slapped him on the shoulder and exclaimed, "THIS IS WONDERFUL. TUESDAY? I WAS SURE IT WAS THE 5TH. THE LADDER IS IN THE BASEMENT. I BUTCHER THE RABBITS ON A STUMP DOWN THERE."

Sigured seemed to, once again, notice the line of people standing against his front wall. "WHO ARE YOU. YOUR TEE TIME IS NOT UNTIL THREE. SO, GOOD TO SEE ALL OF YOU, MEL. LOVE MICHELANGELO BUT I'M TIRED OF LAYING ON THE FLOOR TO VIEW HIS WORK. HAH-HAH. IT WAS A BOX CAMERA."

"GOOD BYE SIGURD," yelled Colby. He opened the front door and everyone filed out, anxious to leave Sigurd Borndahl. As Colby was closing the door, Sigurd continued his banter "THIS IS WONDERFUL. HAH-HAH. THIS IS WONDERFUL." Even after the door was closed, Sigurd could be heard, "WEREN'T YOU IN CAT ON A HOT TIN ROOF WITH LIZ?"

Colby led the way next door to the apartment of Adolf Brummel. Colby knocked very quietly on his door. The door opened immediately, perhaps one inch. One eye could be seen in the narrow opening.

"Adolf, I'd like to check your toilet," said Colby in a very soft tone. "HAH-HAH. THIS IS WONDERFUL," could be heard coming from the apartment next door as everyone was scrutinized by the single eye ball. "NEW YORK CENTRAL? NO. LIONEL."

Then the door was flung open, banging hard on the wall. Adolf backed off a precise three steps, clicked the heels of his black boots together, raised his hand in a Nazi salute towards those standing outside his door and said softly, "Heel Heetler." Colby responded with his version of the Nazi salute, clicking the heels of his tennis shoes together which made no sound at all except for the squeak made on the wooden floor. He raised his hand in a half-hearted salute and muttered, "Go Gophers." That appeased Adolf, for he dropped his salute immediately, but maintained his position of attention.

Nazi Swastikas adorned every wall. There was one on the front of his fridge, one on a coffee cup sitting on the kitchen counter, and another on his Mr. Coffee. One entire wall was a 1940 painting of a Hitler youth rally in front of the Nazi Headquarters in Berlin. Every little stick figure was a swastika with a head, arms and legs. It must have been Mr. Brummel's attempt at re-creating a happy time in his younger days. A german bayonet, sheathed, was proudly positioned in the center of the kitchen table.

Adolf was still standing at attention in the center of the room as Colby and his guests departed. The only sound they heard upon leaving was, "THIS IS WONDERFUL. HAH-HAAH," coming from next door.

Colby stood in front of his six guests and said, "I have been in this building since I was 14. I can't tell you how many times I have visited Mr. Borndahl and Mr. Brummel. It has always been what you just saw. It never changes with either of them. "THIS IS WONDERFUL," echoed down the hall.

Mr. Dillard asked, "How do they survive? Do they go out to a store?"

"Mr. Borndahl's daughter comes once every two weeks with groceries. He acts around her the same way he acted with us. Mr. Brummel has an old friend who brings him food and a bottle of whiskey every week. I don't see him much. He usually comes in the middle of the night. They practice their 'goose step' in the halls into the wee hours of the morning."

Hedrick Gordon asked to see where Colby lived. Colby led the way to the basement, to his area close to the furnace. "Do you pay rent to live here?"

"No sir. I shovel snow in the winter and try to keep the place up as best I can. I understand the furnace. I am allowed to stay here for nothing."

Mrs. Goethe was staring at a piece of paper pinned to the wall above Colby's little bookcase. "May I ask you about this?"

"That's my Christmas present from Louise this year."

"What does it say?"

"It says, 'Jesus loves you and I do too.'"

"How beautiful."

"Yes. It is that."

"It's almost 3:00. I must be getting home. We're having guests for dinner. I've seen all I need to see," said Mr. Dillard.

"I didn't realize it was that late," said Mrs. Goethe.

"Yes. I think we've got enough information to take back to the board," said Mr. Gordon. "Colby thank you for today. And thank you for what you are doing here. God bless you."

"Thank you for coming. May I offer a prayer before you go?" Every head bowed. "Dear Jesus, I thank you for these people and what they are doing for your cause. Bless their church and the multitude of good people that worship you there. Be with us all as we continue our labor of love, to take the message of your love to those who have not yet accepted, and to those who suffer daily in so many ways. Thank you for the fruit of the spirit that brings us kindness, goodness and faithfulness and joy. Those are the reasons we have gathered here today. Bless us now as we continue down the paths you have put before each of us. In Jesus precious name I pray, Amen."

All said, "Amen." There followed the handshakes and hugs of farewell. Mrs. Goethe, filled with emotion tried to say the words, "I don't know how you do this everyday." The words came out with accompanying tears and a wave of her hand to everything in the basement of the old and run-down apartment building. Everyone knew she was referring to all that had been witnessed this day.

Colby led the group up the stairs and towards the front door. The board members continued forward while Arvie, Brooks and Brenda remained behind with Colby.

At the door, Rick turned and said, "Arvie, can we talk to you a moment?"

"Sure. I'll be right there." Arvie turned back to Colby. "Is there anything we can do to help you, while we're still here?"

Colby took a deep breath and shook his head. "No. I just need to clean up and change and then I need to see the rest of my people for today."

Arvie gripped Colby's shoulder for a moment, and then he, Bren and Brooks followed the others outside.

When they stepped outside, Bren whispered, "Look at the windows. It's just like Colby said." Arvie looked up; sure enough, every window had at least one face peering out, watching the ambulance load up and drive away.

Rick Gordon and the others were waiting beside his car. Their faces were solemn.

"So, do you think my description was accurate, at the meeting the other morning?" Arvie asked as he approached them.

"Not by a long shot," Rick said. "You seriously understated the magnitude of the need here, Arvie."

The other two nodded.

Rick continued "What Colby does here, every day—and, I assume, what Henry did here for many years—is beyond anything I could have ever imagined," he went on. "This is … it's …

"It's where the people of Christ need to be," Miles Dillard finished Rick's sentence. His voice sounded firmer than it had since he'd gotten here. "This is exactly where Jesus would be, and so it's where his people must be."

"The need is so … so terribly immense," Signe Goethe said, almost whispering.

"Yes, it is," Mr. Dillard said, "but our Lord took five loaves and two fishes and fed thousands. If we don't at least offer what little we have for his use, we don't deserve to call ourselves His people."

"You took the words out of my mouth, Miles," Rick Gordon said. "We've got a lot to think about here, and we've got to figure out how best to bring this need before the church. But it must be done."

"Thank you all for coming," Arvie said while shaking hands with each of them. "I really appreciate it."

"Arvie, thank you for allowing yourself to be used by God to bring these people to the church's attention," Rick said. "We wouldn't be here if you hadn't obeyed the prompting of the Spirit in your heart."

Arvie wanted to say something, but right then, he didn't trust the way his emotions felt. So, he just nodded. Rick, Miles Dillard, and Signe Goethe got in the big, black Lincoln and drove away.

As they pulled away from the curb, everyone waved farewell. *That car in this neighborhood looks absurd* thought Brooks. Arvie, Brooks and Bren shared a group hug and went their separate ways. Before departing, he asked Bren if she had enough information to take back to the hospital. "Oh Dad, I've got more than enough."

* * * * * * * *

Once in the car, Arvie dialed Hannah to let her know it was over and that he was leaving for home. She asked if he was ok. He stated that it had been a difficult day for everyone, that they had not had any lunch and he was hungry. He said he'd stop at the deli for their usual and that he would give her all the details of the day's events when he got home.

* * * * * * * *

It was very quiet in the Lincoln as it made its way north amid the early rush hour traffic. The vehicles' occupants were all immersed in their own thoughts. In the parking lot of the Dove Creek offices 30 minutes later, Mr. Gordon let both passengers off at their vehicles. There were the usual and customary words such as 'thanks for driving' and 'we'll be in touch.' All three wanted nothing more than to get home. Mrs. Goethe said upon departing, "I don't believe I'll recover from this day for some time."

Before leaving the parking lot, The President of the Dove Creek Board of Directors placed a call to Senior Pastor Wylie Hoyt. Pastor Hoyt picked up immediately with the words "Hi Rick. I've been waiting for your call."

"Where are you Wylie?"

"I'm at home."

"I'll be right over."

* * * * * * * *

Arvie managed to get the car into the garage but it was not without a struggle. On the way home, he realized how very tired he was. There were several times when he had to re-adjust his position in order to not fall asleep. He usually traveled in the fast lane of 35W but not this afternoon. He settled in the right lane. His mind began recounting all that had happened over the past weeks, beginning with the days at the cabin. It was only after a red Lexus streaked by on his left and sounded a lengthy blast of the horn that he realized he had moved too close to the left lane. He forced himself to focus on driving. He sang hymns all the way home, fighting hard to remember words to some verses that had been forgotten over the years.

He parked the car and pushed the remote to close the garage door. He could very easily have fallen asleep right there. He dragged himself into the townhouse. Only when he shut the door did he remember that he was supposed to have stopped at the deli for food. Oh well.

"Oh, my dear. Are you all right?"

"I'm so tired. It just hit me on the way home. Everything that has happened. And today. Today was the worst. You can't imagine. Oh, I forgot to go to the deli."

"Don't even think of it. I can run up there. I'll do that right now. Why don't you get comfortable on the couch and take a little nap if you want to?"

"Thanks. I think I'll do that. I have so much to tell you. We saw so much today. I have never cried so much. The heartache was awful. Louise killed herself. It was too much. If this day didn't convince those church people to do something, nothing would. I'll tell you all about it later."

"Here. Let's get you comfortable." She settled him on the couch, fluffed the pillows just so, and threw the little blanket over him.

"Thanks," he said. One breath later and he was snoring.

Hannah left the room and headed to the Deli.

* * * * * * * *

Hannah returned 20 minutes later to find him standing in front of the patio doors.

"You're up. I thought you were gone for the night."

"I heard the garage door when you left and suddenly all the images of the day came to life. I couldn't go to back to sleep. I think I have to go through the day with you in order to clear it all out."

"It's a beautiful evening. Would you like to go out on the patio or sit right here?"

"Let's sit right here."

"What would you like to drink?"

"A big glass of water."

"You sit down. Here are the sandwiches. I'll get two waters and some napkins. So, I'm all ears."

* * * * * * * *

It took a long time to complete the telling. He had cried. She had cried with him. She liked a lot of detail and had therefore asked numerous questions along the way. The events surrounding Louise had been the most emotional moments of all, even for Hannah.

"What was the reaction of the board people by the end of the day?" she asked.

"I think Mrs. Goethe was stunned. Mr. Dillard was much more reserved and though he didn't ask as many questions, took many notes and seemed more business like about everything that happened. I noticed him wiping his eyes several times. Rick Gordon was taking everything in. He's an active man and he seemed to miss nothing."

"Next steps? Was anything said about that?"

"No. But I've got to believe that something will be done after all that happened today. Colby is absolutely amazing. The way he handles it seems so mature and well beyond his years. Those people had to be amazed by what they saw him do. But it's the plight of those old people living as they do that's got to be addressed."

"Are you prepared should they decide there is nothing they can do or that they can't do anything right now – maybe next year?"

"They have to do something and they have to do it now. Why wouldn't they?"

"That wasn't my question, my dear. Are you prepared should they decide there is nothing they can do or that they can't do anything now, but maybe next year? Can you handle that?"

"I don't know because I wouldn't be able to understand why they wouldn't do something now. No matter how much money they don't have, no matter how many questions still remain, after what was seen today, passing on this, for whatever reason, is unthinkable."

"Do you remember what you tell me all the time, what you've told me since this anxiety thing was diagnosed?"

He looked at her with a blank expression on his face. She reached over and wrapped her fingers around his wrist. She leaned closer and looked deep into his eyes and said, "You have told me repeatedly to *stop trying to understand everything and learn acceptance. What part of that don't you understand for yourself?*"

"But if they do nothing I'll never be able to accept that. Mr. Elston shouldn't be living the way he is forced to live; Mr. Schilling, Mr. Borndahl, and Mr. Brummel don't even know how they are living; Louise killed herself today because of how she was living; Beulah isn't living any more because she is dying; Mr. Bjorkman and his twin sisters may be dying right now because of food poisoning; and Mrs. Koepke isn't living at all and hasn't for many years. And this situation will be overlooked and left to continue? How can I accept that?"

"Now you listen to me" Hannah commanded, squeezing his wrist even tighter. You are not a young man any more. You are 75 years old – do you hear me? 75 and soon to be 76. You've worked your whole life and now its retirement and by gosh, you are going to learn how to enjoy it if I have to shove it down your throat. Ever since you went up to that damn cabin three weeks ago for that damn "Olga" or whatever you call it, you've been driving yourself into the ground with worry and concern over your stupid magic coffee that a dead Indian sold to you and stressing over what does it heal or not heal, and you've got to pour a cup for every drug dealer on every drug corner in town, and then when they put you in jail you've got to pour coffee for everyone who locked you up and every inmate in there with you. This is all just plain unadulterated crazyness! There is only so much you can do – my ignorant old husband. *Can* you understand that? No. Sorry. Can you accept that? Let me put it this way: pouring your coffee led you to the drug dealer. Giving coffee to the drug dealer led you to jail. Going to jail led you to Henry. Meeting Henry led you to his flock. Learning about his flock led you to the Dove Creek Board. You have now introduced the Dove Creek Board to Henry's flock. Don't you think that's enough? Can't you see that's all you were supposed to do? You brought this issue to the Board. That's enough, Arvie. That's enough. Now take some deep breaths, open a dictionary and learn how to spell acceptance. And while you're in the dictionary, look up faith. Maybe I've been mistaken all these years but I thought you knew how to spell that one. Do you think that this church is not going to do something? Do you think that what these people saw today meant nothing to them? Do you think that what is happening with those people down there means nothing to God? Do you think all that suffering means nothing to Him? What do you think God put you in this pickle for anyway? To stress out and have a heart attack over all of this? There is only so much one old fart can do. And you have done it. Let go and let God!

" Now go upstairs and take a nap and when you get up let's see if we can have a conversation about how we might possibly be able to enjoy our *Golden Years*. It's fine with me if you want to continue to try to get everyone in the state of Minnesota to drink your coffee so nobody in the state will ever get sick again but please learn how to bring hope to the world in a more relaxed manner. Now go upstairs and whenever it is that you come back down the stairs, be ready to begin to act like an old skinny, bald senior citizen again. I want that man back and I don't want to still be waiting for him at noon tomorrow. Do I have to explain this to you again or is once enough? Now go." She pointed to the stairway. Her eyes open as wide as possible and scary looking. He stood, looked at her for a long moment, leaned over to kiss the top of her head, squeezed her right cheek, and headed for the stairs.

Chapter 26

"Ya. Bad things do happen to us all. Life is tough. It's a troubled world. We all know that. Wars, killing, mutilation, starvation, prisoner abuse. World War II, ya know. The Bulge: 'member that battle? Bataan: 'member that hellacious march? Bad things happen: Hitler. But every time there's a bad thing, there's a good thing. Life works that way ya know. Stick around cause ya don't know what tomorrow brings."
- *Ole*

"Be joyful because you have hope.
Be patient when trouble comes, and pray at all times."
Romans 12:12

It was 8:00, Friday morning when Dove Creek board members were notified of an emergency meeting that would be held at 6:30, Monday evening. All members confirmed their attendance with one exception: Frieda Charlson. She was leaving Sunday, along with 60 others, on a Dove Creek sponsored mission trip to Haiti and would therefore be absent.

* * * * * * * *

Arvie was on the road by 6:30 that Saturday morning. He had three State of Minnesota road maps and his GPS but none of that would do him any good because he had no clue where he was going. He couldn't find a County Road JW on any map and his search of Google Maps hadn't found anything either, but Jacob had seemed to be very thorough. Perhaps he would put out a sign, or signs. If so, Arvie hoped he'd make it obvious. *They seem to know when I'll be at a certain convenience store so why won't they know when I'm coming to look for County Road JW?*

The concern about finding the place was upsetting to him. He had decided the night before, to do it; make the drive. He told himself that it would be fine whether he found it or not. He'd had the thought, on more than one occasion, that he'd eaten some bad pizza the night before that dream and it really meant nothing.

But still, if there was a chance to talk with Jacob again, Arvie would make the effort.

It's expecting a lot to think that Jacob would know I'm coming on August 10th, the dream said October 10th. I'm afraid I'm wasting my time, he whispered to no one.

He gave me the clues but I don't understand. And yet, he was hopeful. He believed that once he got up around the big lake, he'd see something that would make sense.

He turned north on 169 at Princeton. 50 miles left to the big lake and then a few more to Garrison. He decided at that moment that he would turn west on 18 at Garrison, as if he was heading to the cabin.

He had only seen Jacob once and that was the day the coffee journey had begun.

As I was leaving his store he said, "Enjoy... gasp... your... wheeze... reunion." He giggled a bit at the recollection of that meeting.

It was as if the old guy knew where I was going and why? Yes, today I will drive to the cabin. If Jacob knows I'm a little familiar with that trek, perhaps the county road sign will be on the way there. So, if there are messages or signs along the way, what might they look like? "Be patient and be alert," he said out loud.

He would be driving by the places where he had purchased the coffee: two separate places. He was convinced that they didn't exist, were gone, had vanished but was also sure that if he saw one or both, he would be going in.

* * * * * * * *

No. Not here anymore. They are gone. How is that possible? Arvie was up to the big lake where 169 turned from a four-lane separated highway into a two-lane road. There had been no sign of the two roadside establishments. He was disappointed but not surprised. The message from their disappearance was that this is truly a God-directed mission. *Someone bigger than all of us is in charge.*

He was going past the entrance to the Casino when he noticed something. It was well off the right side of the road and sitting on top of, perhaps, a five-foot tall metal post. It was a small, rather nondescript sign, maybe 18 inches tall and 12 inches wide. The background was shiny and black and the letters "JW" were printed in red. Underneath the "JW," was a red arrow pointing up, or straight ahead. The post, itself, was leaning to the right and appeared about to fall to the ground. He could have missed it very easily. He reached down to the dashboard and pushed the button to begin a trip meter then pushed it again to reset the numbers to 0. *Let's see how far up the road the next sign is.* It was exactly three miles. That sign also leaned to the right and the arrow indicated he should continue straight.

Three more miles and another sign appeared. Then another, another, and yet another. He passed the, "Welcome to Garrison," sign and was approaching Highway 18, which he would take to the left. *Will there be a sign? Is there a sign?* "There," he said aloud. Yes, a sign with the arrow pointing to the left. He turned West on 18. "Well now, this is no sweat," he mumbled. *I'll just follow the signs until I get where I'm going. This is too easy.* But he still didn't understand. How could anyone have known he would be going out there that day? *Wait a minute. The date today is August 10th, 8/10. Perhaps there is a meeting on 8-10-10. The signs must be here for them. Well, it's a possibility.*

It was almost exactly six miles west on 18 when he saw the next arrow. It directed him to take Highway 6 north. He made the right turn. *I must be getting close,* he thought. *Slow down. There is no rush. The next sign could be on either side of the road.* His head was back in the army: right, left, right, left. *Whoa.* He thought he caught a glimpse of a sign back by a narrow trail he had just passed. He pulled onto the shoulder, put the car in reverse and slowly backed up. He found a single, narrow lane heading into the trees. He put it in park, got out and made his way over to the black and red "JW" sign, lolling to its right in the late morning shadows. So easy was it to extract from the dirt that it was obvious it would have fallen into the weeds within minutes. He looked at the letters "JW" closely. The print style was exactly the same as on every can of coffee. He returned to the car, opened the hatchback and laid the sign inside the car. He didn't think Jacob would mind. And then he realized he could not take the sign. If others were coming for the meeting, if there was a meeting, they would need to see this sign. He marched back and re-planted it.

It was then that he noticed a street sign up against the trees proclaiming, "Aninaatig Rd." *Must be Ojibwe,* he thought. He turned into the forest and proceeded ahead on Aninaatig Road. He stopped very quickly, backed up enough to take a closer look at the street sign. The colors and script were identical to those he had grown used to seeing.

He got out again and walked up the lane 50 yards or so to get a sense of the road. He couldn't really see it when he was driving because of the weeds, but now, standing still and looking directly down at the surface, he could tell that it was crushed rock. So, he would be driving on rock and weeds.

He returned to the car, put it in gear and continued slowly down the lane for about a half mile. He stopped when the lane ran out. He was surrounded on all sides by forest, but directly ahead of him was another street sign. It was the longest street name he had ever seen: Makominagaawanzh Lane. There was only one way to go and that was to the left. He turned left slowly.

He was getting the idea now. This had all been laid out many years ago. Perhaps it was going to be developed into streets and houses. The crushed rock was put in for the streets, but it did not appear that there were any houses. It appeared that the whole idea had been abandoned and the weeds had taken over.

The forest continued without a break and the narrow one-lane road took him to the north for perhaps a mile. As he crunched along the narrow path at maybe five miles per hour, he came upon the faint outline of a driveway on his right. It was overgrown so thickly, it was obvious it had not been used in a very long time. He could see the dark outline of a shed back there in the tangle of trees and foliage. There was a mailbox nailed to a tree with an unreadable name upon it, washed away by rain and snow and wind over many seasons. He continued along Makominagaawanzh Lane very slowly.

Makominagaawanzh Lane petered out. Again, he stopped. Before him, on the other side of the road was another street sign with the 2nd longest name of a street he had ever seen – "Gaagaagiwaandag Way." The only option he had here was to take the turn onto Gaagaagiwaandag Way and navigate his way to the east. The pines were so tall and stately. The road continued straight in front of him. He stopped the car again because of the beauty in front of him.

Gaagaagiwaandag Way was barely wide enough for one car. He had seen back on Makominagaawanzh where some trees had been taken out to provide a space for one car to pull over so another could pass. Frankly, it appeared that no one had been back in here in years. The weeds he was driving over were four and five feet tall, with some even taller. His vision was severely restricted, so much so that he felt he had best get out of the car and walk down the Way for a bit just to make sure there wasn't something hidden in the grass that he wouldn't want to hit, like another car, or a 20 foot deep canyon, a river, or anything at all.

He left the car running and strolled through the weeds. He studied the surface of the 'road' again and was satisfied that it was the same crushed rock base. Therefore the foliage growing up through the rock was an indication that the rock was not as thick as it could or should have been. What really concerned him was how easily a depression could be concealed. And, what if a depression did not have a rock bottom and was just mud and water. He could be stuck out here for an eternity, never to be found.

"What happened to Arvie" they would ask?"

We don't know. He went off one day to meet up with a dead Native American who had sold him coffee one day. He never returned. Sure could have used that car. It was an AWD.

The weeds around the car were the tallest so far. He had not taken many steps when the weeds became only about a foot tall and there were not as many of them. He went back to the car confident that he could see better, and proceeded forward.

The forest was so thick. Pines, birch, evergreen, with blue spruce mixed in. The smell of it all – Wow. You can't find a smell like this back in the Twin Cities. He was moving forward, though slowly. He realized that he could see where the road went because of the tunnel of trees he was driving through. They had taken out a lot of trees to put in this road.

Up ahead, Gaagaagiwaandag dipped and made a slight turn to the left. The scene reminded him of a picture hanging in their living room at home. If he were to guess, at the bottom of the upcoming dip will be a little stream. And sure enough, there it was. At the sound of it, he stopped, got out and walked forward in order to see it. He would have to drive through it. It was six feet across and very shallow. It was all the same rock on the bottom as was used on this road though the rock appeared slightly larger.

Ok. "Here I am" he mumbled to himself, "and I don't want to be forced to back all the way out of here. I could if I had to but then I would never know what is out there in front of me." So, he got back in the car and rolled across the little stream uneventfully. The road turned a little left and almost immediately back to the right, still basically going east. After the road straightened out, there was another street sign for Gaagaagiwaandag Way. He stopped the car thinking they don't need that one. He got out, pried the sign out of the sandy forest soil and laid it across the back seat. He got back in the car, put it in gear and continued forward. Gaagaagiwaandag Way was going to end in about 400 feet, because he could see nothing but a wall of trees up ahead.

Another street sign appeared. "Miskwaawaak Blvd." Boulevard? Ok. Someone had had some very high hopes for this development to name this a Boulevard. He could only turn right, or south. The road seemed more obvious, all because there were fewer weeds. Suddenly he realized that along the right side of the car was a rock outcropping, about five feet high and continuing to rise, while the "Boulevard" seemed to be dropping down. The trees on the left side of the road appeared to be thinning somewhat. And then the trees stopped altogether.

He stopped the car again and got out. Before him was a valley as beautiful as any he could imagine. On his right, the rock wall continued on, perhaps reaching as high as 60 – 70 feet or so before dropping under the canopy of the forest again and disappearing in the haze of the distance. The valley might have been a mile wide in all directions. Snaking its way through the center of the valley, was the little stream, winding its way to the rock face, and then flowing along the rock face before disappearing somewhere.

There were no buildings to be seen. The grass floor of the valley was the greenest grass he had ever seen. He had played and watched a lot of golf over the years, but never, even at the Masters, had he seen this color green. There were no weeds, just beautiful grass, ringed by the forest.

He turned off the car and then set off on foot to explore. He found two things down by the stream. Four blackened circles with no grass inside the circles and what appeared to be small pieces of charred wood. All the circles were surrounded by rocks. Fire pits, he presumed. He found no firewood, but of course there was plenty of that over there in the woods. And secondly, a small bridge made of wood over the stream. Someone had been here before him. A wooden bridge, made with wooden pegs. No nails. No screws. Nature didn't do that.

He had left the car with the intention of walking the outside edge of this valley. He was hoping to find another way out of here. But the more he looked around this circle, the bigger it grew. It would take him longer to walk all the way around than he had originally thought. He didn't think to bring his binoculars today. That was not thought out well. He could have used them right now. Standing in the middle of the valley he could not see anything that would indicate a passage through the trees. Of course, that really didn't tell him much because if it weren't for the fact that his car was parked up there, from the look of it standing here he wouldn't have known there was a passage there either.

Is this the place where he is supposed to be on 10-10 at 10? Getting in here in the dark could be interesting. Where is the barbed wire that was in his dream? He didn't see any of that. There were a lot of trees in the dream and there are a lot of trees right here. Ok, so should he be concerned about not seeing any barbed wire? There could have been some back by that property he drove by with the shed and the mailbox. He decided not to worry about barbed wire.

"So Arvid, is this the place?" he asked. He had followed JW signs to get there. The colors used on the signs were identical to that used on the cans of coffee. All things considered, he was good with this. He felt he had found it and that he would be meeting Jacob again.

He was about to climb the gradual slope to the car when he noticed an indentation in the wall of trees. *That doesn't look natural* he thought. It was about 100 yards or so up ahead, along the wall of trees on his right. As he walked along the edge of the forest, he came to the conclusion that someone had mowed this grass within the past two days or so. *Who might be taking care of this piece of property and why? It can't be public because there is no access, or at least he didn't think so. So, is this private land?*

He was still a few yards away from this variation in the tree wall when he was stopped dead in his tracks. A huge owl left a branch somewhere nearby and buzzed him, very close to his head. He had jerked his head to the right to avert whatever it was. His heart was beating rapidly as he turned slightly to watch as the graceful owl with a wingspan of perhaps five or six feet climbed lazily into the sky towards the trees by his car. He wondered if that scary moment took one or two years off his life. The way his heart was pounding, he thought it likely that he would die two years earlier than he would have before he met the owl.

As he paused for a moment to settle himself, his eye caught something back in the trees. A cross. A wooden cross. And then multiple crosses came to his attention deep in the shadows. He moved closer to the opening in the trees. It was about 15 feet wide and 15 feet deep. A well manicured pathway leading to a cemetery buried in the trees.

He stopped at the end of the mowed path and peered into the woods. There didn't appear to be anything organized about the layout of this cemetery. It seemed that plots had been selected wherever there was room amidst the trees. He didn't know much about trees, but he knew all of those were pines; tall, stately pines. He thought he remembered that the roots of a pine tree were vertical as opposed to horizontal. Or did he have that backwards? Looking closely at the closest cross to him, he could see a space where a casket could fit, or a body.

He stepped into the woods. The crosses were at most four feet tall by two feet wide. The crosses were oak and were made with 2 X 2's. They appeared to be carefully crafted. The cross piece and the upright had both been cut to fit perfectly where they came together. There was no nail to hold them together. There was no screw. *Glue. Had to be Glue.*

He walked around a tree to see what was on the cross piece. "Running Bird," was engraved towards the left side of it. The date next to the name was, "1922."

He made his way to the next cross. It was tricky going because of all the undergrowth: Ed Crooked-Beak 1931. The next was Bjorn Nilsson 1919. He wondered how a Swede came to be buried there. Norl Sitting Bear 1920. Cooba Falling Star 1904. Deer Tall Tree 1876. Jacob Whitefeather 1963.

He never imagined seeing that. He was shocked, and yet it shouldn't have been entirely unexpected. He knelt close to the cross and ran his hand over the oak, reading those letters again.

"What're you doin in there? Hey. You come outa there right now."

Arvie stood up as fast as his knees would allow. He searched the edge of the trees for the source of the voice. There.

"Yes. I'm coming," he replied. He made his way slowly through the trees and the underbrush, glancing up when he could to take note of the man waiting for him. Tall, and broad. Native American. Arvie came around the last tree and stepped carefully out onto the grass, "I'm sorry. I was just looking for someone."

"You are not allowed in this valley. And this burial ground is very sacred. You could be severely punished for this breach of honor."

"Oh, I'm so sorry. I meant no disrespect."

"You are an old one."

Arvie realized that he was being addressed by "an old one." At first glance, the man appeared to be quite young. The closer he came, the more advanced in age the man became. They studied each other. "Perhaps we are much the same age," said Arvie hesitantly.

"Perhaps we are. I am Julius Flying Eagle." He extended his hand.

"I am Arvid Ellison." They shook hands.

"We have had vandalism here. Some of the young ones have not learned respect. Who were you looking for?"

"Jacob Whitefeather."

"I think you found him back there."

"I did."

"Did you know Jacob?"

"I bought coffee from him at a convenience store on 169 two weeks ago."

"I see," said the big man with a hint of a smile appearing at the corners of his mouth. "I thought the date back there on the cross said he walked the path of spirits in 1963. Yet you say you bought coffee from him two weeks ago. I find that a bit confusing."

"As did I," Arvie said. "Any idea about how that could've happened?"

"No sir (a broader smile). That's above my pay grade. How did you get in here?"

"I took a right turn off 6 when I saw a sign that had "JW" written on it."

"You got here that way?" He laughed. "So that's your car parked up there?"

"Yes."

"Did you make good time coming through the subdivision?"

"It was a little slow going."

The old man laughed again. "You didn't tell me why you were looking for Jacob," he said.

"Ok. I had a dream. I saw the numbers 10-10-10 encircled by a halo of fire. That's what I called it anyway. I saw a county road sign, or I thought that's what it was, with the initials JW. I assumed it was County Road J, West. I had thought the 10-10-10 was a date – October 10, and the 3rd 10 meant night time because I also saw a moon. Actually, it was a friend of mine who suggested that."

"So why are you here in August? October 10th is two months away?"

"Yes, well, I thought if I had interpreted things correctly, I'd better come during daylight hours to find the place because it might be difficult to find it in the dark. I had thought that I might meet Jacob then, even though I did see that newspaper clipping about his death in 1963. I guess that year etched into the cross back there pretty well confirms that, huh?"

"What kind of coffee did he sell you a couple of weeks ago?"

"Forever. Now I have Reunion, Mercy, Redeemed and just the other day I received Joy."

"Yes. Joy is our most recent. You're the one we read about in the papers. You're the one that was with Henry."

"Yes. Did you know Henry?"

"No. I've only heard of him. He is a legend among us. Well, he and Mary. You were going to pick up the ingredients report from him that night weren't you?"

"Yes, I was," Arvie said haltingly. "How did you know that?"

"Jacob told me that Henry had it inside his shirt. It got shredded in death."

"Oh, dear God." Arvie leaned over, put his hands on his knees and felt as if he was going to wretch.

Julius Flying Eagle continued: "To speak to your curiosity, the ingredients are all natural. You can walk around in these woods and find everything."

"You know about the coffee, I mean, healing things?"

"Yes. I do."

"Does it really heal things in us?" Arvie asked as he stood upright once again.

"It is a mystery, isn't it? Did it heal anything in you?"

"Yes. It did."

"Then the answer is yes, it heals things in us. It is no longer a mystery."

"But does it really, or is it just the hope we have that makes it seem so?"

"You said you were healed of something."

"I was."

"You have your answer."

"One of the Native Americans who handed me a sack with a can of coffee inside said these words to me, 'He will know when you are in need and he will get it too you.' What does that mean?"

"Just that. I fear you have difficulty accepting the obvious. I suggest you simply accept. By the way, when you drive out of here, continue along the row of trees by your car. It's a straight shot to the road though it doesn't look like it from where you are parked. Take a right at the road you come to and it brings you right down to 18."

"Thank you for the directions. I'll sure do that. Sounds much easier than going back through the subdivision. Do you come here often?"

"I do. I come to have fellowship with the spirits of the old ones. Many of these, Jacob included, were friends. Oh, and by the way, if you turn to the left out there on that road and drive about a block, you'll see a red barn tucked back in the trees on your left. On the 10th of every month we have tribal meetings there and 10:00 those nights is when we have our monthly raffle. It sounds like someone was sending you an invitation to the October raffle. Tonight's the August raffle."

"So, there will be people coming tonight?" He was glad he put the sign back.

"We hope so. I'll bet that's it. You've been invited to the October raffle. Come early because the buffet opens at 6:00."

"You've got to be kidding."

"No. I'm not kidding. Spend a few bucks on the raffle. They usually have something pretty nice. The buffet is really good."

"Can I ask you one more question?"

"Sure."

"That convenience store where Jacob sold me the coffee. Did you take that away at the end of that week?"

"Why would we do that?"

"I can't find it now."

"The county commissioner up here doesn't like seeing old buildings on the main roads. Says it's bad for business during the tourist season. Maybe he tore it down?"

"I thought you put those stores out there to serve a purpose and when there was no longer a need, you took 'em away and stored 'em someplace."

"I love your imagination. That'd be a lot of work, I think. I've got to be getting home. It's been nice talking. And I will not give you a ticket for trespassing." He stuck out his hand.

Arvie took it and said, "Thank you for what you have told me. I enjoyed meeting you."

Julius Flying Eagle turned and walked away in the general direction of Arvie Ellison's car. He raised a hand in parting and said, "Drink the coffee." And he was gone.

Arvie stood for a moment and then walked after him. He stopped where Julius Flying Eagle had turned into the trees, except there was no path. There were no leaves bent, no twigs broken. Where did he go? He walked back and forth for a few minutes, looking for something, but found nothing. "So be it," he muttered and proceeded to his car. "Accept the obvious," Julius had said.

It was perhaps a mile before he found the road. He stopped to think for a moment. "I can turn right and head for home, but if I turn left, I'll find a red barn." He decided on the latter option.

Had he been driving faster, he most assuredly would have missed it. There were a few buildings along here, but all seemed abandoned. A small road sign was coming up on the right: "JW" was all it indicated. Not county or state, just "JW." Yes, it was black with red letters. There was a red arrow pointing to the left. Maybe the dream was accurate after all.

While accelerating slowly, he found the narrow two-lane gravel road entering the trees. Perhaps 200 hundred yards into the woods, he saw the color red. *The Red Barn*, he thought. He turned quickly to the left. These are the woods he saw in his dream. All the different varieties of trees as the dream indicated.

As he approached the barn, he drove through an open gate. He saw the barbed wire fencing all around the perimeter of the parking lot. He pulled up in front of the door, got out and tried the door. It was locked. He realized that the parking lot extended around back, so he got back into the CRV and went around back. There were two abandoned cars and a pick-up truck parked in one corner, fully rusted. There were also two small storage sheds, also painted red. The barn was typical; two stories high. *I've been invited to the raffle on the 10th of October at 10 p.m. Maybe I'll come. Maybe Brooks would like to come. We'll see.*

He headed out the lane, took a right and headed for home.

* * * * * * * *

"Honey, I'm home."

"Out on the patio."

"Hi you two. Brooks, good to see you. (Hug) Hi hon." (Hug and kiss)

"I hear you've been up in the woods again. Did you find it?"

"Yes. I did."

"Really? What did it look like?"

"Well, it's like a beautiful green valley, perhaps a mile across, in the middle of a dense forest. I suppose you could call it a valley. There's a little stream running through it, and the grass is so green. You know how green it is at Augusta every April? Well, the green in this valley makes Augusta look burned out. It is so pretty."

"When is it - this clandestine rendezvous?"

"Two months from tonight. 10 pm on October 10."

"I remember now. The 10-10-10 in your vision, your dream. You want some company?"

"Sure. I'd love that. But let me tell you what I found out today. I happened to find a cemetery in that valley and I found Jacob's grave. And then I ran into Julius Flying Eagle who answered all my questions. I told him about my dream and he said on the 10th of every month at 10 in the evening, they have a raffle at their club house which is a red barn on a road that does have a sign proclaiming it as, "JW.""

"A raffle?"

"That's what he said. And then he said, 'Apparently you've been invited to the raffle on October 10th." He also told me that Henry had stuffed the 3M report on the contents of the coffee inside his shirt and that it had been, 'shredded in death.' Those were his words. *Think* of that. Julius was helpful. I'll tell you all about it sometime.

436

I'll tell you how I found the valley, too. That was fun. Oh, wait. I've got something to show you."

He went to the car for the street sign. When he came back through the patio doors, he held it up and went, "TaaDaaaah."

"Good grief," said Hannah. "Is that an Indian name for a street? Gaagaagiwaandag Way. How on earth do you say that? Gaa – gaa – gi – waan – dag? I think I got it"

"I think you did to. Ojibwe, I think. Isn't that something? I drove several streets with names like this."

"I assume," said Hannah, "that you are planning on going to the 6:00 service tonight, since you just got home now."

"Is that ok? I kind of lost track of time."

"It's all fine. We already called Kate and Bren to let them know."

Had Arvie remembered to turn on his phone, he would have taken a call from Hedrick Gordon regarding the emergency board meeting which had been set for the following Monday evening. He listened to the message and was quite elated over the news. Rick had said he and Pastor Hoyt had met on Thursday night and, after telling the story of his day, Pastor Hoyt was in total agreement to get everyone together and go to work. Rick's last comment was, "Keep the faith, Arvie. This is the beginning of what might be a long journey. Oh, and by the way, we began tearing out the insides of 204 Lake today. Talk to you soon."

Chapter 27

"I want to believe what I can't see. Sometimes it's difficult to do that. That's one reason why I drink so much coffee because when I got a cuppa in front me and I'm stareing down into it and stirring, I can see it all. And it's wonderful." - Ole

"Faith means being sure of the things we hope for
and knowing that something is real even if we do not see it."
Hebrews 11:1

Arvie had just poured the morning's first cup of Mercy when the doorbell rang. He peeked out the front window and saw one of those ugly black sedans.

He opened the door. "Agent Settles. What is it that brings you here so early?"

"I need to speak with you, Mr. Ellison. It is very important. Is your wife still asleep?"

"I believe she is, yes."

"Good; let's not disturb her. May I have a cup of your coffee, and can we talk out here on your porch?"

"Certainly. I'll be right back." Arvie hurried to the Mr. Coffee and poured another cup and returned to the front porch. "What is this about, Agent Settles?"

"Mr. Ellison, I have a request to make of you. Someday soon, you and I are going to sit down over another cup of this coffee and have a long talk, but now is not the time. I need your help, and I need it now."

"And why is it me that you need?"

"All I can tell you is this: you are a man of faith, and that is what I need from you now. I can also assure you that what you will be doing is of utmost importance. I want your trust, and I really can't answer any questions, at least not yet. May I have your help, Mr. Ellison?"

Arvie took a sip of coffee and looked at Agent Settles. Agent Settles took a sip and looked at Arvie. *When he puts it like that, what else can I do?*

* * * * * * * *

Special Agent Titus Woodhull felt a sense of grim satisfaction. He always felt this when he was about to close a case. This one had been tricky, but matters were now coming together as he thought they should. He stroked his mustache as he stepped over to the doorway of his office.

"Agent Owens, have you heard from Settles yet? Has the suspect been arrested and charged?"

"Yes sir. Settles called in maybe twenty minutes ago. Ellison should be printed and dressed in orange by now. Arraignment is scheduled for first thing tomorrow morning. Everything is on schedule."

"Very good, Owens. Perfect. When they assign the judge, will you let me know, please?"

"Yes sir."

Yes. It was all coming together. It always did.

A few minutes later, there was a knock on the door. Woodhull looked up from the file he was studying. One of the other agents; *what was her name? Baines, that was it.* He motioned her to come in, and she handed him a note. Woodhull studied it, then gave her a confused look.

"The boss is coming here?"

"Yes sir. Colonel McIlroy arrived late last night, and he'll be here any minute."

"Why wasn't I informed of this earlier?" asked Special Agent Woodhull.

"I don't know, sir. I was told of this just now. He will come to your office when he arrives, sir."

"Thank you, Baines. Please send in Agent Owens, would you?"

"I'm sorry, sir. Agent Owens said he had to meet someone. He left a few minutes ago."

Special Agent Woodhull pivoted in his chair to look out into the workroom; indeed, Owens's desk was vacant.

"Fine. Please ask him to come in as soon as he returns."

"Yes sir."

As Baines closed the office door, Woodhull leaned back in his chair, a nervous tick attacked his left eye brow.

* * * * * * * *

This was a little different from his previous incarceration. This time, they stood him in front of the wall for pictures. They took one of him facing the camera, and then he turned to the left and they took a profile. Arvie was standing in front of a vertical yardstick. As he looked at it, he was pleased to see that the top of his head was still 72 inches off the floor. *Funny the things I think about at a time like this.*

Next, they fingerprinted him - messy. Two officers walked him back to a holding cell. He couldn't figure out why they needed two guys; he was seventy-five, and neither one of them looked to be more than thirty-five—and they both looked like big, strapping boys. *What did they think I was going to do?*

* * * * * * * *

"Colonel McIlroy. How good to see you, sir. What brings you to town?"

Special Agent Woodhull realized that in order to look McIlroy in the eye, he had to tilt his head back. He didn't enjoy this, but the broad-shouldered, silver-haired older man had walked in very briskly and was standing very close, and Special Agent Woodhull couldn't change to a more advantageous position without being obvious - something he was reluctant to do.

"Special Agent Woodhull. Haven't seen you in awhile." He extended his hand.

"No sir. Welcome to our town."

"Well, Titus, I'm here on official business. It's an official inquiry, and it has to do with you."

"With me, sir? How can I help you?"

440

"Come with me, please. Agent Owens has a car waiting for us outside."

* * * * * * * *

Arvie had the holding cell all to himself, and he also had a cot, a pillow, and two blankets. *Practically a luxury suite.* It was very different from his first night in jail, sitting on the bench next to Henry. *I wish Henry was with me right now.* One of the uniforms offered him a book to read: *Twelve Angry Men.* He had seen the movie years ago but had never read the book. *The book is always better.*

They asked if he had had breakfast, and he replied that he had only coffee. A female uniform brought him a breakfast of thinned orange juice, tasteless coffee, scrambled eggs, and two strips of very crisp bacon. The toast was cold and dry, without jelly, but at least it was kind of filling. His first time in jail, he had nothing at all to eat.

After a while, they came for him. They shakled him and then assisted him to a van, where Agent Settles waited in the front passenger seat. Arvie got in, Settles nodded at him and apologized for the shackles saying, "Sorry about that but its necessary for a little while. I'll explain it all." They drove towards downtown.

* * * * * * * *

Special Agent Woodhull was very confused and more than a little miffed. He had several important items on his schedule for today, and none of them included an unplanned ride downtown with his superior.

"If I may ask, where, exactly, are we going, Colonel McIlroy?"

"We have a meeting at the courthouse."

Special Agent Woodhull took several seconds to consider various implications of this information. "A meeting? With whom, sir?"

"You'll see."

* * * * * * * *

Arvie recognized the courthouse building; he had served on a jury here maybe two years ago. But this time he would be entering the building in a different way – around back and underground. The only other vehicles down there were police cars and vans from the correctional center with bars across the windows. *It was definitely not public parking,* he thought.

They helped him down from the van; *very courteous, these guys.* He shuffled inside alongside Agent Settles, surrounded by police, both uniformed and plain-clothed.

They stepped onto an elevator and started up. When the elevator stopped at the first floor, several people got on. Arvie couldn't help noticing the way they looked at him, standing in the middle of all those law enforcement types. *They probably think I'm Hannibal Lecter, or someone of a similar nature.* He was pretty sure they'd be relieved when he and his entourage got off.

They exited the elevator on the third floor, and then he shuffled down the hall and into a courtroom. They escorted him to the front, through the swinging, hip-high doors to a table in front of the judge's bench where he was seated behind a large table. "The judge would be in shortly" he was told. Two of the uniformed officers stood in front of the little doors and the plain-clothed guys sat behind him in the front row of the courtroom. Two more uniforms were stationed just inside the doors to the courtroom. Agent Settles sat beside him. He whispered so only Arvie could hear "Hang in there, Arvie. Just a little longer."

A couple of minutes later, the courtroom doors opened, and Special Agent Woodhull walked in. He was flanked by a tall guy with silvery hair. He looked like somebody who would play a rich, powerful guy on TV or in a movie. Agent Owens was with them.

When Special Agent Woodhull saw Arvie sitting at the table with Agent Settles, his eyes got a wide, surprised look. It was the first time Arvie had ever seen Special Agent Woodhull look so plainly surprised, unnerved and very quickly, unsure.

As the three of them were seated at the second table at the front of the quiet courtyroom, Arvie could overhear Agent Woodhull say to the big white-haired man, "I don't understand, sir. Why was I not informed of this meeting earlier? And why is he here?" Woodhull nodded in Arvie's direction. "I was told he was under arrest."

"Let's put it this way, Titus," Silver Hair said. "In a few minutes, Judge Gilfillen will come in and sit down. Until he gets here and we start our little meeting, I am in charge of your activities. So, take a seat and wait for the judge."

For a second, the thought crossed Arvie's mind that Woodhull was going to do something dramatic, pull a weapon or make a break for it. However, after a few seconds with eyes darting around the room, *probably taking stock of all the guns in the vicinity,* Woodhull seemed deflated. Arvie thought he could see something physically drain out of him. Woodhull sat down at the table between Silver Hair - whose name, Arvie soon learned, was McIlroy - and agent Owens.

The judge came in shortly thereafter and took his elevated seat up on the dais. The elderly man wasn't wearing the usual black robe. He was dressed in a very nice suit, the fit of it paled in comparison to Woodhull and his suit. The judge carried two thick folders that he arranged on the desk in front of him. He opened them both, put on some reading glasses, and looked everything over for what seemed like a half-hour, but was probably less than five minutes. He looked up over his glasses at Special Agent Woodhull.

"Is this Titus Woodhull, Colonel McIlroy?"

"Yes, your honor," McIlroy said.

Then the judge looked at Arvie. "And you are Mr. Arvid Ellison?"

"Yes, your honor," Arvie replied.

"Mr. Ellison, do you have any idea why you are in my courtroom this morning?"

"No sir, I can't say that I do. I was only told that it was important for me to be here."

"Yes, that's correct. And on behalf of the United States government and the people of the State of Minnesota, I'd like to thank you for your trust and your willingness to assist with this matter."

"I'm happy to help, sir."

"Bailiff, please unshackle Mr. Ellison."

A uniform appeared, released Arvie's wrists and ankles, collected the chained together apparatus, and left the courtroom.

"I apologize for that inconvenience Mr. Ellison but it was a necessary inconvenience" stated Judge Gilfillen. Arvie went to massaging his wrists as Agent Settles leaned in and whispered, "I'll explain about that later."

The Judge looked down at his files and without looking up asked, "Mr. Ellison, about a week and a half ago, were you at or near the Chariton Street exit off Interstate 35W?"

"Yes sir."

"What did you do while you were there?"

"I gave some coffee to a man I had frequently seen there who appeared to be a panhandler."

The judge went on to ask him all about his conversation with the man, and Arvie shared everything he could remember.

"And did you return to that intersection several days later, Mr. Ellison?"

"Yes sir."

"What happened this time?"

Arvie recounted the moments with a younger man who wouldn't drink his coffee, followed by his encounter with Agents Settles and Owens, and then his trip to the FBI field office and his meeting with Special Agent Woodhull.

"Your honor, I am compelled to point out ... " Woodhull began.

"Mr. Woodhull, I don't recall asking you a question," Judge Gilfillen said, staring over his glasses. "But rest assured, I will have several questions for you, here in a bit. And I will be very interested in what you say at that time."

Arvie thought it interesting that the judge called him, "Mister Woodhull," instead of, "Special Agent."

The judge looked back at his files. "Now, Mr. Ellison, I have a number of records here ... your birth certificate, your school records, your selective service registration ..." He leafed slowly through the two-inch-thick stack of papers in the folder to his left. "Every bit of which indicates clearly to me that you were born, educated, and lived for a number of years in and around East Moline, Illinois."

They found me. "Yes sir," Arvie stated, somewhat hesitantly.

"Right." The judge looked to Arvie. "Did Mr. Woodhull ever suggest or insinuate that you had lived or worked somewhere else?"

"Yes sir."

"And where was that, may I ask?"

"He said … well, I mean, he seemed to believe that I had lived or traveled quite a bit in South America. Peru, I think. And maybe Colombia." Arvie realized that he had begun to perspire and his nerves were taught.

Judge Gilfillen nodded, and for several seconds he didn't say anything. "Yes. Interesting. And yet, these documents in front of me here, which I obtained rather easily at the suggestion of Agents Settles and Owens, along with the assistance of a very helpful local member of the news media, all tell me that you have, in fact, never been outside the borders of the continental United States, except for a brief foray into Juarez, Mexico, during a family vacation in the mid 1940s."

"Yes sir. It was just after the war, and my mom wanted to go to California to see her sister. We traveled Route 66 and, well, my dad wanted to see Mexico."

"In fact, Mr. Ellison, my careful inquiries with the State Department indicate that you have never even held a US passport."

"No sir. I never needed one, I guess."

"No, I guess not." For a while, Judge Gilfillen looked down at Arvie's folder, flipping pages back and forth. He closed it and reached for a second folder in front of him, opened it and leafed thought it for a minute or so.

"Mr. Woodhull, your parents were missionaries in Venezuela, is that correct?" the judge said, still looking down at the contents of the folder.

"That's correct, sir."

"And you were born and raised in the suburbs of Caracas."

"Yes sir."

"But you did not attend the public schools there. Rather, your parents placed you in the mission school, where you received your education through the sixth grade. Is that correct?"

"Yes sir."

"At the age of twelve, you were sent to Lima, Peru, to a private boarding school for the remainder of your education through high school?

"That's also correct. Sir, you have all of this information in my file …."

"I don't require your commentary, Mr. Woodhull; simply answer my questions."

"Yes, your honor," Woodhull responded haltingly while picking at his mustauche.

"Would you happen to recall the name of your roommate, Mr. Woodhull?"

Woodhull stared at the table top for so long that Arvie thought he was not going to answer. And then, in a husky tone –

"César Cifuentes."

"Thank you. When you graduated from high school, where did you attend college?"

"I attended Universidad de Li—uh, the University of Lima."

"Very good. And whom did you room with during those years?"

It was several moments before Woodhull uttered a quiet answer – "César Cifuentes."

Judge Gilfillen kept asking questions, and Woodhull kept answering, but his pauses were getting longer and longer. As the questioning went on, Arvie could see Woodhull's shoulders drooping more and more and for a while, he thought Woodhull might, actually, keel over onto the table. The special agent never looked at the judge or anybody else. His voice became more and more monotone, husky; like a robot. *But he sure lived a more interesting life than me,* thought Arvie.

It turned out that his boarding school and college roommate was the son of the head of one of the biggest drug cartels in South America. Oscar Cifuentes had a lot of money and power and, most importantly, he had vision. So much so that he decided the best way to conduct business in the very lucrative North American market was to acquire several highly placed legislators and law enforcement officials. From there, it was easy to place the equally ambitious and visionary Titus Woodhull, his son's schoolmate and best friend, in the elite ranks of the FBI's drug task force. As Arvie listened, he slowly began to realize that he was sitting in on the trial of Special Agent Woodhull. It was all coming out. *This was the reason Settles had whispered that "it would be over soon."* Arvie felt the stress of the last days begin to let up.

"Now, Mr. Woodhull, I have to ask … What made Mr. Cifuentes's offer so attractive to you? After all, you had a very religious upbringing, your parents must have certainly taught you right from wrong. Yet, when the opportunity was presented to go to work for the Cifuentes cartel, it seems that you barely hesitated at all. Can you help me understand your thought process?"

Woodhull's eyes were closed. His voice was very quiet when he finally spoke. "Mi madre y mi padre eran pobres y estúpidos, al igual todas las personas religiosas. Y no quería ser como ellos. Nada como ellos …"

It was the strangest thing Arvie had ever heard; it was almost as if a completely different man was speaking - as if Woodhull had suddenly been possessed by the spirit of a Spanish person. Or maybe that personality was inside him the whole time, and he had just kept it hidden.

"We'll need that in English, Mr. Woodhull," Judge Gilfillen said.

Woodhull paused, then began again, his eyes never leaving the floor. "I had no desire to be anything like my parents. Like all religious people, they were poor, superstitious, and ignorant. I wanted something better. Something much more. And César's father offered me that." Then he stared directly at the judge. "There was really no question as to what I would do, once given the opportunity."

Judge Gilfillen looked at Woodhull for several quiet moments, and then he nodded. "Yes. I'd say that was accurate." He took off his glasses and rubbed the bridge of his nose. "I'm going to take a few minutes to consider what we've learned here, so far. Mr. Ellison, you're free to go if you wish."

Arvie had gotten so drawn into the drama that he'd forgotten where he was. "Your honor, if it's okay with you, I'd like to see this through to the end. Today, I mean, at least."

"That's certainly reasonable, and I'd say you've earned the right. All right, let's take, say, five minutes. Mr. Ellison, I believe there is a break room just down the hall; you might be more comfortable waiting there; some of the agents might wish to accompany you. Mr. Woodhull, I'll ask you to remain right where you are." Judge Gilfillen got up and left.

Agent Settles leaned over and said, "Arvie, I don't think they've got any of your coffee in that break room, but if you want, I can fill you in a little bit while we're waiting on the judge."

Already Arvie was feeling better. He was happy he was not Woodhull, and he was very happy to not be wearing those shackles. "That would be great," he replied and couldn't hide his smile.

* * * * * * * *

Once seated at a small plastic table in the break room, Agent Settles began, "Owens and I have had Woodhull under surveillance for about six months now. For several years, the Bureau has been conducting an undercover investigation of a suspected infiltration by South American drug interests in this country; particularly within the Twin Cities area.

"Once the trail started leading toward Woodhull, Owens, Wong, and I were placed under his authority, supposedly to staff up for the big operation he was directing. But everything he did was under observation; our directive was to allow him to operate as if we suspected nothing until we had airtight evidence of his guilt.

"In a way, Arvie, you were the final piece of the puzzle that we needed. Woodhull somehow sensed we were closing in, I think, and he started to get desperate. He needed someone to pin everything on, and I think he was preparing the way to pin it all on you and your homeless friend."

"Me and Von Barstow?"

"Zeke. There was never any such person as Henryk von Barstow. That persona was entirely a fabrication of Woodhull's creative imagination. But when you came along with your free coffee and conversation, we believed Woodhull decided you were a more likely candidate. That's when Owens and I picked you up the first time - at Woodhull's request."

"But why me?"

Settles took a deep breath. "Well, you heard what he just said in the courtroom; somehow, his upbringing turned him the wrong way. In his twisted imagination, he decided that all religious people were – ah - simple-minded."

"I think he used the word 'stupid.' But I'm not sure since it was in Spanish."

"Yes. Well, you get the idea. I think he thought he'd be able to bull his way through, using the fabricated evidence he concocted. Of course, he didn't realize that Owens, Wong, and I were feeding him what he wanted, just waiting for him to put the noose around his own neck."

"Wow. And I was the bait."

"Yes, and I am personally sorry that you were the one who got tangled up in all this, Arvie. I hope you realize, now, that most of the reason we kept you under surveillance - and why we picked you up this morning - was for your protection. We simply weren't sure what Woodhull might do if he felt threatened. Until he was in the courtroom, we wanted him to believe that you had been arrested this morning; that's why the shackles and the orange jump suit. We didn't want him to know that this had anything to do with you until he got into the courtroom."

"Did he have anything to do with the death of von Barstow—I mean, Zeke? And that other guy?"

"Quite likely. That business about the Black Widow of the Jungle is for real; the killings here matched the MO used for the executions in South America carried out by the Black Widow. I suspect that will be part of what Judge Gilfillen plans to ask Woodhull, after the break. That, and the names of the other people within the Bureau and in Washington who are on the Cifuentes payroll."

"Wow." Arvie exhaled a huge sigh and he felt himself relax.

Settles continued - "If he cooperates, he might get off with spending the rest of his life in prison. If he doesn't … "

"Wow." Arvie was repeating himself, but he couldn't think of any other words.

"Arvie, before we go back in there, use my phone and call your wife; let her know you're okay, and that you'll be home soon."

"Thank you, Agent Settles, for everything. I believe I heard that your first name is John. May I call you that?"

"Absolutely," said John Settles with a big smile.

* * * * * * * *

The Dove Creek Monday evening emergency Board meeting *was* indeed the beginning. An action plan was put in place to locate any and all resources in the church and throughout the extended community that may have relevant expertise in the area of caring for seniors, government agencies included. Over the course of the next several months, weekly meetings were held and gradually a plan emerged. It was some time later that the plan was finalized and announced to the church. Arvie had been made privy to the plan, in advance, thanks to Rick for continually keeping him apprised.

As he sat in church on the weekend of the announcement, he watched the 15-minute video that contained many of the elements of what was to be done. As Pastor Hoyt narrated the video, Arvie began to weep. When Pastor Hoyt interviewed Colby while standing in front of the apartment house furnace, he could hardly contain himself. Also included was a picture of Henry and Mary. It was an old grainy picture that they had given to Colby. And then there was a picture of Arvie and Henryk von Barstow, standing on the corner of 35W and Charitan. They had received that picture from an Agent with the DEA. When the picture appeared on the big screen, it was Colby's voice he heard saying, "This is how it all began. The Coffee Man giving a cup of coffee to an old man he had seen begging on a street corner." There were no more details than that. Pastor Hoyt concluded the announcement with "Some of the most amazing, dramatic and important stories begin with a simple act of kindness."

Arvie had played his role well.

Pastor Hoyt's message that weekend was taken from Matthew 25: 35-40. *"……anything you did for even the least of my people here, you also did for me."*

There were three major inclusions in the announcement: three nursing homes, owned and operated by church families that had agreed to play a major role in providing the solution:

1)   Plans were announced for a new nursing home with maximum occupancy of 48, with construction to begin in the early fall.

2)   Funding for the program had been accounted for. Contributions from local businesses for the effort had surpassed the original goal, with individual contributions still to be counted.

All of what was taking place was beyond Arvie's ability to understand and so he made no effort to try. It was Julius Flying Eagle, with some help from Hannah, who had convinced him that he needed to accept; he need not understand. Arvie thought acceptance made sense, especially after listening to Hannah's lengthy, loud and passionate rant on the subject. Attempting to understand brought about too many questions and an abundance of confusion. He need not understand.

17 seniors were the first relocated to area nursing homes. Included were Mrs. Koepke, Mr. Elston, Caroline Hasterlitch, Beulah Goyanovitch (though she died before the move), Sigurd Borndahl, Hjalmar Bjorkman and the one sister who survived food poisoning, Maizee Roush, Jim Schilling and his friend Bertil.

The biggest issue occurred when Sigurd Borndahl refused to leave his apartment because he couldn't leave his paintings behind. A special meeting of the Dove Creek Board was called to outline a plan designed to explain to Sigurd that he had no paintings. Colby was asked to communicate that reality to Sigurd. What Colby actually told Sigurd was that he could take all the paintings with him. That way, it would cost no money to ship the paintings and no physical effort would be required and the paintings arriving at their new home would be guaranteed to arrive undamaged. Even the moving truck was not needed. Sigurd was very happy when they arrived.

Arvie and Brooks continued to devote Saturdays to Colby, helping him wherever needed. Though the flock was being depleted slowly by the relocation, there were new faces appearing on a regular basis. Colby was correct in his assessment regarding losing his job – as some are relocated, others will move in to replace them; the ebb and flow, as he called it.

Brenda and her friends began working the neighborhood, with Colby's help of course, on Thursday afternoons. All told, 14 nurses and four doctors had signed up for the task. Colby made a list for them each week; people who needed medical help of some kind. The medical team made the rounds, several sharing Jesus stories and Bible verses as well as medical services. Promoting hope was at the top of their list. Brenda also carried a bag of thermoses of coffee along with a supply of Styrofoam cups.

The Barn

Arvie and Brooks journeyed to the red barn on 10-10. Since Julius Flying Eagle said something about a good buffet being served at 6:00, that was when they arrived. It seemed as though everyone in Minnesota was there. The barn was packed with people and, other than the buffet, most were focused on the raffle. A huge gas grill was being raffled off at 10pm. Raffle tickets cost $1 a piece and Brooks and Arvie each bought 10 tickets. Brooks thought he'd seen a grill like that at Home Depot for $600. Arvie didn't know about that, but was impressed that it had a built-in sauce rack. Brooks told Arvie that if he won, he'd have to petition the Townhouse Association to build him a bigger patio.

They spent the evening playing air hockey, pin ball and shuffle board and then spent some money betting on a roulette wheel. Julius Flying Eagle introduced them to the "Raffle Executive Committee" and many others. All in all, it was a fun evening making new friends, eating good food and sipping a beer or two.

Edgar Half Moon had the winning lottery ticket. He was Jacob's great, great grandson.

It was a most enjoyable evening. So much so, that they made plans to return 11-10-10 and bring the wives along.

Samuel's Coffee House(s)

Arvie got his coffee house. He actually got several. It took eight months to finish out, but by the following April, "Samuel's Coffee House" opened at 204 Lake Street in Forest Lake, complete with drive-through service. He poured Forever, Mercy and Joy in those early months and then, along came Grace, Peace, Eternity, Worship and Victory.

Oh, and by the way, the view out the three-story window over the lake was beautiful and yes, Rick was right: people came from miles away because Samuel's was located in the perfect spot. His vision was proved correct.

Arvie also began receiving a monthly stipend from Rick. Brooks and Hannah both commended Arvie on the character of his newest best friend.

Arvie continued to take his coffee to the hospital on Mondays. He became very adept at moving the little cart. His proudest moments were when he received messages that so-and-so, "in 619 needs to see Samuel and enjoy a 'cuppa.'"

The "Wicked Witch" is no longer. Wilda had been a very sick lady for several months. But something had worked for her; either the magic of medical science or the magic of the coffee. Whatever the cause, the brilliant halo was no more. Wilda no longer wore one stitch of black and she and Arvie became close friends. They began every Monday morning with the Bible on the table, sharing devotions together and inviting Jesus into their day; their week.

Arvie continued with his coffee duties at the Wednesday Organ Concerts. He continued to carry his three thermos bottles every Saturday when he and Brooks drove south to work with Colby and he found additional time to visit the new Assisted Living Homes, bringing hope to all the seniors who lived there.

Every six months or so, Rick opened another Samuel's Coffee House. The second was on Lake Calhoun in Minneapolis. Arvie was there for the Grand Opening, as he was for the third Samuel's, which was located on the East River Parkway. What a view.

Hannah attended these functions and helped pour the coffee, as well. They had an enjoyable time. She encouraged Arvie to focus on acceptance and he returned the favor. Together, they were learning how to live with anxiety.

While Arvie's schedule remained busy, Sundays continued to be wonderful days of rest with Hannah; days filled with golf, football, volleyball and basketball.

Hedrick Gordon was busy with his design plans for more Samuel's. The first three had gone so well, he had decided the fourth would be located north of Milwaukee; somewhere on the west shore of Lake Michigan near Sheboygan and would be an expanded version of the first three.

The demand for coffee never slowed down and trucks continued to arrive when inventory ran low. No orders were ever placed, no deliveries were ever scheduled and no coffee house ever ran out of coffee.

The first time Arvie saw a delivery truck, he was overwhelmed with a feeling of purpose and fulfillment. On the sides and the back of the trucks, written in bright red letters were three lines. The first line gave the name of the coffee being delivered such as, Mercy. Below, on the second line, and not surprising, was written, "A Fine Coffee Product of Northern Minnesota." It was the third line, however, that seemed to strike a chord deep within Arvie, "Found only at Samuel's Coffee Houses."

It took Arvie a long time to believe it could work, but miraculously it did. He worked on trust and fought the urge to follow each truck after a delivery, to find out its origin. He met several of the truck drivers and thanked them for their work, but soon realized that they delivered the coffee and would not take time for conversation. Throughout the process, Arvie has learned about faith and works to accept, fully, that which he cannot see.

Colby

And Colby? Well there will be a huge star in his crown one day. He continued giving himself to his people every minute of every day. He took a semester off from his studies because he had too many priorities. "I'm cutting back," he said. "I need more time for my people." He confided in Arvie one day that he had not been able to forgive himself for Louise. Had he been around that day, "she might still be alive." He wasn't going to allow that to happen ever again. God continues to bless him richly.

Sandy's Last Entry

The Coffee Man
Touches Everyone, Even Me
By Sandy Marsh (final submission)

Hello loyal readers. It is because of you that I feel some reservation in sharing this news. You have continued to be supportive of my work here at The Daily and for that, I will be eternally grateful. The management here at the paper and the readership have been better than I could have hoped for and I thank you from the bottom of my heart.

Even though it is difficult to say goodbye, I am excited and at peace with my decision. If you are a regular reader, you know the recent storyline revolving around "Samuel," The Coffee Man. If you have missed this man's story, I encourage you to go back and find the previous articles to become familiar with an average, every-day man who demonstrates the power that one man can have in making a difference for others. While I would love for each of you to get to know him personally, I can only share my experience and move forward in a way that best exemplifies the purposeful living that I have witnessed.

One day, Samuel shared a cup of coffee with a homeless man. I knew neither man at the time, but this single act, changed the trajectory of my life. With that one act, Samuel and I were put on a crash course with one another, the FBI, the police and those that our society would consider, "the least of these."

Samuel led me on a journey of self-discovery, growth and spiritual awakening. That may all sound a bit, "fluffy" for a hard-nosed reporter, but in the end, it is simply the truth. Growing up, I went to church. It was what we did. I didn't hear anyone say that they walked with God or had a relationship with God. What would that even look like?

Because of Samuel, I have met people with nothing who give what they don't have to others who have even less. And more than this, they do it with a happy heart. They are grateful for the gifts that God gives and carry on doing their work for others with only faith and love to carry them through.

Because of Samuel, I have seen the effect that one human being can have on another without millions of dollars or a grand education. Armed only with a jug of coffee, I have seen Samuel engage with hundreds of individuals and bring faith, hope and healing where doctors would claim it impossible.

Because of Samuel, I have seen hundreds of individuals come to be baptized with two thousand witnesses over the course of one weekend. Growing up in my church, I may have seen five or ten babies baptized over the course of a year and I'd never seen an adult do it. This experience tugged at my heart and brought me to a realization: I was changing or being changed.

Because of Samuel, I have found a stirring deep within. I've always believed there was something more; I knew I was missing something. I stuffed that feeling down inside and just pushed harder at work. But now. After Samuel… After God…

Because of Samuel, I witnessed a "mega-church," the kind of place that could be judged by society as bloated and lining the pockets of its staff, jump in with both feet to help those less fortunate. There was no bump to the bottom line or payback for the church in any visible way. Help was given by its volunteers and with resources and money because that is what God asks of His believers: Truly I tell you, whatever you did for one of the least of these brothers and sisters of mine, you did for me. Mathew 25:40

I have not just heard people preach and quote scripture. I have seen people live what is written in the Bible. I have seen the results that follow when one, "walks with God," and lives with this purpose.

I don't know what my future holds. No, I am not headed to the Monastery or into a dark cave to meditate for enlightenment, but I have come to the conclusion that I want what these people have.

I will continue my investigations but with a focus on the grander purpose. I want to make this effort because I believe it truly matters and I want my life to matter. It begins with some baby steps for me. Surprise, surprise: I'm going to church. Wish me well. Perhaps even pray for me or join me in the quest. When I get organized, I will share my journey online somewhere: just google me and we'll find a way to stay in touch.

For the time being, wherever you find me, you can be sure that I will be enjoying a good "cuppa" coffee, thanks to Gitchi Manitou and Samuel.

The Tribute

On the night of October 11 at 10:30, Arvid and Hannah and Brooks and Kate took their positions in front of Colby's apartment building. All the candles had been distributed.

It was a beautiful night, partially overcast and perfect for candlelight.

The church bell, high atop St. Marks Catholic church four blocks away began to play the first of its 11 chimes.

At that precise moment, a lit candle was placed in the front window on the 4th floor across the street; another in the next apartment to the right. Then one appeared on the first floor to the right of that. Behind them, three quickly appeared in three 1st floor apartments. Mr. Hapenstiel's building down the street seemed to light up all at once. The Nesterling building, next door, followed suit. Soon, candles were seemingly everywhere. A high-rise, three blocks away, lit up; candles in nearly every window. Henry's building behind them only had one darkened apartment – his own.

How can little candles bring this much light? They looked in all directions. Hannah couldn't stop the tears from flowing. Kate was much the same. Brooks and Arvie fought the battle bravely, but could not hold out. How meaningful could something like this be? Henry, are you watching? Mary? Those in your flock are thinking of you both tonight and thanking you.

Truth be known, Colby had an army of helpers lighting many of the candles and getting them positioned in the windows. He wanted to make sure that none went unlit just because a senior mind forgot the time and the duty.

Truth be known again, this is not something that Henry and Mary would have desired. For all those years of service to their neighbors, they never once wanted a thank you. They did not think being thanked was appropriate. They had the courage, the patience, the faithfulness and the obedience to do what Jesus asks of us all.

And then voices in song were heard amid the candle-lit darkness. A church choir, perhaps 40 voices strong, walked slowly down the street singing old familiar hymns.

When I survey the wondrous cross
On which the Prince of Glory died,
My richest gain I count but loss
And pour contempt on all my pride.

Forbid it Lord that I should boast
Save in the death of Christ my God.
All the vain things that charm me most
I sacrifice them to his blood.

See from his head, his hands, his feet
Sorrow and Love flow mingled down.
Did e'er such love and sorrow meet
Or thorns compose so rich a crown.

Were the whole realm of nature mine
That were a present far to small,
Love so amazing, so Divine,
Demands my soul, my life, my all.

Hannah leaned into Arvie, tears running unashamedly down her face. She whispered, "How appropriate those words. They gave their souls, their lives, their all." Her emotion continued as Amazing Grace began.

Dove Creek produced a video of the tribute and it was used at the following weekend services. Local TV stations also reported the event and the news captured the attention of local audiences for several weeks.

The Final Chapter

"I've always loved playing games—almost any game.
The beginning is tough, when you don't know the outcome. But you
persevere. You keep pushing forward and when you overcome, if
you overcome, glorious! Heh heh."
- *Ole*

On a cool, crisp Friday in mid-September, all the old boys and
spouses gathered at Richy Patterson's farm west of New Richmond,
Wisconsin, for the annual corn boil. The previous year, the boil was
at Old Will's farm in Wataga, Illinois. Will and Richy would
continue to trade the celebration each year.

Richy's 1840's farmhouse occupied a hilltop with a spectacular
view of the rolling countryside. At sun-up and sun-set, it looked like
a painting. Over the years, Richy had made wonderful updates to the
original farmhouse and he had added a spacious, guest quarters in the
back of the property which was now called the bunkhouse. When
Richy hosted, everyone stayed in the bunkhouse together. The
women got the nicer room with a valley view and didn't have to
climb ladders to go to bed. The guys got the real bunkhouse feeling
in the opposite room with a farmyard view and double-decker built-
in bunk beds. On Friday evening, after everyone had arrived, they
grilled Wisconsin bratwurst, sat in a big circle around the fire pit and
talked halfway through the night.

That year, Forever coffee was a main topic of conversation.
Arvie retold the story, which started at the old convenience store the
previous July. He did his best Jacob Whitefeather imitation and all
enjoyed a good laugh.

Arvie brewed several pots that night and several more in the
morning. He also presented everyone with a shiny black can of their
own to take home. Old Will, Vidor, Richy, and Freddie had not yet
received the mysterious deliveries, so they were glad to get some
coffee to try. Even Bert, the resident skeptic, was willing to take a
can, mainly at Gayle's insistence. Carl, Freddie, and Arvie kidded
him a little bit about it but they were glad he accepterd it. All the

boys who had been at the cabin told their stories about some ailment that had gone away: either there own, a friend's, or a family member's. Hope was alive and well.

Saturday morning was set-up day for the corn boil. Richy brought in members of the local high school football team to lug tables and chairs. Late afternoon, when groups of locals began arriving for the event, old friends pitched in wherever they could. They made sure everyone's plate stayed loaded with fresh, hot ears of corn. They disposed of the gnawed cobs and provided a never-ending supply of butter, salt, and pepper. Richy and Old Will provided aprons and kept their pockets filled with additional supplies, especially napkins. It was a real community event.

They had all attended their share of corn boils over the years, both at Richy's and Old Will's. Many familiar faces were recognized and hugs were exchanged. Arvie watched Hannah and the other wives circulate, doing their job. *How blessed*, he thought, *that we have lost no one since we gathered last year down at Old Will's place.*

Richy had even brought in a local band. They played from 5:00 until 6:30 on a stage set up in front of the barn. They were pretty good, too. They even knew a few of the tunes that the Mount Holy Waters Class of '60 had danced to, back in the day. After a couple of encores, the festivities came to an end, the barnyard slowly emptied of local guests and the band packed up to leave.

Ole's group pushed tables together, set up the supply of beverages and relaxed in conversation. As darkness settled in, the lights in the barnyard came on and candles and torches were lit. A few crickets chirped in the cool evening air. It was just about as perfect a scene as one could want.

Arvie sat next to Hannah. They held hands and looked down the hill and across the darkening countryside. The scattered lights from the houses and barns down in the valley looked lonesome in the middle of all the darkness. He leaned in and planted a big kiss on Hannah's lips.

"My goodness, a kiss? Are you not well?" Hannah asked.

"Thanks for standing up for me and putting up with me, all those times over all the years. Particularly with everything that happened recently. You've been wonderful. I love you. It hit me up side my head, just now. I had to tell you—and kiss you."

Old Will clapped him on the shoulder and asked if they could use a quality alcohol product from Richy's special cabinet. Hannah said, "Yes, and please hurry."

Will and Bert soon returned with several bottles and a tray of glasses. Sitting there with college buddies and their wives, Arvie thought he could almost feel the years fall away. He half-expected Ole to come wandering up, telling everyone it was time to get back to work.

During a lull in the conversation, Hannah said, "I've been thinking about Mr. Woodhull."

"Whoa. Why would you want to do that, dear?" asked Arvie. "What do you mean?"

"Well, based on what you told me and what Agent Settles said, it was almost like Woodhull became a different person. He was one person when he was in South America, and then when he joined the FBI, he was a different person."

"Yes. I had a similar thought, that day in the courtroom."

"Maybe he was playing different parts for so long that he started to really believe himself," Carl said.

"Could be," Hannah concurred. "But then, I started thinking about myself. I wonder if, for these last few years anyway, the same was true for me? My problems with anxiety; it happened so quickly."

Gayle, Bert's wife, reached across the table and put her hand on Hannah's arm.

Hannah continued, "In the blink of an eye, I had gotten … old. Everything I had grown comfortable with was gone. I was afraid of … everything."

"I think we all have to deal with fear and anxiety at some point," said Joyce, Freddie's wife. "For a while a few years ago, I could barely get myself to leave the house by myself to go to the store."

Hannah nodded. "Yes. I've realized how hard it is to go from someone I've known to someone I don't know, almost overnight. And as hard as I would try, as much as I would tell myself 'just snap out of it,' getting better is a process. It takes time. And then I've wondered if it takes the coffee a little longer to heal the mind than the body. Arvie and I have talked about that a little, haven't we?" She looked at him. "What do you think?"

"Well, I will say that you have seemed much better, these last couple of months," Arvie replied. "What do you think, dear? Is it gone? Can you say that you are over and done with it?"

She thought for a moment. "I don't know if that's even possible. I'm afraid that it won't ever totally go away. But I think that over time I'm getting used to dealing with it. Does that make sense?"

"I think it does. And I think Dr. Blower has helped you a lot."

"You know, this is kind of a weird thought," Carl said, after a moment of quiet.

"That's the only kind you have, Carl," Bert said. Everybody groaned.

"But seriously, Hannah. If not for your anxiety and going to your therapy group at the University, Arvie would never have noticed the homeless guy, by the highway."

"Right. Zeke," Arvie said, nodding.

"And the whole adventure with the crooked FBI agent wouldn't have happened," Carl continued.

"And we would never have gotten to rib Arvie for being in jail," Freddie said. More groans, with a few chuckles thrown in.

"Well, speaking of having experiences you never expected," Gayle said, "I've been trying to decide if I should say anything about what happened this past summer in the library."

"What are you talking about Gayle? Everybody in the world knows what happened at your library. You were on TV more than Walter Cronkite used to be. You're famous," Richy concluded.

"Oh, come now," Gayle said. "But maybe you could all plan to come down to Robinswood during the upcoming holidays. Then you could see where this man lived for forty-two years ..." For a moment, Gayle was lost in recollection. She looked up and continued quietly, "It is such a special place and so very beautiful and unusual. Yes, and it's also very sound-proof. You have to see it in person. I could tell you all about it, but you wouldn't realize the enormity of it. The TV cameras couldn't do it justice."

"Well, I'm intrigued," Richy said. "Sounds like we have a plan."

464

"Yeah, you should all come," said Bert. "Everyone can stay at my brother's place on the Mississippi. He'll give us all a good deal on cabins. I'll check with him for dates and let you know. It'll be great fun to have you down there."

"Hey, Arvie," Freddie said, "you never said anything about the analysis you got done on the coffee. Remember? Henry's 3M friend?"

"Oh. That. You know, in the tragedy around Henry's death, and with everything that happened after, I guess I just forgot about it. I never saw the report. But one of the Native Americans I met later told me that it's made of all natural stuff. Can you imagine, and it's the best coffee I've ever tasted. What really happened to the report is sobering. Henry had tucked it inside his shirt that night. It was shredded in death."

"Oh, how awful," said Joyce, closing her eyes and shaking her head.

"But don't you want to know?" Bert asked. "Don't you want to see the actual report?"

Arvie smiled. "Bert, in Hebrews chapter 11, verse one says, 'Now faith is confidence in what we hope for and assurance about what we do not see.' All I know for sure is that I have hope—more than I've had in a long time. And so, I'm content to trust in that, even though I can't see everything clearly. Hope was what kept Henry going and what keeps young Colby going. And hope is enough for me; for us." Hannah nodded in agreement.

After a few seconds of silence Carl said, "Well, I hope that Arvie doesn't snore as loud tonight as he did last night." Everybody laughed.

"Okay, you guys, I think I may depart on that note, 'cause I'm beat," Arvie said. He stood up from the table and extended a hand to his bride. "Come on, Hannah; we're both yawning. I'll escort you to the bunkhouse. How do you like sleeping in the same room with a bunch of old grandmothers?"

More hoots of derision.

"I love them all, but I'd rather be sleeping with you."

Even more hoots.

"Well now. That's nice to hear," Arvie said putting his arm around her.

They bid all a good night and walked toward the bunkhouse in the quiet, enjoying it together. "Look down there," she said, pointing toward the valley below the hilltop. "So beautiful and peaceful."

"Yes. This is a beautiful setting. It's easy to see why Richy loves it so much."

They stood in the dark, looking into the valley. "You know," he said, "there really was something snazzy about that earlier you, but there is something extremely endearing about the current you. I love them both, you know."

"I know. Both of us thank you for that ... and we've both loved you, too. All this time we've had together ... all the years ... you've made it fun, Arvid. Do you know that?"

"I was born with a talent for fun, Hannah, my dear. I'm very special that way."

"Yes, you are. It's time to get some sleep. See you in the morning."

They shared a hug and a tender kiss. Life was good. She turned and entered the girl's side and he walked around the bunkhouse to the boy's side. *Tomorrow's another day,* he thought. He hoped so.

On the back wall, behind the coffee counter
at every Samuel's Coffee House is listed the names of all
the coffees from Northern Minnesota:

Forever	*Reunion*	*Redeemed*	*Mercy*	*Forgiveness*
Grace	*Peace*	*Faith*	*Love*	*Praise*
Eternity	*Prayer*	*Salvation*	*Hope*	*Trust*
Worship	*Obedience*	*Strength*	*Joy*	*Freedom*
Victory	*Repentance*			

"Let's face it boys: we don't know much.
Matter of fact, we know nothin'. It ain't knowledge that gets us
where we want to go anyhow. Only grace, faith and love.
Might as well relax and drink the coffee. Heh heh."

- Ole Ekdahl

"The joy of Jesus will be my strength –
it will be in my heart. Every person I meet will
see it in my work, my walk, my prayer – in
everything."

~Mother Teresa~

Questions for Reflection or Discussion

Chapter 1

1. What is hope? How does the definition change throughout life or does it change? In other words, is hope different for the 17-year-old and the 77-year-old?

Chapter 2

1. After drinking Forever at the cabin, all four of the old boys talked of physical conditions that had improved or disappeared. Even Bert, the cynic, agreed. Is it difficult to believe in a magical coffee? What about miracles? Do you believe they happen? Have you experienced any yourself?

2. Arvie realized that something had changed since his acid indigestion didn't occur after the big steak dinner the first night. Has this happened in your life – an unexpected change? If so, share the experience.

Chapter 3

1. Why do the old boys have a special place in their hearts for their former boss? Do you have a revered former boss? How was he or she similar to, or different from, Ole?

2. Have you had the opportunity to be a leader? Would you like to emulate Ole? What characteristics could you develop further or eliminate to become a better leader?

3. Arvie and Carl discussed Forever as a Fountain of Youth. What do you think of that possibility? Would God object to them providing a "Heaven on Earth" scenario with healing coffee?

4. Was Arvie justified in pouring Forever for everyone – especially seniors? How would you have handled the situation?

Chapter 4

1. When Arvie returned home, he introduced Hannah to Forever. Has someone important to you asked you to believe the impossible? How is faith in a loved one similar and different to faith in God?

2. Arvie had a wild coffee inspired dream. What might cause these kinds of dreams? Have you had a similar dream? Could it bring about a sense of doubt? Why or why not?

Chapter 5

1. Arvie had an appointment with the urologist to review test results. Are you at a point in life that brings you into physicians' offices more frequently? If so, does it bring about a sense of anxiety? Why or why not? How is faith helpful? Are there times when it lets you down? If so, why do you think that is?

Chapter 6

1. Arvie went to a street corner to share Forever with a beggar. When was the last time you tried to share a cup of coffee with someone you didn't know? How about volunteering for people that were in need? How can we move further beyond ourselves?

2. Arvie stopped for gas at an old station and the attendant didn't know how much he had purchased. Arvie considered telling her the wrong amount to save a few dollars. Has there been an opportunity for you to do something similar? If so, what was it? Describe that opportunity and what you did with it? Thinking back, are you pleased with your decision? What might "harmless little fibs" do to our character? How might they affect our lives?

3. Are you familiar with churches that provide book stores and coffee shops? What opportunities exist within your church for volunteering? Do you volunteer or would you consider volunteering? For those who have, does volunteering give you the feeling that you are assisting in reaching others for Christ?

Chapter 7

1. Early in their marriage, Arvie and Hannah didn't enjoy NFL football together all day on Sundays. However, in these later years, Hannah eagerly participates and instigates this time: many times, popping the corn and adding extra butter. If you are married, have you experienced such pleasant surprises over the years? How important is this type of togetherness or is it simply a waste of time?

Chapter 8

1. Arvie received a little brown bag from Cassie at Walmart. No, it did not contain a can of coffee. Instead, it held a can of soup which was a message of hope for Hannah. Do you know someone like Cassie who can make a meaningful gift from a can of soup? Who is it and how do they do it? Have you been this person? Could you be? What ideas come to mind?

2. Arvie spoke with Pastor Noah about pouring his coffee at the senior Bible study every Wednesday morning. Was there any part of this conversation that you found interesting? If so, what was it and why was it interesting?

3. Arvie received Forever at convenience stores frequently. How would you feel if that happened to you? Knowing that *with God, all things are possible*, could you accept God working directly with you/through you? Perhaps you've experienced it. Have you talked about it with others? If not, why not? If you have, how did it make you feel? How did it affect your faith?

4. Talk with someone about your most recent experience at an *organ concert*. Did you participate in the concert? Why or why not?

5. Pastor Noah knew exactly what Arvie was talking about with a God-directed mission. Have you ever accepted a God-directed mission? If so, think back on that experience. What did it feel like? Was there doubt in your mind about what you were doing? How did you overcome it? If not, do you wonder why not? Didn't feel the nudge? Were you too busy to listen; too scared to step out in faith? Why might it be scary?

6. Are you familiar with an anxiety diagnosis? After a particularly difficult day for Hannah, Arvie criticized her by saying "If you are a Christian and have Jesus, how can you have these emotional times? Is your faith not strong enough?" Do you feel that Arvie was justified in talking to her in that manner or doesn't he fully understand anxiety? How might he have approached it differently?

7. What do think of Arvie wanting to be baptized by immersion? He and his church believe that it is an act of obedience, completely different than the baptism he had experienced as a baby. Do you believe it is an act of obedience or is it really not necessary?

Chapter 9

1. Arvie met a cynical FBI agent on Zeke's corner. How did Arvie talk about things that cannot be seen? How did his side of the discussion hold up against the cynic? What would you add to the discussion?

2. Arvie met Special Agent Titus Woodhull and was accused of criminal activity in South America. Have you been accused of something you didn't do? How did it make you feel? Were you able to prove your innocence? If so, how?

Chapter 10

1. Arvie dreamed of an explosion, a gash in his head and a circle of fire. Do you remember your dreams? If so describe one and discuss. What do you believe about the meaning of dreams?

Chapter 11

1. After Arvie blew up his grill and was struck in the head by the grill lid, he saw *halos of fire*. How would you feel if something similar happened to you? Would you think that you were given a special responsibility or just had some medical complication? Might you try to ignore and hope it would go away?

2. Have men in dark suits come to you and taken you away? If yes, explain what happened. If no, good for you.

3. Can you imagine being told that your past, as you remember it, never happened? Arvie feared that Woodhull was about to prove that he was guilty of a life he had never led and that he might be locked away for the rest of his life. How would you feel in that situation? What would you do? What could you do if that realization came while you were locked in a jail cell?

4. Has a human-interest newspaper article been written about you? If so, what was the reason? If you had been seen pouring coffee for someone in an effort to heal something for them, would you be embarrassed? How would you feel?

5. Have you met people like Henry and Mary? If yes, who was it? What did they do? How did they make you feel and why did you feel the way you did?

6. Henry described himself as a, "Handyman for Jesus, harvesting lost souls." Has there been a time in your life when you would have considered such a career? Why or why not? Might you consider it now? Age is not a disqualifier.

Chapter 12

1. What did you think of Corliss Unger Diddle of the Food and Drug Administration? In Arvie's place, would you have talked to her in the same way? What might you say differently?

2. Brooks went off on Special Agent Woodhull. Did you agree in principle with his rant? Would you have handled the moment differently? How so or why not?

Chapter 13

1. Brooks was with Arvie at a convenience store when Arvie received cans of Mercy. How did Brooks react? How would you react?

2. At the baptism, while still in the pool, Arvie looked out into the darkened church and noted many halos of fire. Do you think a simple hit on the head by a flying grill lid could have been responsible for this odd circumstance? Might it have been a miracle?

Chapter 14

1. Arvie stood in front of his patio door looking at an ugly black Ford sedan and daydreamed about being a master of the covert and Hannah as the Black Widow of the Jungle. Did you wonder, for a moment, if what he was spouting could be true? Did you wonder if Woodhull was right? How did that make you feel?

Chapter 15

1. Arvie heard on the car radio about a shooting at a school: three children shot. Are we growing callous about such reports? Should we try to maintain a tender spirit or work to be strong and "deal with it?"

2. Arvie witnessed Henry's death and expected to die the same way. Have you been a witness to an event where someone died violently and unexpectedly? How did it effect you?

3. How do you feel about *serving others*? Do you think it is important? How is it similar to/different from *loving others*?

4. Do you know what ingredients are in your coffee? Do you care?

Chapter 16

1. After Henry was killed, Arvie was hospitalized for several days due to emotional or physical trauma. Have you or a family member experienced anything similar?

Chapter 17

1. Reporter Sandy Marsh told Brooks about another murder thought to have been committed by the Black Widow. Brooks asked Sandy if the Black Widow was still doing her thing down in South America. Why might he have asked that question?

Chapter 18

1. Think of the faith of Henry and Mary. Have you ever taken a moment to wonder about that kind of faith; the beauty of it? Could you live on faith alone?

2. Hannah visited Mary in the hospital. She told Arvie, "It was a one-sided conversation but it was a chance to say some things that were on my heart. I don't know that she heard me, but I want to believe that she did." Think of those friends and family members you love. Are you prepared to say what you want to say? Take a moment to think of a loved one and the words you will say. Why not say them now before you may have to wonder if they were able to hear you?

Chapter 19

1. While in the hospital Arvie met a young nurse named Alexandra. She asked him some serious questions. Are you ready to witness at any time, any day, any place? How might you have counseled Alexandra?

Chapter 20

1. Arvie and his son, Brooks, drove to Henry's apartment to help Mrs. Koepke. Were you surprised at Mrs. Koepke's physical and mental condition and what tasks they performed for her? If so, why?

2. As Arvie and Brooks were leaving Mrs. Koepke's apartment, they met Colby. How did you receive his message relating to the condition of the seniors in Henry and Mary's flock?

3. Brooks asked his dad if he began each day with God and the Bible? Do you? Why or why not?

4. Arvie and Hannah paid for the niche at the Mausoleum for Henry and Mary. Would you do that?

Chapter 21

1. Arvie had very little notice about a presentation to the Dove Creek board the next morning. How would you have dealt with such news? Would you have trusted that, as Noah said, there was no need to prepare something formal and simply prayed the night before? Would you have skipped the golf tournament and prepared for as long as it would take to feel sure about carrying the burdens of all those people? Is one answer better than the other?

Chapter 22

"So don't worry, because I am with you. Don't be afraid, because I
am your God. I will make you strong and will help you; I will
support you with my right hand that saves you."
~Isaiah 41:10

1. Arvie was unsure about bringing the issue of Henry and Mary's
   people to the Dove Creek Church board. He had prayed about it.
   Do you go to prayer before making important presentations? Do
   you take the words of Isaiah 41:10 seriously?

2. What was the most meaningful section of Arvie's presentation?
   Would your presentation of this matter have differed in any way?
   If so, how?

3. Have you experienced a real miracle? Arvie experienced the
   miracle of pouring more coffee from his three thermos bottles
   than was possible. Did you believe that it was a real miracle or
   did you discount it as not possible? Are all things possible with
   God, even simple things like pouring coffee, or do you think not?

Chapter 23

1. Arvie's prayer was the longest of his life. What is prayer to you?
   Do you pray simply or do you pour it all out, as Arvie did here?
   Do you think any prayer is better or worse in God's eyes?

2. When praying for the health of a friend, we are accustomed to
   praying for *restored* health. How would you have prayed for the
   people in Henry and Mary's flock? Would you have prayed for
   restored health or perhaps, for the Lord to take them?

3. Arvie received a call from the Chairman of the Dove Creek
   board, Mr. Gordon, who presented a job opportunity to Arvie.
   Arvie was taken by complete surprise. Have you ever received
   such a call?

4. Why was Brooks suspicious of the call from Mr. Gordon? Is it a question of faith or simply realistic to question something that seems too good to be true?

5. Arvie was doubtful his church would be able to take on the project. He said if they couldn't, he'd take it to the Democrats. Did you enjoy his political rant?

Chapter 24

1. Do you believe that it's possible for seniors like those in Henry and Mary's flock to be living in your community? Why or why not? How might you find out?

2. Brenda asked if she and a group of her fellow nurses and a doctor or two could be of help to the seniors in need. Have you experienced a time when assistance showed up when there was a need? If so, how did it happen and did it have an impact on your faith?

Chapter 25

1. Arvie kept asking himself what he would do if the church wasn't able to get involved. Hannah preached a sermon to him about acceptance. How did her comments resonate with you? Have you ever given or received such a "sermon"? If so, how did it affect you?

Chapter 26

1. Arvie found Jacob's grave from many years before, proving that Jacob couldn't have sold him Forever, but Arvie knew he had. With all the questions that arise, how would you have reacted?

Chapter 27

1. How did you feel when Agent Woodhull was found out? Was it a surprise? If so, why? How did you feel when it was uncovered that Arvie had been used as a pawn to trap Agent Woodhull; how about with the discovery that drug money had paid off enough government people to place Woodhull in such a position?

2. How did you feel when Dove Creek announced the plan for Henry's (Colby's) flock? Could (would) your church step up in such a situation?

Additional

1. Are you willing to accept a mission that is put in front of you? Do you believe ordinary people can accomplish extraordinary things? If so, how?

2. Were you surprised when you read Sandy's last column? What emotions would Arvie have felt?

3. What one thing about this story might you remember?

The Quiet

Book II in the "Hearty Boys" Series

Bill Pearson

There is a bad smell in the Public Library and Head Librarian, Gayle, is bound and determined to find the source.

The library occupies the top three floors of the building while commercial establishments fill the first floor. With restaurants beneath, Gayle wonders if it is rotting food in the basement or an animal that got trapped in a small space somewhere. Could it be sweat socks and an old jock strap jammed behind some books?

Gayle calls her husband because men are experts at smelly stuff. He calls in his friends: plumbers, builders, electricians, police, dogcatchers, "What is that smell?"

Officer Brownsrud has smelled this once before. "I think you'd better call the coroner. There is a dead body in here."

"WHAT?" Gayle screams just before sliding from her chair to an unladylike sprawl behind her desk in a dead faint.

The police conduct a search of the entire complex. No dead body is found in the library, the restaurants or the shops. The smell persists and a multitude of theories are proposed.

Gayle knows there is an answer to this dilemma. Surely somebody knows something. The days fly by, and then ….

Coming Soon